Praise for the Whiskey Creek novels of
New York Times bestselling author Brenda Novak

"Novak is always a go-to author for sassy romance set in small
towns loaded with charm. Her latest in the Whiskey Creek series
is naughty and nice, and readers will fall in love with the magic of
the season."
—*RT Book Reviews* on *The Heart of Christmas*, Top Pick

"If you haven't started reading the Whiskey Creek series, get
going! Novak's…gift for writing about passion never ceases to
amaze, and fans of romance will be hooked with just one visit to
Whiskey Creek."
—*RT Book Reviews* on *Come Home to Me*, Top Pick

"Once again Novak's Whiskey Creek springs to life in all its
realistic, gritty Gold Country glory…. This poignant, heartfelt
romance puts a refreshing spin on the classic reunion/secret baby
theme."
—*Library Journal* on *Come Home to Me*

"[Brenda Novak] weaves a tight story of human weakness and
longing, with cross threads of passion and hope. One needn't
wonder why Novak is a *New York Times* and *USA TODAY*
bestselling author."
—*Examiner.com* on *Come Home to Me*

"The worst part of any Brenda Novak book is the last page.
I always want more… The Whiskey Creek series is an absolute
delight and this newest installment is…so satisfying I ran out of
superlatives. Brenda Novak outdid herself."
—*Fresh Fiction* on *Take Me Home for Christmas*

"[*Home to Whiskey Creek* is an] engrossing, character-rich story
that takes a hard look at responsibility, loyalty and the results of
telling (or concealing) the truth."
—*Library Journal*

"It's steamy, it's poignant, it's perfectly paced—it's
When Lightning Strikes and you don't want to miss it."
—*Happy Ever After* on USATODAY.com

BRENDA NOVAK

This Heart of Mine

MIRA

MIRA®

ISBN-13: 978-0-7783-1672-5

Recycling programs
for this product may
not exist in your area.

This Heart of Mine

For questions and comments about the quality of this book, please contact us at
CustomerService@Harlequin.com.

www.MIRABooks.com

Printed in U.S.A.

To my children.
The love I feel for you made this story what it is.

Dear Reader,

I've now written more than fifty books, so when I get the question "Which book is your favorite?" it's even more difficult to answer than it was before. I like different books for different reasons. The Stillwater Trilogy will always be among my favorites (*Dead Silence*, *Dead Giveaway* and *Dead Right*). So will *A Home of Her Own* from the Dundee series and *Inside* from the Bulletproof trilogy. Some stories are just easier to write. Or certain characters are more accessible to me, which creates a stronger bond. This novel is one of those standout stories that poured right onto the page (how I wish they could all do that!). I think it's because, as a mother of five, I can so easily relate to Phoenix in her desire to have the chance to show her teenage son the love she feels for him.

Those of you who've read my books before probably know that I often focus on redemption themes. After what Phoenix has been through, she deserves the best of happily-ever-afters, and I thoroughly enjoyed giving her one.

I love to hear from my readers. Please feel free to contact me online at brendanovak.com, or by snail mail at PO Box 3781, Citrus Heights, CA 95611. If you sign up for my mailing list, I'll be able to alert you to special sales and giveaways and send a reminder whenever I have a new book out. You can also find me on Facebook (BrendaNovakAuthor) and Twitter (@Brenda_Novak).

Here's hoping you enjoy watching Phoenix and Riley rediscover each other!

Brenda

WHISKEY CREEK Cast of Characters

Phoenix Fuller: Recently released from prison. Mother of **Jacob Stinson**, who is being raised by his father, Riley.

Riley Stinson: Contractor, father of Jacob.

Gail DeMarco: Owns a public relations firm in Los Angeles. Married to movie star **Simon O'Neal**.

Ted Dixon: Bestselling thriller writer, married to **Sophia DeBussi**.

Eve Harmon: Manages Little Mary's B & B, which is owned by her family. Recently married to **Lincoln McCormick**, a newcomer.

Kyle Houseman: Owns a solar panel business. Formerly married to Noelle Arnold. Best friend of Riley Stinson.

Baxter North: Stockbroker in San Francisco.

Noah Rackham: Professional cyclist. Owns Crank It Up bike shop. Married to **Adelaide Davies**, chef and manager of Just Like Mom's restaurant, owned by her grandmother.

Callie Vanetta: Photographer. Married to **Levi McCloud/Pendleton**, veteran of Afghanistan.

Olivia Arnold: Kyle Houseman's true love but married to **Brandon Lucero**, Kyle's stepbrother.

Dylan Amos: Owns an auto-body shop with his brothers. Married to **Cheyenne Christensen**, and they have a baby boy.

1

It was the first time she'd seen her son since the day she gave birth to him. Phoenix Fuller had spent an eternity waiting for this moment. She'd counted every single breath, it seemed, for sixteen years, waiting to lay eyes on Jacob again.

But as anxious as she was, she'd promised herself she wouldn't cry, or try to hug him, or do anything else that might make a teenage boy feel uncomfortable. She was a stranger to him. Although she hoped to change that now that she was back in town, she couldn't come on too strong or he'd likely shut her out— even if his father didn't make sure he kept her at arm's length. She had to be an embarrassment to both of them. They were all from the same small town; it wasn't as if they could hide the fact that she'd spent Jacob's entire life in prison.

Her heart leaped into her throat as she watched Jacob and his father, Riley Stinson, get out of a large Ford pickup and stride toward the entrance of the restaurant.

God, her son was tall, she thought, hungrily devouring the sight of him. How he'd gotten so big, she had no idea. She barely topped five feet. Even at thirty-five, she could be mistaken for a much younger person when she wasn't wearing makeup and had her hair pulled back.

But Jacob took after his father in size and shape, had the same broad shoulders, narrow hips and long legs.

"Excuse me. Your table's ready whenever you are."

Phoenix wouldn't have heard the hostess if the woman hadn't touched her arm when she spoke.

It required real effort, but she dragged her gaze away from the window in order to respond. "Thank you. The rest of my party will be here in a second."

"That's fine. Just let me know when you're ready." With a polite smile, the young woman seated a couple standing nearby.

Once again, Phoenix's eyes were riveted on her son. Only this time, she felt such a surge of emotion she almost darted into the bathroom. She could *not* break down.

Please, God, don't let me cry. He won't come within ten feet of me if I do.

But the harder she tried to hold back her tears, the more overwhelmed she became. In a panic, she slipped around the corner, into the small alcove by the bathrooms, and leaned her head against the wall.

Breathe. Don't blow this.

The bell over the door jingled, telling her that Riley and Jacob had stepped inside. She imagined them looking around, maybe getting annoyed when they didn't find her. But she was frozen in place. She absolutely could. Not. Move.

"Hey," she heard the hostess say with a familiarity that hadn't been present in her greeting to Phoenix. "We're busy this morning, like we are every Saturday. But if you can wait for a few minutes, I'll get you a table."

"We're actually meeting someone who should be here."

That had to be Riley, but Phoenix couldn't say she recognized his voice. Her memories of him were vivid. But they'd both been so young, and he'd changed a great deal. No longer the skinny teenager she'd known in high school, he was a man with plenty of hard muscle on his solid frame, a man in his prime, and that had been more than apparent as she'd watched him walk, shoulder to shoulder, with their son a few seconds earlier.

"Who are you here to meet?" the hostess asked.

"Name's Phoenix Fuller," came his response.

"What does she look like?"

"I'm not sure these days," he said, and Phoenix winced. Her shoulder-length dark hair wasn't bad. It was thick, probably her best asset. Her hazel eyes weren't unattractive, either. She didn't feel she was ugly. But the scars on her face would be new to him. She hadn't had those when she went to prison.

"She wasn't very tall," he added, as if that might be the only detail still applicable.

"There was a woman who said she was expecting two more to join her," the hostess said. "But I don't know where she went..."

Determined not to miss this opportunity after waiting so long for it, Phoenix curved her fingernails into her palms, took a deep breath and stepped around the corner. "Sorry I...I had to wash my hands."

The frown that appeared on Riley's face brought heat to her cheeks. He wasn't happy to be in her presence. No doubt he'd spent the past seventeen years hoping he'd never have to see her again, especially since her release date had been extended twice beyond her original sentence.

But she'd known this first meeting would be difficult. Squaring her shoulders, she ignored his disapproval and turned to Jacob. "Hello, I'm your mother."

She'd practiced saying those words so many times and still almost choked up. Only by sheer will did she manage to retain control. "You can call me Phoenix, though, if that feels more natural to you. I don't expect..." Her tongue seemed so thick and unwieldy, she could hardly speak. "I don't expect you to do anything you don't want to do, not when it comes to me."

He seemed surprised she'd throw that out there right away, but she also thought she detected a slight lessening of the tension gripping his body. So she extended her hand. "It's very nice to meet you. Thank you for coming. I hope this restaurant is okay. Just Like Mom's was always a favorite of mine when I lived here so I hoped maybe...maybe it'd still be popular."

Jacob glanced at his father before shaking her hand. "Hello," he mumbled, but wouldn't quite look her in the eye.

Telling herself that was normal, that a certain amount of reluctance was to be expected, she let go as soon as they touched. She didn't want him to notice how badly she was trembling.

"Are you folks ready to sit down?" The hostess, who'd been distracted saying goodbye to some departing patrons, was now watching them with avid curiosity. She'd probably figured out that this was "the" Phoenix Fuller everyone had been talking about—the one who'd been convicted for running down a rival with her mother's old Buick just before graduating from high school.

"Yes, please." Supremely conscious of the two people trailing behind her, Phoenix followed the hostess across the restaurant to a corner booth.

Once they sat down, she leaned back as another woman came to bring them water.

"You can have anything you want," she told Jacob as he opened the menu.

It was too soon to mention that. But she was nervous. And she'd worked so hard in the weeks before she was released to be able to provide this meal. She really wanted him to enjoy it.

"I like the Belgian waffle with the ice cream and strawberries."

Grateful he'd chosen something rather celebratory and elaborate, she smiled. "Then you can have it."

Belatedly, she realized that his father should have a say in the matter; it wasn't a healthy meal and she held absolutely no power in Jacob's life. So she appealed to Riley. "If that's okay with your father."

Once Riley had given his permission, she dropped her gaze. It was easier not to look at him. If she could've invited Jacob on his own, she would have. The emotions she felt where her son was concerned were poignant enough. Adding his father to the mix just complicated an already complicated situation.

"You can get whatever you'd like, too, of course," she told Riley. "My treat."

The second she got those words out, she felt her face burn even hotter. What a stupid thing to say! Riley was a successful building contractor. He didn't need an ex-con to pay for his breakfast. And she knew that although she'd sent every dime she could spare to the support of her son, her contributions had been paltry compared to what he'd done for Jacob over the years. Riley probably found her offer to buy him breakfast laughable. But she'd meant to be generous. She was struggling so hard to get by that thirty dollars was a lot of money to her.

"The shrimp omelet's good," he said, and set his menu aside without really studying it.

The shrimp omelet and the Belgian waffle were the two most expensive meals on the menu, but Phoenix didn't mind. She quickly calculated how much money she'd have left over and started looking for something under five dollars.

"I'm not very hungry," she mused so they wouldn't find it strange when she ordered light. "I think I'll just have some toast and coffee."

The minute she lowered her menu, she nearly raised it again to use as a shield. Both Riley and her son eyed her appraisingly, skeptically. Although she'd expected close scrutiny, it was still difficult to be examined like some kind of unusual—and not particularly welcome— bug. Not only that, but she was self-conscious about the scars on her face, didn't want them to become a focal point.

"How long have you been home?" Riley asked, breaking a silence that was growing awkward.

She slid her menu to one side and folded her hands in her lap. "Three days." She would have contacted him immediately, but it had taken some time to summon the nerve. He'd made it clear that he wished she'd settle anywhere but Whiskey Creek.

He clutched his water glass. "Who picked you up?"

She'd had to pay for a taxi, but she didn't want to admit that. "An acquaintance who…who's sort of a friend."

That was nebulous, but he didn't seem to question it. "I thought maybe your mother…"

"No. She can't—doesn't—drive these days." At nearly six hundred pounds, she couldn't fit inside a car. Her mother had been a recluse since Phoenix and

Riley were dating. In addition to her weight, Lizzie had significant issues with hoarding and depression. She didn't own a working car or have internet service. If not for the kindhearted guy from the Baptist church who'd brought groceries and performed the occasional vet run—for only ten dollars a week—while Phoenix was in prison, Lizzie might not have survived. It wasn't as if Phoenix's father cared about either one of them. Or her brothers, for that matter. He'd left shortly after Phoenix was born; no one even knew where he was these days. And her two older brothers, who'd been so devastated when he left, had washed their hands of Whiskey Creek and everything that went with it when she was still in school.

Riley had to be aware of Lizzie's situation. So was he merely trying to reiterate the point he'd made in his last letter—that he believed Jacob would be better off without her involvement in his life? He'd mentioned her mother as a less-than-positive aspect of associating with her. Lizzie's many problems were the reason Jacob hadn't been allowed to visit his grandmother more than three or four times during his life, and of course her mother had never reached out. Although Lizzie often couched it as a gruff rejection, she felt too unworthy, especially when she came up against a well-established, well-respected family like the Stinsons.

Riley took another sip of his water. "How's she doing?"

Phoenix refused to be drawn into a conversation about her mother. She wasn't willing to address *any* subject that might make him less likely to let her see Jacob. "Fine."

"Fine?" he repeated. "That's it? I haven't seen her around town in years."

Jacob scowled at him. "You know what she's like, Dad."

Phoenix cleared her throat. "She'll be better now that I'm home. I'll see to it. And she won't bother you or Jacob. I'll make sure of that, too."

"How can she bother us if she can't leave the house?" Jacob asked, glaring at his father. "Has she bothered us so far?"

"I'll handle this," Riley said, but Phoenix felt the need to chime in. She couldn't allow Riley to think Jacob was supporting her side of any argument. Riley held her heart in his hand because he controlled what she wanted most—a relationship with Jacob. So, first of all, she had to protect her relationship with *him*.

"Your father's right. She can be…an embarrassment. I remember what it was like when…when I was in high school. But she's, um, well, like you say, she doesn't go anywhere, so I highly doubt she'll be an issue." Except for when he came to her place, but she'd figure out how to handle that if and when it happened.

Obviously annoyed that his father was being so protective, Jacob grumbled, "*I'm* not worried about it."

She hoped that was true. He had enough to cope with just being her son. Not many other kids had to live with the stigma of having their mother labeled a murderer. "I hear you're a talented baseball player," she said, eager to change the subject.

This elicited a shy smile—one that revealed how very handsome and charismatic her son was. He looked even more like his father than she'd initially thought, with those amber-colored eyes and his nearly black hair.

"I like to play," he said.

"It's really something to be the starting varsity

pitcher as a junior," she told him. "Baseball's a big deal around here."

Riley's mood seemed to improve as he gave his son's shoulder a little shove. "Last week he almost pitched a no-hitter."

Jacob lifted his eyebrows. "Almost but not quite."

"The season's young," Riley responded.

Phoenix loved the pride in Riley's voice. She felt that same pride. But right now, carrying on this conversation was a chore. For one thing, except for a few close friends she'd made in prison, she'd kept to herself. She didn't consider herself particularly entertaining. For another, she just wanted to sit and stare, memorize all the details of her son's face. The pictures she'd been sent had been far and few between and hadn't done her boy justice. He'd had braces on in the last one, which had come in a Christmas card two years ago. Small effort though it required on Riley's part, she was grateful to him for sending that. She still had both the card and the photo. They were among the scant belongings she'd brought home from prison.

"Do you have plans to play in college?" she asked.

"Definitely," he replied. "I've got a few universities interested in me. Great ones, too. I'm hoping for a scholarship."

He had so much going for him, so much to look forward to. She owed Riley for that. He'd done a great job with their son. "How exciting!" she said. "I'm sure you'll get one."

The waitress came to take their order, so Phoenix quickly added up what the tab would be, after they asked for orange juice with their meals. She didn't want to embarrass herself when it came time to pay by running short. "Just coffee for me," she said to be safe.

"That's all you want?" Jacob asked.

"I don't usually have much for breakfast." Hungry though she was, she was too nervous to eat, anyway.

"No wonder you're so small. Most of the girls in school are twice as big as you," he said. "And some of them aren't finished growing."

"I might be small, but I'm strong," she teased, flexing one arm.

"I heard. You got into a few fights in—"

"Let's not start with that." When Riley interrupted, her son flushed and fell silent.

"It's okay, he can say what he wants," she told Riley before answering Jacob. "I was forced to defend myself, but...I managed." Sometimes better than others. It always depended on how many people jumped her at once.

"What happened?" Jacob asked.

During which incident? She supposed the one that had left the scar on her lip. She didn't want to get into what life was like on the inside, but she also didn't want him to feel there were subjects he had to avoid.

"The women in that prison could be...territorial," she said. "There were times I had to fight or I'd be picked on for the rest of my stay, you know? I'm sure you've seen that type of behavior in school." The fact that she was fighting for her life had given her little choice in the matter, but she didn't want to make it sound quite so dire.

Jacob wrinkled his nose, clearly doubtful. "So you didn't start the fight?"

"Would you start a fight if you were my size?" she asked with a laugh, hoping she could get him to smile.

He didn't, but some of his doubt seemed to slip away. "No. I can't even imagine how you defended yourself."

"I told you." She winked to cover a reservoir of much deeper feeling. "I'm stronger than I look."

He studied her for a few seconds. "Is that what those scars are from?"

Phoenix's tongue automatically sought the one on her lip. She'd gotten it just before she was due to be released two years ago—the cut and twenty stitches. The scar had come later. "Yeah."

"From a *fist*?" he clarified.

"No, it was a razor blade." She shifted in her seat, conscious that Riley couldn't approve of her describing such a gruesome scene. But she wanted to satisfy Jacob's curiosity so they could move on. She didn't want him feeling she'd brushed his questions aside.

He frowned at her. "Must've hurt."

It had, but the pain hadn't been the worst of it. Those women, with the help of one guard who'd always had it in for her, had purposely set her up. She'd been blamed for starting the fight, which had added more than two years to her sentence. That had to be why Jacob was questioning her so carefully. He must've been told she was a troublemaker when she didn't get out.

Although that day had been one of the darkest of her whole life, Phoenix shrugged so he wouldn't have to know it. "Not too bad. Anyway, I'd like to see you pitch sometime, if you wouldn't mind having me at a game." She waved a hand before he could respond. "I'll sit on the visitors' side, so don't worry about that."

Confusion created lines in his forehead. "Why would you sit on the visitors' side?"

Because she couldn't imagine he'd want a mother who'd been in prison for murder showing up where people might recognize who she was and connect them. "I'd rather not cause a stir."

She looked to Riley for confirmation. He'd used the stigma of her crime as one of the reasons Jacob would be better off without her, so she was hoping to reassure him that she wouldn't make things difficult. But he didn't comment one way or the other, didn't say she couldn't come as she feared he might. He covered his mouth for a few seconds, rubbed his jaw, then straightened his silverware. It was Jacob who insisted she could sit wherever she liked. But a polite boy *would* say that.

"Okay, just...just let me know when you have a game." She figured if he never came forward with that information, she'd have her answer as to whether he preferred she stay away from him in public.

"How am I supposed to let you know?" he asked. "Do you have a home phone or a cell?"

She didn't. She couldn't afford either. She had far too many other necessities to buy first. "Not yet. But I have a laptop, and I learned that Black Gold Coffee has free Wi-Fi. I could set up a Facebook page, and you could message me that way—with your father's permission." He could also get hold of her through her mother, who lived in a separate trailer on the same property, but she hesitated to suggest that, given Riley's disapproval of Lizzie.

"You have a laptop?" he asked.

"I do. It was a gift from one of the correctional officers when I was released. It's an old one, but...it works."

"So you'll friend me? You know how to do that?"

She sipped more coffee. The caffeine was making her jittery on an empty stomach, but it helped to have something to do with her hands. "I took some computer classes when I was... I took some classes."

"Oh."

"What are your plans now that you're home?" Riley asked. "Are you looking for a job or...?"

"Not quite yet," she replied. "I have to finish cleaning out the trailer where I'm living before I do anything else." She almost expounded on how bad it was, how unsanitary. Her mother's hoarding was worse than ever. But she caught herself. If her primary goal was to provide a room for Jacob that Riley would deem safe—in case her son ever agreed to stay with her for a night or two—it wouldn't be wise to regale his father with the gritty details. When she'd first begun cleaning it up, the trailer hadn't been fit for pigs. Although it was a lot better now, it would be *spotless* by the time she was done.

"Where will you apply after that?"

"Anywhere there's an opening." Riley had also pointed out how difficult it would be for her to make a living in Whiskey Creek, a town of only two thousand. The school had allowed her to graduate in spite of the fact that she'd missed the last three weeks of her senior year, but a high school diploma wouldn't do much to offset her criminal record. She hadn't mentioned the business she'd started while she was still incarcerated. She had no idea if it would succeed. But she'd established a small income making leather bracelets for men and boys. The woman who'd given her the laptop, Cara Brentwell, had been putting the bracelets up on Etsy.com and eBay for the past three years. That was where, most recently, she'd gotten the bulk of the money she'd been sending to Jacob. She and Cara had split the profits but, as a free woman, she no longer needed Cara's help.

"I, um, have a small gift for you," she told Jacob. "Don't get excited, it's nothing big. You don't even have to wear it if you don't like it. I just wanted to see if... you know, maybe you'd think it was cool."

She reached into her bag and pulled out the leather pouch she'd put the bracelet in instead of wrapping it. Somehow that seemed more masculine than paper and bow.

"Thanks," he said as he accepted it.

She didn't say that she'd made it. She didn't want to give him or anyone else any reason not to like it. "If you'd rather open it later," she began, but he had his hand inside and took it out before she could finish.

"What is it?" Riley asked.

"A bracelet," Jacob piped up, and the pleasant tone of his voice was slightly reassuring. He didn't sound as if he *hated* it.

"So you've seen them before?" she said, trying to gauge whether he was just trying to salvage her feelings.

"Yeah, but none quite like this." He turned it over in his man-size hands. Fortunately, the braided leather she'd embellished with a piece of petrified wood that was carved in the shape of a bird—a play on her name that she wasn't sure he'd understand—fastened with a tie so it couldn't be too small. "It's awesome. Where'd you get it?"

The waitress arrived with their food, and Phoenix pretended she hadn't heard the question. Jacob became so distracted putting on the bracelet, and then eating, that he didn't pursue an answer.

From there the conversation became a bit stilted. Phoenix asked about his grades, expressed pride that he was doing so well and encouraged him to continue. Then she asked if he had a girlfriend. He said he didn't, that he was interested in a few different girls, but mostly just as friends, and then the conversation lagged again. It would've been more natural to talk to Riley, too, but Phoenix was careful not to direct a single question to him. She didn't want him to worry that she might still have feelings for him. Sometimes their brief relationship played out in her mind, usually late at night. Those memories were some of the best she had. But she told herself they continued to matter simply because she hadn't shared the same kind of intimacy with any other person. She'd been barely eighteen when she went to prison and, although she'd been approached by various male guards over the years, which some of her fellow inmates resented, she'd never even kissed anyone besides Riley. One guard sent her a few letters after he quit his job at the prison, but she never responded. He lived in the Bay Area, and she'd planned to return to Whiskey Creek; she'd realized all along that she'd have a very brief period to get to know her son before he reached adulthood. She didn't want to waste time on a man, especially considering how fickle and unreliable they could be, judging by the speed with which Riley had fallen in and out of love with her.

Even without being addressed, Riley added a comment here and there to support what Jacob said. Whenever that happened, Phoenix would turn a polite smile on him to acknowledge his remark. But she kept her attention on her son, which worked fine—until the check came. Then she had to engage Riley because he tried to pluck it off the corner of the table.

Thankfully, she managed to grab it before he could. She wouldn't allow him to buy her a meal, to buy her anything. This was a matter of pride, what little pride she could salvage, anyway. She'd extended the invitation; she'd pay the tab. Anything else might make him believe she was out to get something from him when, other than his blessing for her to see Jacob, she definitely wasn't.

"I don't mind," he said, as if he wasn't sure whether to insist while she counted out her money.

Even with the tip, she had enough—thank God. "It's my treat, but I appreciate the offer," she said firmly.

Leaving the money on the table, she slid out of the booth.

"Breakfast was good," Jacob said.

A jolt of hope and happiness shot through her that he seemed to have enjoyed himself. The path ahead of them would not be smooth, but she'd survived her first breakfast with Jacob and didn't feel she was about to fall apart. It probably helped that she'd had a lot of practice with disappointment. She hoped the next encounter would be easier, and the next even easier and so forth. She had to start somewhere.

"It was my pleasure," she told him.

Although she tried to lag behind, they waited for her to precede them. She didn't own a car, which meant she'd be walking five miles to the barren spot of land her mother had inherited from her own parents. Lizzie had two old trailers on that property—the one she'd filled so full of junk she could no longer live in it, which was now Phoenix's home, and the one she occupied herself, with her five dogs, two hamsters and a parrot.

Once they got outside, she stepped out of the way so they could move past her and into the parking lot. "Thank you for meeting me."

Riley squinted against the bright spring sunshine and gazed around, as if he expected someone to be there to pick her up. "How are you getting home?"

She didn't answer that question directly for fear he'd take it as a hint that she wanted a ride. "Oh, don't worry about me. I've got it covered."

"You've got what covered?"

"Aren't we talking about a way home?"

"Someone's coming to pick you up, then? When will they be here? Do you need to use my phone?"

Now that he'd pinned her down, she had to tell the truth. She couldn't use the cell he offered. She had no one to call. "There's no need to bother anyone. It's such a nice day I'm happy to walk."

He glanced down at her strappy sandals. "You can make it that far in those?"

"I made it here," she said. "They're very comfortable." Whether that was true or not wasn't important. They were all she owned.

He didn't seem convinced, but when she waved and turned to go, he started toward his truck. Jacob was the one who called her back.

"Mom?"

Phoenix's heart hit her chest with one giant thud. He hadn't addressed her as anything yet, let alone *Mom*. She hadn't expected to hear him say that, not right away, especially since she'd given him permission to use her first name instead. "Yes?" She hoped her voice didn't sound as strangled to him as it did to her.

"You told me I could say anything."

"Jacob." Riley spoke their son's name as a warning, but Phoenix ignored that, along with his frown.

"You can. It's absolutely okay."

"No matter what it is?"

She swallowed hard. She hadn't expected the questions to begin quite this soon. "Of course."

Jacob looked at his father, but his inner turmoil was obviously driving him to disregard the quick shake of Riley's head. "Did you do it?" he asked. "Because I have to hear that answer from you. *I want to know the truth after wondering about it all these years.*"

She didn't mind him asking. She longed to tell him the truth. But it would've been much easier to discuss this some quiet night when Riley wasn't with them, because she knew Riley would doubt every word she said. She was afraid he might even scoff at her denial, if not in front of her, then once he and Jacob got in the truck.

Still, now that she had the chance to tell Jacob she was innocent, she had to take it. Kids didn't always wait for the best time or place, and if she missed this opportunity, maybe she'd never have another. Not like this, with her son so...open.

Tempted to grab his arms or do something else to impress on him just how fervent she was, she stepped forward. But she was still afraid that coming on too strong would scare him away. So she stopped there and lowered her voice for emphasis. "I *didn't* do it. I *swear* I didn't do it."

"But you were driving the car! You *had* to have done it." Although he sounded argumentative, he spoke as if he wanted her to persuade him otherwise, and she appreciated that more than he could ever know.

"There was someone else in the car, Jacob. Have you heard about this?" He must've been told bits and pieces over the years. But he hadn't even been born when the trial took place, and he would've been ten or twelve before he was old enough to hear what had happened. That meant that whoever told him the story had very likely simplified an incident that was over a decade old. And once Jake entered his teens, maybe he felt it was a subject his father didn't want to touch, so he didn't push.

"No," he said, shaking his head. "Who was it?"

Did this mean that Riley was so convinced she'd been lying when she gave her side of the incident that he didn't even present it?

She didn't know how else to interpret it. "A girl my age—a friend of sorts that I was supposed to be doing a homework project with," she said. "My mother let me take the Buick so we could go to her house after school. When we spotted Lori Mansfield walking back to the high school after finishing her cross-country run, the girl who was with me said we should give her a little scare. I laughed. Maybe I said something that she took for agreement—I don't remember—because the next thing I knew, she yanked on the steering wheel."

His Adam's apple moved as he swallowed. "Someone else turned the wheel?"

"Yes. I don't think she meant to kill Lori. She had no reason to harm her. I'm guessing she thought I'd be able to correct in time, but I couldn't." She winced at the memory. "It all happened too fast."

He spread out his hands, beseeching her. "Why didn't you tell everyone that?"

Another group came out of the restaurant. She fell silent until they'd regained their privacy. Then she said, "I tried." She'd told everyone in the courtroom. Riley hadn't been there the day she testified, but surely he'd heard what she'd said from someone. "No one would believe me."

She wondered how Riley was taking all of this but was afraid to look at him. "It's the truth, but the girl who was with me denied it."

"You're saying she *lied*?"

Penny Sawyer had left Whiskey Creek right after high school and never come back, and Phoenix knew she probably never would. "Yes. Under oath."

"Why would she do that?"

"I'm sure she was scared, Jacob. She didn't want what was happening to me to happen to her."

"So she let you take the fall."

"Essentially."

"But…why would her word be any better than yours?"

At this, Phoenix couldn't stop her gaze from shifting to Riley. She found him watching her as intently as Jacob and got the impression he was trying to figure out whether he could believe her any more than he had before. So she decided to tell the down-to-the-soul truth, regardless of the embarrassment certain admissions might cause her. "Because they knew I had a…a terrible crush on your father. They called it an obsession, and maybe it was. They also knew by then that I was pregnant. You see, I hadn't told anyone about you before the accident. I was too scared my mother, the school counselor and anyone who knew your father would want me to…to end the pregnancy or put you up for adoption. I wasn't willing to do either."

"They thought you were jealous of Lori."

She guessed he'd heard that part before, since the entire story hinged on it. But had Riley provided the information? Or was it Riley's parents? Or even others in town? She'd always wondered what people were telling Jacob about her. "They assumed I thought your father would come back to me if she was out of the picture. And the girl in my car had no motive. She was just being…silly."

"That's so unfair!" Jacob turned as if to gain the support of his father, but Riley remained silent, his hands jammed into the front pockets of his jeans.

"If what you're saying is true, you served all that time for nothing," Jacob said when he faced her again. "Why didn't you fight harder to get people to believe you?"

Because she'd been an odd, unfortunate eighteen-year-old girl struggling to grow up with an obese, hoarding mother who wouldn't even leave the house. Without champions, without the money to hire a decent attorney instead of the public defender who'd done a halfhearted job at best, she'd had nowhere to turn. To make things worse, Riley's parents were so sympathetic to Lori's family that they complained about how many times she'd phoned Riley or driven by their house, told everyone how she'd followed him around town. The fact that she'd also crank-called Lori after Riley had started dating her, had become a big part of the case against her.

Everything that could go wrong simply had.

"I didn't have the tools," she said. "I was only two years older than you are now and I was pretty well on my own. There wasn't a lot I could do." Especially because she couldn't claim that she hadn't been absolutely consumed with Riley. The day he came into her life everything had changed; it'd been like feeling the sun on her face for the first time. But after only six weeks of an intense "I have to be with you every second" affair, he'd suddenly broken up with her.

As rocky as her life had been, she'd never felt pain to equal that.

But she hadn't killed anyone.

"The girl, the one who lied, this is all her fault," Jacob said. "Do you know where she is? Are you going to try and find her and make her admit the truth?"

Phoenix had spent seventeen years thinking about getting out of prison and going in search of Penny. She craved vindication. But she knew chasing after it would be a waste of effort. Even if she could find Penny, it would still be her word against that of someone more credible. No one wanted to consider the possibility that an innocent woman might have been in prison for so long. And even if Penny suddenly and miraculously came forward on her own, it wouldn't change what Phoenix had been through. It probably wouldn't convince the people she needed to convince, since they didn't want to believe the truth, anyway.

"No." In the beginning, she'd sent so many letters to Penny, pleading with her to tell the truth. All the ones she'd mailed after the Sawyers left Whiskey Creek had been returned. She didn't even know whether the early ones had reached the girl who could've made such a difference. "I have to focus on moving forward, forget the past."

Jacob stared at his feet. When he lifted his head and spoke again, he sounded torn. "I'm not sure I can believe you."

"That's okay." She forgave him easily, was grateful he was actually trying. "I understand how hard it is. I won't put any pressure on you. We don't have to talk about it again, if you don't want to. We—"

"I think that's enough for today," Riley broke in. "Jacob, let's go. We've got to work."

Anxiety-induced sweat rolled down Phoenix's spine. But she smiled so her son would know he could leave without feeling bad about anything. She didn't blame him for being confused, and she certainly didn't want to detain him any longer and get him in trouble with his dad. She'd known from the beginning that she'd have to earn Jacob's trust over time.

Clasping her hands in front of her, she watched them get in Riley's truck. She'd just taken a deep breath and was about to start her long walk home when Jacob turned and waved—and she knew she'd carry the memory of that tentative smile for the rest of her life.

2

Jacob sat in silence as they pulled out of the parking lot. They had a job today, a remodel of one of the older Victorians in town, and needed to go to the lumber store, about ten miles away. On Saturdays, Riley hired his son to help out so Jacob could learn the trade, in case he cared to become a partner in the business when he was older or wanted to get his own contractor's license. They had a lot to do, and they were getting a late start because they'd met Phoenix for breakfast, but right now it was difficult to concentrate on anything other than the past hour. Riley was so torn about what he'd seen and heard, he knew Jacob had to be really confused.

"You okay?" he asked as they rolled to a stop at the traffic light in the center of town.

Jacob gave him a morose shrug.

"Could you use your voice?" Riley asked.

"I feel…weird," Jacob replied.

He looked sullen and unhappy. "Weird in what way?" Riley could guess, since he was so conflicted himself, but he felt it was important to get his son to talk to him about Phoenix. It hadn't been easy to become a father at eighteen. Other than the help he'd received early on from his parents while he was commuting to college three days a week, he'd raised Jacob alone.

But Riley had a feeling that he was facing a much more formidable challenge now. He didn't want Phoenix back in his life or his son's, didn't want to cope with all the old questions and doubts.

"I met my mother for the first time a few minutes ago, and I can't decide how I should feel about her."

Because he had no frame of reference. Riley hadn't even given Jacob the many letters she'd sent, other than a handful of the less emotional ones. In his mind, he'd been protecting his son, hoping she'd move on and just leave them alone when she was eventually released. But if she *was* innocent, maybe standing between her and Jake had only hurt them both.

If so, that was a lot to feel responsible for.

"It'll take a while to adjust," he told Jacob.

"How would *you* feel if you were me?" his son asked. "Do *you* think she killed Lori Mansfield?"

The light turned green and Riley gave the truck some gas. Jacob had asked this question several times over the years, but Riley had always been able to say he wasn't sure and leave it at that. Phoenix hadn't ever been present in Jacob's life, so Jacob hadn't pushed the issue. But with her back home, he needed a more definitive answer.

"She wasn't herself when all of that happened," Riley said.

Jacob leaned forward to look into his face. "What does that *mean*? Are you saying yes or no?"

Riley had no idea whether she'd killed Lori. He only knew that everyone else insisted she must have, and the scenario created at her trial seemed logical. Lori was the girl he'd started dating right after Phoenix, and Phoenix had acted terribly jealous. "I'm saying she became a little...intense after I broke up with her."

He'd often relied on her erratic behavior during that time as a reason to withhold another one of her letters.

"She *could* have done it."

"Yes."

The expression on his son's face made it clear he didn't like that answer. "But 'could have' isn't proof!"

"There were witnesses, Jake."

"Who saw her behind the wheel! She admits she was driving."

"Penny Sawyer was a witness."

"The friend she told us about? Penny, the one who might've grabbed the wheel?"

"Penny had no motive."

His scowl deepened. "How come I don't know any Penny Sawyer?"

"She moved away after the trial."

"Why?"

"Because she'd graduated from high school, so she left for college like almost everyone else."

"*You* didn't leave for college."

"I went to UC Davis three days a week because it's only an hour away, and I had you. I wanted to be able to come home at night and take care of you. *My* situation was different, not hers."

Jacob didn't respond right away, but he didn't sound any more convinced when he did. "Has she ever returned?"

"Not to my knowledge."

"*That's* unusual, isn't it?"

"Not if her family relocated during those four years, which they did. She had no reason to come back here."

"She could've lied about what happened."

"Or Phoenix is lying. Like I said, she wasn't in the best frame of mind when Lori was killed."

"So her frame of mind clinches the deal? Makes her guilty? Or did my mom go to prison just because she was heartbroken and jealous? She was pregnant at eighteen, with no one to turn to except a weird mother she was embarrassed by—a mother who couldn't really do anything to help, anyway. From what I've seen of *that* grandma, you were the most normal thing Mom ever had in her life. *Of course* she'd try to grab on to you. She probably felt like she was drowning. And you *were* the one who got her pregnant."

The fact that she'd been a virgin until he came along still made Riley feel ashamed of breaking up with her the way he had. But he hadn't known she was pregnant when he told her he didn't want to see her anymore. He'd only been acting on the advice—the *insistence*—of his parents. They'd been so positive that he was about to ruin his life by getting involved with a girl who wasn't worthy of him they'd threatened not to pay for college if he didn't listen.

"I wasn't there that day," Riley reiterated. "I can't say what happened."

"You must believe *something* deep inside."

Riley wished his heart told him she was guilty. Then everything would be simple; he could condemn her without reservation. But…damn all the doubts. He'd always wrestled with them, as well as the question of how much involvement he should allow her to have in Jacob's life. He'd been trying to act in the best interests of his son. His parents agreed with keeping her as far away from Jacob as possible. In the beginning, they were the ones who'd suggested it.

But had he done the right thing?

"I don't know what to believe," he admitted. "I hope she didn't serve seventeen years for a crime she didn't commit."

"You'd rather believe she's a murderer?" Jacob broke in, pushing him to commit himself one way or the other.

Riley gripped the steering wheel tighter. "No, of course not. There are no for-sure answers in this, that's all. Trust me, if there were, I would've found them. I've nearly driven myself crazy with all the wondering and the second-guessing."

"You helped put her away."

He shot his son a glance that let him know he didn't appreciate being reminded of that. He'd only spoken the truth when he testified about her incessant phone calls and her attempts to get back with him. But the last thing he wanted to believe was that she might have been wrongly punished and he'd had a hand in making that happen. "The DA put me on the stand. It wasn't my choice." He'd cared enough about her to want to stay out of the whole mess.

Jacob knocked his head against the passenger window. "God, I hate this! I'm tired of thinking about it, tired of everyone watching to see what I'm going to do now. Part of me wants to go on with my life and pretend she doesn't exist. We've made it this far without her, right? But…if she's not evil, I don't see why I can't have a mother."

Riley sighed. He'd screwed up so badly when he'd gotten involved with Phoenix.

Or…maybe not. He loved Jacob too much to regret those six weeks. And it was hard to regret them for a different reason—he'd never had another girlfriend with whom he'd felt such an immediate and solid connection. He'd dated plenty of women who were more "suitable," especially since then. But he had yet to find someone who was as engaging as Phoenix had been.

"I liked her," Jacob said without being prompted, his voice sulky. He obviously hadn't expected softening his heart to be such a temptation. Maybe he even resented it.

"I can see why. She was very nice at breakfast."

"That's not how she usually is?"

Riley turned down the radio. "It's been seventeen years, bud. I can't say how she usually is." Prison might have twisted her if she wasn't already as twisted as everyone thought.

Jacob twirled the leather bracelet she'd given him around his wrist as he tried to puzzle out how he was going to react now that his mother was back. "She tried to make this morning easy for me. Did you notice?"

"I did."

"That was cool, after everything she's been through. Don't you think? She didn't try to make us feel sorry for her or like we had to do anything we didn't want to…"

"I agree. I thought that was…admirable." Riley didn't want to reverse his opinion or his policies on the basis of one meeting, but he'd been impressed with Phoenix—*really* impressed. She obviously took care of herself physically. She'd looked…not beautiful but attractive. And she'd said all the right things, done all the right things. She'd even paid for their meal, despite the fact that she had so little. Seeing her pick up the check, Riley wished he'd made arrangements with the waitress beforehand so he wouldn't have to feel as if he'd taken her last dollar.

But did her behavior in this one instance mean he should foster a relationship between her and Jacob?

Would that be good for his son or the worst decision Riley had ever made?

"What was she like in high school?" Jacob asked.

In an attempt to relax, Riley slung one arm over the wheel. "She was different from the other girls. Aloof. One of those people who watches the world and everyone around them with a certain amount of skepticism and distrust." They'd been over this before. But, apparently, Jacob needed to hear it again.

"She wasn't part of your crowd."

"No."

"Was she popular?"

"Not at all."

"But you were popular. So why'd you go out with her?"

"I've told you. At first I saw only what everyone else saw. But one of our teachers asked me to tutor her in math, and after I started getting to know her, I learned that different isn't necessarily bad. She was more interesting than the other kids. She wasn't that great in math, but she was smart in other ways."

"Did you think she was pretty?"

He pictured her as she used to be, in her dark clothes and big army boots, the black fingernail polish, the eyeliner and bloodred lipstick. "Not really." She looked a lot better now, but he didn't add that.

"Why not? What was wrong with her?"

"Nothing. She just refused to conform, wasn't fixed up like the other girls were. She always wore baggy, secondhand clothes. Didn't come to many school functions. Ate alone."

"But…"

The tone of his voice must have suggested that he wasn't revealing everything, and Jacob was once again pressing for more. "She didn't have a lot to begin with, as you've pointed out," Riley went on. And somehow she'd made it work, managed to create her own style. He'd come to admire that—and more—while they were together. He'd considered her someone who dared to go against the norm and disregard the dictates of the "in" crowd.

At least, that was what he'd thought of her until everything went so horribly wrong. Then it was easier to believe, like everyone else, that she didn't have the conscience of a normal person.

"*I* think she's pretty," Jacob said.

"She's okay," Riley muttered, but these days she was much better than "okay." Despite two or three scars, which didn't detract from her appearance, there was a sophistication to her face that hadn't been there before. And her eyes... They were more guarded than ever, but a measure of strength, maturity and determination shone through that set her apart. So he wasn't fooled. Although she'd been very respectful this morning, almost deferential, there was still some fight left in her. All he had to do to find out how much was deny her the chance to be part of her son's life. That was another reason he felt so torn. She wouldn't be easy to dissuade where Jacob was concerned. He'd tried—to no avail.

"And I like the bracelet she gave me," Jacob said.

"I can tell." Riley pulled into the parking lot of Meek's Lumber. "Are you going to invite her to one of your games?"

"Why not? Anyone can go to the school." He hesitated with his hand on the door latch. "You'll let me, right?"

As much as he wanted to refuse, if only to keep their lives simple and moving forward on the same track,

Riley didn't see how he could continue to enforce his will. "If having her there is what you want."

"I can't see how it'll hurt anything," he said.

Riley hoped that was the case.

Phoenix spent the first half of the walk home in a daze, reliving every minute of breakfast and thinking about Jacob—what it'd been like to meet him, to speak with him, to see him put on the bracelet she'd made. But after a couple of miles, she could no longer ignore the blisters that were forming on her feet. It was so hot today; every part of her body felt sticky.

She wiped the sweat from her forehead with one arm and considered removing her sandals. She would have, except there were too many briar-like plants and sharp rocks along the side of the road. And she couldn't walk on the pavement without getting burned.

"Not much farther," she told herself, but that was hardly encouraging when she had another three miles.

Why hadn't she been more practical with the pittance the state had given her on her release? She could've bought some cheap running shoes. She'd tried on a pair. But she'd had her first encounter with Jacob in mind when she chose these sandals. She'd wanted to look her best.

She wondered if she'd hear from him on Facebook…

At the sound of a vehicle approaching from behind, she stepped off to one side, kept her face averted and waited for whoever it was to pass by. She didn't want anyone to see how badly she was limping. She felt too many people in Whiskey Creek would take pleasure in her distress.

And what if it was one of Lori Mansfield's parents or another member of her family?

They might try to take revenge. They'd certainly sent her enough ugly letters once they found out she was going to be released, warning her not to return to Whiskey Creek, threatening her if she did.

She tensed as the vehicle drew closer. It didn't whiz by with a blast of hot air, as she expected. It slowed and came to a stop a few feet ahead of her. Then the driver— a dark-haired man from what she could see through the back window—leaned over and opened the passenger door. "Would you like a lift?" he called out.

Because she had no idea who this person was or what he might do to her, she almost waved him off. But this was Whiskey Creek; there wasn't any violent crime here to speak of. As long as he wasn't connected to the Mansfields, she should be okay. Not *everyone* in Whiskey Creek these days had been around when she lived here before. This could be a complete stranger, his offer the simple kindness it appeared to be.

Grateful that she wouldn't have to continue the painful journey on foot, she hobbled to the truck. "Thank you. It's so hot out today. And these darn sandals…"

As soon as she recognized him, she choked back the rest of her words. He wasn't connected to Lori Mansfield—thank God. But he *was* connected to Riley. This was Kyle Houseman, one of the many friends who'd hung out with Riley all through school.

Phoenix didn't want Riley to find out that Kyle had discovered her in such a pathetic state, so she backed away. "Actually, never mind. I just realized there's no way we could be going to the same place. But thanks!"

She slammed the door, praying that would be the end of it. But he didn't drive off. He reached over and opened the door again.

"You might not be aware of it yet, but you're getting

sunburned," he said. "And it looks like we're traveling in the same *direction* at least. I don't mind going a little out of my way."

If he knew who she was, he didn't let on. But he would figure it out if she had him drop her anywhere close to her mother's property. And getting close to her mother's property was the whole point of accepting a ride. "I'm fine. Really. It's not much farther."

His eyes narrowed as recognition dawned. "Wait a second...you're Phoenix."

"Yes. Another reason you should go on your way." After closing the door, she forced herself to walk without favoring either foot. But he lowered the window and rolled along beside her.

"I know where you live. Let me give you a ride."

"I can walk a couple of miles," she said.

"You seemed to be struggling when I came up behind you."

He'd noticed? From so far away? "These sandals are new, that's all. I'll break them in."

"So you don't need a ride."

"No, thank you."

"Come on!" he argued. "I can't leave a woman limping on the side of the road."

"According to most folks around here, I'm not a regular woman."

"What does that mean?"

"I'm a murderer, remember? Surely, you can leave *me*." Instantly regretting the harshness of those words, she glanced over and attempted a smile. "I didn't mean to be rude. I just...I'd rather not trouble you."

"But it's no trouble!"

Refusing was making a bigger issue out of this than

simply giving in. Besides, she couldn't tolerate the pain of marching beside him anymore.

When she stopped, so did he. "Fine. I guess I will take that ride," she said, and climbed in.

As she put on her seat belt, he studied her with avid curiosity, and she supposed that was the price of his help. She was a freak in this town—the one person more reprehensible than all the rest.

"I'm sure you've got a camera on your cell phone," she said. "Go ahead and take a picture."

"I'm sorry." He sounded a little abashed. "It's hard not to stare. You look...different."

So did he. Like Riley, he'd filled out, not that she cared. Anything that had to do with Riley—except Jacob, of course—was off-limits. She couldn't even be friends with this man. "I'm nearly seventeen years older. Of course I look different."

"What I mean is you look *good*," he clarified. "You've aged better than the rest of us."

He must not have noticed her scars. "I'm sure that's not true."

He leaned over to examine her feet. "You're bleeding."

Embarrassed, she raised the foot that hurt the most so it couldn't touch anything, but he was increasing his speed, so he obviously didn't expect her to jump out. "You're the one who made me get in."

"This is a work truck, nothing fancy, so don't worry about that. But you might want to grab a napkin from the glove box."

She did. Trying not to show how badly it stung, she patted one of those napkins against the blister that had burst.

"How long have you been home?" he asked as he drove.

"If you're still friends with Riley, you know the answer to that question," she replied.

He grinned as if she'd caught him. "Right. I admit he's mentioned it. You got back…what? Two, three days ago?"

She kept her eyes on her foot. Kyle was nearly as handsome as Riley, but she didn't want to acknowledge that. "Look, I'm not sure why you're helping me. But if it's because you want the chance to warn me not to cause your buddy any trouble, I assure you I won't. I'm not going to cause anyone any trouble, least of all Riley or Lori's family. I plan to keep to myself, mind my own business and…and see if I can't get to know my son before he's an adult and off to college." She almost added, *That's not too much to ask, is it?* But she understood that for many people here, it was too much to ask. They didn't think she deserved anything—even to breathe the same air.

"You don't have to be defensive with me," he said. "I have no hidden agenda. I'm curious about you. Everyone is. But I don't wish you any harm. And I'm pretty sure Riley can fend you off, if necessary."

She folded her arms, wrapping them tightly around herself as she watched the scenery fly past her window. "He won't have to fend me off."

They'd almost reached the entrance to her mother's property when Kyle said, "It was nice of you to send money to Jacob. I don't think many people in your situation would've bothered."

Riley had told him about her child support, too? He and Kyle must be as close as ever, she decided, but said nothing.

"The amounts you sent had to have been a sacrifice," he added. "It's tough to earn much inside."

"I did my best." God, wasn't that the truth. She'd worked long, hard hours in the laundry, made bracelets on the side, thanks to the craft class that had inspired her business, and gone without everything she possibly could to provide that pittance for Jacob. "I wanted to do my part."

"What did you say?"

Apparently, she'd spoken too softly. "I was happy to do it," she said in a louder voice.

He pulled through the gate, which was sagging so much it couldn't be closed, and her mother's dogs, the three that weren't inside Lizzie's trailer, went wild.

She opened the door, which drew them, barking and jumping, to her side. The dilapidated condition of both trailers, not to mention the state of the yard, made her even more self-conscious about her situation here at home. She didn't want Kyle to take note of all the junk, but she didn't get out immediately in spite of that. He'd been surprisingly nice and, since she was prepared to meet hostility around every corner, she felt she hadn't responded as politely as she should have. "Thank you for the ride. I apologize if I seemed…reluctant or ungrateful at first."

With that, she managed to hop to the ground despite her blisters. Then she stood on one foot to watch him leave—it hurt too much to use the other—and was puzzled when, after he put the transmission in Reverse, he didn't leave.

"If you ever need a ride, especially before your feet have healed, call me," he said, and wrote his number on a scrap of paper, which he handed her.

3

The noise of the dogs brought her mother to the door. Because of Lizzie's tremendous weight, she moved slowly and ponderously, so Kyle was gone by then. Phoenix was glad of that. But it was never easy to contend with her mother.

"What the hell's going on out here?" Lizzie shouted, her words and tone containing the caustic edge she was so famous for.

Phoenix pocketed the slip with Kyle Houseman's number, removed the sandal on the foot that hurt the most and limped close enough that she wouldn't have to shout. She'd promised herself before she left prison that she'd be unfailingly kind to her mother. As ornery as Lizzie could be, she hated herself more than anyone else did. After what Phoenix had been through, she had greater empathy and understood that Lizzie sounded worse than she actually was. It was smarter not to react to all the cussing and yelling and the harsh things her mother said to drive people away.

Fortunately, the dogs stopped barking and settled down, so it became possible to speak in a normal voice. "Everything's okay, Mom. Don't worry," she said, but a few calm words would never reassure Lizzie. She took nothing on faith and was always ready to fight, even if she was only shadowboxing some imaginary enemy.

A scowl creased what Phoenix could see of her face through the narrow opening. "Thought I heard a car."

"You did." Phoenix picked up her sandal. "My feet were hurting, so I caught a ride home."

Now that she was no longer in danger of revealing herself to anyone else, Lizzie opened the door wider. "From *who*?"

"Just some guy who passed me." Phoenix shrugged. Her mother didn't need to hear the details. *She* wasn't even sure what to make of Kyle, whether or not she could trust his kindness. She had few friends in this town and that probably wouldn't change.

"You hitchhiked?"

"More or less."

Her mother tsked. "You better watch out. Folks around here hate you, and you have no idea how they might decide to show it," she said. Then she shut the door.

Phoenix stared at it, wondering why her mother had to be so difficult. Before she left this morning, Phoenix had told Lizzie she'd be having breakfast with Jacob. Why couldn't she have shown a little interest in that momentous occasion?

She could have at least asked how it went…

Except that Lizzie thought reaching out to Jacob, holding on to any shred of hope that he might accept her, was a waste of time. She insisted that Riley would never allow either one of them to play a significant role in Jacob's life and Phoenix was a fool for trying to prove she cared.

Maybe it was true.

With a shake of her head, she started back to her own

trailer, which wasn't easy with one bare foot. She had to thread her way through the refuse that had been dumped in the yard since before she was born. That meant circumventing old tires, two broken-down vehicles from when her mother did drive, a decrepit, hand-powered lawn mower, a washing machine. But it wasn't the big stuff that worried her now that Kyle wasn't there to see it. She was afraid she'd step on a nail or a piece of broken glass.

If she hadn't been looking so carefully, she might've missed the banged-up bike peeking out from under an old mattress. Once she'd pulled it out, she saw that it had two flat tires and the frame was rusty, but…maybe she could fix it. Then she wouldn't have to walk every time she needed to go to town.

Pushing the bike, she reached the trailer and leaned it up against the side. This was a project she'd have to tackle later.

She was just climbing the three steps to her door when her mother screeched her name.

From her new vantage point, Phoenix couldn't see Lizzie's steps—or Lizzie, either—but it wasn't difficult to tell she was standing where she'd been before. She rarely came all the way outside.

"Yes?" she called back.

"My toilet's plugged up!"

Phoenix allowed herself a grimace but was careful to keep the impatience out of her voice. "Did you try to plunge it?"

"You know I can't bend over like that!"

So who'd played the role of plumber before Phoenix got home? The guy who'd delivered the groceries? Or did Lizzie call—and somehow pay—for a professional? Maybe she got a cut rate, like at the vet's…

Phoenix didn't bother asking. She went back and un-clogged the toilet. Then she washed the blood off her feet and found some Band-Aids to protect her blisters.

"I'm hungry," her mother announced as soon as she was done, so she warmed up some soup, hoping her mother would eat a healthy meal instead of the cheap pizza, soda, chips, cookies and candy she normally consumed. Only when Phoenix had finished cleaning out a small section of her mother's kitchen—the one part not buried beneath all the things her mother hoarded—did she feel free to return to her own place, and by then it was after two in the afternoon.

The day was getting away from her, and she still had several bracelet orders to fill. She also planned to make some progress on the overhaul of her trailer. She'd been living out of the kitchen, bathroom and one bedroom—all she'd managed to put right so far. That alone was a major improvement over what she'd known in prison, but she was determined to turn her humble abode into a home she could be proud of, for its cleanliness if nothing else. People in Whiskey Creek might not believe that she was innocent of Lori Mansfield's murder, but at least she'd show them she wasn't willing to live in filth, like her mother.

She'd eventually have to clean the yard, too, if Lizzie would let her. It hadn't been easy to talk her mother into allowing her to move the junk from the trailer into an old shed. Lizzie was terrified some of it would be thrown away, since the shed was full, too. And that was exactly what Phoenix had done. There wasn't room for all the newspapers, plastic bags, paper sacks, balls of aluminum foil, empty soda bottles and other garbage her mother had collected. So when Lizzie wasn't looking, Phoenix had made piles behind her trailer. Then she'd gone out early yesterday morning, on trash day, and dumped everything in the county's container.

Phoenix was still frightened her mother would find out. Lizzie couldn't bear to part with a single scrap of anything for fear she'd need it later. But she wasn't as mobile as she used to be. Phoenix hoped that would save her from discovery. She had enough battles to fight at the moment. She didn't need a big argument with her mother.

Once Phoenix removed her brown linen shorts and crisp blue cotton blouse—more damp than crisp after her walk home—she pulled on a T-shirt and a pair of old jeans she'd cut into shorts and belted because they were too big for her. The clothes had belonged to one of her brothers. She wasn't sure which. She hadn't seen Kip or Cary since she was ten. They'd both left town as soon as they could and never looked back. Kip hadn't even been eighteen.

Phoenix had thought they might return one day, for her sake, and maybe they would have, if she hadn't gone to prison. Her mother had spoken to them during her trial and asked them to send money for her defense. They'd helped a little, but it hadn't been nearly enough to do any good, and they'd only written her a couple of times since. She guessed they considered her a lost cause, like their mother.

Finally beginning to relax after her anxious morning, she started the bracelets that had to be shipped on Monday. She planned to paint afterward. Although the gallon she'd discovered in the old shed at the back of the property wouldn't go very far, there were another couple of gallons out there, and she found rehabbing the trailer to be a soothing exercise. She loved seeing the place transformed, figured she might as well do what she could with the paint while her mother had her favorite shows to entertain her and was less likely to need anything.

But she couldn't work as fast as usual. She was too absorbed in thinking about her son, kept stopping to look at the picture of him with braces. She was just planning how she'd decorate his room, which was something she enjoyed imagining, when she put her head down on her wobbly excuse for a desk. She was only going to rest for a few minutes…

"What do you mean you gave Phoenix a ride?" Although Jacob had helped Riley do the prep work for the shower they were putting in the Victorian that was their current project, Riley had dropped him off at the high school so he could do some weight training with the rest of the baseball team. He'd purposely waited until he was alone to follow up on the text he'd received from Kyle at noon.

"She was walking along the side of the road when I was heading out to see Callie, who has some interesting news to share, by the way."

Riley opened his mouth to ask for more information about Phoenix but was distracted by the mention of Callie.

"What kind of news?"

"I want to tell you, but…on second thought, I'd better wait and let her."

"Is something wrong? She's okay, isn't she? I mean… nothing's wrong with the transplant?"

Due to nonalcoholic fatty liver disease, their good friend had a liver transplant a couple of years ago, just before she married her husband, Levi. She seemed to be doing well since, but she had to take immunosuppressant drugs every day, and they had some unfavorable side effects. Riley had always been a little uneasy about her, terrified that there might be a problem with her new liver. If the transplant hadn't become available when it did, they would've lost her.

"She's fine. It's not necessarily a *bad* thing."

So what, then? Riley reflected on what they'd been talking about yesterday, when the entire group met at Black Gold Coffee, like they did every Friday. "She's been planning to expand her photography studio. Is that what's going on? Did she find the right location? Are you looking over the lease for her?"

"No. I'm sorry I brought it up. I spoke without thinking, because it's been on my mind so much. But it's her news. I should let her share it."

"Why would she tell you and not me?" Riley asked. "If the space she's considering needs improvements, she'd come to me."

"You'll understand later," Kyle replied with a laugh.

That laugh reassured him. Kyle wouldn't be jovial if Callie's life was on the line again. "As long as her new liver is functioning properly..."

"It is. I swear."

Riley took a deep breath. "Then back to Phoenix. She was probably walking home from Just Like Mom's, where we had breakfast this morning. I told her it was too far in those sandals."

"By the time I saw her, she'd gotten about halfway and had such bad blisters she could hardly walk."

The mental picture made Riley wince, since he could've spared her that. "Did she recognize you?"

"Immediately. That's what made it so difficult to get her into the truck."

"Why? You don't have any history with her."

"But you do, and I'm part of your circle."

Riley had gone from being the object of her desire to being anathema to her. At breakfast, she was careful not to show her dislike, but she'd barely looked at him. "How'd you convince her?"

"I wouldn't take no for an answer. I couldn't bear to let her continue walking on those bloody feet."

Riley supposed *he* should've insisted on giving her a ride. She wasn't his responsibility, and yet she sort of was. "Did she tell you we met up this morning?"

"No. She didn't say much of anything."

Then what was the purpose of this call? "That's all you wanted to tell me? That you gave her a ride?"

Kyle cleared his throat. "Actually, no. I wanted to see if you'd mind if…"

"What?"

"If I bought her a few things."

Riley pulled to the side of the road and sat there with his engine idling. He had his Bluetooth on, so he could legally talk while he was behind the wheel but at the moment, he couldn't concentrate on anything besides the conversation. "What are you talking about? What kind of *things*?"

"A few necessities. Nothing big."

"Why would you do that?"

"Because I feel sorry for her, okay? She has nothing. I don't know how long it's been since you were out at Lizzie's place, but…it doesn't look good. When she gets rid of something, she just throws it in the yard. With that kind of start, it won't be easy for Phoenix to rebuild her life. She couldn't have saved much in prison, not with the money she kept sending you."

Riley shook his head in disbelief. "Since when did you develop such compassion for my ex-girlfriend?"

"Since I saw her hobbling down the road, and she was hesitant to accept even the slightest kindness for fear…I don't know, for fear it would turn out to be another kick in the teeth. She reminds me of an abused animal, the way she tries to avoid people or skirt around them."

"You learned all this from one encounter."

"Even after she got in, she hugged the door. She looked like she'd jump out if I so much as raised my hand to scratch my head. She's got a difficult road ahead of her, especially here in Whiskey Creek. But she's facing down her detractors for the sake of her son. That takes guts, man. I can't help admiring it."

Riley felt the same grudging admiration, but he hated to acknowledge it. Hated to acknowledge that he'd probably go anywhere *but* Whiskey Creek if he were in her shoes. Not many people could withstand so much negative sentiment, and that wasn't her only challenge. "Her mother lives here, too," he pointed out, as if Lizzie gave her a second compelling reason to return.

"If anything, that impresses me more. It's damn noble of her to come back to that kind of situation."

Noble wasn't a word he'd ever heard in conjunction with Phoenix. "You're serious."

"I don't want to debate whether or not she's really a murderer, Riley. As far as I'm concerned, that's in the past. Who can say what was going through her mind when she did whatever she did? I only know that according to the judicial system, she's paid her debt to society. Maybe the Mansfields aren't satisfied, but seventeen years is a long time and I, for one, am ready to let her move on."

Riley rubbed a hand over his face. If what she'd said in court—and reiterated this morning—about her friend yanking on the steering wheel was true, she wasn't even responsible for what had happened. But he didn't see anything to be gained by dredging that up. The truth was, Kyle's offer to help her bothered him for other reasons, none of which he wanted to examine too closely. "What are you thinking of buying her?"

"New shoes, for starters. Since she doesn't have a car, she's going to be on her feet, walking a lot. And some clothes. Just a few things. I'll spend three, four hundred dollars, tops."

Riley winced again, this time at the memory of her buying *his* breakfast this morning, remembered how carefully she'd laid out the bills. "She won't take charity, particularly from me or one of my friends."

"I don't plan to give her a choice."

A line of other cars flowed past. "How are you going to avoid that?"

"I'll buy the stuff and leave it on her doorstep anonymously—if I can get to her doorstep without being bitten by Lizzie's dogs."

"How do you know her size?"

"I was hoping *you'd* have that information."

"No. I haven't got a clue." He suddenly remembered a lazy afternoon when they were hanging out together, and he was teasing her about how small her feet were. She'd told him she wore a six. That jumped into his mind, but he didn't retract his initial answer. Kyle was going to need more than her shoe size.

"Then I'll guess, pay cash and include the receipt so she can return or exchange the stuff."

Riley pinched the bridge of his nose. "You've put some thought into this."

"It's been all I can think about since I dropped her off."

"Fine, if that's what you'd like to do," he said. "I'm not sure why you're even telling me about it."

"You're *not*?"

"It's not as if she's my enemy!"

"Really? Because I distinctly remember you not wanting her to come back. You spent years dreading the day."

Riley couldn't keep from feeling defensive. "I have a lot on the line," he said.

"I understand. I'm not faulting you. I just felt I should let you know, because making things easier for her might also encourage her to stay when you'd rather she left."

He had a feeling she'd stay regardless. She was *so* stubborn. "I don't care if you help her."

"Good. Thanks. And if it's any reassurance, she told me she's not out to cause you any trouble."

"She volunteered that?"

"Pretty much."

"Why?"

"My guess? To make it clear that she's on her best behavior. That she wouldn't ask you for anything, wouldn't expect anything—even a ride from a friend of yours. She just wants everyone to leave her alone. And she wants to get to know Jacob, of course."

Riley thought about how quiet his son had been all day. "I think he wants to get to know her, too."

"Are you comfortable with that?"

He leaned his head back on the seat. "He's sixteen. I don't feel it's my choice anymore."

"Then we'd better hope her intentions are as good as she claims."

No kidding. "I guess we'll see, huh? I'll talk to you later."

"Riley?"

He hesitated before hanging up. "What?"

"She's a lot prettier these days."

A flash of anger shot through him, and he sat up straight. "That had better not be why you're helping her!"

"Calm down. It's not," he said. "I just wondered if you'd noticed."

"I've noticed," he responded, and hit the end button.

"What about this?"

Riley grimaced at the blue dress Kyle had pulled off the rack. He was beginning to wonder what had possessed him to call his friend back and offer to go shopping with him. Just because Kyle had decided to play Santa in the middle of spring didn't mean Riley had to get in on the act. "I don't know. I don't even know what I'm doing here," he grumbled.

"I do," Kyle said. "Phoenix is your son's mother. So there's that. And you feel bad about letting her buy you breakfast this morning, knowing she's got to be living on pennies."

"No, it's your fault," he said. "You dragged me into this."

"*Dragged* you? You're the one who suggested we stop at the grocery store on the way over here and get some canned goods. Thanks to you, we spent nearly fifty bucks on soup and chili and crackers and shit, and walked out of there with almost two boxfuls."

The memory of Phoenix sitting at Just Like Mom's in probably the only nice outfit she owned, counting out the money to cover his breakfast, made him squirm. But this wasn't *just* about that. Spending a couple hundred bucks to help her get a start was the least he could do, *especially* if she was innocent. "Food makes sense. She probably needs that most of all."

The sales assistant approached, a woman by the name of Kirsten, according to her badge.

"Clothes make sense, too," Kyle said. "So...should we buy it?" He shook the dress to bring Riley's attention back to it.

"That's part of our new spring line," Kirsten volunteered. "The cap sleeves are darling. So is the print. And with the way cotton breathes, it's perfect for the warmer months. Any woman would love it."

Riley figured she'd know better than they would. The girl he'd dated years ago would never wear something so feminine. But Phoenix was a woman now, and judging by what she'd had on at the restaurant this morning, her tastes had matured.

Even if it wasn't the *perfect* choice, he doubted she'd be too critical. No one could ever accuse her of being spoiled. "I guess it's fine." They'd already been shopping for two hours and had agonized over their other purchases just as much. Now the mall was about to close, and they still had a ninety-minute drive home. He was anxious to be done.

With a sigh of relief, Kyle turned to the sales associate. "We'll take it."

She was heading to the register when Riley stopped her. "Wait! I don't think that one will fit." They hadn't even looked at the tag.

"What size do you need?" she asked.

"A small one," he replied.

"That doesn't tell me a lot." She chuckled. "*How* small?"

"We bought something in a size three at the last place," Kyle told her.

Her heels clicked on the floor as she approached the rack where Kyle had found the dress. "I'm afraid this brand only comes in even numbers—zero, two, four. And I doubt we have a zero. We don't get many of those. Is there someone you could call or text to ask?"

Kyle took out his phone. "Maybe one of our female friends has seen Phoenix since she's been home," he said, but Riley stopped him before he could dial.

"I doubt they have. And it doesn't matter, anyway, because no one's supposed to know about this, remember?"

"We can trust Callie, Eve or Cheyenne!" Kyle said.

"The fact that I'm pitching in on this is just between you and me," Riley insisted.

Kyle scowled. "If it's not going to get back to Phoenix, what does it matter?"

After everything he'd said through the years, it would seem like too much of a contradiction. And he didn't want to deal with the questions his buying clothes for her would raise, or what the rest of the gang might surmise from his answers. "We agreed."

Kyle shoved his phone back in his pocket. "So…what do we do? Make another guess?"

"That's what we've done so far, isn't it? You said yourself she can always return or exchange." At least he'd known her shoe size…

"If she can walk all the way to Sacramento," he muttered. "I wasn't really thinking of the logistics when I said that."

"With any luck, all the stuff will fit or she'll figure out how to get back here and return the things that don't." Riley picked up the bags he'd put on the floor. "We're just dropping this shit on her doorstep and leaving it at that."

Kirsten obviously didn't overhear a conversation like this every day. "Who's the lucky recipient?" she asked, her gaze darting between them.

"An old acquaintance." Riley had no intention of explaining more than that, even though he could tell she was curious.

"Maybe someone could give her a ride if it doesn't fit," she said, as if she'd easily solved that problem.

Riley ignored the comment. She couldn't know that after spending nearly seventeen years in prison Phoenix had far fewer resources and friends than most people. "We'll take a two or a four. Your choice."

"*My* choice?" she said in surprise.

"If it helps, she's small, maybe a hundred pounds, but she's not flat or anything," Kyle told her. "She's got a really nice, um, figure."

"I see." As Kirsten turned to sort through the rest of the dresses, Riley shot Kyle a dirty look.

"What?" Kyle murmured.

"She's got a really nice figure?"

He spread out his hands. "It's the truth!"

"A hundred pounds isn't much," Kirsten mused, concentrating hard enough that she seemed oblivious to what they were saying behind her. "I haven't weighed that since I was twelve. So…I'm thinking a two."

"That'll work," Kyle said, but he would've responded the same way no matter what she recommended. They had no idea what they were doing.

"Here we go." A pleasant smile curved her lips. "Will there be anything else?"

"We'd like one more outfit," Riley said.

"For the same woman?" she asked.

"Yes."

She draped the dress over her arm. "Something similar to this or…?"

"Maybe some shorts?"

"Got it."

When she set off to fulfill Riley's request, Kyle lowered his voice. "What about underwear?"

"What about it?"

"Don't you think we should get her some?"

"Hell, no!" He wasn't about to look at lingerie with Phoenix in mind.

At his unequivocal response, Kyle frowned. "Look, I'm not an only child, like you. I have a sister, so maybe I'm more comfortable with this. But a woman's got to have underwear. And we passed a Victoria's Secret store. I say we stop there on our way out, grab a handful of panties and a bra and be done with it."

Riley stretched his neck. To continue to refuse would only make him seem immature. Kyle was just being practical. But Riley had slept with Phoenix. Of course he'd conjure up images and memories best forgotten. He'd been with only one other girl before her, an older girl who'd approached him at a party with one thing in mind. It had been more of an initiation than anything. But as much as he didn't want to acknowledge it, even to himself, what he'd experienced with Phoenix had been different—all about mutual discovery and young love. She didn't realize it, but their breakup had been almost as hard on him. He'd trusted his parents to know what was best for him, and yet he'd never felt sure they were right. "No one had better find out about this."

Kyle slapped him on the back. "They won't."

"Including *her*."

"It's a doorbell ditch. She'll never catch us."

"We're not ringing the damn bell. She can find whatever we leave in the morning. It's not like it's going to rain."

The saleswoman was on her way back, arms full. "Do you like any of these?"

Kyle sifted through the various styles of shorts and shirts she'd collected. "I bet the cutoffs would look nice."

The saleswoman seemed pleased with his choice. "Would you like to purchase them, too? Maybe with this purple shirt?"

He scratched his head. "I'm not sure about the shirt. I'm not big on purple."

As they walked over to see about getting the shirt in a different color, Riley wandered through the rest of the store. They'd already bought Phoenix an expensive pair of running shoes, some flip-flops, a pair of "skinny" jeans and a white, lacy tank top. As far as he was concerned, except for underwear, they were finished. But when he turned around to go over to the register, he caught sight of an aquamarine top that looked as if it would match those stormy eyes of hers.

"You coming?" Kyle called.

Riley almost walked off without it. They had enough. But at the last second, he changed his mind and went back.

"Do you want that instead of the pink one we just got?" Kyle asked when he saw what Riley was carrying.

"No, we'll get this one, too," he replied. "I'm sure she could use an extra top."

"You're spending a lot of money," his friend complained.

"What are you talking about?" He took out his wallet. "I'm paying half, so you're still in it for less than you planned."

"That's all well and good. But I don't want you to blame me later for what this cost you, just because it was my idea. You're the one who's running up the bill. You insisted on getting the more expensive tennis shoes." He checked the tag on the shirt. "And this is sixty dollars!"

They could swing sixty bucks for someone who'd never had much of anything. He'd used the same rationale when considering the running shoes. Although he was probably a fool for getting involved in this—it made Phoenix sympathetic to him when he was hoping to keep her at a distance—he was starting to get excited now that they were finished with all the style and size choices. He kept imagining the relief these things would bring her, and that made him feel good despite the ambiguity of the past—or perhaps because of it. "It'll only be thirty dollars since we're splitting it," he said, and watched the salesgirl ring it up.

4

A noise startled Phoenix. Earlier she'd awakened with a crick in her neck after nodding off at her desk and had stumbled to her bed, where she'd been sleeping ever since. She'd gotten very little rest the past few days; she'd been too busy, too anxious, too worried. Apparently, her exhaustion had overcome all of that. But she was still uneasy enough not to allow herself to sink *too* deeply into unconsciousness. At the back of her mind were those letters from Lori Mansfield's family and the threats they contained. This was *their* town, they'd said. *Lori's* town. Phoenix had no idea if Buddy, the brother who'd sent the worst of the letters, would actually "make her sorry," as he claimed. But this sound... it wasn't just the dogs, although she could hear them barking from her mother's trailer.

She blinked into the darkness as the wooden steps leading to her door creaked again. Was someone looking for a way in? The fact that finding one wouldn't be hard made her supremely aware of her own vulnerability. She'd opened her windows because it had been so warm in the afternoon and she didn't have a working air conditioner. Then she'd been too out of it to remember to close them when she went to bed. Buddy could easily cut the screen on the large living room window beside the steps and hoist himself through...

Her heart in her throat, Phoenix scrambled out of bed and rummaged around until she found the bat she'd brought in from the yard her first night back. It was all she had to defend herself with, but she was determined that she would not let Buddy stop her from being part of Jacob's life. She'd suffered enough for what had happened to Lori Mansfield. Since she hadn't done anything wrong, besides make a couple of stupid crank calls to Lori before the accident, she'd basically been punished for falling in love with Riley Stinson. Her crush on him was what had given her the supposed "motive."

"Who is it?" She hated the tremor in her voice. She needed to sound strong in order to convince Buddy— it had to be him—not to try anything. But he didn't seem to be breaking in. She heard a thud, as though he'd dropped something on her porch. Then there was another thud and the *tap, tap, tap* of receding footsteps.

Holy shit! It sounded as if there were *two* people on her porch! What had they left behind? And what would it do to her?

Wielding the bat with single-minded purpose, she charged down the hall and through the front door, screaming like a banshee. "I'm not going anywhere, you sons of bitches!" she yelled.

Her mother had had a floodlight installed to discourage teenagers from coming out and throwing beer bottles at her trailer, so Phoenix could see the back of a tall figure dressed in black and wearing a hoodie. She thought he called out, "Shit! Let's go!" But she couldn't see anyone with him, and there was no way she could catch him. He ran off the property and sprinted down the road, too far ahead for her to even give chase.

"Phoenix?"

The dogs—and possibly her shouting—had awakened her mother.

"It's nothing," she told Lizzie, and squinted into the darkness, trying to make sure that was true. There wasn't anyone else on the property, was there?

No one she could see. If there'd been two people, they'd both run off—but they'd left two medium-size boxes outside her door.

She wondered what mean thing her fellow Whiskey Creek residents had gotten up to as her mother reprimanded the dogs. "Settle down!"

Using her bat to poke the boxes so she wouldn't have to get too close, Phoenix pushed them onto the ground. She was convinced they contained a bomb or a snake or something that was just unpleasant, like dog crap— so convinced she almost didn't want to open them. She knew she wasn't welcome here, didn't need any more warnings. But one of the boxes broke apart when it struck the ground and what spilled out didn't look dangerous *or* unpleasant.

From what she could tell, it was...*clothes*. And *canned goods*, which was why they'd hit the ground with such force.

She peered at the man—or men—who'd run off. Why would Buddy, or anyone else, bring her clothes and food?

Was there something wrong with it? It would be far crueler to make her believe this was a nice gesture, only to let her discover later that there were words written on the various articles, like *Murderer*, that he'd urinated on everything or that the canned goods were rotten or poisoned.

And what was in the other box? The one that *hadn't* broken open?

Slowly descending the steps, she made her way around to find out, but she kept looking over her shoulder, checking to see whether whoever it was would come back. If Buddy had dropped off something intended to be hurtful, he'd want to stick around to make sure it had the proper impact.

There was also the possibility that he'd been hoping to draw her outside…

But everything remained quiet. There was no movement, no noise.

Just to be certain they were gone, she walked to the gate and stared as far down the road as she could. Nothing.

"Phoenix?" Her mother had managed to quiet the dogs. "You still out there? What's goin' on?"

Phoenix returned to study what lay on the ground, searching for movement. Had Buddy filled those boxes with cockroaches or earwigs or some other kind of bug? "I told you, nothing. Go back to sleep."

"The dogs heard somethin' or they wouldn't have gotten themselves worked up like that!" her mother insisted.

"It was just me, chasing off a raccoon." Whatever her visitors had brought, her mother didn't need to know about it. Lizzie had been tormented enough for being odd, difficult, overweight, a recluse.

"You best be careful, girl," her mother warned. "There ain't nobody in this town who likes you."

"I know, Mom. You tell me that every day," she said, but not loudly enough for her voice to carry to the other trailer.

"Did you hear me?" her mother yelled.

Phoenix spoke louder. "I heard you. Don't worry. I can take care of myself." Tough talk for someone acutely aware of her own weakness. Fighting with other women was one thing. That had been frightening enough. But Buddy? He was a huge man, positive she'd killed his baby sister, who'd been only a year younger than he was, and he seemed to believe that justice meant an eye for an eye.

"Get inside and lock the door," her mother urged. "The bastards who run this town would love nothing more than to catch you out at night."

"I'm going," she said, but circled the boxes that had fallen instead. Whatever they contained—bugs or snakes or rat poison—she needed to get rid of it.

Once again using her bat, she nudged the box that had broken open. It was clothes, all right. As she'd noted before, it also contained canned vegetables, beans and soup. And a shoebox. She thought that might be where she'd find the dog shit, but when she knocked off the lid, she saw that it was...*running shoes*?

"What's going on?" she murmured. The clothes were for a woman. There wasn't any writing on them or blood that she could see. She couldn't smell urine. Everything looked nice and new. These were name-brand items with the tags still on them.

More of the same, as well as some packaged food, filled the second box.

Who'd brought her these things?

Whoever it was had included a receipt. Whoa... someone had spent a great deal and left her the option of return or exchange.

That sure as hell wouldn't be Buddy.

Were these gifts, then? Everything was in her size, or close, and had been dropped at her doorstep. It had to be for her. But she was afraid to trust what she saw. She couldn't remember the last time anyone had given her anything, other than the small handmade gifts she'd exchanged with her friend Coop and a few of the other women in prison at Christmas. Cara had given her that laptop, but she'd also made Cara a fair amount of money for helping facilitate the bracelet business.

"Look at this stuff!" she muttered as she began to dig through everything in earnest. This was better than any Christmas she'd ever had.

She held up a pair of lace panties. *Victoria's Secret?*

Returning those to the pile, she pulled out a sundress, carefully brushed off the dirt and hugged it to her. It was a two. She was fairly sure it would fit. And it was so darn pretty…

Eager to try it on, along with everything else, she started gathering up what had spilled. But she couldn't stop thinking about the dark figure in the hoodie. She figured it had to be Kyle and felt bad for misjudging him. He was the only person who'd shown her any kindness so far.

"Thank you," she whispered, and was suddenly so overwhelmed with gratitude all she could do was sink down on her knees and cry.

Afraid the dogs would start barking again, Riley held very still. When Kyle had run off, Riley had hidden. Now he was pressed up against the back of Lizzie's trailer, taking advantage of the deep shadows, and couldn't go anywhere until Phoenix went inside. He'd thought he'd just wait until she went in, then slip out of the yard. But she was too overcome to be in any kind of hurry. And seeing her, someone who was so distrustful, so prepared to battle some unknown assailant, break down when she finally realized she had nothing to be afraid of made Riley's chest tighten to the point that he could barely breathe. He could only imagine what it must be like for her, to have so little in the way of resources and yet feel as if she had to take on the whole world.

There ain't nobody in this town who likes you.

And yet she'd come back...

He clenched his fists and leaned into the rusty old filing cabinet that helped provide his cover. He refused to tear up—but fighting his emotions left a huge lump in his throat. Damn it! He'd known better than to get involved in this.

But it was the burning behind his eyes and the empathy that made his heart ache that caused the anger. He'd never been happier to give someone a gift.

Grateful to Kyle for thinking of it, for bringing it to his attention and making him feel responsible for meeting at least some of her needs, he watched as Phoenix wiped her cheeks, dusted off each item and restacked the cans inside the boxes.

The lights inside her trailer snapped on as soon as she carried the heaviest carton through the door. Then she returned to collect the other one.

After her door closed for the second time, Riley could have left without giving himself away. Instead, he was tempted to creep up to her window to see if she was trying on what they'd bought. It would be gratifying to see how it fit. His interest wasn't sexual, so it didn't seem all that reprehensible. But he decided that peeping through her bedroom window wouldn't be appropriate despite his intentions.

Besides, Kyle had to be impatient waiting at the truck, which they'd parked half a mile or so away.

With a final glance at the bat she'd left on the ground, Riley was moving toward the street when he spotted a piece-of-shit bike leaning up against Phoenix's trailer. She must have plans for that, he decided. She probably intended to fix it so that she'd have some transportation.

Noah, one of his best friends, owned the bike shop in town. Riley could get it fixed quicker and cheaper...

One of the dogs barked, making him a little anxious, but he couldn't stop himself. He grabbed the bike before he left and was carrying it with him when he met Kyle on the road.

"What the hell is that?" Kyle asked.

"What does it look like?" he replied.

"Is that where you've been? Trying to steal her bike? I was beginning to think she caught you."

"It wasn't the bike that held me up."

"Then what did?"

"It took her a while to open those boxes and figure out they were safe to accept."

Kyle's expression showed interest. "You saw her open them?"

"Yeah. After she chased you off, she thought whoever had left the stuff was gone."

"But...how did she not see you? With that damn floodlight it wasn't even very dark."

"That's why I couldn't move. I was hiding in the shadows behind her mother's trailer." And she definitely hadn't seen him. If she'd known he was there, she would never have broken down. That was what had made her relief and gratitude so honest. Here was someone who'd withstood so much tragedy without flinching. She hadn't complained or railed at him when he didn't bring Jacob to see her in the correctional facility, even though she'd requested it several times. She would simply wait a few months and politely ask him again.

Now he felt like shit that he hadn't shown more consideration. But he hadn't wanted to confuse Jacob, hadn't wanted to do anything that might cause his son to stumble. His parents, who'd been so much help when Jacob was small, had convinced him that allowing any kind of contact with Phoenix would be a grave mistake. And there was something about believing that she'd gotten what she deserved that neutralized compassion in general—and in him, too—especially when so many people he respected stood united in that opinion.

"So what did she think?" Kyle asked as they walked toward the truck.

Riley shifted the bike to his other hand. It wasn't heavy, but it was awkward to carry. "She liked everything."

"Really?" He seemed pleased, and Riley understood why. He'd felt the same way when she'd held that sundress to her chest as if it was the most beautiful thing she'd ever seen. "How do you know?"

Riley grinned at him. "Trust me, it was obvious."

"She's too guarded to show much emotion. But you could tell, huh?"

She wasn't guarded when *he* saw her because she'd thought she was alone. All her walls had come crumbling down. But he felt it would violate her privacy to share the moment he'd witnessed, with those tears streaming down her face, so he kept it to himself. "Yeah, I could."

"I hope I get to see her wear something we bought," he said.

They reached the truck. "That felt great," Riley admitted as he climbed into the passenger seat. "Thanks for including me."

Kyle looked surprised. "Seriously, man? I know it's hard for you to have her back."

Riley had had his own challenges, but he'd never been through anything even close to what she had—and maybe none of it had been her fault. "Seriously."

Riley almost ignored the knock that sounded early the next morning. He'd been up most of the night, and Sunday was his day off.

Jake can get it, he thought, and rolled over. It was probably one of Jacob's friends, anyway, rousting him to go mountain biking or out for a hike.

But when the knocking continued, he remembered Jacob wasn't even home. He'd stayed with his best buddy, Tristan Abbott, last night and Riley had been happy to let him. He'd known that if Jacob stayed elsewhere he wouldn't have to explain his own whereabouts or actions.

"Coming!" he called as he dragged himself out of bed and yanked on a pair of jeans.

"Where's your shirt?" his mother snapped once he opened the door.

He shoved a hand through his hair. "You're lucky I have my pants on. Anyone who bothers me this early deserves to see me in whatever state I decide to answer the door."

"Have you seen her?" she asked as she brushed past him and into the house.

He didn't really want to have this discussion. He knew who "she" was, and he knew that he and his mother were going to have very different opinions on Phoenix, especially after what he'd witnessed last night.

He wished everyone would leave her alone, let her live in peace.

"She took Jacob and me to breakfast yesterday morning at Just Like Mom's. Why? Is that the reason you're here? Did someone tell you about that?"

"No. But I'm surprised *you* didn't."

"This is the first time I've seen you. Did you want me to file a report?"

She perched on the edge of his couch. "That would've been nice. You're not the only one who has a stake in this, you know."

"Where's Dad?" he asked.

"On his way to the golf course with his friends."

"He was willing to miss the 'Phoenix' talk?"

"He'd miss my funeral for a good golf game."

Riley couldn't help chuckling.

"So?" she said.

"So, what?"

"How did she act?"

They were back to the nitty-gritty details of his first visit with Phoenix. "She was very...polite."

"Of course! She wants to impress you."

"She wants to know her son, Mom. She's made that clear, wouldn't you say?"

"That's what she'd like us to believe, but she hoped to get you before, and I'm sure she'd be thrilled to land you now. You remember how fixated she was on you." She picked a piece of lint off her slacks. "You wouldn't want to start something like that up again, would you?"

Even that aspect of Phoenix's actions had been exaggerated over the years. "She deserves the chance to prove she's changed."

"What are the odds she changed for the better *in prison*?" his mother responded.

"Don't make it sound like that's impossible. Otherwise, why would we let anyone out?"

"Because there aren't enough cells to keep all the murderers locked up. But I didn't come here to debate the penal system. I was hoping to get you to reconsider being so flexible. She's probably seen things you and I can only imagine. Who knows what kind of people she met in that place? I don't want her to become a negative influence on Jacob after all we've done to raise him right."

Riley's temper was beginning to chafe. "Mom, Jacob's sixteen. Almost an adult. We can't protect him forever."

"He's at a very impressionable age!"

"Still, we need to trust in who he is. It's up to him to decide whether he wants his mother in his life."

"But he doesn't know what's best."

"Neither do *we*! That's the thing!"

"We have a lot more to base our decision on than he does."

With a sigh, Riley slouched into the chair opposite her. "I'm not so sure. I've been wondering if we were wrong to keep them apart. It hurt Phoenix deeply, and I honestly don't think she's all that bad."

His mother's eyes widened. "Maybe you need to talk to Lori Mansfield's family, to be reminded of how much they've suffered from losing their beautiful daughter."

"I'm sympathetic to the Mansfields. I know you and Corinne are close friends, that her happiness is important to you. But they're not the only ones who've suffered. And if Phoenix has been telling the truth about the events of that day, her punishment was completely unjustified. I'd hate to add to that."

His mother got to her feet. "Now you believe she's innocent?"

"There's nothing to prove her guilt *or* her innocence."

"Then look at the facts. That's what they convicted her on, isn't it? She was jealous when you started seeing Lori. So she tried to take her out of the picture. It was Phoenix's car that ran her down, and Phoenix was behind the wheel. There was even a witness inside the vehicle!"

Who might have been lying, but he could tell the argument was only going to escalate if they continued talking about this. "We don't know exactly what happened," he insisted.

"What's gotten into you?" she asked. "Just last week you were wishing along with the rest of us that Phoenix would go *somewhere* else."

That was before he'd met her for breakfast, before last night. Both encounters had had a profound effect on him. It was much easier to malign someone who wasn't around. Now that he'd seen the contrast between the real Phoenix and the monster they'd created in their minds, he understood that everyone's negative comments and opinions had fueled fears in him that might not be well founded. "I *didn't* want her to come back. I wrote her and told her as much." He didn't say that was one letter he wished he could *unsend*. "But Whiskey Creek is her home as much as ours. She can come here if she wants, and there's nothing we can do to stop her."

"So you've made up your mind? You're going to support a relationship between her and Jacob?"

"If that's what he wants, yes—unless she does something that seems…wrong."

"By then it might be too late."

"That's the chance I have to take."

"When they'd *both* be better off if she'd just move somewhere else?"

He thought of the shopping he and Kyle had done. His mother would not be happy if she learned that they'd helped Phoenix, but he didn't regret it. Giving her those things had felt right.

"How would they *both* be better off?" he asked. "She has nothing to start over with. At least if she stays here she'll have a free place to live until she gets on her feet."

"That dump out there isn't even sanitary. A normal person wouldn't want to stay there."

He felt slightly defensive. "She's doing what she can to clean it up." She'd told him as much.

"Either way, the Mansfields won't put up with her living in this town."

Riley scooted forward but rested his arms on his knees. He didn't want to come on too strong. "There's nothing the Mansfields can do."

"Of course there is," she said.

"What are you talking about?"

"I'm saying someone should warn her. Maybe that'll make her think twice about burdening us with her presence."

He'd been uncomfortable with this conversation from the beginning, but now he was downright concerned. "*Warn* her? Really?"

"Yes! I've heard Corinne say that Buddy won't allow it. You know how close he was to Lori. They were thirteen months apart and did almost everything together growing up."

"I know he's angry that his wife left him last year. He always seems to be out causing trouble now that she's gone. But Phoenix has nothing to do with his current misery."

"How can you say that? She's at the root of it. He's never been able to get over Lori's murder."

"So it's also Phoenix's fault that he goes from job to job? That he's currently making minimum wage working as a clerk at the hardware store and living with his parents?"

"You can't judge him!"

Although Riley had spent a lot of time around Buddy through the years—thanks to the friendship between families—he'd never cared for him. Buddy had always been an egotistic braggart. "But he can judge others."

"In this instance, I think he's got the right. Anyway, he wrote Phoenix before she was released. But either she didn't get his letter, or she ignored it, like yours."

Riley felt his muscles tense. Buddy was six feet four inches tall and weighed probably 230 pounds. A single blow from his meaty fist could cause significant damage. Even with a bat, Phoenix would never be able to defend herself. "What did Buddy say in that letter?"

"I don't know. It's not as though Corinne read it to me. But it was something to the effect that she'd regret it if she came back here."

No wonder Phoenix had reacted the way she had when she'd heard them on her porch last night. She must've thought the Mansfields were coming for her. "He'd better not hurt her," Riley said.

His mother frowned at the firmness in his voice. "*I* have no say over what he does," she responded.

"Then maybe *he* should be warned."

"About…what?"

"If he hurts her, he'll answer to me."

His mother's mouth dropped open. "You're taking

her side? Coming out in opposition to my best friend's son? When *he's* the one who's lost a sister?"

"Phoenix is Jacob's mother," he said, as if he'd be doing it for the sake of his son. But he knew in his heart that Jacob wasn't the only reason he was willing to defend Phoenix. He admired her guts and determination almost as much as he admired her desire to be a mother to her child. Whether she was guilty or not seventeen years ago, she deserved the chance to prove herself.

He was drawing the line.

5

"What's wrong with you?" her mother snapped.

Phoenix set the frying pan to one side and turned in surprise. It wasn't easy to cook in Lizzie's trailer. Hemmed in by stacks of packaged goods—trash her mother, for some strange reason, found valuable—plants, a bevy of dog bowls and giant bags of dog kibble and an overlarge hamster cage that took up most of the table, she had barely enough room to move on the sticky linoleum. Maybe that was why her mother never bothered with real food—she could no longer fit in her own kitchen. "What do you mean?"

"You're smiling and humming and acting all…happy. What have you got to be happy about?" Lizzie absently petted one of her five dogs, this one a poodle, as she narrowed her eyes. "Did you have a man over last night? Was that the fuss that woke me?"

Phoenix felt her face flush. "No, I didn't have a man over."

Lizzie studied her more closely. "Then why are you blushing?"

"Because you're embarrassing me!" For the past seventeen years, she'd rarely allowed herself to even *think* about sex. She hadn't wanted to miss physical intimacy as much as the other women seemed to; that was all some of them talked about. She also hadn't wanted to get involved in the kind of romantic relationships that sometimes sprang up between them as a replacement. "I'd rather not talk about my sex life—especially with you," she added as she dished up the scrambled eggs she'd made for breakfast.

"What is it, then?" her mother pressed. "What's put you in such a good mood?"

"Nothing! It's a beautiful Sunday, that's all. And I have plans to go into town." She was going to use the internet to create her Facebook page so Jacob could message her. She was looking forward to making contact with him again without having to go through Riley.

"Yesterday was a beautiful day, too," her mother said with a saucy lilt, as if there had to be more to it.

And there was. Her lift in spirits had nothing to do with the weather and everything to do with the fact that at least one member of the Whiskey Creek community didn't have hard feelings toward her—that and how feminine she felt in her new clothes. Who would've thought a lacy bra and a pair of matching panties could make a woman feel so...attractive?

She was beginning to think that maybe it wouldn't spell doom to have a man's hands on her body—as long as she waited until after Jacob went to college. At that point, she could probably start dating and, possibly, get serious.

"You're not a lesbian, are you?" her mother asked.

Phoenix slammed the drawer after getting them each a fork. "Stop. No."

"Did those women in that prison ever try to touch you?" Lizzie accepted her plate grudgingly, but Phoenix guessed that, deep down, she enjoyed the care she was receiving. At any rate, Phoenix hoped she did. It wasn't readily apparent, wasn't as if her mother ever said anything to show her appreciation.

"Did they?"

"No," Phoenix insisted, but that wasn't strictly true. Although no one had gotten very far, in the beginning she'd had to fight to keep herself from being used—and that had earned her some dangerous enemies, which hadn't made the time she'd served any easier.

"So you still like men."

Phoenix refused to meet her eyes. She was afraid her mother was saying, *So you still like Riley*, and she wasn't going anywhere close to that question. She *didn't* like Riley, not in that way. Anyone would think he was handsome, because he was. "Right now I'm only interested in Jacob, okay? I'll worry about everything else in a couple of years."

"You're what...thirty-five?" Her mother spoke around the bite she'd just taken. "That's getting up there, but you could have more children if you don't wait too long."

The toast popped up. Grateful for the distraction, Phoenix turned to butter it. "I'd better figure out how to support myself first."

"You look like you're doin' fine to me, all dolled up in those tight jeans. They must've cost a pretty penny."

She'd been thinking she'd help support her mother if she could. Lizzie had trouble getting by on her disability check. But that comment made her wonder why she'd even consider it. "They were a gift."

"From *who*?"

Phoenix hadn't been planning to tell her mother about last night. But if she did, maybe Lizzie would quit reminding her how much everyone hated her. It was difficult to hear, even though, for all intents and purposes, it was true. "Kyle Houseman."

Her mother's fork clanged on her plate. "Why would Kyle Houseman give *you* anything?"

"To be nice," she said with a shrug.

"Don't you believe it!" she scoffed. "He's Riley's friend."

Already, she regretted revealing her secret. "I'm aware of that."

"Then why would you accept anything from him? If you get involved with Kyle, you can kiss your chances of a relationship with Jacob goodbye. Riley won't put up with you messin' around with his friends."

"I'm not going to be 'messing around.' Kyle's not coming on to me, Mom."

Her mother gave her a "stop lying to yourself" look. "Then what is he doing?"

"Trying to be generous, I guess." She wasn't really sure. He just didn't seem as judgmental as everyone else. Or maybe he wasn't as close to Lori's family.

"No one's *that* generous to an ex-con," her mother said. "He expects a return on his money, or he wouldn't have spent it."

"That's *so* jaded!"

"I'd rather be jaded than a fool who learns the hard way."

Phoenix could no longer taste her eggs, but she shoveled them down, anyway. "He's a friend," she muttered. "And I could use a friend right now."

Her mother hooted, making Phoenix feel like the biggest idiot in the world. "He's the kind of friend who'd like to get inside your pants and then drop you on your ass the same way Riley did. Boys like Riley and Kyle don't date girls like you, Phoenix. It's time you faced up to that. It'll save you a lot of heartache later."

Her mother just had to be crass. "I don't even want them," she said, and left her plate in the sink instead of cleaning up because she couldn't bear to remain in Lizzie's presence.

It was a lazy Sunday morning, the kind of perfect spring day when people breezed in and out of Black Gold Coffee in twos, threes or fours, talking and laughing. The laid back feel of the place, as well as the trendy atmosphere with its wooden floors and chalkboard menu, helped take the edge off the residual anger Phoenix felt after that encounter with her mother. Lizzie had issues. Phoenix tried hard not to let them affect her. Still, there were times when Lizzie's negativity washed over her like a tidal wave, threatening to drown her. She had so much difficulty dealing with her mother. Even when she was young it had been tough. At least prison had taken her out of that situation, not that she ever wanted to go back to living behind bars.

Now she was getting a short break from Lizzie and using the internet, as she'd wanted, but she couldn't completely relax. Whenever she was in public she worried about running into a member of Lori's family. She felt certain the Mansfields would cause a scene. So far, she'd been lucky. She hadn't bumped into them—or Riley's parents, who'd come out in such strong opposition to her seventeen years ago.

Coop, a friend she'd met in prison, would call a reprieve like that "a tender mercy," and Phoenix was inclined to agree. Coop spotted tender mercies everywhere. Although she readily admitted to shooting her father when she caught him molesting her two-year-old daughter, and had three years left on her sentence, she managed to retain her optimism and keep fighting. It was her encouragement that'd helped Phoenix through her darkest times. *You're young and you're beautiful and you'll get out of here someday,* she used to say. *Then you can do anything you want with your life, and don't let anyone tell you different.*

For a second, it was almost as if she could hear Coop's voice. That brought on a moment of nostalgia, made her miss Coop and a few of her other friends.

She decided to write them. She'd promised she would. But first she had to set up a Facebook account, she told herself, and focused more intently on the screen.

She wasn't particularly good with a computer. She had barely enough knowledge and experience to be able to post her bracelets on Etsy and eBay, to manage her PayPal account and to respond to the people who contacted her, but millions of others had gotten on to the social networking giant, and she was sure she could figure it out, too.

The only problem was the bell that jingled over the door whenever anyone walked in or out. It was distracting. That noise signaled a change in her environment, alerted her to something new and potentially dangerous, and that made her tense—until she saw another individual or small group she didn't recognize.

Fortunately, she had her coffee, so she could sit in the corner and try to go unnoticed behind her computer screen.

She was reading Facebook's instructions when the bell went off yet again. She leaned to one side to see who it was—and did a double take. The last person she'd expected to come walking through that door was Jacob. He strolled in with a friend, both of them wearing beanies and looking so cute she couldn't help feeling a sense of pride. That was *her* boy and he was big and handsome and smart. He seemed like a really nice person, too.

But she didn't want to put him on the spot. She was afraid that singling him out might embarrass him. So she kept working as if she hadn't noticed him. She thought he and his friend would grab their lattes or whatever they were getting and head out without glancing in her direction. But Jacob spotted her while they were waiting for their order and surprised her by saying, "Hey! It's my mom."

He'd spoken loudly enough that it would seem strange if she didn't look up. So she met his gaze and smiled. She was just trying to decide if she should walk over, or if he'd rather she just waved. But she didn't have to make that choice; he brought his friend to her.

"What are you doing here?" he asked.

She turned her computer so he could see it. "Trying to navigate Facebook for the first time."

"Piece of cake," he said. "Let me help you."

He pulled a chair from another table and slouched into it while Phoenix nodded politely to the boy who was with him.

"I'm Tristan," his friend said.

"Tristan's on the baseball team with me," Jake explained.

She extended her hand. "Nice to meet you."

"It's cool to meet you, too." He gave her a bashful smile. "Jake told me you were pretty, but…I didn't think you'd be *this* pretty."

"Dude, are you hitting on my *mom*? Sit down!" Jake said with a shocked laugh.

Phoenix was slightly embarrassed but flattered at

the same time. It was good to know Jacob was proud of her, at least in one respect. And she was even more grateful to Kyle, if indeed it was Kyle, for providing the jeans and blouse she was wearing. Otherwise, she'd be in the same clothes she'd worn on Saturday.

"One iced coffee, one mocha," the barista called out, and Jake asked his friend to get their drinks.

"See? You click on this," he told her, shifting so they could both view the screen. "Then you choose a username and put your personal information in here."

"My real name is different enough that I'll stick with that."

"Okay." He typed it for her.

"Do you set up the page the same way if it's for a business?" she asked.

"You want one for a business, too?"

She saw that he was wearing the bracelet she'd given him. "Yeah. I have a little something going and thought a Facebook page might help."

"I'm pretty sure it would be the same."

Tristan returned with their coffees, but instead of getting up and heading out, Jacob continued to prompt her through the Facebook process while Tristan looked on.

A few minutes later, her personal page went live.

"We did it!" she exclaimed.

"I'll friend you when I get home," Jacob said.

"So will I," Tristan piped up.

Jacob cocked an eyebrow at him. "Dude, you're not friending my mother."

Tristan went beet red. "Why not?" he muttered, but Jake's attention had already shifted back to her Facebook page.

"What are you going to use as your profile pic?" he asked.

"Just a photo of some scenery I can grab off the web, I guess. I don't have a camera."

"That's a problem I can fix." He stood up and pulled out his smartphone. "Smile."

The optimism and happiness she'd felt this morning, before her mother had quashed it, swelled inside Phoenix again. She grinned up at him, and he snapped a picture before returning to his seat.

"How'd it turn out?" she asked.

He leaned over so they could both look at it, and she breathed deep, taking in the scent of her child and wanting so badly to put her arms around him—to feel him against her just one time, since she'd never been able to hold him when he was a baby.

"It's good," he said, oblivious to all the chaotic thoughts and motherly desires he was rousing in her.

"That should work," she said, and he emailed it to her so she could load it.

"Does your father work today?" she asked as they waited for the photograph to hit her in-box.

"No. He takes Sundays off, which means I'm off, too." He rocked back and stretched out his legs. "Hallelujah!"

"You don't like working with him?"

He shrugged. "I don't think it's too much fun when all my friends are out messing around. But...I like being able to do what I can do. Nobody else my age can install a water heater or frame a house or put on a roof. And giving up my Saturdays is how I saved enough to buy some wheels." He motioned to the window, and she glanced out to see a white Jeep. It wasn't brand-new;

it had some miles on it. But he was proud, and she admired Riley for making him earn the money.

She could only imagine what the girls thought of her son and was so glad his high school experience seemed to be better than her own had been. "That's a nice Jeep," she said.

"Would you like me to give you a ride?" he asked.

Even at this late date, he seemed open to getting to know her. She wasn't going to miss this opportunity. "Sure." She closed her laptop, slid it into the backpack she'd found at her mom's and appropriated for her own use and stood as he took out his keys.

"It's a sweet ride," Tristan said.

She followed them out. "Your father won't mind you taking me for a test-drive..."

He made a face as if it was ridiculous of her to ask. "Why would *he* care? It's *my* Jeep."

But Riley wasn't convinced yet that she was good for him. Jacob had missed that nuance, and she was so excited that he wanted to share something with her, she chose to ignore it. Riley didn't have to know about the next few minutes. It wasn't as though she was doing anything wrong by letting Jacob show her his Jeep.

"You can sit in the front," Tristan volunteered, and hopped into the back without using the door.

Phoenix felt a huge smile stretch across her face. This was "a moment," she decided, *the* moment she'd dreamed about for so long. She was with her son, and he seemed okay with having her there.

As Jake started the engine and pulled out, he managed the vehicle so effortlessly she had to marvel at how grown-up he was, and that he had so many abilities.

"I owe your father a lot," she said, and meant it.

He didn't seem to follow. "For what?"

"He's done a great job with you."

The cocky grin he flashed made her laugh, so then he laughed, too.

She loved the feel of the wind blowing through her hair as they drove, sometimes a little too fast but not so fast that she had to say anything. She was glad of that.

"Have you ever driven a stick?" he asked.

"Me?" Phoenix brought a hand to her chest. "No." They didn't teach that in prison. She'd missed out on so much. She hadn't even been able to name her son. Riley had done that. But more than anything, she regretted not being there to watch Jacob grow up.

He pulled to the side of the road. "Come around. I'll teach you."

She shook her head. "No, I can't. I haven't been behind the wheel in a long time. I've got to get used to driving an automatic before I attempt a stick."

"Are you sure you don't want to try?" he said. "It's not hard…"

"Just riding around with you is fun for me."

"Okay," he said, a bit reluctantly, and drove them to a muddy spot outside town to go off-road. As they lurched around, Phoenix clung to her seat belt. But he wasn't getting too crazy, so she could enjoy it. By the time they returned to the pavement, her stomach was sore from laughing so much, and she wished she had some money she could offer him for gas.

Maybe next week, she thought. If she had enough bracelet orders. She sold most of her bracelets for fifty dollars, but she'd considered adding some new models, with various silver beads and options to personalize them, and planned to charge seventy-five dollars for those.

"You're a good driver," she said.

She expected him to thank her. When he didn't, she looked over to see him watching his rearview mirror with an expression of concern.

"What's wrong? Don't tell me it was illegal to do those doughnuts." If he got a ticket while he was with her, that wouldn't please Riley, not when he was so concerned about the kind of influence she'd be.

Jacob didn't answer that, either. He just changed gears and sped up, so she twisted around to see for herself.

She didn't find a police car following them—but there was someone driving so close behind them, she was afraid they were about to be rear-ended.

"What's going on?" she asked. "Why is that guy trying to hit us?"

Jacob's jaw tightened. "That's no 'guy.' That's Buddy."

Fear blasted through her, wiping out all the laughter and fun. *"Mansfield?"*

"Yeah." He spoke through gritted teeth. But she could recognize the driver herself now, even with the limited view she had through the front window of his oversize truck. Buddy had changed a lot. From what she could see, he was now sporting a full beard.

"Pull over, Jake," she said.

"That wouldn't be a good idea," he responded.

"Why?" Tristan shouted. "He's gonna crash into us!"

Phoenix was too focused on her son to explain. "You have to let me out."

"No way," Jake said. "That's what he wants. Then he could do anything."

This was so dangerous. She was terrified that Jake or his friend would get hurt—because of her. "Stop now. Please!"

Her son's eyebrows jerked together. He was obviously thinking fast, trying to decide the best course of action. But she just wanted to get him and Tristan out of this situation as soon as possible, before something tragic could occur. "What will you do?" he asked, sounding torn.

"Don't worry about me. I can take care of myself."

"Against someone like that?"

Buddy tapped their rear bumper, giving them a small jolt.

"I don't want you in the middle of this!" Phoenix cried, "Do what I say! Now!"

"No!" he snapped, suddenly adamant. But they'd reached town. He had to brake at the light, so she released her seat belt and jumped out, not even trying to take the backpack that held her laptop and purse.

"Mom!" Jacob tried to stop her but she slipped out of his grasp.

"Get out of here!" she yelled back. "Go home!"

6

Riley had just finished mowing the lawn and was leaning against the kitchen counter, cracking open a cold beer, when his cell phone went off. Leaning over, he slid it toward him so he could see who was trying to call him.

As he'd expected, it was Jacob.

"'Bout damn time," he muttered. His son had chores and homework to do before school tomorrow. "There you are," he said after pressing the talk button. "Where've you been? I thought you were going to drop Tristan off and come home after you picked up a coffee."

"Dad! You got to come now!"

At the panic in his son's voice, Riley slammed down his beer, which splashed all over his hand. "What's going on? What's wrong, Jake? Are you okay?"

"I'm okay, but…"

Although he couldn't be sure, it sounded as if his son was crying, and that nearly paralyzed him with fear. He hadn't heard Jake cry in a long time. "Did you get into an accident?" He rinsed off his hand and grabbed his keys. "Are you hurt?"

Jacob cleared his throat, obviously struggling to get

the tremor out of his voice. "No. But…Buddy saw us and was…and was acting crazy. So she jumped out. Then he veered toward her. It didn't look like he hit her hard, but she fell. And now she's bleeding!"

He was speaking so fast he was leaving out pertinent details. "Who's *she*?"

"Mom!"

Phoenix? Riley was at the front door, but at this revelation, he paused. He couldn't help feeling betrayed, as though they'd held some kind of secret meeting. "What were you doing with her?"

"I ran into her at Black Gold, and I…I just wanted to give her a ride in my Jeep."

Riley could easily see that happening. Jake was so excited to have his license, so damn proud of that old Jeep. And of course, Phoenix would never refuse his offer.

He threw open the door and hurried outside. "Where are you?"

"At the corner of Sutter and Kennedy, just as you come into town."

"I'm on my way."

"She fell into a ditch, Dad. I think she hit her head on a rock, but she won't let me call 9-1-1. Tristan says I should do it, anyway. I would but she doesn't like him to even mention it. And she keeps trying to get up."

Riley climbed into his truck, fired the engine and threw the transmission into Reverse. "Where's Buddy now?"

"Gone. He took off as soon as he did it."

"Sit tight," he said. "I'll be right there."

The drive took only a few minutes, but it felt like forever. Jake's Jeep, when he finally found it, was parked off the road, halfway in a field, as if he'd pulled over and stopped wherever he could. Next to it, Riley saw Jake and Tristan leaning over someone else, who had to be Phoenix, although they were blocking his view.

Riley left his truck next to the Jeep and hopped out.

Jake met him before he could even round the back bumper. "I'm glad you're here. She's hurt, but she says it's not bad, that head wounds bleed a lot."

Riley didn't say anything. He didn't know what to say until he'd seen her injuries.

"I'm okay." Phoenix waved him off when she caught sight of him. "I told Jake there was no need to bother you. I'm just a little scraped and bruised, and embarrassed to have caused a scene."

She'd hit her head, all right. There was blood running down the side of her face. Jake pressed her back when she tried to get to her feet. Riley got the impression he'd been doing that since it happened.

"What do you think, Dad? Shouldn't she go to the hospital?"

"There's no need for that," she said.

Riley crouched beside her and examined the gash above her temple. He was no paramedic. He wasn't sure how deep it was or if she needed stitches. It was even possible she had a concussion, but she seemed coherent, and that was a good sign. He'd seen a friend get hit pretty hard during a football game in high school and could still remember how he'd repeated himself over and over and babbled on about strange things that weren't even taking place.

Phoenix wasn't doing any of that.

"What happened?"

"I told you…" Jake started, but Riley cut him off.

"I'd like to hear her tell it." He wanted her perspective, but he also thought this might be a good way to judge whether or not she was thinking as clearly as it seemed.

"It was Buddy," she said. "He was trying to run Jake off the road to get him to stop, and I was afraid…I was afraid he'd wind up causing an accident. So I got out, but it was just as the light turned green, which gave Buddy the chance to gun his motor and come straight at me. I jumped into the ditch, so he didn't actually hit me and I…fell awkwardly and banged my head, I guess."

"Then he took off?"

She nodded, giving him a wan smile. "I'm sorry about this. I never intended to put Jake in danger. We were only taking a ride in his Jeep."

"It's not your fault," he said gruffly, so angry with Buddy that he could hardly speak. He could understand the terrible loss Buddy had suffered. He wasn't unsympathetic to that. But Buddy had no right to drag the past into the present, to act as judge, jury and executioner. Phoenix had been through due process and served her full sentence.

"It sort of is," she insisted, blinking back tears. "I knew he might have it in for me. He—he sent me a few letters, so it isn't as if I was completely unaware. But I never dreamed he'd do anything to threaten Jacob or anyone else. To be honest, that never crossed my mind."

"I'll deal with Buddy," Riley said. "But first, I'd like you to see a doctor, even if it's not at the hospital."

She touched her face. When there was more blood than she expected, she wiped her hands on the weeds and dirt to avoid getting it on her new clothes. "I'd rather go home," she said. "I can make it."

She started to stand, and Riley tried to help her, but she flinched when he took her arm and nearly fell back. "You'll get blood on you," she said, using the Jeep to support her weight. "You should take Jacob and Tristan home. I keep telling them they need to go in case Buddy comes back, but they won't listen because they think I'm really hurt."

She *looked* hurt. And she wasn't very steady on her feet. She tried to disguise her wobbliness by leaning into the vehicle, but Riley could tell how shaken she was.

"And what will *you* do if he comes back?" he asked.

"I'll hide and then keep heading home."

"By walking."

She wiped away the blood that was beginning to run into her eyes and looked around as if she wasn't sure where she was or what direction she needed to go. "I'll take my time. You know, walk slowly."

"That's bullshit," he said, and addressed Jake. "Are you okay to drive?"

He nodded.

"Drop Tristan off and go home. I'll take care of your mother."

"I can't believe Buddy did this," Jake muttered.

"I'm sure he acted without thinking," Riley said. But he planned to make sure Buddy thought about the consequences of his actions in the future.

Phoenix staggered away from the Jeep so the boys could leave, but she wouldn't allow Riley to steady her. Every time he tried, she lifted her hands and said, "It's okay. I'm all right."

Jacob hesitated, still upset. "Shouldn't I stay with her?"

"No, I've got this," Riley said, and Jake reluctantly walked around to the driver's side.

Phoenix waved to reassure their son.

Riley had to hand it to her. She was tougher than any

woman he'd known. It was impressive how determined she was not to lean on him—literally or figuratively.

As soon as they were gone, Riley grabbed Phoenix's elbow, hanging on even when she tried to avoid the contact, and guided her to his truck. "Let's get you to a doctor."

The second he mentioned doctor, she wrenched away from him. "No, I—I don't need a doctor."

"He'll check out that cut, tell us if it needs stitches."

"A doctor will cost money. And I...I have other plans for...for my income in the next while."

What income? He doubted she had any, but he couldn't say that. "Phoenix..."

"Stop," she said. "I've had worse than this. This is nothing."

Watching her closely, he could see that she was dizzy. "Do it for Jacob's peace of mind, then."

"Please, don't."

"Don't what?"

"I haven't got the money for a doctor. I'm sure you know that."

"*I'll* look after the bill," he said, but he should've known that wouldn't convince her.

She edged farther away from him. Then she started down the street at a faster clip than he felt she should. "I'm okay," she called back. "Go take care of Jacob."

"Damn it, Phoenix." He hurried after her. "Why do you have to be so stubborn? It won't cost that much."

She hadn't bothered to turn when he spoke, so he'd been talking to her back. "It's a waste of money," she told him over one shoulder. "I'm fine, like I said."

"It's five miles to your place. You'll never make it."

She made no comment.

"Soon you won't even be able to see where you're going, what with all that blood."

Again, she didn't respond. She'd managed to put a little distance between them and obviously thought she was getting away. But he wasn't about to let her go. He had no idea whether she'd make it. So he jogged after her and swept her into his arms, which wasn't hard since she didn't weigh much.

"Ah!" she cried. He'd startled her. She hadn't expected that move. He guessed her head hurt, too, and being jarred hadn't helped.

"We're doing this *my* way," he said, and carried her to his truck.

Phoenix felt like throwing up. The pain, coupled with a heavy dose of embarrassment and regret, were getting to her. She never should've gotten into Jacob's Jeep. Riley wouldn't want to let Jake spend any time with her if he wasn't safe in her company. That was all she could think about as she kept wiping the blood streaming from somewhere near her right eyebrow in an effort to keep it from staining the upholstery in Riley's truck. She'd long since given up trying to save her new clothes.

Riley looked grim as he drove. She could all too easily imagine what he was thinking. That he'd known it would be a nightmare to have her come home. That she should've gone anywhere but here. That she had no right to ruin his life a second time. And, worst of all, that Jacob was indeed better off without her.

Too bad she didn't feel well enough to change the situation. She'd have to wait it out and hope she'd still be allowed to communicate with Jacob on Facebook, and maybe go to his games, after this was all over.

When they came to a stop at the only other light in

town, Riley glanced over and must've seen that she was fighting a losing battle with the blood. She had nothing to wipe it with, so he took off his T-shirt.

"Here. Use this."

She averted her gaze so she wouldn't see his bare chest. Just accepting the T-shirt seemed too intimate. If she'd had a choice, she would've refused it, but the damn bleeding wouldn't stop.

Closing her eyes, she pressed the soft cotton to her head and then rested against the window to help keep it in place.

"You okay?" he asked as they parked in front of a house she didn't recognize.

She didn't bother to answer. She wasn't okay, but that wasn't entirely due to her injuries. She was more upset and disappointed than anything else. "Where are we?"

"Dr. Harris's. It's Sunday. We're not going to catch him at his office."

"We can't bother anyone at home!" she protested, but Riley was already getting out of the truck.

"Damn it," Phoenix muttered as he hurried to the door—and felt even worse when the doctor answered, looked out at her and nodded to Riley. She could tell from the expression on Riley's face that she was going in.

When he came for her, he didn't help her out, as she'd expected. He carried her again, only this time it was worse because he was bare-chested. She had his shirt wadded up in her hand.

She could feel his warm skin against her cheek, so she tried to move her head away from him. But that hurt so much, she couldn't manage it for long, and he seemed to grow impatient with her attempt to avoid contact, because he tightened his grip so she couldn't manage it at all.

"You took a hard knock," the doctor said as they entered the house.

"It's not bad," she said.

He motioned Riley through to the kitchen and followed closely behind them. "Let's take a look."

The doctor pulled the bloody T-shirt away the moment Riley sat her at the table. "We'll have to clean you up before we can tell what we're dealing with."

She steeled herself against the pounding in her head, which was getting worse now that the shock was wearing off. "It's just a little cut."

"I'm guessing that little cut needs a couple of stitches," he said drily.

"A butterfly bandage will do. Then I'll get out of your house. It's Sunday. I'm sure this isn't what you want to be doing."

"Relax," he said. "It shouldn't take long."

Even if it went quickly, she had nothing to look at other than Riley, who stood nearby, clearly unhappy, with his arms folded over his chest.

The doctor cleaned her wound and then deliberated as to whether he'd stitch it. She hadn't seen a man in any state of undress for so long that she was tempted to stare at Riley. So she did her best to focus on her feet, her lap, the floor, the doctor's everyday clothes, especially the house shoes he wore. In spite of that, she'd gotten a long enough glimpse of Riley to be able to tell that all the physical changes since high school had been for the better. His work kept him in great shape. There was no doubt about that. Most women would find him extremely attractive.

But not her, she told herself. There was no way she could afford even the slightest admiration or attraction.

"You'll heal with less of a scar if I stitch it," the doctor told her.

"It doesn't matter. I'll be okay. Just put a Band-Aid on it," she said. "I have other scars."

Riley asked Dr. Harris for a minute alone with him. Then they both went into the living room, where they spoke in such low voices she couldn't hear them.

God, she hated this. It went against everything she'd promised herself she'd do when she got out. She did *not* want to give Riley any reason to complain about her, or be unhappy that she was now living in town. Didn't want to cost him any money or aggravation. She just wanted to steer clear of him and have peace between them.

"The stitches won't take more than a few seconds. I keep a bag here at home," the doctor said when they walked back into the room.

She wanted to continue her argument, but they were obviously united against her, or he wouldn't have come back intent on giving her stitches.

She'd have to figure out a way to pay for his services, she decided. At this point, that was the only dignified course of action. So she kept her mouth shut and let him work. And when he was finished, she allowed Riley to drive her home.

Fortunately, her mother's dogs weren't out when they turned into the property, but all the junk she'd been embarrassed to have Kyle see was right there for Riley's view. She hated that he couldn't possibly miss it.

The doctor had given her a local anesthetic when he stitched her up and some pills for the pain. Because her head was no longer pounding, she was able to get out before Riley could come around to open her door.

"Thank you so much for your help," she said as she moved past him. "I don't know what kind of arrangement you made with the doctor about the bill, but I'd appreciate you sending it to me when it comes. I might have to make payments, but I'll handle it over time. And I'll buy you a new shirt, too." The doctor had returned Riley's, but it was balled up on the rubber floor mats, too soaked with blood for him to put on.

Realizing that he probably wouldn't want to touch it, with biohazards being as dangerous as they were these days, she walked back to the truck and started to reach inside. "Here, I'll just…throw this one away so you won't have to…"

He grabbed her arm. "Leave it."

She did as he asked in case he was planning to try to save it. Maybe it was a personal favorite. "I was tested for AIDS and other communicable diseases before I was released, and I don't have anything."

"Good to know," he said, but he didn't sound concerned. "Let's get you inside."

Much to her chagrin, he insisted on helping her to the trailer, which made her regret that she hadn't finished fixing it up. She'd worked as hard as she could, but the rest of the improvements required money she didn't have.

Riley held the door as she stepped inside. "You need some sleep, like the doctor said," he told her.

"I'll go straight to bed." Anticipating the relief she'd feel when she could crawl into bed and try to forget the humiliation of having Riley rescue her, she turned to say goodbye. But he didn't stay on the landing. She had to move back because he was following her into the house.

"He also thinks you're not getting enough to eat," he said with a frown.

Why the heck was he in her living room? She didn't want him there. The place didn't look good enough yet. She'd planned to get it just right before he came over to inspect it. "I've never been very big."

"Malnourishment is something else."

Why had they been talking about her diet? That was none of their business. "Well, you know what they say about prison food." She said that as if she was joking, but she'd purposely eaten as little as possible. Meals were handled by other convicts, and she'd heard too many stories about what some of the food contained.

"He also said someone needs to wake you every few hours."

"I heard him. But I don't have a concussion." It was difficult not to let her gaze fall to his chest. All those muscles were appealing, even though she didn't want them to be...

"We don't know that," he said. "It's better to be safe than sorry."

"Okay." She stood at the door. Maybe *now* he'd leave and she could quit fighting the urge to ogle him. The hunger she felt had far more to do with physical touch than food.

"Okay what?" he said.

"I'll...be careful."

"I'm asking who's going to wake you up."

"My mom. Of course." She gestured at the other trailer. "She lives right there."

He frowned again. "And never comes out."

Lizzie felt safer staying out of the public eye.

"She'll check on me," Phoenix said, but that was a lie. She didn't even plan on telling her mother what had happened. She was going to take a nap. Then she'd pull herself together long enough to make some bracelets so she could pay off her doctor bill.

"You're sure," he said.

She put more energy into her voice, hoping to convince him. "Positive. You should get home. I'm sure Jacob's wondering where you are."

He seemed offended that she was in such a hurry to get rid of him. "Look, I can tell you don't like me much, Phoenix. And I don't blame you. You've been through hell and it's all associated with me. But...I don't want to make things worse. I'm just trying to help."

"Because you think there's a need, but there's not," she said. "And I don't know what gave you the idea that I don't like you when I'm so grateful for all you've done for Jacob. You've been a fabulous father."

"Nice segue," he murmured.

Thanks to the pain meds the doctor had given her, Phoenix's headache was gone, but she still wasn't completely lucid. She knew that because she was looking at Riley's chest without even trying not to. Worse, she wanted to touch it—touch *him*. "Excuse me?"

"Whether or not I've been a good father has nothing to do with what I just said."

"Yes, it does," she argued, struggling to remain coherent. "It's important that you understand how much I appreciate your efforts—all you've done to make life so good for him. He's a great kid. And now you're being sympathetic to me because I'm his mother. But that isn't a burden you need to carry. I'm not as helpless as I seem. This bandage just makes me *look* pathetic."

She laughed even though he didn't laugh with her. "Bottom line, I'm no one you have to bother with. And just to reassure you...since we've never had the chance to discuss it, at least as adults…what I did before, becoming such a nuisance. Please don't feel that could ever happen again. Honestly, it was nothing more than a schoolgirl crush that got out of control." The damn pain meds were making her babble, but she figured she might as well get this out in the open while she had a private audience with him. It wasn't as if she'd ever call him to say any of this. She wouldn't call him for *any* reason—unless it was an emergency and she needed to reach Jacob. "You were the first boy I ever…well, you know…"

He was staring at her so intently she could no longer meet his eyes. "I remember. I was there, too."

"I thought maybe you'd blocked it all out. But it's probably not so unusual for a girl in that situation to feel some sort of…attachment, right? You can understand that."

He didn't say he could. He didn't say anything, so she stumbled on.

"I was just too naive to realize that…that 'I love you' for a…for a guy means something different than it does for the typical girl, that's all. I thought we both meant it, although how could we, at that age?" God, what was she saying? Was she making any sense? She tried even harder to explain. "I put *way* too much store in those three words and…sex. I completely bought in." She added another laugh to let him know how ridiculous that had been. "And then I panicked when I learned I was going to have a baby." She tucked her hair, caked with blood, behind one ear. "I'm not excusing my behavior, don't get me wrong. I shouldn't have called you so many times or driven by your house. 'Go away' is 'go away.' Not that I heard you say it very often, but maybe that was because I didn't *want* to hear it. Anyway, I hope you understand that I'd never try to force my affections on you again. I'm a little wiser about how the world works these days, despite my lack of experience with men. So there's no need for you to worry."

"You understand how the world works," he repeated.

She'd said so in that diatribe…somewhere. But why had he picked out that particular comment? Was she getting through to him or not? "Yes. Probably better than most people."

"And 'I love you' means something different to a boy."

His voice had a rough edge that made her fear he wasn't taking what she'd said as the apology she'd intended. "Right. Sex and love are two different things, and boys can make that distinction more easily than girls. That's all I'm saying. I get that now."

"I see. What a great thing to learn."

Was he being sarcastic? She was so confused. "It was a lesson I needed. And learning it the way I did means I'll never forget."

A muscle moved in his cheek.

"I'm sorry," she said. "Did I say something wrong? I was trying to apologize for…for falling in love with you. Or for holding on to you when I should've let go." None of this was coming out right. She could tell that much, so she stopped trying to explain and opted for the direct approach. "Regardless of anything else, know this—I *promise* I'll never single you out like that again or do anything else to make you uncomfortable."

There. That had to be clear. She smiled up at him, hoping what she'd said would finally meet with his approval. But there was that damn frown again. "What's wrong?" she asked.

"Nothing. Don't worry. You nailed it. And so innocently, too."

She pressed her fingers to her temples. The pain meds had *really* kicked in. "I admit my thoughts are… somewhat disjointed. What, exactly, did I nail?"

"That you can't trust a guy," he replied. "That a guy doesn't know what love is."

That sounded a bit harsh. Had she actually said those things? "Maybe not *all* guys," she clarified.

"Okay. Only me," he said, then walked out.

"I was trying to apologize!" she called after him.

He shook his head as he turned back. "For ever loving me?"

She tried to follow him out onto the stoop but felt too weak to move that far. She leaned against the door instead. "But you didn't *want* me to love you! I swear I'm not finding fault with you or blaming you for anything. I'm trying to figure out a way to coexist here. I don't want you to be miserable just because I'd like to get to know Jacob, don't want you to feel as if that's going to cost you anything. Even what you did today." She pointed at her head. "That trip to the doctor. The ride home. I feel bad that you had to go to the trouble and I wish you would've let me handle it."

"You think you can handle Buddy?"

"I'll have to," she answered. "He's not your problem."

"Yes, he is. He's not going to get away with what he did."

His remark propelled her outside despite her shaky legs. "Don't say that. You can't get involved. You don't want to lose his friendship on my account."

"Because he'd be a much better friend than you."

She laughed again, hoping to *finally* lighten this up. "Not many people could offer you less than I could."

He shook his head as he gazed back at her.

She used her fingers to comb the tangles out of her hair. She had to look a sight covered in the blood from her cut and the dirt from her fall. "There's no need to feel conflicted, Riley. You've got it all. Just enjoy life and carry on the way you always have," she told him, and shut the door.

7

On the drive home, Riley cursed softly to himself as everything Phoenix had said ran through his mind. Her words wouldn't have affected him so deeply if she'd been accusing or resentful. Then maybe he would've felt defensive. But she'd assumed responsibility for everything, going all the way back to when they'd been together—even though he *had* told her he loved her and taken her virginity. Of course she would assume she could count on what he said, because she'd been sincere with him.

It was easy to see why she'd felt sucker punched when he broke up with her. But he honestly hadn't intended to put her in that position. She had no idea how much pressure he'd been under—from his parents, from everyone, including his teachers—to distance himself from her. No one wanted him to get mixed up with "Lizzie's girl." It was his mother who'd wanted him to date Lori, her best friend's daughter. Riley had never been that interested in Lori. Phoenix had been every bit as special to him as he'd told her at the time.

Maybe that was why it had stung to hear her discount what he'd said and done—categorize his part in their relationship as throwaway, the difference between boys and girls, sex versus love. Although it was logical that she would. He'd let her down, hadn't been old enough or mature enough to know how to stand up against his parents. He hadn't even been convinced that he should! In his eyes, at that time, his parents were always right, the guiding beacon he relied on. He hadn't wanted to lose their love and approval. And he certainly hadn't wanted to "ruin his future" as they'd insisted he was doing.

So he'd unwittingly ruined Phoenix's future. If he hadn't set that chain of events in motion, Lori would still be alive.

He thought about that occasionally, late at night when he tried to work out how he should treat Jacob's mother. But with his parents' support—with everyone's support—he'd always been able to justify his behavior, to believe she had indeed reacted out of jealousy and done something unforgivable.

The more he dealt with Phoenix as an adult, however, the easier it was to believe her explanation of that tragic event.

Parking his truck in the driveway instead of the garage, since he was planning to leave again, Riley hurried inside the two-story house he'd built four years earlier to put on a clean T-shirt and check on Jacob.

"Is Mom okay?" Jacob asked, coming out of his room the minute he heard the front door.

"She's going to be fine." Riley hoped. The doctor had indicated she *should* be. But it seemed crazy to leave her over there all by herself, drugged up and with a possible concussion. That trailer had no air-conditioning, and she didn't have a phone. How would she call for help if she needed it? What if she couldn't get over to her mother's? And who would she call even if she did reach Lizzie's?

There was a chance she might not be able to get out of her bed, so Riley planned to go back and check on her. No way could he count on Lizzie to take care of anything or anyone. She was the most dysfunctional person he'd ever known. If he didn't return, he wasn't sure Phoenix would even get dinner, and that worried him. For one thing, she was supposed to have something in her stomach when she took more of the pain meds the doctor had sent home with her.

Jacob stepped out of the way so Riley could get past him on the stairs, then followed him to his room. "Did you take her to the doctor?"

"I did." Riley pulled a T-shirt from one of his drawers and yanked it over his head. "He cleaned her wounds and stitched her up."

"She needed *stitches*? How many?"

"Six. It was quite a gash but not as bad as it looked. Head wounds bleed a lot, like she said."

Jacob dropped onto the bed while Riley went into the master bath to wash his hands and face. "That whole thing scared the crap out of me," he said, speaking loudly enough that Riley could hear him over the running water. "When I saw Buddy racing up on me in that Excursion of his, I thought he was playing with me at first. But then I saw the look on his face and knew we were in trouble."

The fear his son must've felt in that moment made Riley angry all over again. Jacob had only been driving for six months.

"Can you believe Buddy would do something like that?" Jacob asked.

Riley couldn't. He'd known Buddy wasn't pleased

to have Phoenix back in town, but this was ridiculous. "I'm going over to the police station to talk to Chief Bennett right now. Why don't you come with me, so you can explain exactly what happened?"

"You're going to report him?"

"You're damn right I am. He had no business doing what he did."

Jacob seemed hesitant. "But you don't even like Mom."

"I've never said that."

"You weren't very happy about her coming home. And you didn't want to meet her for breakfast."

"I wasn't sure what kind of person she turned out to be. That's all."

"And now she's okay?"

"Let's just say I'm giving her the benefit of the doubt. As long as she doesn't break my trust, I don't have a problem with her being here."

"But if you stick up for her, it'll get us in a fight with Buddy, and that won't be good. Grandma really likes the Mansfields. She hangs out with them all the time, and that means we have to see Buddy once in a while."

"Sometimes you have to do what you think is right regardless of the fallout."

He didn't comment, so Riley thought maybe he'd left. "Jacob?"

"I'm here."

"Don't you think that's true?"

"Yeah, I do."

When Riley reentered the room, Jacob was still on the bed. "You'd better get your shoes. We need to leave right away."

His son got up, but didn't head to the door. He walked over and gave Riley a hug. It was a man-hug—a brief clasp. But it was meaningful because it was so unexpected.

"Thanks, Dad."

When Riley returned to Phoenix's trailer, all appeared to be quiet. He didn't want to drag her out of bed and down the hall to answer if she was sleeping, so he knocked softly and, when no one came, tried the door. It was locked. He thought he'd have to rouse her, after all—until he realized that the door wasn't quite latched. He was able to open it without a problem.

The trailer was hot, but not so hot that he considered it dangerous. He was more concerned about the fact that it didn't appear as if she'd been up since he left four hours earlier. Nothing in the trailer had changed.

After setting the soup he'd bought at Just Like Mom's on the counter, along with the backpack and purse she'd left in Jacob's Jeep, he walked down the hall, knocking gently on the cheap paneling to alert her. He didn't want to scare her.

"Phoenix? It's me, Riley."

There was still no response, but her bedroom door stood ajar, so he poked his head in. She'd showered, but that was about as far as she'd gotten. She'd fallen into bed with a towel wrapped around her head; she didn't appear to be wearing anything under the sheet that covered her. Hot as it was, he couldn't blame her, but the sight of her bare arms and shoulders, and the profile of her face, made him pause. She was pretty, all right— even when she was beat up.

"Phoenix?"

Nothing.

He moved to her side and took her hand. "Hey, Phoenix. Are you okay?"

She mumbled something about being fine and rolled over, jerking her hand away. The sheet dropped in the process, baring her shoulder blade, which bore a tattoo of Jacob's name and the date of his birth written in cursive. A bit lower he found an oddly shaped scar, as well as the fresh scrapes from having dived into that ditch.

Averting his gaze before he could see anything more revealing, he muttered a curse. She looked so small and fragile lying there. Damn Buddy for making a difficult situation even worse.

"Phoenix," he said, shaking her. "It's time to wake up. I brought you some dinner."

"Later," she grumbled.

Figuring he'd fulfilled the doctor's orders by getting her to talk, Riley decided to give her another hour. She'd been through a lot. Maybe, right now, rest was more important than food.

"Okay. I'll wake you again in a bit," he told her.

As he closed her bedroom door, his phone vibrated in his pocket. He had an incoming text. It was Jacob, wanting to know about his mother.

She's fine. Just sleeping, he wrote back while walking to the living room. Jacob had wanted to come with him, but he'd had a group homework project. Riley had said he could stop by after.

So what to do until then? Phoenix didn't have a television. She didn't have much of anything, he saw as he wandered around the place. There was a bedroom on the far side of the living room, which she'd furnished with the same type of broken-down furniture that filled the rest of the trailer. He found a warped chest of drawers, a bed that was set up on cinder blocks and some homemade bookshelves. It all looked as if it had been retrieved from a junkyard, but it was clean. The whole trailer was clean. He could smell the ammonia from whatever she'd used to scrub the place.

In the kitchen he came across a small, cheap microwave, but he wasn't sure what she used it for. Other than the food he and Kyle had delivered, her cupboards were bare. When he opened the fridge to put away the soup, he discovered that it was almost as empty as the cupboards. A half-eaten bowl of oatmeal, an apple and some hummus sat on one shelf, which made it easy to see what she'd been surviving on. But that hardly constituted a balanced diet. How she'd had the strength to do the cleaning she'd done, and in such a short time, was a mystery. There was evidence of her work all over. For instance, she was in the process of removing some old wallpaper in the living room, but she didn't even have a scraper. From what he could tell, she'd been using a butter knife and a razor blade, both of which were sitting on the corner of a wobbly side table.

He shook his head at how tedious and painstaking a process that would be, and yet she'd made significant progress—through sheer determination. She was used to making do with whatever she had, he thought, which reminded him of her bike. So he called Noah.

Noah answered with "What's up?"

Caller ID had identified him. "Not much. What's going on with you?"

"I'm closing the shop for the day so I can go home and have dinner with my wife. I think she's cooking her famous meat loaf. Want to join us?"

"No, I'm tied up. I was just calling because I have an old bike I'm hoping you can fix."

"What kind of old bike?"

Noah sold mostly high-end mountain bikes, so he was assuming Riley would be able to name the make and model. "It's a twenty-year-old ten-speed, if it's that new. And it needs tires, maybe a lot of other work."

"Dude, what are you doing with a piece of shit like that when I own a bike shop? Come on in. I'll set you up with the perfect ride at my cost."

"Actually, it's not mine."

"Whose is it?"

He stood at the window of that extra bedroom and gazed out at the depressing sight of Lizzie's yard. "It belongs to Phoenix."

There was a slight pause. "I can help her out, too, if you want."

"She doesn't have any money. But she doesn't have a car, either, and needs a way to get around."

"I see." There was another brief silence. "How's that going, by the way? When we were at the coffee shop on Friday, you weren't too excited about her being back in town."

"I don't mind," he insisted, feeling guilty for having bitched about her impending return.

"Really?"

"Yeah."

"Does that mean she *doesn't* have horns on her head and carry a pitchfork?"

"She's not so different from everyone else." He considered telling Noah what Buddy had done, and how apathetic Chief Bennett had been when he and Jacob had gone to complain. Of course there was going to be some resentment, he'd said. Buddy would get past it. The Mansfields were good people. Buddy was just having a hard time since his wife walked out on him. Yada, yada. Although Bennett had said he'd look into it, Riley had gotten the distinct impression that he didn't plan to do much more than issue Buddy a cursory warning.

As much as that irritated him, Riley didn't want to get into a long discussion right now. Despite how disoriented Phoenix had seemed when he tried to wake her, there was always the possibility that she might overhear him.

"I'm glad," Noah said. "That should make things easier for Jacob."

"I agree."

"So when do you plan to bring in the bike?"

"Tomorrow okay?"

"Tomorrow's fine with me. We open at ten, but if you have to be at work earlier than that, leave it on my front porch. I can take it around to the shop when I walk over."

Riley turned his back on the piles of rubble he could see from the window. What a place to grow up... "I'll do that. Any idea when you might be able to get to it?"

"Biking season's started, so we're swamped. But you don't need to worry, since you know the owner."

Riley smiled at his jocular tone. "It's nice having friends in high places. Thanks."

"No problem. If I ever need my roof repaired, I'll expect the same treatment," he joked. "See you tomorrow."

Riley sighed as he hung up. Then he realized he didn't have to stand around being bored. He had his tools in the truck; he could finish removing that old wallpaper.

The wallpaper was gone within the hour, but Phoenix still hadn't stirred, so he began to look for other odd jobs. He fixed the hinges on some of her cupboards so they'd close properly, replaced a broken screen so the mosquitos couldn't get in and repaired a leak under her sink. He was in search of more small repairs he could

make when he opened a door off the hallway and discovered her workroom.

"What the hell is this?" he muttered, but it was quite
obvious. That bracelet she'd given Jacob? She'd made
it. Apparently, she made a lot of them. Several different
types—some braided, some with carved pieces of wood
or silver beads, some personalized—hung on a coat
hanger dangling from a nail above her desk, and a pile
of packages, all addressed and ready to be mailed, were
stacked along the far wall. A shelf consisting of a length
of board supported by two cinder blocks held an array
of stampers, hole-punchers and heavy-duty scissors.
On another shelf he saw several bowls of beads, metal
pieces, fasteners, even feathers. And the whole room
smelled like the leather strips that filled an old suitcase
lying open on the far side. There was also a chalkboard
leaning against the wall with names and checkmarks
and what he decided must be a style number.

Phoenix hadn't mentioned that she ran a business.
Why had she kept that to herself?

He had no idea, but the sight of her little bracelet fac-
tory made him smile. What she'd accomplished was impressive, considering everything she'd been up against.

He wondered where she sold them…

Suddenly her door banged against the wall, hard
enough to rattle the whole place. She was up.

Assuming she was ready to eat, he ducked out of
her workroom.

Then he stopped dead in his tracks.

8

Phoenix was so disoriented. She was fairly certain the doctor had given her too much pain medication. It should've worn off by now, she told herself. She couldn't even walk straight. She had to use the walls to steady herself and feel her way along, since her eyelids were so heavy.

Or maybe some of it was the aftereffects of her tumble. She'd landed really hard...

She was staggering in her attempt to reach the bathroom in the hall, since the one in her bedroom didn't work—until she heard a choked sound. Then she froze, shoved her hair out of her face and looked up to see Riley standing, big as life, in the doorway of her office less than three feet away, his jaw practically on the floor.

She screamed before she could stop herself, and the grogginess evaporated. She didn't have a stitch of clothing on! Even the towel she'd wrapped around her head was in the bed somewhere.

Whipping around, she tried to dart back into the bedroom, but when the door hit the inside wall, it had bounced back so hard it'd slammed shut—and that must've jarred the lock because she couldn't open it.

All she could do was cover as much of her breasts as possible while trying to break through the door using her shoulder.

"Wait! Stop!" Riley cried. "You're going to hurt yourself even more. Will you calm down? You're freaking me out!"

He took off his T-shirt and, for the second time that day, offered it to her. But she was shaking too badly to put it on, so he stepped up to help. After righting the sleeves so she could poke her arms through, he yanked it over her head and pulled it down, and she felt the warmth of the cotton cover her body.

Then they both stood there gaping at each other and breathing as hard as if they'd just run a mile.

"What are you doing here?" she asked when she could find her voice.

Thankfully, he was so much bigger than she was, his shirt came to midthigh. She no longer felt exposed. She was, however, writhing with embarrassment. He was the only man she'd ever slept with, which suddenly seemed far too significant.

Looking a bit rattled himself, he wiped his face with one hand. No doubt her bloodcurdling scream had shaken him up. "I'm sorry. I thought you knew. I came in a couple of hours ago to check on you. I spoke to you, and you answered me. I've been going in and out and hammering and stuff…"

She had no recollection of any of that. She only remembered falling into bed. *"Hammering?"* That caught her attention because it was the last thing she'd expected him to say. Why would he be hammering at her house?

He shrugged. "Figured I might as well make myself useful."

"By…"

"Fixing a few things while I'm here."

Did he really have to see how she was living? Hopefully, she hadn't asked for his help when he'd spoken to her earlier. She certainly hadn't meant to. "How'd you know where to start?" she said, as if she wasn't painfully aware of how pathetic she must seem to him.

"It's quitting that's the hard part," he said. "There's so much left to do. But I haven't been quiet, which is why I felt my presence wouldn't come as a shock."

"I didn't think I'd see you again," she explained. "I mean…not today. I'm trying to prepare a room for Jacob, in case you ever let him stay with me for a weekend now and then. I planned to ask you to come out and inspect it when I'm through, but…it's not nearly ready."

"That's the room on the other side?" He motioned toward the far end of the trailer. "It's for Jacob?"

"Only with your permission, of course. I'm hoping he'll be able to visit once in a while—that's all. Nothing…nothing that would upset you or…or threaten your relationship with Jake."

The way he studied her made her wonder if she should've kept her mouth shut.

"I don't always think the worst, you know," he said.

She shook her head. "I wasn't accusing you. I just want to be clear about my intentions so you can maybe…come to trust me…a little."

"It sounds like you could trust me a little more, too. Anyway, I brought you some soup. Can I talk you into eating it?"

Soup? When she'd left prison, she'd been prepared to overlook his many slights, had been determined to repay even cruelty with kindness. That was the only way she'd felt she could build a relationship with Jacob. But Riley was being much nicer than she'd anticipated, and she wasn't sure how to deal with nice. She hadn't had much experience with it. "You didn't need to do that, but I appreciate the gesture. I'll eat after I get back into my bedroom so I can return your shirt. I don't want to hold you up."

She tried the knob again, kept jiggling it, hoping it would somehow release, but it didn't work. Apparently, nothing could go right for her.

He rested his hands on his hips as he watched. "Is there some sort of trick to it?"

"I guess it locks when you slam the door, which is news to me. But I'll think of something." She stopped bothering with it, since her efforts weren't being rewarded. "The windows are open. I could cut the screen and crawl through. I'll do that. Wait here."

"You want me to *wait*? Wouldn't it be easier if I hoisted you through?"

The image that went through her mind, of his hand under her shirt, made her burn with fresh embarrassment. "That's okay. I'm not…dressed for that."

"Isn't it more important to get back in your room than to preserve your modesty?"

She felt her face flush. "I didn't mean for this to happen. I hope you believe that. I honestly wasn't aware I had company."

"I know."

"*Do* you?" she asked. "Really? Because I'm afraid when you get home you might start thinking I walked out with no clothes on purpose to…to entice you or something. But I swear that wasn't the case. I mean…if I was seriously trying to get a man's attention in *that* way, I'd at least make sure I'd combed my hair." She chuckled, hoping he could see the logic—and the humor—in what she'd said. "No woman would come on to a man looking like she'd just been hit by an Excursion."

"I don't think you did it on purpose," he responded. "The terror on your face, and the fact that you nearly broke your shoulder trying to escape, pretty much told me that your panic was genuine."

There was a huskiness to his voice that made her curious as to what, exactly, was going through his head. It didn't sound like relief, as she'd assumed. But he *did* seem to believe her, so she let the rest go in hopes that she could make up for the fact that he'd just seen a great deal more of her than he wanted to. "Thanks for understanding. I may have told you earlier, but in case I didn't, I have no designs on you, no residual feelings or anything. You and everyone else in town must be wondering, but you can relax. You're *completely* in the clear."

"*Completely*," he repeated, mimicking her emphasis.

She wasn't sure how to react to that. Wasn't what she'd said *good* news? "Yes."

His face grew shuttered. "You wouldn't sleep with me again even if I were the last man on earth. Got it. Thanks for putting me on notice."

There was that odd element in his voice again. It confused her. She thought she was telling him what he wanted to hear, what would make him the most amenable to allowing her back into his life, if only for the sake of their son. But he seemed more offended than relieved.

Was it an ego thing? Did he want her to continue to worship at his feet?

"It's not that I think you're unattractive or anything," she said. "I didn't mean to offend you."

"Of course you didn't. Any woman would be lucky to be with me. Any woman but you, right?"

Her breath caught in her throat. This was somehow going sideways again. "Even I think you're handsome, Riley."

"God, Phoenix." He rubbed a hand over his face. "Will you…*stop*? Just say what you really think and feel? I'm not as big an ogre as you're making me out to be."

She cleared her throat. "Okay. Sure. That's fair. I thought I was being honest, but I'll just…climb through the window and give you your shirt so you can go home."

He folded his arms and leaned against the wall. "You'll need a ladder if you don't want my help. You realize that."

"You've seen the yard. There's got to be a ladder somewhere. So if you'll…excuse me." She waited for him to move down the hall so she wouldn't have to brush by him, but he didn't.

"I have a better plan," he said, straightening.

Her eyes lowered instinctively to his chest and the muscles that rippled beneath his skin, but she jerked them up again. "What's that?"

"I'll pick the lock."

"You can do that?"

"I don't see why not. My tools are here."

True. They were hanging on the leather belt that rode low on his hips. "You don't mind?"

"Stop being so damned polite!" he snapped.

"Okay."

"It's driving me crazy."

"Got it. I'm sorry. I just…know that none of this is reflecting well on me. I shouldn't have gotten into that Jeep with Jacob. I feel…terrible that I endangered him. I won't let it happen again."

"You tried to draw the danger away from him as soon as you could. I'm grateful for that. What happened wasn't your fault, anyway. Buddy's to blame."

"I appreciate your understanding," she said, and meant it.

"And just so *you* know something, I'm not going to use Jacob as a weapon against you, so you can stop walking on eggshells around me. I don't like feeling that you view me as the bad guy. I'm not your enemy."

He'd certainly seemed like her enemy in court. But she didn't say so. She'd long since decided he'd had a right to end their relationship. Maybe he'd thought he loved her and realized later that he didn't. At seventeen and eighteen, relationships went that way sometimes— on-again, off-again, I love you, I hate you. They were both so young. And anyone was entitled to break up with anyone else, regardless of age. She should've just let him go.

"Thanks."

"Go eat."

"I'm going. If you'll—" she indicated the hallway "—let me pass."

He scowled. "I'm not blocking you," he said. "Go!"

By turning sideways, she managed to slip past him without any contact. But being naked under his shirt and so close to him was bad enough.

"What? Now I bite, too?" he asked. He'd obviously noticed how carefully she'd tried to circumvent him, but she pretended he hadn't said anything. He didn't understand what going seventeen years without that kind of touch did to someone. She was so…empty, so lonely. She didn't want to end up doing exactly what she'd promised she wouldn't do—crave his touch.

* * *

Riley stood still for a few seconds, trying to regulate his breathing. He had no business being turned on by what he'd seen, but his body didn't give a crap what his brain said, probably because he didn't get to enjoy many romantic encounters. As a single dad, it wasn't appropriate to bring home random love interests, and he hadn't been in a serious relationship for quite some time—actually, none that he'd ever incorporated into his life with Jacob. No one he'd dated felt to him as if she could become Jacob's stepmother, and it seemed unfair to introduce him to one possibility after another, especially if Riley didn't have much confidence the relationship would last.

That, together with living in a small town, had seriously impaired his sex life. Which was why he was sweating right now, he told himself. He'd just seen a naked woman, one he'd slept with in the past, and that conjured up all the old, erotic memories he'd locked away.

"This is it, in the fridge?" she asked from the kitchen.

He drew a deep breath before answering. "Yeah, it's chicken tortilla. After you heat it up, add the cheese, chips and cilantro that are in the white bag on the counter."

"I've never had this kind of soup, but it sounds good. Would you like some? It's a big container. There's plenty for both of us."

"No, it's for you." He had no idea when she might feel strong enough to walk to town for more groceries. What else was she going to eat?

"You really don't want any?"

"I'm not hungry." For that. He was suddenly starving for the feel of a woman's body as his mind's eye once again focused on the way her hands had tried to cover her breasts.

He'd seen them despite that…

"Where's Jacob?" she asked.

She was so sure of his contempt for everything about her that he knew she'd never guess he was contending with an unwanted erection.

"He has a group homework project," he said, and forced himself to find a nail he could insert through the hole in the center of the lock. This was Phoenix, he told himself. He *couldn't* be attracted to her.

But that didn't seem to change the fact that he was.

"Stupid door." Her voice filtered back to him again. "You'd be home and able to help him if not for that."

"Jake handles his studies without me these days."

"He's such a great kid. I hope he wasn't too upset about this morning."

"He's worried about you."

"A little fall is no big deal."

A *little* fall… From her perspective, that was probably true. As she'd said, she'd weathered far worse. He could tell that when he saw her bare back, but he hadn't noticed any scars while she was in the hall. He'd been far too interested in other things.

He fished around for the trigger in the knob. He figured if he couldn't find it, he'd break the door open. Had she been any bigger, she could've done that herself, it was so flimsy.

He managed without too much trouble, swung the door open and gazed around, taking note of how neatly she'd piled her few belongings in one corner, including the items he and Kyle had purchased for her. She didn't have a chest of drawers, and yet she'd put one in Jacob's room. That detail didn't slip past him. It looked as if Jacob had the more comfortable bed, too.

"Did you get the lock to open?" she asked from the end of the hall.

"Yeah." Conscious of his lingering erection, he turned only partway to answer. Then he acted as if he was doing something with his tool belt and adjusted himself.

"Thanks."

When he glanced up again, he noticed that she was waiting expectantly, eager to get into her room. No doubt she wanted to change into an outfit that made her feel less vulnerable. But she didn't approach, and he knew she wouldn't as long as she had to come anywhere close to him. She'd made her escape when she maneuvered past him in the hall and was bent on keeping her distance.

Who could blame her? She'd been punished enough for sleeping with him seventeen years ago.

"The soup's delicious," she said, leaning against the wall and holding the bowl as she ate. "What do I owe you for that?"

"Nothing. It's my treat."

"You got it from a restaurant. Let me pay you back."

That damned pride! "With your bracelet money?"

She seemed startled by the comment. "That's just a little something I started in prison. I don't know how it will go."

"Looks like it's going pretty good right now."

"Better than I expected," she admitted with a shy smile.

"How'd you get into that?"

"They offered a class on working with leather at the prison. I took it and…came up with a few things that some of the other women liked and wanted to buy. So I sold them, took the money and bought more supplies. Then I sold those and did the whole process over again. There was a prison guard who especially liked them. After she bought several for gifts, she talked to me about posting them on Etsy.com and eBay. I had to share the proceeds with her, but I couldn't have done it on my own. And that's what gave me most of the money I sent you."

He chafed at the reminder. That money must have been such a sacrifice, and he hadn't really needed it. Most of it was still in a savings account for Jake's college fund. Jake knew she'd sent money once in a while, but he didn't know Riley hadn't spent much of it.

"Now that you've been released—is it strictly your business?" He hoped the prison guard wasn't still getting a cut.

She nodded. "That was always the understanding."

"That's nice. So people pay you via PayPal?"

"Yeah. And it goes right into my account. I'm not earning a lot, but…it's something."

"Why didn't you tell Jacob you'd made what you gave him?"

"No reason," she said, but he knew that was a lie. She must've been afraid he'd reject it—or she didn't want him to feel obligated to accept it.

She tried hard not to expect anyone to love her, he realized.

"Thanks for…coming to the rescue yet again," she said.

If she apologized once more for the trouble she'd caused him, he was going to throttle her. "Like I said before, I don't mind."

Finally satisfied that his body was no longer demanding sexual fulfillment, he returned the nail to his pouch and approached her. But the closer he got, the more she backed up, until they were both in the kitchen.

"I told Jake he could stop by when he was done with his homework, so you might want to go ahead and get dressed."

She stiffened. "Jake's coming here?"

The panic in her voice surprised him. "Where else?"

"But…I'm not ready. I don't want him to judge me by…by what he sees around here. And look at me!"

"He's not going to judge you at all," he said, but thanks to her mother, she'd been judged her whole life. He knew he wasn't going to convince her.

"His room isn't ready," she went on. "I'd like to repair some of the furniture I have in there. And paint. And clean up outside." She did a double take when she noticed the wallpaper she'd been removing was gone. "What happened to— Did you finish it?"

He shrugged. "It didn't take long."

"Thank you. That was really hard to get off."

"It helps to have a scraper."

"What else did you do?" she asked.

He listed the various chores, but she didn't seem pleased. "You didn't need to do all that."

"I didn't have anything else to keep me busy."

"Still…"

"It's not a big deal. So what do you want me to do about Jake? Would you rather I told him he can't come?"

She worried her bottom lip. "If you wouldn't mind. I'd like to have everything perfect before he sees it."

He couldn't help responding to her earnest expression. "Of course."

Her body softened in relief. "Thank you."

"I'll head out, then." He stepped to one side.

"Okay. I'll be right back with your shirt."

While she was gone, Riley checked the soup container and was gratified to see that she'd eaten quite a bit. She must've been starved...

"Phoenix!"

Riley couldn't see Lizzie, but he could hear her shrieking her daughter's name, and then, *Where are you?* Where the hell is my dinner? You want me to starve in here?"

Phoenix didn't respond, but Riley was quite certain she could hear; all the windows were open. If he had to guess, she was hesitant to scream across the distance as her mother was doing.

He imagined her in the bedroom, changing as fast as she could so she could hurry over to the other trailer, where she'd do whatever Lizzie asked, just to shut her up. But Phoenix had a possible concussion, with six stitches, and Riley felt she should be left alone to rest.

Telling himself he'd bring more food for the next day, he grabbed the leftover soup and stalked over to Lizzie's with it. "Here you go," he said. "Phoenix told me to give you this for dinner. She's been meaning to bring it by but she was too busy with bracelet orders."

Lizzie's eyes just about bugged out of her head as she recognized him. And when her gaze lowered to his bare chest, he knew he should've at least put on his shirt. What had happened was so innocent, and he was so used to working without a shirt, that he hadn't even considered how it might appear.

"What are *you* doing here?" Lizzie asked, as if the devil had shown up at her door. "Don't tell me you've been sleeping with my daughter again! Surely, she isn't *that* stupid."

Footsteps padded on the packed earth and Phoenix

came running around the corner, dressed in a pair of denim shorts that were far too big for her and a simple tank top. "Thank you for this," she said, thrusting his shirt at him. "I'll take care of my mother. Don't worry."

"Did *he* do that to you?" Lizzie demanded the second she saw the scrapes and bruises and the stitches on her daughter's forehead.

Phoenix tried to come between the two of them. But she faltered and her hand went to her head as if she might pass out.

Riley took her arm so she wouldn't fall. "You shouldn't be out."

She ignored him but didn't jerk away as she normally would have. Since she'd been home, she wouldn't let him get within two feet of her. The way she'd behaved when she'd had to pass him in the hall was proof. But he could tell her head was swimming; she needed the support. And she was focused completely on her mother.

"No. He didn't hurt me," she said, struggling with the effects of having moved so fast in her current condition. "Of course not. I…I fell and he lent me his shirt to…to mop up the blood."

Except there wasn't a drop of blood on it, and Lizzie didn't miss that. Contempt curled her top lip as Phoenix rushed on. "Wait, that was actually a different shirt." She was getting flustered in her attempt to explain. "But still. Riley gave me a ride home. That's all."

"And then you let *him* have a ride, huh?" she snapped. "I guess seventeen years in prison didn't teach you what spreading your legs for the Stinsons' coddled boy will do?"

Riley glared at her. "That's enough," he growled. "I don't care what you say about me, but watch how you talk to your daughter."

"Oh, that's right. You're the only one who's allowed to treat her like shit," she said with a cackle, and backed her considerable bulk into the house.

The slamming of the door echoed in the ensuing silence.

Phoenix seemed to realize that he was supporting her and reached for the railing instead. "Sorry about that."

"Don't worry about it. Let's get you back to bed." So he could leave. He wasn't sure what the hell he was doing here, anyway.

Gingerly, Phoenix began to go down the steps. "She's not as bad as she seems, you know. She's just… protective of me in her own way."

When she stumbled, he caught her and would've swung her into his arms. She was so light it would've been easier to carry her. But he knew she'd protest. "You need to go to bed, and you need to stay there until you feel better," he said.

"I will," she agreed. "But…don't go home upset, okay? She's wrong. You've had the best life has to offer because you deserve it. I'm *glad* you have so much."

The crazy thing was that he believed she meant what she said. She wanted him to be happy despite the disparity in their situations, despite the past. Not many people could be as generous. Which brought a question to mind—if he deserved what he had, did that mean she deserved so much less?

His mother would answer that with a resounding yes. But it sure as hell didn't feel that way to him.

9

When Phoenix woke up, it was the middle of the night. Since her windows were open, she remained still, listening for sounds that might indicate trouble. She should get up and close them, she told herself. Hot was better than unsafe. But all she heard were the cicadas and frogs down by the creek.

It's okay. Everything's okay. She hoped Buddy would be satisfied with the damage he'd caused, that her injuries would somehow dissolve his anger...

Unwilling to focus on that frightening event, she remembered that instance with Riley when she came out of the bedroom and the door locked behind her—and nearly laughed out loud. What were the chances of something like that happening? Especially when Riley was around?

He must've thought she was up to her old tricks—as if she hadn't learned her lesson!

Phoenix hoped she'd been able to convince him that it was an accident, because it honestly was.

She rolled over and tried to go back to sleep, but she should never have allowed herself to think of Riley. Once she did, other thoughts and images intruded—memories, too. She remembered how reverently he'd touched her the first time they'd made love, how he'd trembled when she'd touched him...

That was in another lifetime, she reminded herself, when she was another person. She could no longer think about it, even occasionally, even deep in the night, or she could rekindle that desire and destroy everything she was trying so hard to build.

Maybe she should go out to Sexy Sadie's sometime this week, and drink and dance—possibly get laid. Maybe that would put a stop to these inappropriate thoughts and memories.

But she couldn't risk the gossip that kind of behavior would cause. She wasn't even sure she *could* have sex with a man she didn't know. Riley was her only experience.

She'd just have to continue stumbling along and do the best she could.

Dragging herself out of bed, she went into her office. She needed money, and that meant she had to work. The incident with Buddy had cost her an entire day. But she didn't start with anything that would make a profit; she started by creating a bracelet for Kyle. His late-night visit to her place, and the clothes and food he'd brought, gave her a kindness to cling to, one that came without the risks associated with being grateful for Riley's soup and repairs.

She didn't want to make Kyle feel he was now obligated to treat her as a friend when they bumped into each other in town. She thought he'd be smarter to stay away from her and planned to make that clear. But she did want to thank him, and give him what she could, little though that was.

"Did you tell her?"

Riley sat back on the floor joists. He'd just climbed

into the attic of his current project to fix some wiring when Kyle called. "What are you talking about?"

"Phoenix! Did you tell her we left those clothes and things?"

Riley brushed insulation from his shoulders. Attics were hot, hellacious places. "No, of course not. I was more concerned about keeping that a secret than you were. Why would *I* tell her?"

"Then how'd she find out?"

The heat pressed in from all sides. "What makes you think she did?"

"She dropped off a small thank-you gift sometime during the night—or early this morning, before I got up."

Riley pictured Phoenix staggering toward him completely naked and shook his head—but that image had popped up repeatedly since he'd left Phoenix's last night. She had a beautiful body despite the scars; there was no denying that. "What kind of gift?"

"A leather bracelet."

That was from Jacob's mother, all right. "Anything else?"

"A note."

Too anxious to remain seated, especially in such a confined space, Riley stood and accidentally banged his head on the ceiling. "Shit!"

"I know."

"It's not that. Never mind," he grumbled. "Read me what she wrote."

"One sec." There was a brief pause, then Kyle came back on the phone. "'Dear Kyle, thank you. It couldn't have been easy for you to break ranks with everyone else (don't worry, I won't tell anyone). I just had to let you know that I'm very grateful for what you gave me and will pay you back once I get on my feet. In the meantime, I hope you can accept this small token of my appreciation. (Please don't feel you need to acknowledge me in public.) P.'"

Rubbing his head where he'd whacked it, Riley mulled over what he'd heard.

"You still there?" Kyle asked.

"Yeah."

"So? What do you think?"

"I'm trying to figure out how she caught on."

"I gave her a ride home a little while before we went back with those clothes. Maybe that was enough to tip her off. Did *you* get a bracelet?"

"No."

"Then that has to be it. The good news is she probably has no idea you were involved, so you're in the clear like you wanted to be."

And the bad news was that she probably thought Kyle was some knight in shining armor.

Not that he cared, Riley told himself.

"It has to be the ride," Kyle was saying, growing more confident that his assumption was correct. "But...I don't live all that close to her. How do you suppose she got over here?"

"She must've walked." Riley had dropped her bike off at Noah's before heading to work, so she couldn't have found a way to fix and use that.

"In the dark?" Kyle exclaimed.

That she'd go to so much trouble to thank someone for a little human kindness was crazy. "And with six stitches in her head," Riley added.

"What are you talking about?"

As much as he wanted to stand and move around,

the lack of space forced him to crouch down as he told Kyle what Buddy had done.

"That pisses me off," Kyle said. "What are you going to do about it?"

"I went to see Chief Bennett. I'm going to let him handle this one. He's asked me to stay out of it, and so has my mother. But Buddy had better not do anything else."

Kyle didn't immediately respond.

"What are you thinking?" Riley asked.

"I'm thinking you're in a tough spot with your mother. Maybe I should be the one to deal with this if it comes up again."

"No, I want you to stay out of it." He hung up, but Kyle called right back.

"What?" Riley said.

"That was an offer of help, you know."

"I'm sorry."

"What's going on with you, man?"

"Nothing. This is a difficult time for me. It's been an adjustment since Phoenix got out."

"But you're reacting in a way I never would've expected."

"I have no clue what you're talking about."

"Don't tell me you're suddenly attracted to her..."

Suddenly? He'd been attracted to her since he first got to know her when he tutored her in math. Other things, other people, were what had come between them—his friends, parents and teachers, and then all that far more terrible stuff. Everything had worked together to convince him that she was evil or crazy or both, unworthy of him or any other normal person. And with time, he'd managed to forget the incredible chemistry they'd shared, how unassuming and real she could be, how delighted she was with the smallest kindness.

With effort, he'd minimized what he'd felt and assumed that was all in the past.

But he was feeling *something* now that she was back. "Why do you say that?" he asked, hoping to dodge a more direct answer.

"Um, the fact that you're *jealous*?"

"I'm not jealous! It's just that…I've slept with her before. She's not someone I'd like to see you get involved with."

"I'm not interested in her romantically. That would be too weird considering I'm one of your best friends. And to be honest, I don't know if I could put up with all the negative crap I'd get from my own friends and family. Whoever ends up with her is going to have a battle on his hands. I'm only trying to be fair and do what I think is right. This can be a hard place to live, with so many people united against you."

"She's Jacob's mom. I'll look after her," Riley insisted.

"*You'll* look after her? That's nuts," he said, and disconnected.

Riley dropped his head in his hands. It *was* nuts. Why had he reacted so negatively to Kyle, who just wanted to be kind?

When his phone rang again, Riley was so sure it was Kyle calling back yet again he answered without looking at caller ID. "Hey, I'm sorry, dude. I'm confused as hell right now," he said, but this time it wasn't Kyle.

"What are you talking about?"

Riley sucked in a quick breath when he recognized his son's voice. "Hey, Jake. Why aren't you in school?"

"I *am* at school. I'm between classes."

"Then…what's going on?"

"I checked my schedule. I have a home game on Wednesday."

"What time?"

"Right after sixth period."

"I'll be there, like always."

Following a slight hesitation, he said, "Are you still going to check on Mom like you said at breakfast?"

Given the conversation he'd just had with Kyle, Riley knew he should keep his distance. If she'd walked all the way to Kyle's and back, she must be okay. But the fact that she had no one to even check in on her, and no phone in case she needed help, made him worry. There was nothing to stop Buddy from going out to her place and raising more hell. "Yeah, I guess. Over lunch. Why?"

"Will you let Mom know? About my game? I sent her a message on Facebook but I'm not sure she'll get it."

Riley hung his head as he rested his elbows on his knees.

"Did you hear me, Dad? 'Cause I gotta go. The bell's gonna ring."

"I'll tell her about it," he said.

"How much would it cost me to get her a phone?" Jacob asked.

"You're not old enough to get anyone a phone."

"We could put her on your plan."

Riley shook his head. His world was going crazy. "She wouldn't let us even if we offered."

"Why not?"

"She's a very independent person."

"That's good, though, isn't it?"

When Jacob said that, Riley realized Phoenix's independence and strength, her determination to fight back without leaning on anyone, was partly what drew him to her. He doubted he'd met anyone else with so much resilience. "Yeah, that's good."

"Tell her I can pick her up if she needs a ride."

"You won't have time to get her. I'll see if she wants a lift."

"I'm excited that she might be there. I hope I have a good game."

"Me, too," he said, then ended the call. Phoenix was doing a better job of winning over his son than he'd anticipated—and that made Riley feel as dubious as he did about all the other changes going on.

When Riley arrived at Phoenix's trailer, her face was devoid of makeup, her hair was pulled back and she wore those ugly cutoffs that were several sizes too big.

"Hey." She held the door, but her eyes immediately took on that wary look she seemed to reserve for him—as if he was a poisonous snake that had just slithered within striking distance.

He handed her the chicken sandwich he'd bought for her on his way here. "Lunch."

When she didn't take the bag, he scowled. "*Your* lunch, which is why I'm handing it to you."

"Riley, I don't want you to keep bringing me meals. I can't afford it."

"It's *food*, Phoenix. Everyone's got to eat."

She gestured in the general direction of her kitchen. "I have some canned goods."

Which he'd also bought; she just didn't know it. "This will taste better. How's your head?"

Finally accepting the sack, she moved out of the way when he walked in. Heaven forbid they should ever come in physical contact. "Good as new."

Maybe the pain was gone, but the bruising was more apparent. She looked like she'd been beaten up.

"You're black-and-blue all over."

"I'll heal."

The smell of fresh paint registered, and he noticed some beige splotches on her clothes and in her hair. "What are you painting?"

She pointed to the farther bedroom, the one she'd designated as Jacob's. Of course she'd apply herself to his room before any other.

Riley thought of all the money she'd sent over the years, and the cards and letters for Jacob. Jacob got the best of whatever she had. Riley had once chosen to view that as manipulative, but he was beginning to see her attempts to reach her son in an entirely different light…

"How's progress?"

She frowned. "I'm not much of a painter, and this paint is pretty old. Someone gave it to my mom years ago. To be honest, I'm not sure it's going to work. But I decided to try it out."

"Let's see."

She shook her head. "That's okay. It's not finished yet."

He moved toward the bedroom, anyway. She followed and stood behind him as he surveyed her work. "Did you stir it?" he asked.

"As well as I could."

It needed more vigorous stirring. And she needed masking tape. "You're trying to do this freehand?"

"It takes more time, but I'm being careful."

She hadn't done a *bad* job, considering that she'd probably never painted a room before. But he'd painted so many things, he could do better in just a couple of hours.

He thought about the rolls of tape he carried in his truck, in case he ran into something that required a quick coat, and was tempted to offer them to her. But if she was leery of a chicken sandwich, she wouldn't thank him for getting involved in her latest project.

"It's that bad, huh?" she said when he didn't speak right away.

"It'll be fine." He turned back to her. "Is the pain in your head gone?"

"For the most part."

"And you've heard nothing from Buddy?"

"No. Is that why you're here? You didn't say anything to him, did you?"

"I went to Chief Bennett. He said he'd handle it."

"That won't turn out the way you want if he says the wrong thing. You know what a hothead Buddy is."

"It's where we have to start. Or *we* look like the troublemakers."

Concern entered her eyes. "There is no *we*. This has nothing to do with you. I've tried to tell you that."

She'd also told Kyle not to acknowledge her in public. She knew she was considered poison.

"The other reason I came by is because of Jacob—he asked me to tell you he has a home game on Wednesday at four-thirty."

She didn't seem as excited as he'd thought she would.

"You wanted to come, didn't you?"

"Of course, but...I hope some of these bruises are gone by then, or I'll attract too much attention, even from people who don't know I'm an ex-con."

"Ex-con or not, you're prettier than most women," he said. "I wouldn't worry about it."

She looked more skeptical than flattered. "I'd wait for the next game, but I've been dying to see him in action, so…maybe I'll be able to find a hat, one that'll hide the bandage over my stitches."

"A hat's a good idea. It's been damn hot this spring. You could get sunburned sitting out there."

"I'll see what I can do," she said as they moved to the front door.

"Okay, I'll pick you up at three-thirty."

She grabbed his arm as he stepped out, then immediately let go as if she'd caught herself doing something she shouldn't. "Wait, what are you talking about? Pick me up for what?"

"The game. What else?"

"I don't expect a ride. I can get there on my own. There's no need."

"Of course there is."

"No, there isn't! It's not like this is on your way. Which reminds me. I had a bike out here." She indicated the spot from which he'd taken it. "You didn't happen to see it, did you?"

He considered denying it but didn't want to give her any reason to call Kyle. "It's at the shop."

"*What* shop?"

"Do you remember Noah Rackham?"

She nodded. "His brother died not long after Lori did. That was a tragic summer…for all of us."

Riley didn't want to talk about Lori. He still wasn't sure who to believe about what had happened that day— Phoenix or his mother and everyone else. "He owns the bike shop in town."

"So?"

"He's fixing it."

"How? You mean…*you* took my bike to him?"

"You need to have some way to get around."

Her expression hardened. "But I don't want you to provide it."

He grimaced. "Don't let your pride stand between you and the things you need, Phoenix."

"*Pride?* All I have left is my self-respect. You want to take that away, too?"

Suddenly uncomfortable, and feeling more responsible than ever for his part in her trial, he shifted his feet. "That was never my intention."

"Good." She raised her chin. "Because I can get by on my own. I don't need your help."

He thought of mentioning how grateful she'd been for Kyle's compassion but was afraid that if he did, she'd make Kyle take back all the stuff they'd bought. "Fine," he said with a shrug.

"That means no more food," she insisted, handing him the chicken sandwich. "No more anything. And please leave my bike at the shop until I can afford to pick it up."

"Noah's my buddy. He's fixing it for free."

"I don't care. I don't want pity—especially yours."

"It's not pity. It's…"

"*What?*" she demanded. "Why would *you* ever want to help *me*?"

To relieve some of the guilt he suffered for letting his parents talk him into breaking up with her, and for not being kinder while she was in prison. There'd been times when he'd been tempted to reverse his policy, to give Jacob her many letters. But after convincing himself that she had too many character flaws, he couldn't. Also, the future—when she might get out, what she might do when she did and what she would be like— had been *such* an unknown. He'd felt Jacob would be safer if they stuck to the familiar and ignored all the doubt, all the questions.

Besides, being friendly with her opened him and Jake up to the possibility that they might come to believe her side of the story, which would saddle him with even more guilt. "I'm sorry I hurt you."

She gestured dismissively. "At that age…"

"Don't make excuses for me," he broke in. "I knew what love was, and I was in love with you."

He didn't wait for her response. He wasn't asking her to forgive him. He thought that might be too much. And yet he did want her to know she hadn't been crazy for trusting her heart.

She'd come out onto the steps and that caught his attention as he climbed into the cab of his truck. She didn't say anything, didn't even wave.

But she smiled, and he smiled back.

10

When Kyle showed up at Jacob's game, he was wearing the leather bracelet Phoenix had made for him. Riley tried not to let that bother him, but he found his eyes straying to it again and again.

"She's not here yet?"

"Who?" Riley asked, pretending Phoenix hadn't been on his mind just about every second since she'd come back.

"You know who. Jake's mom."

"No."

Kyle rested both fists on his hips. "Maybe I should go by her place, see if she needs a ride."

"I dropped off her bike last night." Since it had been late, and all her lights were off, he'd left it leaning against the side of the trailer, where he'd found it when they'd brought over the clothes and food. He'd also left her a Whiskey Creek Miners baseball cap, in case she hadn't been able to find a hat to hide her stitches.

Kyle continued to search the crowd. "It's a long ride," he said.

"Not as long as it is a walk. I'm sure she'll be here soon." He didn't want Kyle giving her a ride if she wouldn't accept one from him.

Kyle didn't seem to like his response, but he sat down and propped his feet on the bench below them, as Riley was doing. "It'll take guts to come here, especially on a bike."

"There's nothing wrong with riding a bike," Riley said.

"When you're doing it to stay healthy or for the environment, no. But riding a bike because you're an ex-con and don't have any better transportation? That only gives people something else to look down on you for."

"The people in this town feel as if they have plenty to look down on her for already."

"That's why I'm worried. I don't like the idea of everyone pointing and staring."

"She's not even here yet, Kyle."

"If she comes."

"She'll be fine. She just wants to see Jacob play."

"So she'll brave it. I get that. She braves a lot of things. But this won't be easy."

Riley scowled at him. He wasn't pleased by how defensive of Phoenix Kyle had become. They were the only two in their circle of friends who weren't married. Neither one of them had met the right woman. But Riley wasn't about to let Kyle start thinking *Phoenix* might be a possibility. "She's none of your concern, bro."

Kyle threw him a disgruntled look. He obviously found that comment unnecessary, but Riley didn't retract it. He pretended to focus on watching his son warm up—until Kyle muttered, "Oh, shit."

Riley followed his friend's line of sight to see his parents approaching with their padded bleacher seats and cooler, and said the same thing to himself. They came whenever possible. Now that they were retired, that included at least half of Jacob's home games. But

Riley had hoped they'd miss this one. He hadn't mentioned it to them, hadn't mentioned that Jacob had invited Phoenix, either.

"Hello!" His mother lifted up her chair so he'd come take it from her and help her get situated. He did that while his father visited with the parents of another kid on the team. But Riley had a hard time acting happy to see his folks. Phoenix was going to have it rough enough, being noticed by everyone else. The last thing she needed was for his mother to be staring daggers at her.

At least Corinne Mansfield hadn't come. Corinne and his mother were close enough that Corinne attended some of Jacob's games. They'd sit and talk through most of it, but Helen felt she was doing her part just by being there.

"Who are we playing today?" she asked.

"El Dorado High," Riley said.

"They're from Placerville, aren't they?"

"Yeah."

"Jake can handle them Cougars." His father, having finished his conversation, joined them.

Riley hoped his dad was right. He always got a little nervous for his son. So much of the game depended on the pitcher. It was a great deal of pressure, especially since Jake hoped to play college ball.

But today there were other, bigger things to worry about, he realized as he spotted a lone woman making her way to an isolated spot in the visitors' bleachers.

Phoenix had arrived.

Phoenix felt so many butterflies in her stomach, she thought she might be sick. She kept telling herself that everything would be fine, that if Buddy Mansfield had any reason to attend the game, he wouldn't attack her in front of so many spectators. Most sporting events were well attended in Whiskey Creek. There weren't many other things to do. They didn't even have their own movie theater.

But who could say what might happen? And as much as she feared getting hurt again, she was even more worried that her coming here might turn out to be an embarrassment for her son. She couldn't imagine Jacob would invite her back if her presence caused too much of a scene.

Pulling her hat low in hopes that she wouldn't be noticed or recognized, she sat as far as she could from the home crowd, along the edge of the opposite bleacher, where she could see her bike. She didn't have a lock and didn't want it to be stolen. She doubted any of these people would be tempted to take it for its financial value, but if they realized it belonged to her, there was no telling what they might do...

Taking a deep breath, she searched the baseball diamond and spotted her son in the bull pen. He looked so mature in his uniform. She smiled as she rested her chin on her hand and listened to that solid *whomp* as the ball hit the catcher's mitt over and over.

Fortunately, no one on the visitors' side seemed to care about her. She wasn't causing a stir even on the home side. If she was lucky, the whole game would pass this way.

That gave her a bit of confidence, so she grabbed the backpack she used to carry around her computer and took out the sunflower seeds and sports drink she'd purchased for Jake by scrounging up all the change she could find in her mother's trailer. Lizzie had complained about the "mess" Phoenix made searching through everything, but she'd done it while eating the breakfast Phoenix had prepared for her, so she hadn't been too serious about it.

Anxious to give her son these treats, like the other mothers were doing, she waited for the right moment. She'd hate to get him in trouble with the coach...

When the game was about to start, she decided it was too late. Better to forget her little offering than to create a problem. But the way Jake kept looking into the stands as if he was searching for someone made her wonder if he could be looking for *her*.

She waved to get his attention, and he waved back, apparently satisfied. Taking courage from that, she kept her eyes trained on him and walked down to the fence.

"I brought you some seeds," she said when he met her there. "But maybe you already have some."

"I can always use more." He came around the fence to accept the Gatorade, too. "Thanks!"

"I'm really excited to see you play," she told him.

He flashed her a grin. "I hope I don't screw up."

She slipped her hands in the pockets of the shorts Kyle had purchased for her. She'd worn them with the pretty turquoise blouse that was her favorite. "You won't. But it doesn't matter to me either way. I'm proud of you just for getting out there."

The coach called him, and he put his Gatorade and seeds in the dugout before taking the mound to finish warming up.

She stood at the fence awhile longer. She could see him so much more clearly when she was this close—until the opposing team filled the dugout, blocking her view, and someone started calling out the batting order.

"You can do this," she murmured for Jacob's sake.

That was when she first noticed Riley. He was sitting directly across from her, wearing the same kind of ball cap she was. She couldn't be sure because the bill of that cap shaded his face, but she thought he was staring at her. And he wasn't the only one. Kyle was sitting with him. So were his parents. Phoenix hadn't seen Helen and Tom for seventeen years, but she recognized them. The fact that she'd come out of the stands to speak to Jacob had alerted everyone to her identity.

Feeling far too conspicuous, she let go of the chain link—she hadn't even been aware that she'd been clinging to it—and forced her legs to carry her back to the unobtrusive spot she'd selected. She figured if she didn't do anything else, they'd eventually look away. So she leaned over to check on her bike, which was, thankfully, still leaning against the pole that supported the back of the bleachers. Then she clasped her hands in her lap and tried to ignore everything except the game.

She might've managed that, except she caught sight of some commotion and couldn't help another nervous glance in Riley's direction. His mother had started toward her, but Riley had gotten up and taken hold of Helen's arm.

Phoenix couldn't hear them, but she knew they were arguing—about *her*—and that brought a fresh onslaught of self-consciousness and concern. Should she leave? Others were beginning to study her and whisper. Even Jacob, who'd thrown three pitches, had stopped to look over at them, then at her, as if he understood exactly what was going on.

Afraid she might blow his concentration if she stayed, she hurried down the bleachers, hopped on her bike and pedaled home.

* * *

Jacob didn't say much after he got home from the game. Riley had grilled him a burger and opened a can of green beans, but he refused to serve the mashed sweet potatoes his mother had dropped off earlier, even though that was their favorite dish. He was mad at her for the way she'd reacted to seeing Phoenix at the ballpark. Largely because of her and the upset she'd caused, Jake had struggled at the mound and been pulled from the pitcher's mound. Even worse, they'd lost the game.

"Will you want another burger when you're done with that one?" he asked as he watched his son chewing glumly.

"No."

Riley had eaten earlier when the burgers first came off the grill. The coach had kept Jacob late—talking to him about his poor performance, no doubt—so Riley had to keep his son's food warm until he got home. "You okay?"

"I've been better."

"It's hard to pitch when you can't focus on the game. You had a lot on your mind."

Jake said nothing, so Riley assumed he'd finish his meal in silence. But his son suddenly blurted out, "I feel bad for her! Doesn't anyone care that she might've been innocent?"

Riley didn't want to have that debate again. He'd believed she was guilty; he couldn't have stopped her from going to prison, anyway. But now that she was back, he was having the same doubts and sympathies Jacob was. "Your grandma shouldn't have made a scene. Phoenix had every right to be there."

"Exactly! I *invited* her! But Grandma thinks it's okay to hate her—that we should all hate her. I saw how mad she got when you wouldn't let her go over to Phoenix. *She* left the park, too."

The public nature of that argument had been embarrassing. Riley owed his parents a great deal. They'd given him so much support with Jacob. He doubted he could've gotten through Jacob's infancy without them; at eighteen, there was no way he could've been the type of father Jacob needed and gotten through college at the same time.

His mother had reminded him of that in front of the whole home crowd. But, damn it, wasn't he justified in telling her to butt out on certain issues? Or was it as ungrateful as she said it was for him to accept her mashed sweet potatoes, for instance, but not her advice?

"Grandpa didn't leave," he pointed out, looking for a bright spot to cheer his son.

Jake sent him a look indicating that didn't help. "I bet he wanted to when I walked my fourth batter!"

It had been difficult to watch his son miss the strike zone so many times, especially since Riley knew that personal issues were getting in the way of his performance. But he didn't want to make a big deal of it. He was sure the coach had already said all there was to say. "Every pitcher has an off night now and then, even the pros."

"I'm not worried about *me*, Dad. Baseball's a game. It means a lot to me, but…I can't quit thinking about how Mom must've felt, being chased off like that."

She'd ridden a bike for ten miles—to the high school and back—in the heat of the day and with six stitches in her head. As Riley watched the game, he kept remembering that. He'd also imagined Buddy spotting her along the road and running her into another ditch.

"I saw she brought you something to drink," he said. "That was nice of her."

"Yeah. She got me some sunflower seeds, too." He toyed with his green beans but didn't seem too interested in eating them. "I've watched other kids' moms do that stuff my whole life—be it the room mom or the team mom or…whatever. Today it felt like it was my turn to have my mom do that, even though it *is* kind of late."

Riley had done all he could to make sure Jacob had everything he needed, but he couldn't completely replace a mother. He'd had to work even harder when Jacob was young, when he'd been trying to get his business started. He hadn't been able to spend much time at the school. He'd felt out of place when he did go, since he was generally the only man and so much younger than the other parents. "Your grandma used to send in cupcakes for your birthday."

That wasn't much of a consolation, but Riley didn't have anything else to say.

"And it was nice of her," Jacob responded, "but… does she have to make me feel bad just because I want to know my mother? I mean, do we have to believe what everyone else thinks, or can we make up our own minds?"

Riley sighed as he took a stool at the island where Jacob was eating. "We owe it to ourselves, and your mother, to do just that."

"Even if we're the only ones who like her?"

"Even if. That's why I stopped your grandma."

Jacob put a green bean in his mouth. "So *you* don't mind if I get to know her."

"I want you to be happy. That's what I want."

He seemed encouraged. "Can we go over to her place, then, and see if she's okay?"

Riley had wanted to do that all evening; he just didn't know what kind of reception he'd get. Lizzie didn't like him any more than his mother liked Phoenix. No doubt she considered him Whiskey Creek's chief devil. Even Phoenix acted as if she preferred he stayed away. And she'd definitely mentioned that she didn't want Jacob to see her trailer in its current condition.

"I'm not sure she really wants us out there," he said.

"Why not?" Jacob asked.

"You know what her mother's like. The place is a mess. That's embarrassing to Phoenix."

"But we don't care about the mess. I'd like to apologize. I don't want her to think I set her up for what happened."

"She knows you'd never do that."

Still, what could it hurt to go over there? Maybe Phoenix would feel self-conscious about a few things, but she had to be used to that. And Riley thought Jacob would see what he saw—someone in a hell of a battle doing everything she could to keep fighting.

"Fine," he said. "Get showered and we'll go."

The lights were on in Phoenix's trailer, but she didn't answer their knock.

So Riley yelled through one of the open windows. "Phoenix, it's Riley and Jake! Hello? You around?"

There was no response and no rustle of movement. But the bike he'd had Noah fix was leaning against the trailer, so he knew she'd made it home.

"Maybe she's at her mother's," Jake suggested, and turned to look at the other trailer.

Riley didn't want to knock there. It wasn't easy for

Lizzie to come to the door. And he had no idea what she might say in front of Jacob. That earlier stuff about Phoenix spreading her legs for him wasn't an image he wanted introduced to Jacob's mind.

"I've got paper in the car. Maybe we should leave a note with our apology," Riley said.

Jacob agreed, but before Riley could finish writing, Phoenix came out from somewhere at the back of the property.

"Riley? Jake?" she called out when she saw them standing beside the truck. "What are you two doing?"

Jacob crumpled the note and tossed it on the floorboard before closing the door. "Nothing. We just...we wanted to make sure you were okay."

She walked toward them, carrying her sandals in one hand. "I'm fine. You don't have to worry about me." She grinned at Jake but Riley could tell that grin wasn't as nonchalant as she wanted them to believe. "You looked so professional in your uniform today. It's hard to believe I have a son who's so big and strong."

Riley noticed how quickly she tried to change the subject. She'd been smart to offer a compliment. But Jake wasn't buying it. He was too focused on what he'd come to say.

"My grandma shouldn't have started anything. I'm really sorry."

"Don't worry about it. I understand that you can't control the people around you. I would've stayed, except I was too afraid it would be distracting for you. We should've thought of that beforehand."

"No, I want you to come," Jake insisted.

"And I will. If your grandparents don't attend the away games, maybe it'd be smarter for me to go to those. We could've been a little more strategic, that's all. There's no need to upset anyone."

"But how will you get to those games without a car?" he asked. "They're all pretty far."

"I should have some money coming in over the next week. I can always take a taxi."

Riley guessed she'd received some bracelet orders and was talking about the money from their sale. But, surely, there were better ways to spend that money.

Still, he was impressed at how hard she tried to relieve Jake's concern.

"You didn't miss anything," Jake grumbled. "I had the worst game of my life, and because of me, we lost."

"You'll win the next one," she said with real conviction.

Riley saw that her feet and legs were wet. "Don't tell me you were in the creek."

"For a few minutes," she said. "I like to wade out there. It cools me off and it's quiet, especially at night. It's also away from all the junk my mother's piled everywhere else, so it has a much nicer view."

"I'm glad you locked your door even though you weren't going far," Riley said. "It might be a pain, but it's better to be safe."

"I do what I can. But if Buddy wants to get in, I don't think locking my front door will stop him. It's too hot to keep the windows closed. I'd suffocate if I tried." She switched her sandals to her other hand. "Buddy and I are going to have to work out our differences at some point."

Riley shoved his hands in the pockets of his jeans. "You haven't heard from him?"

"No."

Maybe Chief Bennett did have a talk with him, and

it had been more effective than Riley had expected. He hoped so. "Good."

"I'd invite you both in, but…it's a school night and Jacob probably needs to get to bed."

"I have homework," Jake admitted.

"Go get it done, and I'll have you over for dinner sometime soon. What's your favorite meal?"

"Spaghetti and meatballs."

"I should be able to manage that. If I practice," she added with a rueful laugh. "I didn't learn too much about cooking before I went…away."

Riley wasn't sure whether that invitation included him, but he wasn't about to ask. "Be careful to pull the door all the way shut. It doesn't always latch."

"I will, but the screen on the big window is right there…"

"So? It might give you a few seconds to prepare or escape, if…if something happens."

She nodded. "Okay."

"Night, Mom." Jacob gave her a brief hug before getting in the truck.

She seemed so overwhelmed by that gesture she didn't say anything, didn't even respond when Riley said goodbye. He started around to the driver's side, but she caught him before he could open his door and lowered her voice. "I'd leave, you know, if I could. I understand that my being in town is hard on you guys."

He glanced at Jake, who was inside putting on his seat belt, to make sure he wasn't paying attention. "We're not asking you to go."

"I'm just saying that would make it easier on both of you, if I could. Move to Sacramento or somewhere not too far away. Jake could come visit me once in a while, and you wouldn't have to see me at all. Then the Mans-

fields, your family, everyone would be happy. But…
it's my mom. She won't move, no matter how nicely
I ask her."

You wouldn't have to see me at all. As if he hated
her that much. "She probably can't afford it," he said.

"She can't. But once I get on my feet, I'm hoping
that'll change, at least to some extent. It's mostly fear
that holds her back. Fear of the unknown, fear of leaving her trailer, fear of people. It runs her life."

"That's tragic."

"She may not be much of a mother, but I can't go off
and live my life and just…leave her here when she's not
even taking proper care of herself."

When he opened his mouth to speak, she cut him off.

"I know, I was gone for seventeen years and she
survived."

She'd assumed he was looking for ways to overturn
her decision to stay, but he wasn't. He'd planned to tell
her to do whatever she felt she needed to, and everyone
else would have to adjust. But she was still talking, so
he didn't get the chance.

"My brothers have already abandoned her. And she's
so convinced I won't be able to love her, either, she's
trying to make sure of it."

"By being unlovable."

"It doesn't make sense. But…I'm going to show her
that I'll stick with her through thick and thin. If she gets
nothing else out of life, she should have that. Family
is the most important thing. That's what I've learned.
Which means I have no choice."

"Jake and I are fine," he said. "Don't worry about us."

Her chest rose as she drew a deep breath. "Thank
you. I just…I wanted you to understand that I wasn't

trying to be a thorn in your side—although it must appear that way."

"I can handle my mother."

"And Jake?"

"He'd rather you were here."

"Thanks."

He reached for the door handle, then paused. "That invitation for dinner you mentioned to Jake…"

"Yes?"

"Does it include me?"

She seemed taken aback. "Of course. You're welcome at anything I do with Jake."

He'd wanted her to say yes, but not for that reason. She seemed to think his only interest lay in policing her relationship with their son.

He wished that was the case—because some of the thoughts that went through his mind when he looked at Phoenix would shock just about everyone.

11

"You're playing with fire."

Phoenix kept emptying the rotting food from her mother's fridge. She almost couldn't tolerate the smell, but she'd been meaning to do this since she got out of prison and was determined to battle through it tonight. It would be much easier to cook her mother's meals if she could stomach opening her refrigerator.

"You have nothing to say to that?" Lizzie prompted from where she sat at the kitchen table behind a stack of newspapers that were God only knew how old.

"What do you *want* me to say?" Phoenix replied. "Riley's my son's father. It's not like I can avoid him."

She dropped a raisin into her hamsters' cage. "You might be smart if you did. Jacob'll come around when he's older."

After what had happened at the game, she'd considered leaving the area—for his sake. But as she'd told Riley, Jake wasn't the only reason she'd come back to Whiskey Creek. Lizzie didn't realize she figured into that decision, and wouldn't believe it if Phoenix told her. "I don't want to miss what's left of his childhood."

"Even if his father's too much of a temptation for you?"

"Cut it out! You already accused me of sleeping with him," she protested. "He hasn't touched me, so I have no idea what you're talking about."

"Oh, yes, you do. Maybe he hasn't touched you yet, but you're thinking about it."

Phoenix hated the fact that her mother was right. She was beginning to feel the deprivation of going seventeen years without a man. She'd thought she'd be able to concentrate exclusively on motherhood, at least for a couple of years. But her hormones were getting in the way, making her long for fulfillment, and Riley was the partner she kept seeing in her mind's eye.

"You said you didn't like Riley. Now you think he's attractive?"

"Just because he's nice to look at doesn't mean he can be trusted."

"You wouldn't admit even that much before." Phoenix wrinkled her nose as she opened yet another container of spoiled food—this one slimy rice. Who knew rice could stink as horribly as rotting eggs? "We were in high school when he dumped me. You didn't expect him to marry me, did you?"

"No, that's what I'm trying to tell you. He won't *ever* marry you. So don't let him in your bed. You won't get anything out of it."

She was starting to think the physical satisfaction would be enough. But she knew Riley would be a poor choice. She couldn't do anything that might complicate their relationship—which was already so complicated—or threaten what was beginning to develop between her and Jacob. "I'm not going to sleep with Riley."

"I don't see any other men coming over here."

"I've been home a week!"

"Doesn't matter. I'd find someone fast if I were

you—just to let Jake's father know he doesn't stand a snowball's chance in hell of using you again."

"*Using* me? We had sex. We both wanted it. We were young. Can't you give him the benefit of the doubt, for crying out loud?"

"The way he and his family have given *you* the benefit of the doubt?"

Phoenix sighed as she adjusted her rubber gloves. "He could be making things a lot more difficult for me, but he's being quite…cooperative." *Surprisingly* cooperative. She hadn't expected him to be so kind.

"Doesn't that make you wonder why?" her mother asked.

"It makes me grateful. That's all."

Lizzie's chair groaned as she shifted. "Oh, come on. You'd love to have him. Still. But he thinks he's too good for you, so don't be fooled."

Obviously, Lizzie thought he was too good for her, too. She kept talking about that. "Thanks for the reminder of my low station," Phoenix mumbled as she dived back into the fridge.

The odor of her mother's fingernail polish—she did her nails almost every day—battled with the pungent smell of liquefied lettuce.

"Can't you hurry?" Lizzie asked. "Or shut the fridge? I can't take the stench anymore."

"That stench is only going to get worse if I don't finish."

"Well, don't throw out anything that's still good."

"I think I know the difference. If *you* did, maybe it wouldn't get like this."

"I didn't ask you to do it," Lizzie snapped.

There's gratitude for you. Phoenix shook her head but didn't comment. Knowing that her mother made herself unlikable because she believed she *was* unlikable didn't make it any easier to cope with her.

"Have you ever considered getting internet service?" Phoenix asked, hoping to guide the conversation to a subject that contained no emotional land mines.

"I don't have the money," her mother retorted without even considering it. "What would I do with it, anyway?"

"You could get a used laptop for cheap and meet people online, make friends or watch old TV shows, new series, movies. There's tons of content available these days for only a few bucks a month—less than what you're paying for cable. Plus, you can get video games."

"I'm too busy for that."

Phoenix bit her tongue. Her mother thought she was busy? All she did was eat, watch television, take care of her animals (fortunately much better than she ever did her children), paint her fingernails (she could no longer reach her toes) and organize and reorganize the garbage she collected as if used tinfoil was gold bullion.

"Right," Phoenix said at length. "Well, I plan to get the internet when I can afford it. I need it for my business. So maybe you'll let me show you a few things. I bet it'll change your mind."

"I bet it won't." Her mother gave her a sharp glance—Phoenix looked up just in time to catch it. "Don't be trying to change everything. I'm fine the way I am."

Sure she was. Everyone had this kind of mold growing in the refrigerator.

Silence fell but, after several minutes, Phoenix broke it. "Jacob hugged me tonight."

She hadn't told her mother, was hesitant to do so now for fear Lizzie would say something caustic and ruin the memory. At the same time, she wanted to show her mother that her son was far more receptive to her than Lizzie had predicted he'd be.

"He did?"

Phoenix heard the surprise in her voice and smiled. "Out front, in the yard. He told me goodbye and gave me my first hug."

There was a long pause. Then her mother asked, more softly, "What'd Riley do?"

"Nothing."

"I wouldn't trust him," she said, her voice returning to her customary one.

She'd said that before, and she was probably right. But part of her mother's problem was that she didn't trust *anyone*.

She had *thirty* new bracelet orders! Elated, Phoenix stared at the proof on her computer as she sat at Black Gold Coffee. She'd never had so many at once, and most were for the more expensive models. She couldn't imagine why there'd be such a dramatic spike. She'd been getting one, maybe two, per day for the past couple of weeks.

But it didn't take long to solve the mystery. As she sorted through the invoices, she realized her bracelets had somehow caught on in a neighborhood, with a group of friends, a college or high school, in Los Angeles. That had to be it, because most of the shipping addresses had the same zip code.

How interesting...

Smiling to herself, she began to email her new clients to let them know when their orders would be completed and sent. Fortunately, she got her money up front, so she had fifteen hundred dollars sitting in her PayPal account. She'd be able to get more supplies, which she'd definitely need, buy some groceries, including the ingredients to make Jacob that spaghetti dinner, and…

The bell rang over the door, and she glanced up to see one of Riley's friends from high school—Callie Vanetta—come in with a guy, most likely her husband, but they didn't seem to be paying attention to anyone else there. They stepped up to the register, so Phoenix relaxed and went back to work. She was so intent on making sure she'd confirmed every order that she stopped monitoring the door for people who might not be pleased to run into her. It was getting crowded, and she couldn't see through the customers who were blocking the entrance, anyway.

By the time she looked up again, however, she realized that Callie and her husband hadn't left with their coffee, as she'd expected. They'd sat down, and several others had joined them. It wasn't until Riley walked through the door that she wished she'd been paying closer attention to who those people were. She should've left when two more of his friends, Noah Rackham and Eve Harmon, arrived.

Riley didn't notice her at first. It took someone at the table to point her out to him. She thought she heard the person say, "Isn't that Phoenix?" Then he did a double take, and got up to make his way over.

"Hey."

She considered closing her laptop and leaving. But she still had a handful of people to email. She didn't want too much time to pass between the order and her response. And she didn't want to have to bike all the way back to town after Riley and his friends were gone to do fifteen minutes more work.

She was going to have to get used to living in Whiskey Creek. That meant she might as well suffer through the point, stare and whisper stuff now. She couldn't run away whenever she bumped into someone who knew her story.

"Hi." She sat back and crossed her legs, hoping to come across as polite but dismissive, so that he wouldn't feel he needed to do anything beyond acknowledge her. Truth be told, she hadn't even expected *that* much, but she thought it was nice of him.

"You look pretty in that blouse."

She was wearing the same shorts and top she'd worn to the game. That was slightly embarrassing, but she didn't have a lot, and no one knew that better than he did. "Thanks."

He indicated her computer. "You working?"

"Yeah. I had quite a few orders come in last night, which means I'll be able to give you some money for Jacob in the next few days."

"Jacob and I are doing okay," he said. "Why don't you keep the extra and use it for yourself? It'll take you a while to get set up, and I'm fine with that."

Riley had never asked her for money, but that was partly why she insisted on giving Jacob as much as she could. She wanted to prove that she was willing to do her part. And she didn't want to give Riley any more reason than he already had to deny her visitation. "Taking care of a kid can't be put on hold. And it won't be a burden. I have quite a few more orders than I was anticipating."

He seemed unsure of what to say, but he nodded. "That's got to be a relief."

"It is. Now I just need to get them made."

"You don't have inventory?"

"Not much. Just what I use to photograph or experiment with."

Before he could say anything else, Kyle walked in, spotted them and bypassed the order line and his other friends to come and say hello. "Hey! How are you?"

His friendliness was so reassuring Phoenix felt her anxiety ease and her smile widen. She also noticed that he was wearing the bracelet she'd made him. "It's good to see you."

"You, too," he said. "You look great."

She'd done what she could to hide her stitches by wearing her hair down instead of pulling it back. "That's because someone has excellent taste in clothes."

A muscle moved in Riley's cheek, as if he wasn't pleased by this exchange, but he didn't interrupt.

"I'm glad you liked it all." He lifted his wrist. "I like what I got out of the deal, too."

She was careful not to allow her gaze to return to Riley. "Thanks. I know it's...different."

"You mean cool."

"Everyone's waiting for us." Riley clapped Kyle on the back a bit harder than usual, judging by Kyle's startled reaction. "And quite a few of us have to get to work."

Kyle's lips twisted as though he was resisting the urge to laugh. "Including me." he said, then nodded in her direction. "Take care of yourself, okay?"

"You, too."

Kyle paused a second longer. "You still have my number in case you need a ride anywhere, don't you?"

"I do."

"Don't hesitate to use it. I don't want you walking or biking after dark."

"She's not going to call you," Riley said, and this time Kyle *did* chuckle.

"You're right," Phoenix said after Kyle had joined

the others. "I won't call him. So don't worry. I'm not trying to horn in on your circle. He's just…a nice guy, so I was being nice back."

"And the fact that you're pretty and single has nothing to do with it."

She wasn't sure she'd heard him correctly. "Excuse me?"

"Nothing. Never mind." He glanced at the menu written on the chalkboard, then at her table, which held nothing but her laptop and the backpack she used to transport it. "Can I get you a cup of coffee or anything?"

She'd spent every dime she had the day of Jacob's game, buying him the seeds and sports drink. But she wasn't worried anymore. Thanks to those thirty orders, everything was going to be okay. "No, I'm fine. I had a cup of coffee when I came in," she lied.

"They have breakfast things, too. Bran muffins and such."

"I'm fine." She hoped her stomach wouldn't growl—and was relieved when it didn't. "Don't let me keep you from your friends."

Those friends were sitting at the corner table, but they were craning their necks to get a good look at her. Although they were smiling as if they were trying to be friendly, she couldn't rely on that.

She figured she'd let them satisfy their curiosity while she finished her work. Then she'd fold up her laptop and get out of there. She didn't like being reminded of the disparity between her social standing and theirs.

"Okay," he said. "Congratulations on the orders."

She gave him a parting nod. "Thanks."

As soon as he went back to his friends, she lowered her head, intent on getting those last few emails sent off. She didn't like being at Black Gold when it got busy like this; that was why she generally came early, before the crowds. She should've left the second she'd spotted Riley's friends, even if it meant coming back later, in the heat of the day. Because five minutes hadn't passed when she heard someone murmur, "Fucking bitch."

Somehow she separated those words from all the other ambient noise. Riley and his group hadn't picked up on them. They were talking and laughing as if the rest of the world could stop turning and they'd hardly be aware of it.

She was glad of that. She didn't want them to notice, because when she looked up, she saw that it was Buddy Mansfield. He'd walked in with a friend. They were both glaring at her, and Buddy's face was completely red.

"Oh, no," she whispered as her heart started to thump. She did *not* want to cause a scene inside the coffee shop. She hated being a spectacle in the first place; she especially didn't want to be embarrassed in front of Riley.

Determined to avoid a confrontation, even if it was only a verbal one, she grabbed her laptop, leaving her backpack behind to save time, and ducked into the women's restroom. She would've preferred to disappear altogether. Unfortunately, that was impossible. Buddy and his friend stood between her and the front door.

She looked up at the only window, hoping she could climb through it. But it was too small, too high and it didn't open by more than a crack.

Praying that Buddy would order and then get out, she hugged her laptop to her chest and waited, shifting from foot to foot.

"Go home," she murmured, willing him to do just that.

The door banged open instead.

"You think I don't have the balls to come in here after you?" Buddy demanded, blocking the doorway along with his friend, who stood slightly behind him.

The memory of the look on Buddy's face when he'd nearly run her down caused her to start sweating. "I don't want any trouble."

She spoke low so that Riley and his friends wouldn't be able to hear, but Buddy didn't follow her lead. "I don't give a shit!" he yelled. "You killed my sister. Do you think I want to see you when I drive through town? When I pick up a coffee? When I go out to dinner?"

His friend seemed interested and supportive, although he didn't say anything.

"I didn't—I didn't…" she started, but her tongue tripped over itself and she couldn't seem to get the words out. Probably because she wasn't sure what to say. She wanted to tell him she hadn't killed anyone, but she knew he wouldn't believe her. It would be much smarter to try and defuse the situation, so that she could escape without further injury. "I'll leave. Now. If you'll just…let me pass."

"*Let you pass?* When you're flipping me off by coming back here? By showing me you're alive and well when Lori is—" his voice broke but he seemed to regain control of it "—when Lori's gone for good?"

He stepped toward her, and she stepped back but came up against the bathroom stalls. "I'm sorry about Lori. I don't want her to be gone. To be honest, there've been many days when I wished she was still around instead of me. But I can't change the past. You and I—we both have to figure out how to go on."

"That doesn't mean I have to put up with your presence in my own town."

She hugged her laptop tighter. "It's my town, too,

Buddy. I have a son here. That's the main reason I came back. For Jake and my mother."

"Jake has his dad. He doesn't need no ex-con whore. And your fat bitch of a mother deserves everything she's got. You're no good—for anyone. Do you understand? You'd be doing us all a favor if you…"

"What's going on in here?"

The moment Riley appeared in the doorway, shouldering his way past Buddy's friend, Phoenix felt tears well up, but she swallowed hard and blinked them back.

"Nothing that's any of your business," Buddy replied. "Tell him, Stan."

Buddy's friend didn't tell Riley anything. He merely shrugged as if he wasn't sure what to do.

Riley ignored him. "Don't cause trouble, Buddy," he said. "How will that help you get over what happened to Lori?"

When Buddy pointed at her, he was close enough that his finger almost jabbed her in the nose. "*She* shouldn't be here!"

Riley moved closer to Buddy. "Do you think she would've come back if she'd killed Lori?"

"What are you talking about? *She* was driving the car!"

"She's served her time. She can go anywhere, even here." With a quick gesture to her, Riley added, "Go ahead and scoot."

Phoenix hated herself for being so grateful to him. Until the relief set in, she hadn't realized just how frightened she'd been. But as soon as she took a step toward the door, Buddy shoved her back, knocking her into the toilet stall and causing her to drop her computer.

She knew she'd broken it the moment she heard it crash on the concrete floor.

"No!" Her entire business depended on that computer!

She scrambled to retrieve it, but Buddy stepped on her hand, twisting his foot as if he hoped to crush every bone.

Then all hell broke loose. Riley grabbed Buddy by the collar, whirled him around and hit him in the face, and the momentum of that punch threw him against the sink.

Buddy's friend yelled, "What the hell!" and took a swing at Riley. Fortunately, one of Riley's friends, who were now crowding the door, stopped the forward motion of his fist and dragged him out.

Phoenix thought it might all be over—until she saw Buddy recover his balance and charge Riley. Leaving her computer where it had fallen, she lunged toward Lori's brother, trying to intercept the blow. The last thing she needed was for anyone else to get hurt. But Dylan Amos, one of the people who'd been sitting with Riley's friends, pulled her against his chest.

"Get her out of here," Riley yelled, just before he and Buddy began to fight in earnest.

Phoenix had never seen Riley come to blows with anyone. He'd always been popular, well liked and well-adjusted. She couldn't believe he was in a scrum now, and didn't want to be the cause of it.

"Riley, no!" she cried. "Stop!"

She struggled to free herself so she could insist he leave the bathroom. Buddy was so much bigger, she was afraid of what would happen if the fight continued. But Dylan held her fast.

"Don't distract him," he murmured in her ear.

"But he's going to get hurt!" Wasn't that obvious? Why wasn't anyone stepping in to stop this? Riley's friends were holding Stan back so it would be a fair match, but that was it.

"He'll be okay," Dylan assured her. "He's mad enough to take just about anybody. *I* wouldn't even get in his way, and I've had a hell of a lot more experience."

"I've never seen him like this," someone else marveled. Phoenix thought it might've been Kyle, but she couldn't turn her head to look. Her eyes were riveted on the two men exchanging blows—until Riley got hit in the face and his nose began to bleed. Then it felt as if she'd been hit herself, and she couldn't bear to watch.

"I'm going to be sick," she told Dylan. "Let me go."

He must've decided she wasn't bluffing. Blocking her so she couldn't change her mind and reenter the bathroom, he released his hold.

Despite her wobbling knees, Phoenix managed to push through the crowd that was gathering but barely made it outside before throwing up.

12

It was particularly hot that night. Phoenix lay in bed, staring at the glow of her mother's floodlight streaming through the window and listening to the whir of the old fan she'd found in the yard. It hummed in perfect rhythm, oscillating back and forth. The air it stirred offered a measure of relief, but she couldn't sleep. Every time she closed her eyes, she saw Buddy's fist knock Riley's head back and the blood spurt from his nose.

Then she felt sick all over again.

Was he okay?

She didn't know. She had no idea what had happened after she left. Once she'd wiped her mouth, she'd grabbed her bike and hurried down the street. She hadn't had the strength to go very far, so she'd slipped into the countryside, where she'd be hidden by the rolling landscape and trees, and had remained there for at least two hours—until she'd felt strong enough to travel more than a few feet. While she was hiding, Kyle had driven by very slowly, as if he was looking for her. She'd glimpsed his truck more than once. But she hadn't wanted to talk to him, hadn't wanted to learn the outcome of the fight in case Riley had a broken nose or jaw.

He's fine. She tried using some of the positive affirmations Coop had taught her while she was behind bars. But nothing seemed to ease her anxiety. She kept imagining Jacob seeing his father come home bruised and bloody, and blaming her. Or Riley cursing her for returning to Whiskey Creek, where no one wanted her, anyway.

He must wish she'd leave town as much as Buddy did.

Maybe she should. After all, it wasn't Buddy's fault that he hated her. He didn't know she was innocent of his sister's murder. Her story about someone else grabbing the wheel—she knew how far-farfetched that sounded. No one had believed it at her trial and no one believed it now.

But what about her mother? Lizzie should receive *some* compassion, shouldn't she? *Some* family love and loyalty despite her problems? Wasn't that where the unconditional part of unconditional love came in?

Your fat bitch of a mother deserves everything she's got...

Trying to stop the echo of those words in her head, Phoenix rolled over. But it was no use. She couldn't relax. She considered going down to the creek to cool off. Then she noticed that there was a light still burning in her mother's trailer...

Phoenix was just wondering whether she had the mental fortitude to keep Lizzie company—she'd made them both dinner but hadn't mentioned the fight—when she saw a pair of headlights turn into the drive.

Was it Riley?

She guessed it was, so she hurried to pull on a T-shirt and a pair of shorts. She was so convinced it had to be him that when she opened the front door, she was surprised to see Kyle's truck and not Riley's.

He got out with her backpack and battered computer, and brought them toward her. "Hey."

She waited for him to join her on the landing. "Hi."

"You okay?" he asked.

"Of course." She didn't ask how things went at the coffee shop. She was too afraid to hear.

"Dylan said you were pretty upset when you left this morning."

She slipped her hands in her back pockets and stuck out her chin. "I don't like anyone fighting my battles for me."

"Anyone?" he asked. "Or Riley, when there's a chance he might get hurt?"

"I don't know what you're talking about." She scowled to show him she didn't appreciate the suggestion. "I'm not carrying a torch for Riley, if that's what you're suggesting. I haven't called him once. I haven't gone over there. I haven't done anything."

"I believe you have no plans of getting back with him, because you think that would be too much to hope for. But that doesn't mean you don't care about him."

"That's...crazy, not true, except...I care about him. Of course I care about him. He's Jacob's father." She spoke in a throwaway tone, as if that were the extent of it—and hoped to God it was. Nothing would be more dangerous to her than feeling what she'd once felt for Riley.

He rubbed his chin as he studied her. "So aren't you curious how it ended?"

"Not really," she lied.

A patient smile curved his lips. "He's fine, Phoenix. He handled himself well. Buddy got the worst of it."

She hauled in a deep breath to temper the relief that

was flowing through her and, oddly enough, suddenly felt like crying.

Fortunately, she was able to hold back the tears. She didn't understand why she was turning into such a big baby after leaving prison. The other inmates would make fun of her if they knew. Even Coop would probably give her a knowing smile. "Who stopped it?" she asked. "Did the police come?"

"No. It was just a brawl between two men. The baristas broke it up not long after you left."

She curved her fingernails into her palms. "Then what?"

"We all left, too."

"Riley was bleeding. I saw…I saw that."

He shrugged. "He got a bloody nose. It'll be swollen for a few days, but Buddy's hand might be broken, and he's going to have one heck of a shiner. You should've seen his eye."

She didn't want to see his eye. She just wanted the past to go away, wanted them all to move on. "Riley didn't need to get involved. I don't know why he did."

"*Someone* had to do something, Phoenix. Buddy can't keep torturing you. I'm sorry for him, sorry about what happened to his sister. But you've served your time."

"I didn't kill her," she said. She'd long ago stopped trying to convince people. It was hurtful and frustrating to be treated to another dose of skepticism and doubt. But she cared what Kyle thought of her. As much as she wished it was otherwise, she cared what Riley's whole group thought.

Kyle studied her for several seconds. "Then that's why Riley did it."

She didn't follow him. "Excuse me?"

"My guess is that he believes you."

Could that be true? Phoenix was almost afraid to hope. It had always been her fondest dream that Riley and Jacob would somehow be able to know or tell, in their hearts since there was no other way, that she was innocent.

"Here." He handed her the laptop. "It's damaged. But I thought you might want it. Maybe it can be fixed."

"It was old to begin with," she said, as if losing it wasn't any big deal. She didn't want Kyle to know she'd suffered yet another terrible setback. She preferred his friendship, perhaps even respect at some point, not his pity. But she had no idea how she'd continue to run her business without access to the internet. There was no public library close by. And she didn't have a car...

"Riley was pretty upset that it got broken. He told me you earn your money making bracelets like this." He pointed to his wrist. "That you need to use the internet. And I told him you can come over to the office anytime and use one of mine. My place is closer than going all the way to town, anyway."

"You have an office?" She didn't even know what he did for a living. When she'd dropped off that bracelet, she'd merely gone to the address listed in her mother's phone book, and it had been dark.

"I do. I have a solar manufacturing plant next to my house, which, as you know, is only about a mile and a half from here. My employees are there during the day, but no one uses the computers before eight or after five. You're welcome to come by and do what you need to. If it's early, knock on my door, and I'll let you in. If you want to work at night, just come before everyone leaves, and I'll show you how to lock up when you're done."

"You'd trust me to do that? To work in your office alone?"

"Of course." He grinned. "But don't give me too much credit. There's nothing to steal except files."

"There are the computers," she teased. "I happen to need one of those."

He laughed. "I'd know where to come looking if one went missing."

She sobered. "It's a generous offer. Thank you."

"Everyone needs a break now and then."

"Have *you* ever needed a break?" she asked.

"I've had my dark moments. You just missed them while you were…away."

She appreciated the euphemism. "It would be nice to hear about someone else's problems for a change. Would you like to come in?"

He seemed tempted but ultimately shook his head. "I don't think Riley would like that."

"He'd rather I didn't make friends with his friends," she said. "And I can't blame him. He wouldn't want his ex, especially such a notorious one, joining his social circle."

A thoughtful expression appeared on Kyle's face. "I don't think that's it at all."

"Then what is it?" she asked.

"You wouldn't believe me if I told you," he said with a chuckle, and walked back to his truck.

Phoenix didn't know what to make of that, but whatever Kyle had meant, he obviously wasn't planning to explain. "I'll come by tomorrow around five," she called after him.

"See you then."

She watched as he drove away. She was fairly certain she could sleep now. But her mother caught her before she could go back inside. "You're flirting with danger," she yelled through the window.

"Why'd you do it?"

Riley studied his scraped knuckles. He'd gone to work after that incident at Black Gold Coffee and hadn't told his parents about the fight, but word had spread. His mother had started calling him around dinnertime. He'd ignored her many attempts to reach him because he hadn't wanted to talk about the fight, hadn't wanted to confront her anger or answer her questions, which might make him examine his own motives—something he was reluctant to do.

But he would've been smarter to address her questions earlier. Now it was nearly midnight, and she and his father were sitting in his living room.

"Keep your voice down," he said. "Jacob's asleep and he has school tomorrow."

She didn't speak any more quietly. If anything, telling her to do that made the volume go up. "You're not going to answer me?"

He sighed. "If you've heard what happened, then you know. Buddy followed Phoenix into the woman's restroom at the coffee shop. He pushed her into one of the stalls and broke her computer. And she needs that to be able to work."

"Work?" his mother echoed. "She doesn't even have a job!"

"She has a business."

As usual when it came to anything intensely emotional, his father remained silent. "What kind of business?" his mother scoffed.

"She makes bracelets."

"Who'd want to buy anything *she* makes?"

He clenched his jaw. "Maybe a lot of people, Mom. Jacob's wearing one right now." So was Kyle, unless he'd removed it.

His mother glared at him. "If Buddy damaged her ability to make a living, then she should complain to the police."

Riley laughed without mirth. "Seriously? How far would that get her?"

"I can't say. But that's how she should handle it."

"She's an ex-con. She'd be unlikely to go to the police for anything. And I can understand why. What would Chief Bennett do? Charge Buddy with a misdemeanor for which there'd be little or no punishment? Make him pay for a new computer? No! All Buddy would have to say is that it was her fault she dropped it. If he could convince his friend to back up his version, he'd even have a witness. When you take into consideration his good family and his lack of criminal history…how far do you think the police will go to help her?"

"That's part of the price you have to pay if you commit murder," she said. "As an ex-con, you no longer have credibility. Anyway, in the version I heard, Buddy hardly bumped into her, and he certainly didn't mean to break her computer."

Riley felt his muscles tense. "I was there, Mom!"

"I can see that! Look at your poor nose!"

"It'll heal. He was in the wrong. And what about when he tried to run Jake off the road with his Excursion and forced Phoenix to jump into a ditch? She has six stitches to show for that encounter!"

"He was only trying to scare her, to give her a taste of what Lori must've felt in her final few seconds. He didn't intend to hit her. But we're not arguing about what happened when she was in the Jeep with Jacob.

I'm not happy about that, either. Buddy was out of line, pure and simple, and the police have talked to him about his actions."

Riley sat up straighter. "So that's it? That's how much good Chief Bennett did?"

"The fact that Phoenix went to him proves she's not as hesitant to complain to the police as you think. Anyway, in Buddy's mind, not only did Phoenix kill his sister, she got him in trouble for being angry about it. That probably riled him up all over again."

"*She* didn't go to Chief Bennett," Riley said. "*I* did!"

His mother's eyes flared, but then she pursed her lips. "Corinne didn't tell me that."

"It's true."

"It wasn't your place to go to Bennett," she said, as if she was pronouncing some philosophical truth. "Phoenix can handle her own problems."

"Mom, she's all of five feet two inches and maybe a hundred pounds soaking wet. I won't let him terrorize her despite his loss."

"I'm not saying you have to let him do anything. Since you got the police involved, they can take care of it—that's all. I don't want to see anyone get hurt, but I also don't want to explain to Corinne why *my* son beat *her* son to a bloody pulp!"

Riley grimaced at her choice of words. "*Bloody pulp?* I didn't hurt him that badly." He would've done more damage, however, if he'd had time. He'd never been so furious in his life.

"By all reports, it took several people to pull you off him."

Riley didn't regret that. He still winced at the look on Phoenix's face when her computer had hit the ground. He'd gotten the feeling she would rather have taken a fist to the jaw. "He went too far, and I reminded him of his boundaries. That's all."

"He did go too far. There's no arguing with that. But what about the mitigating circumstances? His sister was murdered by the woman you were protecting, for God's sake!"

Riley jumped to his feet. "He doesn't *know* that!"

"We *all* do!"

"You weren't in the car, Mom. You have no idea what happened. You haven't even listened, with any kind of open mind, to her side of the story."

"Really? You're going to let her twist the past? Lie to you and manipulate you into fighting her battles?"

His irritation went so deep he threw up a hand. "I won't talk about this anymore. She hasn't asked me for one damn thing—except to bring Jacob to see her when she was in prison. And I feel like shit that I never did it!"

"You made a calculated decision to do what was best for Jacob. You were being a responsible parent. And she doesn't have to *ask* you for anything. You're right there, with your big soft heart, ready to make her life as easy as possible."

"Nothing has ever been easy for her, Mom! That's what you don't seem to understand. Or is it that you don't care?"

She stood, too. "I care about my best friend and her murdered daughter. That's what I care about!"

"What about the fact that Phoenix is Jacob's mother? That he wants to get to know her? That maybe, just maybe, we should give her the benefit of the doubt in case she isn't the monster we've made her out to be?"

His mother gave her head an impatient shake. "We've had this discussion before. He's better off without her."

Riley looked at his father. "Do you agree with that?

Do you think I should've stood by while a 230 pound man pushed her around?"

His father got up. He'd come with Helen in a show of support—no doubt she'd demanded it—but his feelings on the subject didn't seem nearly as intense as hers. If Riley had his guess, his father was probably sitting there wishing he was home in bed. "Perhaps you should let someone else help her. That's all we're saying."

"Who?" Riley demanded. "Who else is going to step up? The whole town hates her. They think she's a murderer."

His father made a sound of regret. "She *was* convicted, Riley. And we've seen the Mansfields' pain up close."

"Yeah, well, maybe I've seen her pain, too. And maybe I see a different kind of person than her jury did—or you do, for that matter."

"Oh, for God's sake!" his mother cried. "Why did you ever have to get involved with her in the first place?"

After twelve months or so of trying to explain how attracted he'd been to Phoenix, and having his mother tell him he was just a kid and didn't know what love was, Riley had dodged this question in all the years since. Helen made being with Phoenix sound so beneath him, so…disgusting. But it hadn't been like that at all. He'd never felt more content than when it was just the two of them. They didn't need to be making love or doing anything in particular. "I was in love with her, Mom. She's the only person I've *ever* been in love with."

"Sex at that young an age can fool you into thinking…"

"Don't patronize me!" he broke in. "I'm not eighteen anymore. I know the difference between sex and love.

Trust me, I've had sex since then. But not love. Nothing close to what I felt for Phoenix."

There was a long silence. Then his mother said, "I'm sorry you feel that way. But I can't help believing there's someone else out there for you. Someone who deserves a great guy."

"You're driving me crazy," he said.

"And you're putting me in a very difficult position with my best friend. I hope you realize that."

"At least you have friends," he said. "Phoenix doesn't even have any family she can depend on."

"She seems to have *you*," his mother snapped, and walked out.

As the door slammed, Riley turned to his father. "And you? What do you have to say?"

"Do what you think is right," he said. "Just…"

"What?" Riley asked.

"Make sure you're thinking with the right head."

Riley felt his jaw drop. "Excuse me?"

"Don't get pissy with me. Word has it she's quite pretty these days."

"Dad?"

Riley cringed as he reached the top of the stairs. He'd hoped his mother's yelling and slamming the door wouldn't wake Jake. The boy could sleep through an earthquake—at least when it was time to get up in the morning. "Yes?"

"I would've stood up for her in that bathroom, too."

The last thing Riley wanted was for Jacob to get into an altercation. "Let me handle your mother's situation, okay?"

"Since you *are* handling it, you're making it easy for me to stay out of it. I'm glad of that."

"I'm happy you approve." His actions certainly weren't going to make him popular with anyone else. But it was time Phoenix mattered to someone, and he was tired of denying, minimizing and ignoring how much she mattered to *him*. "Get some sleep."

He waited to see if his son would offer a rejoinder, but Jake didn't, so Riley went to his own bedroom. As he took his phone out of his pocket, he checked to see if Kyle had answered the text he'd sent before his mother and father arrived, and was pleased to see he had a message. Of course. I went by her place like you said.

Riley dropped onto the bed before texting Kyle back. And?

She said she didn't want you or anyone else fighting her battles for her.

That sounded like Phoenix. What was her plan? Did she think she could take Buddy herself?

She didn't have a plan. She'd just rather be the one to get hurt.

He frowned at the screen before texting back. She said that?

No. I could tell, though. She still worships you.

Riley felt a strange sort of awareness creep over him as he read those words—as well as a certain amount of perverse hope. Don't even suggest that.

Why not? It's true.

She'd be upset if she heard it.

Because she's terrified you or someone else will think she's out to catch you again. But there's no reason to worry about that. She won't come near you unless she absolutely has to in order to see Jacob. She's so convinced her love isn't good enough, she'd die before she'd acknowledge those feelings.

Where are you coming up with this stuff? Riley wrote. He liked reading it, wanted to believe that Kyle was right. And yet the idea of anything between him and Phoenix frightened him. Not because he thought she'd start driving by his place or calling him like she did when she was a teenager, but because he was probably just as attracted to her as he'd ever been, and there was no telling where that might lead. It could lead them right back into trouble, and the last thing he wanted to do was hurt her again.

A ping told him Kyle had responded. Her sheer panic when you got into it with Buddy. Dylan said it was all he could do to stop her from throwing herself in front of you. Had any other guy stepped up, I don't think she would've been quite so desperate to protect him.

Riley rubbed his chin for several seconds as he considered what Kyle had written. *She's afraid something will upset me and I'll refuse to let her see Jacob—that's all. She doesn't have the money to take me to court, and she wouldn't have much of a case even if she did.*

You only want to see the practical side of things. But there's more going on here—on both sides. I doubt you're as indifferent to her as you'd like to believe.

Kyle had been watching him closely, which made sense. If they weren't such good friends, he'd probably be interested in Phoenix himself. Stop with the bullshit, Riley typed. I don't need you screwing with my mind.

Can you honestly tell me I'm wrong?

He couldn't. That was the problem. Don't push me on this.

Fine. You're not ready to be honest with yourself—or me. So let's change the subject. Your birthday's coming up.

And?

That means our big party at Lake Melones is less than two weeks away.

I know when my own birthday is. Don't tell me you're going to ask if you can bring Phoenix as your date. The answer is no.

Because you're still attracted to her. But we're not talking about that, remember? For the record, I'm bringing Samantha.

Riley ignored the part about Phoenix. The chick you met via that online dating site? Isn't that kind of risky? You don't know each other that well, and we're talking about a whole weekend.

We might hate each other by the end of it, but...you

never know. The opposite could also be true. So, who are you going to ask?

Phoenix came immediately to mind. He suspected Kyle was hinting that he should ask her. But that would be crazy. She wouldn't join him even if he invited her.

Still, with almost everyone else in the group married, he didn't want to show up without a date. They'd agreed it would be couples but no kids, which wouldn't be a problem for him, since Jake was older. Jake would spend the weekend with Tristan. He loved doing that, anyway. *Maybe Stephanie will want to come.*

That's the woman you brought when we went to San Francisco last month, right? Kyle texted.

Yeah.

Are you still talking?

We've texted once or twice. But we've both been pretty busy.

Where'd you meet her? I can't remember.

I did a bathroom remodel for her parents down in Angel's Camp, and they introduced us.

She's cute.

She *was* cute. He'd been sort of excited about her after they went out the first time. A nurse at the regional hospital, she fit in well with his friends, was attractive and nice.

So why did he suddenly have so little interest in following up on their date by actually seeing her again?

"Don't answer that," he grumbled to himself as he texted Kyle back. It's late, and I have a headache. I'll talk to you later.

Your nose okay?

Could be better, but it'll be fine in a day or two.

Don't forget to ask Stephanie. You wait any longer, she might have plans, and you'll be the only schmuck without a date. That wouldn't go over very well for the birthday boy.

I'll give her a call, he wrote. But the next day passed, and the day after that—even the day after *that*—and he still hadn't invited her.

13

Riley wasn't sure he wanted to go to coffee at Black Gold this Friday. Now that his son was older, he was normally one of the most consistent in the group. He enjoyed catching up with his friends for twenty or thirty minutes before arriving at his current construction site. But he knew everyone would have a lot of questions for him this morning. The last time they'd gotten together, he'd stormed the women's restroom and punched Buddy Mansfield in the face. And although he'd received several texts from his friends after that incident, as well as a few calls, he hadn't returned most of them.

He told himself he'd skip the get-together. It was difficult to explain what he was feeling for Phoenix; he didn't want to be tied down to anything.

But in the end, he saw their cars in the parking lot and couldn't just drive by.

"Hey!" Dylan was on his cell phone but gave him a nod. Riley waved and got a cup of coffee before sitting down with Eve, who ran the B and B down the street. She lived with her fiancé, Lincoln, in Placerville these days, but still made the thirty-minute drive to run the B and B. Dylan's wife, Cheyenne, was there, too—with her five-month-old baby, who was in an infant seat.

"Skeleton crew this week, huh?" he said, dropping a quick kiss on the baby's head.

Eve checked her watch. "It's early. I bet Ted and Sophia will show. Kyle, too."

That reference to Kyle reminded him that Callie, their friend who'd undergone a liver transplant, had been harboring some sort of information she was supposedly sharing with the group. "What about Callie and Levi?"

Cheyenne nodded toward the door. "Speak of the devil."

Callie and Levi came in, followed closely by Kyle, Kyle's stepbrother, Brandon, and Brandon's wife, Olivia. "Now we're talking."

It took several minutes for everyone to order and settle into their usual booth in the corner, but Riley didn't mind. He liked that everyone seemed preoccupied. He planned to insure they remained that way by mentioning Callie's secret. But Dylan foiled that plan by bringing up the fight with Buddy as soon as he got off the phone.

"How's Mansfield, you maniac?" he teased.

Riley nearly cursed but managed to hold back. "I'm sure he's fine. It was a minor skirmish."

"Not so minor," Eve said. "It scared the hell out of me. I've never seen you like that."

Riley shrugged. "He has no right to bully Phoenix—or anyone else."

There was an uncomfortable moment when he thought someone might take up his mother's argument—"She murdered his sister, remember?"—but no one did. "By the way, your nose looks fine."

"Like I told you…minor skirmish."

"Phoenix was mortified that you got involved," Levi said.

Dylan slid into the booth. "It was more than being mortified. She was so afraid Riley might be hurt she was fighting like a wildcat to get loose. I have no clue what she thought she could do, but she was bound and determined to help."

"She's a fighter," Riley muttered.

"What made you lose your temper like that?" Callie asked. "I mean, we could've just called the police."

"It would've been over by the time they got here," he replied. "I did what I had to do."

"Does she appreciate it?" Olivia asked.

Riley took a sip of his coffee. "She doesn't want me in her life. And considering our history, I guess that's understandable."

Dylan stretched out his legs. "What do *you* want?"

"For everyone to stop tormenting her. She's Jacob's mother, after all."

"That's your only reason for protecting her?" Eve asked.

Riley buried his nose in his cup again before answering. "Of course."

Kyle didn't say anything, but he was smirking the whole time, and that drove Riley crazy. He almost wanted to slug his friend.

"So what's *your* news?" Riley asked, turning to Callie.

She stared at him. "Excuse me?"

"I hear you've got something to share."

She blushed and glanced at her husband. Then a smile spread across her face as she gazed around the table. "Actually, I do. I was going to make the announcement last week, but…we had that fight. Then I thought I'd wait until Baxter could be with us. He's been talking about moving back, as you know."

Cheyenne leaned forward. "But…"

"That could take months. He can't even come to the cabin for Riley's birthday, and since Kyle must've let the cat out of the bag to Riley, anyway…"

"I haven't said anything!" Kyle protested.

Eve gripped the table. "What is it?"

Callie took her husband's hand. "Levi and I are going to have a baby."

Silence fell as everyone took that in. Riley had never considered that her secret might be a pregnancy. He'd assumed she *couldn't* get pregnant, because of her health problems and all the meds she was on.

"Really?" Eve looked dumbfounded but managed to pump her voice full of enthusiasm. "That's wonderful!"

Callie frowned at their lame attempt to show the proper excitement. "Stop it! I know what you're thinking. You're afraid I can't handle this pregnancy—that it'll hurt me somehow, or that the meds I'm taking might affect the baby. But Levi and I have talked long and hard about this, together with my doctor, of course, and we've decided we want to move forward despite the risks."

"What *are* the risks?" Brandon asked, obviously as stunned and concerned as the rest of them. Rarely was it this quiet at coffee.

"I don't want to go into that. I'd rather focus on the fact that there are a lot of people who have experienced what I've experienced, and they've given birth successfully. The doctor says there's no reason Levi and I can't start a family."

Riley happened to glimpse the shadow that crossed Levi's face. But Levi quickly hid that hint of doubt and kissed his wife's temple. "She'll be fine," he said.

"When's the baby due?" Olivia asked.

"Right before Christmas," she announced with a smile. "This is going to be the best holiday season of our lives."

At that point, Riley wished he hadn't dragged the information out of Callie. What was the hurry in learning that they'd now have to worry about her for the next seven months?

It actually made him a little angry, probably because he would never have made the choice to risk any woman *he* loved.

Phoenix had spent the past three days working on bracelets. She'd had so many orders to fill. She'd also been getting up early to finish cleaning her trailer, and to get some healthy food cooked for her mother. At the end of each day, she visited Kyle's office to check for more orders, communicate with her customers and package what she'd finished so far. Fortunately, she'd figured out how to buy postage online, and Kyle had been kind enough to let her packages go out with his business mail. That saved her considerable time. Now she no longer had to bike to town to use the internet or to arrange shipping.

It was getting late on Friday evening when Kyle came in to find her still using one of his computers.

"Wow, it's almost nine," he said. "I thought you'd left and forgotten to turn off the light."

"No, sorry. I've been swamped. But I'm just about done. I need to get home and make three more bracelets."

"*Tonight?* It's the weekend. Don't you ever do anything for fun?"

"I'm taking Jacob to breakfast in the morning, which should be fun." Jacob hadn't said whether his father would be joining them, but she'd let him know he could invite Riley.

"Your boy had an amazing game last night."

A warm feeling passed through her. Jacob had messaged her about it, told her he'd struck out several players and they'd won by five runs. She was sorry she'd had to miss it. She would've pulled away from work for that. Nothing was more important to her than he was. But she hadn't wanted to upset his grandparents or anyone else by showing up again, since it was another home game.

She'd promised to go to the next game, against Ponderosa, instead. That was coming up at Shingle Springs on Tuesday. Now she just had to determine a way to get there. It was a forty-minute drive. Jake had said his father would be happy to give her a ride, but she couldn't imagine spending that much time alone with Riley. She hadn't seen or communicated with him since he'd gotten into that fight with Buddy. For all she knew, he was pissed at her for dragging him into it—even though she hadn't expected, or asked for, what he'd done.

"I'm excited for Jake." She sent off her final email and turned to face Kyle. "You're not going to the Ponderosa game, are you?"

"On Tuesday? No. I've got meetings that won't end until after the game starts—and it's so far. By the time I could get there, it wouldn't be worth the drive."

She nodded.

"Why, what's up?"

"Nothing," she said. "I was just curious."

"Do you need to borrow a vehicle?" he asked. "I've got an old pickup my foreman uses on the property. You can take it if you like."

"Thanks, but I don't have a current driver's license."

"Riley will be going."

"Yeah. Maybe I'll catch a ride with him," she muttered.

Kyle must've heard her sarcasm because he peered at her more closely. "He wouldn't mind. As a matter of fact, I bet he'd like it."

"Sure he would," she said with a laugh.

"It's true."

Kyle obviously didn't have a clue. "That would give the whole town something to gossip about."

"Not really. You *are* the mother of his son."

"I'll figure it out."

"How's your business going?" he asked as she gathered up her stuff.

"Right now it's booming. I have no idea why, but my bracelets seem to have caught on in Southern California. I can hardly keep up with the orders—which is good, since I need the money. And now I can contribute more to Jacob's care. Riley has always had to carry most of that, so I'm glad I can be a better partner now."

"You're one of a kind," he said with a smile.

She looked at him in surprise. That wasn't something she heard very often, yet he sounded sincere. "Thanks. I'll get out of here so you can lock up."

"I'm having drinks at Sexy Sadie's with some friends tonight, if you'd like to join us." He raised his hands. "Don't worry. This isn't a date. Just an offer of friendship."

"Who else is going?" she asked.

"Riley. And the rest of the gang."

She rolled her eyes. "Riley doesn't want me horning in on his friends."

"He doesn't want you getting close to his single *male* friends—namely me, since Baxter's gay—but he'd be fine with this."

Laughing, she walked out ahead of him. "Thanks, anyway. You guys have a great time."

"It's Saturday tomorrow, so my staff's off. But I can leave a key under that plant by the door if you think you'll need the computers."

"If you don't mind, I'd really appreciate it."

"No problem. I'll get you your own key next time I'm in town."

With a smile and a nod, she headed toward the road, but he called after her.

"Can I give you a ride home on my way to Sexy Sadie's?"

"Sexy Sadie's is in the opposite direction," she pointed out.

"Doesn't matter. It'd only take a few minutes, and it would make me feel like a gentleman."

"So I'd be doing *you* a favor," she teased.

He chuckled. "If that's what you have to believe in order to agree."

It was already dark and there were no streetlights out in the country. She'd made the journey three times this week. It didn't take long, but…

"Okay," she said, and let him put her bike in the back of his truck.

But once she was home and he'd left, she had difficulty concentrating on making more bracelets. Her hands were tired, her back ached and she kept thinking about Kyle's invitation to go to Sexy Sadie's. She hadn't been anyplace remotely like that since she was released from prison, and she hadn't been old enough to go before she was convicted.

Just sitting somewhere unobtrusive, listening to the music and sipping a cold drink sounded nice. Maybe

she could ride her bike over, slip in and find a safe corner from which she could watch all the fun.

Phoenix's first concern was whether she'd find
Buddy Mansfield at Sexy Sadie's. She couldn't possibly stay if he was there. One glance at her, and he'd
start another problem.

But as she sidled around the edges of the crowded
bar, she felt safe. She didn't even see Kyle and his
friends. She checked her watch—nearly midnight. It'd
taken her so long to make the decision and get ready,
they must've gone home.

That was *another* reason to be relieved, she told herself as she straightened the pretty sundress Kyle had
given her.

Suddenly glad she'd decided to embrace this adven-
ture, she settled in a corner. She wasn't expecting a
great deal of tonight. She merely wanted to see what it
was like to be out on the town. She thought she might
also have a drink. She wasn't driving; if she fell off her
bike, she'd only hurt herself, no one else. Before she
could approach the bar, a big, bearlike man came over.

He offered to buy her a beer, but she didn't want to
feel indebted to anyone, even for something that small.
So they just talked for a few minutes—or tried to talk
above the music. Then he asked her to dance.

When Phoenix tried to refuse, he grabbed her hand
and tugged her onto the dance floor as Alice Cooper's
"Poison" came on. She wanted to hear the lyrics—
"I want to love you but I better not touch..."—so she
agreed to dance with him. If she didn't, she suspected
he'd talk through the whole thing. She'd missed so much
in seventeen years—hadn't danced since the few high
school events she'd attended—but she remembered lis-

tening to this song over and over and over when Riley broke up with her.

She enjoyed the dance enough to remain on the floor for a second song with her current partner. After that she accepted several invitations from other men. She even had that drink she'd been meaning to have—a glass of wine she sipped while sitting at the bar. She was just beginning to feel warm and loose when she realized that someone was staring at her and looked across the room to see Riley.

Where had *he* come from? Apparently, he hadn't left as she'd assumed. But she had no idea why she hadn't spotted him before. She supposed it was because, once she felt comfortable that there was no one at the bar she had to worry about, she'd quit looking. And it had been more crowded when she'd first arrived.

So where was Kyle? He wasn't around. Riley sat with some guy she didn't recognize.

Curving her lips in a polite smile when their eyes connected, she nodded a hello just as someone else came up to ask her to dance. It was a guy who was almost falling-down drunk, someone she'd been trying to avoid. But letting him lead her onto the dance floor gave her an excuse for not walking over to speak to Riley. She allowed the inebriated stranger to pull her into his arms for a Journey song.

As they turned in a rather clumsy circle, she closed her eyes so she wouldn't be tempted to keep searching for Riley. She needed to let him do whatever he pleased—and to do whatever *she* pleased for a change. But the man she was dancing with kept hugging her too tight and lowering his hands.

"Stop it," she hissed, forcing him to loosen his hold when he touched her ass.

"What's the matter?" With a knowing grin, he pressed her against his arousal, and she nearly broke their embrace. She remembered the thought she'd had a week or so ago—that she should go to Sexy Sadie's and pick someone up, just to see what sex as a full-fledged adult was like. She was hungry for meaningful touch. But she saw how empty such a cheap substitute would leave her.

Who knew? White trash or not, she wasn't the type to go home with a stranger. She supposed that was good information to have about herself.

Frustrated with his groping, she lifted his hands and placed them on her waist yet again. "I won't be able to dance with you if you don't quit feeling me up," she said. She would've left him on the dance floor, but she didn't want Riley to think she was in trouble again.

"What, are you some kind of prude?" he grumbled.

"No, I'm not interested."

"Come on. Give a poor guy a break," he said, and nuzzled her neck.

Before she could react, Riley appeared and tapped her partner on the shoulder. "My turn, friend," he said.

"What?" The guy had to squint to even see him clearly.

"I said I'll take it from here."

The interruption seemed to confuse her partner, but Riley acted as if he had every right, so the guy didn't argue. He muttered something about not realizing she was with someone and stumbled off.

Relieved but confused as to why Riley would help her out—it wasn't as if she were in true danger, like she'd been with Buddy—Phoenix offered him a grateful smile. "Thanks," she said, and started to make her way to the edge of the dance floor.

He caught her by the elbow. "Whoa! Where are you going? The song's not over yet."

She felt her eyebrows slide up. "Does it matter?"

"I came out to dance," he replied, and slipped his arms around her waist.

"This isn't a good idea," she said, but she swayed with him to the music so they wouldn't draw any attention.

"Why not?"

Lowering her voice, she sent a covert glance around them. "We shouldn't be seen together, especially in a place like this."

"It's a bar. Everyone goes here."

"Exactly. And this week you punched out the guy who was tormenting me, which doesn't look good."

"I stopped a bully from beating up on a woman. How is that bad?"

"You endangered yourself in the process. People might assume the wrong thing."

"Which would be…?"

"That you care."

"Maybe I do," he said with a boyish grin.

He'd also had too much to drink. He wasn't sloppy drunk like the other guy, but he couldn't be thinking clearly.

"How have you been after that…altercation?" His nose seemed to be back to normal. "I've been wondering."

"So you had to check in to see if I was okay, huh?"

She heard the sarcasm in his voice. "Kyle told me you were fine."

"Have you heard from him?"

"Buddy? Or Kyle?" He was wearing cologne, and it was a scent she liked…

"Buddy. I know you're going to Kyle's every night."

"Does he mind?"

"Of course not. But we were talking about Buddy."

"He hasn't bothered me since."

"That's the way it should be."

He swayed too far to one side, and she had to catch him. "I hope you're not planning to drive," she told him.

"I have a friend here. He's the DD. But you can give me a ride if you want."

"That's okay. I'm guessing you'd be a bit heavy for me to pedal."

He laughed. "We'll toss your bike into the bed of his truck and give *you* a ride."

"I can get home on my own, thank you." For the sake of appearances, as much as anything else, she kept her body stiff instead of melting into him.

"Can you relax?" he murmured.

"We can't get too close," she said, even though no one seemed to be paying any attention.

"We're just *dancing*, Phoenix. It's not like we're making love."

That comment made her miss a step. Just being in his arms felt...intimate. She wasn't sure why dancing with him would be so different from dancing with other guys, but it most definitely was.

She cleared her throat as she struggled to stifle the memories that were quickly surfacing—of his mouth on her breast, his hand between her legs, the weight of his body pressing her into the mattress.

"I didn't see you when I came in." She spoke to help staunch the flow of those erotic images.

"That's good."

"Why's it *good*?" she asked.

"Because you probably wouldn't have stayed."

"I'm not blaming you for anything."

"So you say."

"You don't believe me?"

"You cringe whenever I get close."

"I'm giving you your space. I wouldn't want you to feel as if…"

"As if you still want me. We've been over this. You don't. Not even a little bit. But do you have to prove it by dancing ten feet away?"

"I'm not ten feet away."

"You might as well be, you're so prickly and defensive."

She had her reasons. But she didn't want to sound accusatory. "I'm not prickly. I've been very nice."

He chuckled. "You could be nicer."

She was afraid of where this conversation was going. "Were you here?" she asked, changing the subject.

"When?"

"Earlier."

"I left for a bit."

"Where'd you go?"

"I was with Kyle and some of my other friends, but they were tired and wanted to go home. Then Sean, a subcontractor I use on occasion, called me up and wanted me to go out."

When the song ended, he didn't let go, even though she tried to step away. "One more," he told her as P!nk's "Glitter in the Air" started up.

As she slid her arms around his neck again, she wished she was as immune to his touch as she needed to be. But he aroused such a deluge of hormones in her, she felt drunk herself.

Hang on. It'll only be another two or three minutes.

Then she could put some distance between them and repair her defenses. "Where's Jacob tonight?"

"Home asleep."

Somehow he'd brought her closer. Those words were spoken with his mouth at her temple.

Think of something else—anything but him. "You don't have to work tomorrow?"

"Not early. Not until noon."

He tried to settle her against him and scowled when she resisted. "You're dancing like a robot," he told her. "Will you quit fighting me?"

He seemed satisfied when she gave in. But she felt her heart speed up, could hear its rapid beating in her ears as he drew her fully against him. And suddenly she couldn't think of anything else to talk about. Nothing that would distract her from the warmth and firmness of his body.

Resting her cheek on his chest, she concentrated on stifling the desire that welled up. *You can't feel that way about him*, she kept telling herself. She'd be asking for a world of hurt if she even *considered* Riley in a sexual context. But his hands slid up her back, as if he was enjoying their embrace. And although he wasn't groping her like that other guy, it all felt very...significant. So significant that she feared this simple slow dance could knock her back to where she'd been seventeen years ago.

She *had* to retain control, had to maintain an absolute "no" where he was concerned. "Hang on..."

"What'd you say?"

She hadn't realized she'd spoken aloud. "Nothing."

He tilted her chin up so she had to look at him. "You know I'm sorry, right?"

"Riley, we're dancing too close. Someone's going to see us and assume the wrong thing. They might even tell your parents, and then you'll have another argument on your hands like the one at the ballpark."

"I won't let my parents dictate how I live my life. We're not eighteen anymore, Phoenix."

"What does that mean?"

"It means you should stop worrying about everyone else."

"I *have* to worry about everyone else. You seem to have forgotten that you're making yourself vulnerable to criticism, disapproval and dislike."

"I'm not afraid."

She glanced around the bar. "You would be if you knew what it was like. Being with me could…could cause the whole town to turn on you. If Jacob's with you, they might understand why you're speaking to me. But you should keep your distance when he's not."

"What if I don't want to keep my distance?" he asked.

She couldn't convince him when he was in this state. Obviously, nothing mattered except the alcohol in his blood, the music and the sense of being able to do *anything* and get away with it. "You're drunk. You don't mean any of this."

"Maybe it's what I mean the most."

"You're not making any sense."

He caught her chin again. "Just tell me this. Will you ever be able to forgive me?"

"You broke up with me when we were eighteen. It would've been nothing if I could've walked away as easily as you did."

"But you stood by your heart. Your feelings."

"So? You meant more to me than I did to you. You can't help that."

"I listened to the wrong people, Phoenix. I loved you. I want you to know I did love you."

Damn it! Just that easily, she felt all jittery inside. She'd wanted to hear him say those words for so long, wanted him to confirm that she hadn't been as alone in their relationship as it had seemed by the end. Everyone had treated her like such a fool for thinking Riley could ever care about *her*.

But this was more than vindication. This was… inviting that old craving to eat her up again. The same desires that'd driven her in the past still lurked inside her—like a monster that slipped back into the shadows whenever she tried to slay it.

"Thanks for that." She stopped talking then and hoped he would, too. She was afraid of what he might say next, and how she might respond. She couldn't worry about the past, or try to resurrect it. She had to focus on the present, and in the present she had every reason to fight what she was feeling.

"You smell good," Riley whispered. Then their bodies moved even closer, and she was completely lost, swallowed up in this moment with him and those poignant lyrics: "Have you ever wished for an endless night…"

She was wishing for one now, and that was why she finally pushed him away. He made her heart yearn for things she couldn't have.

There was no reason to put herself through the torture. No reason she had to let her weakness for one man break her heart all over again.

"It's late. I've got to go," she said, and hurried to the exit without giving him a chance to respond.

14

Phoenix waited anxiously at Just Like Mom's for Jacob to arrive. She looked her best, felt ready in that regard. But she hoped Riley wouldn't accompany their son. Surely, now that he'd had a chance to sober up, he would see it was better if they didn't spend time together. It would be far too easy to fall back into a physical relationship. Easy for her because she'd never really gotten over him. And easy for him because he didn't seem to have anyone else in his bed at the moment. His need and her longing could create another lopsided relationship, if she let it.

But it wasn't Jacob's Jeep that turned into the drive. It was Riley's truck—and, just like two weeks ago, both Jacob and Riley got out.

"Can't I ever catch a break?" she muttered.

"Did you say something?" the woman next to her asked.

Phoenix shook her head. "No. Sorry."

The hostess called for the next party and Phoenix prepared herself for Riley and Jacob to walk in, but she was nervous about facing Riley. She wanted to act as if last night had never happened. And maybe that wouldn't be hard. Riley couldn't have enjoyed dancing with her as much as it seemed—no more than he would've enjoyed dancing with any other woman.

"Morning," she said to Jacob as they came through the door.

Jacob hugged her, and Riley seemed about to do the same. It would've been the standard "hello" embrace, nothing significant. But she pretended she didn't recognize his intent and stepped back before he could touch her. He really did have to be careful about getting close to her, especially in public—or he'd learn what it was like to be an outcast.

"Thanks for coming," she said. "I was afraid you'd decide to sleep in."

Riley was wearing a pair of sunglasses. He'd straightened when she dodged him but said nothing.

"You look great," Jacob said.

She squeezed his arm. "Thanks. I got my stitches out, so that's good."

"You went back to the doctor?"

"No, I took them out myself. I didn't need a doctor for that." She pulled her hair away so he could see the red line—all that was left of her injury.

"You've got to be the toughest mom in the world," Jake said with a startled laugh.

"It wasn't hard," she said. "All I felt was a little tug."

Riley didn't comment, but he took off his sunglasses as the hostess approached and, once Phoenix could see his eyes, she guessed he had a hangover. "Three for breakfast?" the hostess asked.

Riley answered before Phoenix could. "Yes, and we'd prefer a booth if you can arrange it."

"No problem. I have a party that's finishing up now." She looked across the restaurant, saw that a busboy was in the process of cleaning the table she'd had in mind and grabbed three menus. "Actually, we can go over."

"Are you excited about your game on Tuesday?" Phoenix asked Jacob as they settled into the booth.

He sat down across from her; Riley sat beside him.

"I am," Jake said. "Will you be able to make it?"

She smiled. "You bet. I wouldn't miss it."

Riley lowered his menu, which he had immediately opened. "How will you get there? It's too far to ride a bike."

He seemed remote this morning—definitely not the charmer she'd danced with last night. Maybe he regretted some of the things he'd said, was afraid she'd taken them too seriously. "I'll hire a car."

"You'd rather pay good money than ride with me?"

"It's not that I'd *rather* pay, it's just…" She glanced at Jacob, who was watching her expectantly, before returning her attention to Riley. "I don't want to put you out. And I'd rather not give your parents any more reason to be upset with you."

"There's no need to get a taxi," he insisted. "My parents won't even be there."

"They could easily hear that we rode together." What would she and Riley do once they reached the game? Sit on opposite bleachers? That would seem unfriendly after traveling in the same vehicle. And yet she couldn't sit *with* him, or everyone from Whiskey Creek who did show up would wonder if they were getting back together.

"They'll live," he said with a shrug.

The waitress came over with their water. "Hey, Riley. Jake." Her eyes shifted to Phoenix and, when she realized they didn't know each other, she merely said, "Good morning."

"Morning," Phoenix murmured.

She took out her pad. "You ready to order?"

"We haven't had a chance to look at the menu yet," Riley told her. "Can you give us another minute or two?"

"Sure." She treated him to a flirtatious smile before sashaying off.

"Did you see that?" Jake said with a nudge for his father.

"*I* did," Phoenix said. "It appears that our waitress finds your father very attractive."

"Marley's all of twenty-two," Riley grumbled. "Closer to Jake's age than mine."

"She's pretty, though," Phoenix said. "And age isn't everything."

He frowned. "Thanks for letting me know," he said sarcastically and, once again, picked up the menu.

If he wanted a physical relationship, he had options that didn't include her. Despite his sarcasm, she didn't see any harm in pointing that out. Maybe it would give him an outlet until they could adjust to being in the same town. "I'm sure she's not your only admirer."

"I'm aware of what's available to me—and what isn't," he said.

She'd been looking forward to this breakfast with too much anticipation to let Riley's bad mood sour her own. So, drawing a deep breath, she ignored the dark shadow he cast over their morning.

"I had a good week, dozens of customers, so order to your heart's content," she said, trying to tempt them both with her enthusiasm. "*I* might even get the Belgian waffle."

"You should. It's amazing," Jake told her, and asked his father to let him out of the booth.

"Where are you going?" she asked.

"To the bathroom. If the waitress comes while I'm gone, order the waffle for me, okay?"

"Today, breakfast is my treat," Riley said when Jake was gone.

"No, it's not," she insisted. "You're here at my invitation."

"You invited Jake, not me."

"I've told you before that you're welcome to come to anything I do with him." She reached into her purse and pulled out the check she had for him. "And you'll be happy to see that I can put quite a bit more toward his care this week."

He stared at the amount. "*Seven hundred dollars?* That's a lot of money, Phoenix."

"I know." She beamed at him; it felt so good to be able to contribute in a significant way. "You'll have to take out what I owe for the doctor bill first. But the rest is for Jake. It's not cheap to have a kid in sports."

"I don't want your money," he said. "You don't even have a phone. Or a car."

She sat up straighter, taken aback by the edge in his voice. "I have a son. That's my first priority."

"Except your son isn't lacking for anything. Just get your business established, okay?" He shoved the check back at her. "Jake and I are fine."

"I doubt seven hundred dollars is going to buy me much of a car," she said, pushing it over to him again.

"It'll get you a phone," he pointed out, and this time he tore it up.

She folded her hands in her lap. "I can get by without a phone for a while longer. Jake and I are communicating pretty regularly through Facebook."

"Has it ever occurred to you that Buddy could show

up at your trailer, and you might need to call for help? Or that I might like to check in now and then to make sure you're okay?"

"A phone is on my list. I just have a number of things to cover right now."

"Exactly my point."

"I would think you'd be grateful that I'm putting my obligation to you and Jake first." She took a drink of water. "Or is it your hangover that has you a bit...out of sorts? I didn't take anything you said or did last night to heart, if that's what you're worried about."

He didn't answer right away. He just stared at her while turning his water glass around.

"I'm trying very hard to stay out of your way," she added.

"God, Phoenix." He pressed three fingers to his forehead. "I don't know what to do."

His exasperated tone made her slightly nervous. "About..."

"I can't get those few minutes on the dance floor off my mind."

Afraid that Jacob might be on his way back, she glanced in the direction of the bathrooms. Fortunately, she didn't see him. "Why?" she asked, as if she hadn't given it a second thought.

"You felt *nothing*?"

She took another sip of water. "If you're talking about that guy who was groping me, I...I'm grateful you stepped in. It's been seventeen years, but even I'm not *that* desperate," she joked.

His jaw hardened. "You're purposely misunderstanding me."

"Nothing else happened."

He lowered his voice. "I wanted to sleep with you.

I know that's not fair to you, after everything you've been through, which is why I feel like shit—both for having that desire and for admitting it. But there it is. The truth."

She curved her fingernails into her palms. "You were drunk."

"And now?"

What was he saying? And why was he saying it? "It's the allure of the taboo."

"The allure of the taboo," he repeated with a skeptical laugh.

"Yes. You're attracted to the one thing that's not good for you. Or maybe it's—" she grasped for the explanation she'd been giving herself "—that sense of loss some people feel when a person who's always adored them moves on. They can't bear to lose the attention, even though they didn't want that person to begin with."

"I'm not vain enough to expect you to adore me without anything in return," he said with a grimace.

She looked around for Jake again. "Fine. Come up with your own explanation. Or just…ignore the temptation and it'll go away. It did last time."

He sat back. "So you *are* holding the past against me."

"No, I'm… I didn't mean that," she said, growing flustered. "I apologize that my homecoming is so difficult on everyone, but I'm trying to make it as easy as possible."

"Which is what you're doing now?"

"What are you talking about?"

"You're shutting me down."

"I can't believe you just said that. I'm not shutting you down. You don't really want me!"

"How do *you* know what I want?"

"I don't feel any resentment, but we've been through this, remember?"

"We're different people these days."

"Not really. So one of us has to keep the other from making a terrible mistake."

"*Terrible* mistake? Thank God you're so vigilant."

She leaned toward him. "Are you being sarcastic again?"

He sighed. "The thought of us…what it was like… must have crossed your mind, too. You just said it's been seventeen years since you've been with a man."

"I haven't been with a woman, either—in case you're wondering. My mother has certainly been curious about that. But I can wait a bit longer to get together with a guy. Until Jake's in college, anyway."

"So I'm the only one who's ever touched you," Riley said.

Too uncomfortable to continue the conversation, she jumped up. "I'm sorry. If you'll excuse me, I need to use the restroom, too," she said, and made sure Jacob was back in his seat when she returned.

What was he doing?

Riley had no idea. His head was pounding despite the ibuprofen he'd popped before coming to the restaurant. His mouth was dry no matter how much water he drank. He had six to eight hours of physical labor ahead of him remodeling a kitchen, which wouldn't be easy in his current condition. And he was confused as hell.

Should he have kept his mouth shut about what he was feeling? Had he scared Phoenix away?

Probably. But maybe that was what he'd subconsciously meant to do. If she'd been the least bit receptive last night…who could say what might've happened?

He didn't want to hurt her again. He knew that much. He hated how badly he'd hurt her in the past.

"Can she, Dad?"

Jerking himself out of his thoughts, Riley paused with his fork halfway to his mouth to look over at his son. Jacob had been telling Phoenix about a friend who'd smashed his hand in a car door and torn off a finger. It wasn't a pleasant conversation to have while eating, but Riley hadn't wanted to interrupt. Phoenix seemed eager to hear whatever Jacob cared to tell her, so he'd tuned it out. "Can she what?"

"Come over tonight. I told her you'd barbecue some ribs for dinner, and we could watch movies after."

"Um, sure." He didn't mind doing some grilling, but he doubted Phoenix would agree to come—not after last night.

"That's okay," she told Jacob, right on cue. "It's the weekend. Your father might have other plans."

"He doesn't go out that much anymore," Jake said. "I'm always telling him to find someone to date. He'll be alone after I go to college. But I can't remember the last time he even brought a woman home."

"Your mother doesn't need a recap of my love life, Jake." Riley had gone out last night, hadn't he? And lived to regret it.

"I'm just saying you'd *like* to barbecue, right?"

Riley finished his orange juice. "I'm happy to do it."

"See?" Jacob looked back at Phoenix, but when she hesitated, he said, "Don't you *want* to come?"

Riley knew, the second Jake asked that question, Phoenix would do all she could to reassure him.

"Of course I *want* to come!" she said. "What time?"

Jake turned to him. "Six?"

"Sounds good to me," he said.

Phoenix smiled but Riley could tell there was more than a little trepidation behind it. "I'll be there."

"I'll pick you up," Jake told her, and she nodded.

When the waitress came, Riley paid for breakfast, despite Phoenix's protests. Then, as they were walking out, Jake ran into a friend from school and paused to say hello, which gave Riley another private moment with Phoenix.

"Don't worry about tonight," he murmured.

"I can't help worrying," she said.

He grinned. "Why? If you're as over me as you say, I should be easy to resist."

He assumed she'd let it go at that, but she surprised him. "There's always the possibility that I might use you for sex." She smiled sweetly. "Seventeen years is, after all, a very long time."

He could tell that she thought she'd gotten in the last word, which was why he didn't allow her to have it. "If there's someplace I can go to apply for that position, just give me a call," he said, and had to laugh when her eyes widened in shock.

"You're quiet today," her mother said. "Any particular reason?"

Phoenix spoke over the sizzle of her mother's dinner. It was a turkey burger, something a bit leaner than Lizzie was used to, but Phoenix wasn't about to volunteer that. She'd stopped at the grocery store on her way home from breakfast. "Nope, just thinking."

"About…"

"My business. I'm getting so many orders."

Because her mother's recliner was the only chair that could hold her comfortably, she'd long ago moved it into the kitchen, right by the table. It creaked as she shifted her weight. "How much have you made this week?"

Phoenix cast Lizzie a satisfied smile. "Enough that I'll be able to pay that light bill you were worried about."

It sounded as if Lizzie said, "Thanks," but her words weren't very clear. Gratitude didn't come easily for her mother. Her voice was more strident when she added, "How'd it go at breakfast?"

After scrounging up a spatula from one of her mother's messy drawers, Phoenix flipped the burger and sprinkled some salt and pepper on it. She had to serve Lizzie dinner earlier tonight than usual, so she could be ready for Jacob's barbecue—not that Lizzie approved of her going over to Riley's. She'd made that clear when Phoenix mentioned her plans but had finally dropped the subject.

"It was...enjoyable."

"That's it? That's all you've got to say?"

"What do you want to hear?" She couldn't share what had really been going through her mind—the memory of those few minutes dancing with Riley last night and what he'd said to her at breakfast this morning. *I wanted to sleep with you.*

"You could tell me about Jacob. He's being nice to you, then?"

"I've been pleasantly surprised by how receptive he's been."

"Is he as handsome as his father?" Her mother was painting her nails again. She acted completely engrossed in that simple task, but Phoenix wasn't fooled. Lizzie was far more interested in Jacob than she wanted to let on—especially now that Phoenix was getting to know him.

"*I* think so," she replied. "He looks just like his dad."

"And how does Riley treat you?"

Her thoughts reverted to the attraction they were both struggling to overcome. She didn't want to tell her mother about it, but she was definitely concerned. Getting involved with Riley could ruin everything she'd begun to build with Jacob—if it went wrong. And she knew from experience that it was bound to go wrong. "I can't complain. He picked up the tab this morning."

A snort revealed Lizzie's skepticism. "I don't like him."

"So you've said. But as long as I play nice, I'm sure he will, too."

"He didn't play so nice before."

Phoenix tucked her hair behind her ears. "We've been over that, Mom. We have to let the past go."

"Seventeen years in prison? You can let that go and head off to a barbecue at his house tonight?"

"My going to prison wasn't his fault."

"He testified against you!"

"He testified about my behavior at the time. And he told the truth. I did call him repeatedly, drive by his house, beg him to reconsider breaking up with me. I was distraught and too immature to know how to cope with losing him." Not to mention the fact that her brothers had already abandoned her, and she was feeling that heartbreak, as well.

"Does he realize what he's done?" Lizzie asked.

"I think so. He's apologized twice."

"Hmph."

"You'd like him if you ever gave him a chance," Phoenix said.

"As if he'd ever give *me* a chance."

Phoenix didn't respond. She didn't know what to say. Lizzie made it difficult for anyone to like her.

The sizzle from the frying pan filled the silence until Lizzie broke in again. "I finally heard from your brother."

Phoenix couldn't help her quick intake of breath. Although she was glad that Kip and Cary had been able to escape their situation and move on, she missed them. "Which one?"

"Kip."

"What'd he have to say?"

"Not much. It was a short call. That's all I ever get—if he even bothers at all. He's glad you're out."

She got a plate and prepared the bun for her mother's burger. "He say anything about Cary? Do they keep in touch?"

"They always have. He said Cary's getting divorced again. Has two kids with this latest wife."

"That's four in total?" Four children she and her mother had never seen. But she was beginning to figure out that her brothers weren't a whole lot more functional than their mother. "Can he support that many?"

"How would I know?" she replied. "He tells me he's working, but it's not as if he ever sends any money to help *me* out."

Satisfied that the burger was cooked through, Phoenix removed the pan from the stove. "At least the guys seem to be getting by on their own. That's something."

"You'd think they'd consider their mother once in a while." Lizzie said it gruffly, but Phoenix knew that was only because she was hurt by their neglect.

"They have other responsibilities," she said. "Besides, we don't need them. We have each other."

Lizzie eyed her suspiciously. "Until you leave."

Phoenix slid the burger onto its bun. "Why would I do that?"

"You're starting to make money, aren't you?"

"So?"

"So you'll be able to get a car and move."

"You think I'm here because I don't have any other choice?"

"Why else would you come back? Your brothers never have."

"I'm not like my brothers."

Lizzie slipped a carrot through the bars of her hamsters' cage. "Considering how this town has turned on you, you should go somewhere else. You could always drive back here to see Jake."

"Would you move with me?" Phoenix asked, but she had no real hope. She knew what her mother's answer would be.

"I'm too old and fat to go anywhere else. The people here may not like me, but they've grown accustomed to me. I don't want to face a whole new town."

"The devil you know is better than the one you don't, huh?" she teased as she added a salad to her mother's plate.

"I'm comfortable. Doesn't make sense for me to go anywhere else."

Her phobias prevented it. Phoenix understood. "Then I'll stay with you," she said as she put her mother's dinner plate in front of her.

Lizzie didn't look up. She kept her gaze fastened on her food. "You should go somewhere you can start over," she said softly. "You're young and capable of it. And I'm nothing but a pain in the ass."

"Pain in the ass or not, you're still my mother." She gave Lizzie a quick, one-armed hug. She had no idea if she'd be rebuffed. Displays of emotion made her mother very uncomfortable. But Lizzie tolerated this one, and even muttered something about her burger smelling good.

Phoenix smiled as her mother began to eat. "Don't worry about anything, okay?" she said as she let herself out so she could go change for the barbecue. She also had to finish the pasta salad she was planning to bring. She wanted to contribute to the meal, even though neither Riley nor Jacob had asked her to.

15

Phoenix was impressed with Riley's home. It was a nice three-bedroom, two-bath that he and Jake had built themselves, and it had a lot of upgrades—wainscoting, hardwood floors, a rock fireplace, wooden stair railings, stainless-steel appliances and gorgeous cupboards. She had to wonder what it would be like to live in such a place, couldn't help envying them a little, especially when she walked out back and saw that they had a big yard with an expansive deck to go with the pool Jake had mentioned when he picked her up.

"Wow, this is gorgeous," she said.

Riley was at the grill, but he turned to smile at her. He was proud, but not as proud as Jacob, who was showing her around.

"We put the pool in last summer," Jake said. "We'll have some fun parties when it gets warmer."

He waved for her to follow him back into the house. "Come on. I'll show you my room."

She felt it might be too invasive to go upstairs, into the more private parts of the house, but Riley didn't argue. He closed the hood on the grill and accompanied them up the L-shaped staircase as if he was also eager to see her reaction.

"What do you think?" Jake asked as they walked in to what was obviously a teenager's room.

The furniture matched, which was a novelty to her. And there was a ceiling fan, a nice walk-in closet and autographed sports posters hanging on the walls. "You're a lucky boy. That's what I think. Your dad's been able to give you so much."

Her son shoved his hands in his pockets and looked around as if he was seeing it all through new eyes. "Yeah, I know. But that doesn't mean it isn't good to have you in my life."

Touched that he'd say such a thing when she had so little to offer him, she smiled. "Thank you. That was very nice."

Her gratitude must have embarrassed him because he ducked his head and continued the tour. "This is my dad's office," he said as they entered the next room.

Riley's office wasn't as clean as the rest of the house, but it wasn't dirty—just messy. From what she could tell, he ran a very successful business, and she was as happy for him as she was for Jacob. He'd had everything she lacked. But she'd always cared too much about Riley to wish him any less.

"How long have you had your contractor's license?" she asked as her eyes wandered over the expensive computer system, desk and bookshelves.

Other than a brief hello, Riley had let Jake act as host, but he answered this question. "I was twenty-two. I got it just after graduating from UC Davis with a BS in Managerial Economics."

"Managerial Economics?"

"It's basically a business degree."

She touched the smooth surface of the carpentry

work. "What do you think has been more valuable to you? Your education? Or practical experience?"

"In construction, practical experience is more valuable in getting a job done. But there are plenty of good contractors out there who can build a house but can't run a business. So...I'd say it takes both to make a living these days."

"Which is why Jake is going to get his degree, too, right?" she teased, giving her son a nudge.

"That's the plan." He gestured across the hall. "This is my dad's bedroom."

She didn't need to see Riley's bedroom. She expected him to stop Jake and guide her back downstairs, to the living room and kitchen area. But he didn't. And she didn't say anything. She was too curious. Besides, they'd built all of this. They weren't showing her what they could afford to have; they were showing her their workmanship.

Riley had a giant bed—bigger than any she'd seen before. Wooden shutters covered the windows and a set of French doors led onto a large balcony overlooking the pool. The design reminded her of something from one of the *Southern Living* magazines she'd enjoyed in prison—not only because of its size but because of the big ceiling fan that stirred the air overhead.

Jake took her through Riley's bathroom and closet area next, which together were as big as his bedroom.

"It's gigantic in here," she said, half expecting her voice to echo off the marble floor and granite countertops.

"I was thinking about resale when I built it," Riley explained. "I don't need this much space, but most women would like it."

"I'm sure they would." She couldn't resist comparing

it to what she was living in. Her bathroom wouldn't even take up half his closet. "You've done a really nice job."

His eyes met hers. "Thank you."

She pulled her gaze away. "And if you don't sell it, I'm sure your wife, when you find the right woman, will love it."

"*If* he ever finds the right woman," Jake muttered. "It's pretty hard when you don't date."

Riley didn't immediately respond, so Phoenix tried to come up with a soothing rejoinder. "It can be difficult to meet someone when you're out of college and in the work force, especially if you live in a small town."

"Which means you'll have the same problem," Jake said with a scowl. "But there's online dating. That's how most people find a mate these days."

"Most? I didn't realize that." She turned to Riley. "Do you meet the women you date online?"

He shook his head. "Never tried it."

She opened the shower to see that it was big enough for two, with a bench and everything. "I haven't, either, of course. I wouldn't even know where to start."

"It's easy," Jake said. "Like Facebook was. You caught on to that quickly enough. I could help you both get on Match.com."

"Go ahead and act as matchmaker for your father," she said with a laugh. "I think I'll put off that sort of thing for a while. I'm not sure my profile would be too enticing, anyway—broke ex-con, hated by entire community, is looking for love while living in a dump and taking care of her severely dysfunctional mother."

She laughed at the thought of someone responding to something so pathetic, but they seemed troubled instead of entertained. "Oh, stop," she said. "That was humor. I'm fine. I'll get on my feet eventually. And I'll find someone when I do."

"Why not find someone who could help you through it?" Jake asked. "You wouldn't have to mention any of that stuff."

"You mean I could lie, like everyone else?" She laughed again. "No, thanks."

"You're pretty," her son said. "If you put up your picture, you'll attract more than your fair share of guys."

"Because most guys aren't smart enough to know they should care about more than looks?" she joked.

"That's not all you've got," he argued. "There are a lot of good things about you, things that have nothing to do with the past."

"I don't need to tackle dating quite yet," she said. "Your father should get his profile up, though. He's way beyond me when it comes to marketability."

Riley's expression indicated that he wasn't going for it. "I'm not ready for a dating site."

"Do you want to stay single your whole life?" Jake asked.

He gave their son a playful slug in the arm. "No, but I'll run my love life without your help, thanks."

"Fine. I'll help Mom when she's ready. You want to get married, don't you, Mom?"

She pretended to be fascinated with the gold knobs on the vanity. "Someday."

"Do you want more kids?"

That felt like a strange question coming from Jake, but she was glad he seemed comfortable with the idea. "That would be nice if...if you don't mind."

"It's not my decision," he said.

"Time to talk about something else." Riley led them

out of the room. "The meat's got to be done by now, anyway."

Once they were back in the hall, Phoenix paused to look at various pictures of Jake growing up, and was surprised when Riley stopped, too.

"These are wonderful," she breathed, completely taken with the images of her son all the years she couldn't be with him.

"I should've sent you copies," Riley said, his tone filled with regret.

"I understand why you didn't. I bought a disposable camera at the grocery store earlier, hoping I might be able to get some pictures of him tonight."

"I'll send you copies of these, as well. I've already scanned them so I can easily email you the digital files."

"I'd appreciate that."

He went downstairs ahead of them.

"I don't know why he won't let me put up a profile for him on Match.com," Jacob complained.

"Maybe he thinks it'd make him look desperate?"

"But *most* people his age date online."

"You mean *our* age?" She winked at him. She couldn't believe any woman would turn up her nose at a man like Riley. He was handsome, strong, charismatic, successful—everything a woman could want. Not that *she* could afford to see him that way. "We'd better go help," she said.

A few minutes later, they were all on the patio, sitting around the picnic table with their plates full.

"Smells delicious," she said as she pulled her spare ribs apart. She'd thought it would be uncomfortable to have dinner at Riley's house, and it *had* been a bit awkward at first. He'd had seventeen years to build a good life, and she was just getting started. But as the meal progressed and they relaxed around the deck, talking and laughing and snapping pictures, she began to enjoy herself. They discussed Riley's latest jobs, Jacob's classes and friends, her business and all the changes that'd taken place at Whiskey Creek High and the town in general.

It was almost dark when they finally stood to clear the table.

"Dinner was great." At that point, she expected one of them would say they should start the movie, but Riley said they should go for a swim and asked if she'd brought her suit.

"She doesn't have one," Jake said.

Phoenix spoke at the same time. "I'll just watch you two."

"You could wear something we have here," Riley suggested.

She couldn't imagine what they might have. They were both so much bigger than she was. "That's not necessary. I'll take a few more pics, and then I'll wade on the steps."

Riley didn't get a chance to coax her. Jacob tried to push him into the water, and they began wrestling, each trying to gain an advantage over the other.

Phoenix took several pictures of them. Then she put her camera down, intending to walk to the far end by the steps. But when she realized how precariously Riley and Jake were balanced on the edge of the pool, how easily she could push them *both* in, she felt a rush of devilish excitement. With a sudden change in direction, she ran up and gave them a mighty shove—and they went over the edge with a startled cry and a big splash.

She was laughing so hard when they surfaced that she could hardly stand up. But she stopped laughing when she heard Riley say, "You go that way, I'll go this way," and saw the glint in their eyes. They were coming for *her*.

Her levity disappeared. With a panicked scream, she made a dash for the house.

"You want to play dirty, huh?" Riley shouted and caught her while she was trying to get the screen door open.

"I'm not wearing a swimsuit!"

They'd gone in with their clothes on, so he obviously didn't care. Lifting her up with one arm, he hauled her back and Jacob stepped aside as he tossed her into the deep end.

Phoenix hadn't gone swimming since she was a teenager, but she hadn't forgotten how. She could easily have swum to the edge if she'd wanted to. Instead, she broke the surface, gulping and splashing as if she might drown.

She saw the panic that crossed Riley's face a split second before he dived in to save her. But when he grabbed hold, she pushed him away.

"Phoenix!" he called, still concerned.

She laughed as she began to tread water. "Sucker!"

He flipped the wet hair out of his face. "You just about gave me a heart attack!"

She splashed him. "You're the one who threw me in without asking if I could swim!"

"That does it," he said, and dived, dragging her under by one foot.

After that, it was a splashing melee of one person trying to dunk the others. Jacob would drag her under occasionally, but more often they teamed up to get Riley. For the next fifteen or twenty minutes, they were struggling and laughing so much they could hardly breathe, let alone speak. Only when a voice called out to them from the deck did they stop.

"Hey, dude! What happened to you tonight?"

Gasping for air, they all broke apart and looked up to see Tristan.

"What do you mean?" Jacob asked. "Did we have plans?"

"You said you'd help me ask Amber to prom, remember?"

"Oh, right! We were going to put together that treasure hunt to surprise her. I'm sorry. I forgot."

"It's not too late, is it?" Tristan asked.

"Maybe not, but…"

He glanced at his father, and Riley waved him off. "I'll take your mom home. Don't worry. Go with Tristan."

"Is that okay with you, Mom?" Jake asked.

She smiled. "Of course."

"Thanks." He swam for the edge but paused there, a happy yet tired smile on his face. "I had fun. I'm glad you came over," he told her.

"So am I," she said, and watched him walk into the house with his friend.

Phoenix started to get out, but Riley couldn't resist dunking her one last time.

"That'll show you who's boss," he teased.

She had far more drive and determination than he'd expected, and immediately tried to get him back.

They wrestled for several more minutes, until she ran out of strength. Then she said, "Much as I hate to admit this, you win, damn it."

He laughed at her grudging concession. It was funny

to him that she'd even try to best him, weighing about half of what he did. "So say it."

"Say what?" she asked, narrowing her eyes.

"Say that I'm more than you can handle."

"I just did!"

"I want to hear it again. Say, 'Riley, I concede that I am absolutely no match for you.'"

She gave him a saucy look. "You've heard all you're going to hear." He pulled her away from the edge of the pool, which meant she had to put her arms around him or go under. It was too deep for her to stand up. "Then you'll have to give me a prize instead."

"What kind of prize?"

As he held her in the water, his desire to laugh faded. "Riley?"

His gaze lowered to her lips. "You could kiss me."

They were both still breathing hard. He could feel her chest, in those wet clothes, rising and falling against his.

"No, I couldn't."

"Why not? One kiss can't hurt anything."

She closed her eyes as if she couldn't bear to meet his. "How about I…I clean your kitchen instead?"

He waited until she was looking at him again. "That wouldn't be nearly as satisfying."

"It would be smarter."

He could almost taste her. A mere two centimeters and their lips would touch… "That isn't what you want, either."

She shivered, but Riley knew that shiver had nothing to do with the temperature. He guessed that she could feel the pressure of his erection, which he couldn't do much to hide. "Yes, it is."

"No, it's not."

"How do you know?" she asked.

"Because your legs are locked around my hips, as if…as if you like the pressure you feel down there."

Her eyes flared as she released him. "I'm sorry about that. I didn't… I mean…I was…" She didn't finish. He had no idea where she could go with that, anyway.

"It's okay. I don't mind," he said, but she swam away from him.

He reached the edge right after she did. "Phoenix, don't get out," he said from behind her, his mouth at her ear.

Darkness had settled in a little deeper, and the cicadas began to chirp. Now that Jacob was gone and they were alone in the yard, it felt private, especially in that corner of the pool, farthest from the deck.

"I have to," she said.

He could hear a tremor of fear in her voice, but he could hear the huskiness of desire as well, and that made his heart pound. "No, you don't. I'm sorry for what happened before, in high school…"

"I'm not demanding another apology," she broke in. "We just can't screw this up. You need someone else." She began to climb out, but he drew her back against him.

"We could…give it some time…see where it leads," he said.

"Where it leads?" she echoed. "I've already traveled down that road. I know it's not safe."

"It's been seventeen years. You can't say what'll happen now."

He waited for her to insist he let her go. But she didn't, and the desire to touch her more intimately goaded him on. He had a chance with her, or she would've shoved him away.

His muscles tensed in anticipation as he slipped one hand up her shirt and released her bra.

She didn't stop him, didn't speak. At the slickness of her skin and the feel of her soft breast in his palm, he felt a wave of desire sweep through him, through them both. Her nipple was erect before he even touched it, which made him that much harder and encouraged him to undo her shorts.

"Riley," she gasped when he slipped his other hand inside her panties.

"One touch," he said.

Although she was holding herself rigid, he could tell she didn't really want him to stop. She was trembling when he slid his finger into her warm wetness.

"Oh…" she whispered. "We can't…"

"Shh." He wished he could kiss her, but she was facing away from him, and he didn't dare change positions. "It's okay. I won't take it too far. Just—just let me feel you."

Her hand went to his wrist. She seemed undecided, hesitant. He squeezed his eyes closed for fear she'd put a decisive end to a moment that was turning out to be one of the most exquisite he'd ever known. But she didn't remove his finger. She moaned as she pressed it deeper, and then he was trembling, too.

"You don't have to give me anything," he promised her. "This is enough. I just want you to enjoy my touch. Let me feel you come in my arms."

Her head fell back on his shoulder as he began to use everything he'd learned about a woman's body to give her that experience.

"Relax. It's okay," he whispered. He wasn't sure how far she would've let him go—and he didn't get the chance to find out. His mother's voice came from inside the house, at which point they both froze.

"Riley? Jake? Where are you guys? Why isn't anyone answering their phone?"

With a sharp intake of breath, Phoenix pulled away from him and floated along the edge of the pool to the far side, which fell in the shadow of the trees blocking the moonlight. She hadn't said a word—just set about fastening her shorts. That told him, as if it wasn't obvious, that she didn't want his mother to know she was there.

He would've liked to reassure Phoenix that he wouldn't let his mother mistreat her. But she was in a fragile state, trying to return from seventeen years in a hellish place. He supposed Whiskey Creek was pretty hellish for her, too. And his mother had been one of her biggest detractors. He didn't want to expose her presence without her agreement, and there was no time for that.

"Riley?" His mother had opened the screen door to the house and was coming out onto the deck.

He splashed to draw her attention away from Phoenix, who was hidden at the other end of the pool, "I'm here. What's up?" He wished he could get out and guide his mother back into the house, put Phoenix's mind at ease, but his arousal precluded that.

"I've been trying to reach you," she said.

Her imperious tone irritated him, as if he had to be available to her 24/7. "My phone's inside, on the counter."

"What…" She gave him a closer look. "What are you doing swimming *in your clothes*?"

Riley imagined Phoenix slowly sinking beneath the inky-looking water—or at least well below the lip of the pool—to avoid being seen. "Jake threw me in a few minutes ago, right before Tristan dropped by to grab him."

"He left?"

"Yeah, they wanted to go to Amber's. Tristan's asking her to the prom and needed a wingman."

"Amber who?"

Fortunately, he'd managed to turn her mind to other things. "DeVane. You probably don't know the family. What's up?" he repeated.

"I just came from Corinne's."

Riley fought the urge to glance at Phoenix. It would only give her away, and if he did that, he knew she'd go home immediately. Although he doubted she'd allow him to him touch her again, especially where he'd been touching her before, he wasn't ready for the night to end. They'd been having a good time, far better than he'd had in…months. Besides, they still had a movie to watch.

"And?"

"Buddy wants to talk to you. He suggested we all get together, see if we can work something out."

"We don't have to work anything out," he said. "As long as he leaves Phoenix alone, everything will be fine."

"She murdered Lori, Riley. It's not quite that simple."

He didn't like talking about this in front of Phoenix. He no longer believed she was capable of any such thing, but he didn't know what terrible comment his mother might make. The quickest way to get Helen to leave would be to agree to this meeting with the Mansfields. "When?"

"Monday night at seven?"

"Where?"

"Corinne wants to have it at her place. She said she'll make dinner."

"I won't bring Jake."

"Why not?"

"Because I don't want him to hear what might be said."

"Maybe he *should* hear it. He needs to be prepared for any relationship he decides to have with his mother."

Finally safe to let her see the rest of his body, Riley hefted himself out, onto the deck. "He's prepared enough."

"Riley, anyone who gets involved with Phoenix should have his head examined."

He clenched his jaw. "It's chilly out here. Let's go inside." He led her into the house, where she discovered the pasta salad Phoenix had brought to dinner.

"This looks delicious. Did you make it?" she asked, picking up one of the curly noodles and popping it in her mouth.

"Yeah, I did."

"Where'd you get the recipe?"

"You can find anything online."

She pointed at the three plates they'd carried to the sink. "Who were you and Jake entertaining?"

"Tristan was here, remember?"

She eyed him curiously. "You said he dropped by."

"For dinner. Something wrong with that?"

"No, of course not."

"Anyway, I need to clean up and go to bed. I'm fine with meeting the Mansfields for dinner on Monday. Is there anything you'd like me to bring? The wine, maybe?"

"That'd be great," she said, and he walked her to the door.

"Thanks for stopping by."

She gave him another funny look. "You're mad at me."

"I'm frustrated with the whole Phoenix situation."

"We knew we'd have to deal with it someday. It's too bad she couldn't have made it easy on us."

He couldn't respond to that. He wanted to get rid of his mother as soon as possible—and that was what he did. He bit his tongue, agreed with her that it might've been easier had Phoenix settled somewhere else and, eventually, she left. But when he went back outside, Phoenix was gone.

16

"What have I done? *What have I done?*" Phoenix muttered to herself as she walked home, soaking wet and shivering from the drop in temperature that came with nightfall. She'd known better than to let Riley touch her—anywhere. She'd just been...caught up in the moment and that old hunger. She was a healthy woman in her sexual prime. Of course she'd crave a man. It wasn't that she wanted *Riley*. She was over him. She'd spent seventeen *years* getting over him. No way could she allow herself to fall back into the same dark pit she'd climbed out of. She'd vowed that she'd diligently avoid it.

Headlights appeared behind her, so she ducked into the cattails near the creek that ran beside the road. She had no idea what Helen Stinson drove these days, but the Cadillac that passed seemed like a good candidate.

The last thing she wanted was for Riley's mother to see her leaving his place.

She was glad Helen had shown up when she did, though. Who could say what might've happened if not for that chance to come to her senses? She could be in Riley's bed this very instant.

As she returned to the road, she wrapped her arms

around herself. She was freezing cold, and yet her body burned where he'd touched her—as if the heat of his hands was still there.

"Forget!" she ordered herself, mortified by the memory of how she'd clutched his wrist and encouraged him to continue.

Now he'd *never* believe she wasn't out to rekindle their old romance. And what would those few minutes do to her chances of getting to know Jake?

You're an idiot. Tears burned behind her eyes as she imagined Riley taunting her with her own weakness. Had he been testing her? Trying to discover her true intentions—which he'd think would be some sort of reconciliation with him?

What if he put a stop to her visits with Jacob?

"Please don't let that happen," she prayed. "I'll stay away from him. I won't do that again."

Another pair of headlights came up behind her, and she crept back into the underbrush. She wasn't far enough away from Riley's house that she wanted anyone to recognize her, especially when she wasn't sure how she'd explain why she was soaking wet and smelling of chlorine.

But this car didn't pass. It slowed down and parked about ten feet away.

"Phoenix?" Riley called. He'd seen someone or something. And since she was on foot and hadn't left more than ten minutes earlier, she couldn't have gotten much farther than this.

If she could hear him calling her, however, she didn't speak up.

"Come on. Answer me, damn it! I'm sorry about my

mom. But I can't control or change her any more than you can control or change yours."

He batted around the cattails on the bank of the creek, hoping to find her—and finally flushed her out.

"This is completely unnecessary," she said.

At the sound of her voice, he managed to make her out despite the dark. *"Here you are!"*

"I thought you'd give up and go back!"

"Thanks for that."

"I don't mean to be rude. There's just no need to trouble you any further."

"Trouble me?" he echoed. "I can't believe you took off without so much as a goodbye. Or a towel. You must be freezing."

"A little," she admitted. "It's funny how cold it can seem when you're wet."

"I brought you one." He went back to get it, hoping she'd follow him, but she didn't. "You left your camera and your bowl at my place," he called back.

"You didn't bring it? My camera, at least?"

He heard the hope in her voice. But once his mother had gone home, he hadn't bothered with anything other than the towel. He'd been in too much of a hurry. "I've got some extra pictures of Jake I can give you, too, if you go back with me."

He wanted to calm her down, to at least put her back in the happy mood she'd been in earlier.

But she remained where she was, hugging herself and rubbing her arms. "No, that's okay. Maybe you can send that stuff with Jake sometime when we're meeting up if—" her voice dropped "—if you're still going to let me see him."

That was what was going through her head? She thought she'd jeopardized her position with Jake? No wonder she was shaking. He knew how much this chance with their son meant to her. "Of course I'm going to let you see Jake. You think I'm upset about what happened? That I'm blaming you?"

"I should've stopped you."

"I hope you're kidding. You moaned when I touched you. That's exactly what I was hoping you'd do."

As soon as he mentioned that, she turned on her heel and marched down the road as though she couldn't bear the memory of it, but he jogged after her. "Wait! It wasn't a big deal, okay? It might seem like it because you haven't…been with a man in so long. But it's not as if we made love. Will you quit with all the regret?"

He grabbed her shoulder and held out the towel. "Let me give you a ride home."

She was reluctant to come anywhere near him. But she bit her lip as she peered down the road. She was probably thinking about how slow and arduous it would be to get to the trailer on her own. Darkness only made it worse.

"I told Jake I would," he coaxed. "So I'll have to follow you if you refuse. Then it would take us *both* a couple of hours. And imagine the spectacle we'd make to all the people who passed by."

Her chest rose as if she'd taken a deep breath, and she accepted the towel. "Sure. Okay. Why not?"

He wanted to put his arms around her to help her get warm, but she was too spooked to allow him that close. "Great. Let's go."

They returned to the truck, but she waited until he'd climbed behind the wheel to get in. Then she sat as far away as possible and didn't talk the whole way home.

Just before they arrived, he attempted to start a con-

versation. "I'm sorry if what I did in the pool has...
upset you."

"I'm not upset."

"You seem more than upset. You seem to be...filled
with remorse."

"Let's just pretend it never happened. I apologize
that I...got carried away and...and did that."

"*You* didn't do it," he said. "*I* did."

She kept her gaze focused on something beyond the
window. "No one has to take the blame. It was a fun
night. We just got a bit confused at the end."

"*Confused?*" he repeated. "About what? I wanted to
touch you. I admit it." He lowered his voice. "And you
seemed to enjoy it."

"Like you said, I haven't been with anyone in seventeen years. Sometimes I miss that...kind of contact.
Anyone would."

She didn't need to be defensive. He could understand.
It hadn't been nearly as long for him, but he missed that
kind of contact, too. "So it wasn't anything about *me*
that turned you on."

Lines appeared on her forehead. "What?"

"*Any* man could do the same thing for you? Get you
that excited?"

She glowered at him. "It's better if we don't talk
about it."

He sighed. She didn't trust him, and he couldn't
blame her. He couldn't even think of anything to say
that might change her mind, because he couldn't make
any promises about the future. He only knew that he
liked what he'd seen of her so far. Maybe she viewed
herself as a broke ex-con hated by the whole community. But *he* saw a beautiful woman, someone with grit,
honesty, humility, dedication to those she cared about

and the courage to risk almost anything to be part of their lives. So why *shouldn't* he care about her?

"What if I told you I'd like you to go with me and my friends to a cabin next weekend to celebrate my birthday?" he asked.

"I'd say you need to invite someone else."

"You didn't even take two seconds to think about it."

"I don't need two seconds. I'm still sick to my stomach from a few minutes ago, when I thought I'd blown it and you wouldn't let me see Jake. I can't take any chance of that happening in the future," she said, and climbed out.

She'd turned him down flat. Riley was a little surprised. After what Phoenix had been through, it wasn't as if he'd expected her to fall into his arms. Going out with him would, understandably, require a huge leap of faith. But she was lonely and, here in Whiskey Creek, she didn't have many other options.

That was because she was one of the best-kept secrets in town, he realized as he sat in her drive, letting his engine idle. Kyle knew she wasn't what everyone else believed and, as a result, *he* was interested. Only Riley's lifelong friendship with Kyle kept him in his current "hands off" status.

Other guys would want her, too, once they figured out what they were missing...

Shit. He remembered the feel of her lace panties—guessed they were the new ones he and Kyle had bought her—and what he'd found inside them. He'd taken things too far, too fast. No wonder she'd hugged the door so tightly as they drove. What his mother had said in front of her certainly couldn't have helped. She felt hurt and had her guard up, was determined not to put herself back in a bad position.

He couldn't blame her. But it was unusual to feel that getting involved with him would put a woman in a bad position.

His phone rang. Illogically, because he knew she didn't have a way to call him, he hoped it was Phoenix changing her mind.

It wasn't, of course. It was Kyle.

Riley backed out of her drive as he pressed the talk button. "'Lo?"

"There you are! Why haven't you been answering your phone?"

"I've been busy."

"Doing what?"

"Dinner."

"Did you have a date?"

Once again he could feel the softness of Phoenix's breast beneath his hand. "Jake invited his mother."

"Oh." There was a moment of silence. Then Kyle said, "How'd that go?"

"Good. Perfect," he lied. "Why?"

"Just wondering. She's actually the reason I was trying to get hold of you."

"What do you want with her?"

"See?"

"See what?" Riley asked.

"There's that jealousy again."

"I like her, okay? I like her a lot."

"Whoa! And now you're admitting it?"

He rubbed his forehead. "Yeah. I'm admitting it."

"Does *she* know?"

He switched to Bluetooth so he could drive. "It wouldn't matter even if she does. She wouldn't trust me."

"That's not entirely unexpected, I hope."

"Are you trying to make me feel better or worse?"

"What happened tonight?"

He couldn't say anything about what had gone on in the pool, not without compromising her privacy, so he focused on what came after. "I asked her to go to the cabin with us next weekend."

"And?"

"She said no."

"I see. But…that couldn't have been totally unexpected, either."

He shoved a hand through his hair. "It wasn't."

"So…"

"I'm not sure I even want to go anymore."

"What?" Kyle cried. "Come on, man! We've been looking forward to this for months. Gail and Simon don't get to visit us very often. He's always on location for one movie or another, half the time out of the country. Or they have the kids with them and they're busy visiting family. It'll be fun getting together with just our group. You'll see."

That didn't reassure him, but he wasn't about to ruin the weekend for everyone else. "You said you called about Phoenix."

"I did."

"You still haven't said why."

"Because I don't think this is going to improve your night."

Riley turned the radio down. "Tell me, anyway."

"She came by earlier, when I was gone, and left an envelope on my desk."

She'd been going over there pretty often, using Kyle's computers. Did she have a thing for him now? Riley tightened his grip on the steering wheel. "What was in it?"

"A check for twenty-five dollars. She's trying to pay me back for those clothes we bought. She wrote a note saying she'd pay me twenty-five dollars a month until she's covered it all."

Riley released his breath in a long sigh. That wasn't nearly as bad as he'd feared. "Sounds like something she'd do."

"I guess it does. But I feel guilty letting her believe it was just me when you paid for half," Kyle explained. "I wish she'd drop it. We *wanted* to give her those things. But she has so damn much pride."

That was one of the qualities Riley admired about her. Who else, hitting rock bottom as hard as she had, would refuse help from people who obviously had the wherewithal to give it? "Tear up the check."

"Are you sure? If I do, I'm afraid she'll start bringing me cash when she comes to use the computer."

"You can always refuse it."

"Wouldn't you rather I told her you were part of this? So you can work that out, along with all the other… issues between you?"

Somehow the past seventeen years hadn't wiped away what he'd felt for her; they'd merely put it on pause. The truth was, he felt even more attracted to her than before, because now he trusted his own judgment and had been around long enough to identify the traits he wanted in a partner. "No. There's no need for her to know."

"Okay, but…"

"What?"

"I'm concerned."

"Why?"

"She's been hurt so badly in the past. I can't face the thought that your...interest might not be a positive thing for her."

Riley gave the truck more gas. He was speeding, but it was tough to care when he felt so torn and frustrated. "You think *your* interest would be better?"

"I don't see her in that way."

"Then how do you see her?"

"As a friend. She can use some good friends, so I hope you'll consider being her friend, too."

Kyle was right. They'd probably both be a lot better off if he went that route. "I'll try."

"Maybe this will help. I'm going to have my date invite a friend to the cabin. You need a romantic interest."

He needed *something*! It was selfish of him to act on the desire he felt for Phoenix. They'd been so young when Lori Mansfield died. He felt like a completely different person these days—and felt the past shouldn't preclude them from what they might become as adults.

But how could he ever expect Phoenix to get past something like that, something that had taken such a huge part of her life?

"Thanks," he said, and disconnected.

Fortunately, the bracelet orders kept rolling in. That was a bright spot. Phoenix was earning some much-needed money, and she was earning more of it than she'd ever dreamed possible. She'd tried to distract herself from what had happened in the pool on Saturday night by concentrating on her work. She'd put in hour after hour on Sunday and did the same on Monday—until she went over to Kyle's that evening. Then she checked Facebook to see if she'd heard from Jake and found a message asking if she was coming to his game for sure.

She wrote back to say she was. She left it at that, but she hadn't heard from Riley since he'd dropped her off after the barbecue and hadn't figured out how she was going to get there. They'd be smarter to avoid each other than to drive together. Maybe he'd come to the same conclusion.

But they had a son. That made a certain amount of contact inevitable.

Kyle came in to the office to check on her when she was signing off.

"You getting rich yet?" he asked as he breezed into the office.

"I'm richer than I was," she joked. "Especially since you won't allow me to pay you back for the clothes you bought me."

He'd taped an envelope to the computer she used, and it had contained the torn-up check.

"You can let me do you a nice deed."

"What do you call all the rides you've given me?"

"That's no trouble. And it looks as if you're about finished here, so—" he pulled out his truck keys "—you'll be glad to know I'm heading right past your place again."

She grinned at him. "Your timing is impeccable. Too impeccable for me to fall for that."

He grinned at her. "Just get in the truck."

"Why are you being so nice?"

"Because we're friends, and that's the type of thing friends do."

She slung her purse over her shoulder. "What I don't understand is *why* you're my friend. I know how close you are to Riley. Doesn't it feel a bit like you're consorting with the enemy?"

"What are you talking about? Riley's your friend, too. He's told me as much."

If he was just a friend, he wouldn't have stuck his hand down her pants. But she didn't want to think about that. It was hard enough to force the memory out of her mind when she went to bed at night and had to get through all those hours until dawn. "He's the father of my child."

Kyle sorted through some mail he found on his desk. "Which makes it even luckier that you can be civil to each other."

"True." She motioned at the bracelet she'd made him. "You don't have to wear that every day. I won't be offended if you don't."

"I wear it because I like it. Jake does the same. The orders you're getting should tell you they're in high demand."

They seemed to be gaining popularity. She had no idea how long that might be the case, but she planned to make the most of it while she could. "You haven't changed your mind about going to Jake's game tomorrow, have you?" she asked.

"'Fraid not. I have that work commitment. Why? You need a ride?"

"I was hoping to catch one if I could. But…don't worry about it. I'll figure out something else."

"You don't want to go with Riley?"

She cleared her throat. "It's not that I don't want to. I just…I haven't heard from him, and I don't have an easy way to contact him."

That wasn't really the problem. It was a handy excuse, though, which was why she was so startled when he took out his phone, pressed a button and handed it to her. "Now you do."

Oh, jeez… She almost handed it back. But Riley answered immediately.

"What's up?"

Her mouth went so dry it was difficult to speak. "It's…Phoenix."

There was a slight pause, then he said, "How are you?"

"Good. You?"

"Fine."

She turned away from Kyle so he wouldn't see the anxiety on her face. "I was wondering if…if maybe I could still catch a ride to Jacob's game tomorrow."

"Of course."

"Thanks. What time are you planning to leave? Would you like me to meet you somewhere in town to make it easier?"

"No. I can pick you up at your place. I'll be there at three."

"I'll be ready."

"You're calling from Kyle's phone."

She glanced over her shoulder at his friend. "Yeah, I'm at his place right now."

"I'm not going to let it bother me," he said.

"What?" she asked, surprised and a little unclear about that statement.

"Never mind. I'll see you tomorrow," he replied, and was gone.

"Problem solved?" Kyle asked as she returned his phone.

That problem, maybe. But the way she'd melted inside at the sound of Riley's voice once again pointed out that she was fighting something *much* bigger than how to get around without a car. Maybe it made her the stupidest or craziest woman in the world, but she just couldn't get over him. That was all there was to it.

17

Buddy was sitting at the kitchen table, wearing a cast on his right hand, when Riley arrived. From what Riley had heard around town, he claimed it wasn't from their fight, but it had to be. Riley remembered dodging a blow that landed on the cinder-block wall behind him. Judging by the sound Buddy had made, and the way the blood had drained from his face, that was when he'd broken it. He just didn't want everyone to know he'd gotten the worst of their little skirmish. It worked against his tough-guy image that a smaller and far less experienced fighter had walked away without serious injury.

But that broken hand was probably the reason Riley *hadn't* gotten hurt. Buddy had hardly been able to swing at him afterward.

"Thanks for coming, Riley." Corinne's expression was cooler than he'd ever seen, and the set of her mouth told him she was as angry with him as Buddy was. She was just trying to put a civil veneer on it.

"No problem." He handed her the wine he'd brought. "I'm sorry that…that everyone's having such a difficult time."

"Hi, honey." His mother was there, sitting on the sofa

with his father, who also said hello. Helen scooted over to the middle, and patted the spot next to her. "Come sit with us."

Corinne's husband was quite a bit older than she was, but they seemed to have a happy marriage. Although he wasn't the father of her children—her first marriage had ended in divorce a couple of decades ago—he was supportive of the entire family. Like Riley's own father, he didn't talk much. He was quiet, even-keeled. Riley had always liked B.J. far more than the emotional Corinne.

Riley hoped he'd still like him after tonight.

"Can I get you a drink?" Lori's older sister and her sister's husband were there, too, along with their three children, who were in middle school. Riley didn't appreciate that there were young people involved in this. As far as he was concerned, this was an adult matter. Phoenix didn't need the next generation bullying her, too. But the Mansfields thought they were about to discuss a public menace, so they had a completely different take on Phoenix.

"Nothing for me," Riley said. "But thanks."

Corinne perched on the edge of her husband's recliner, and B.J. used the remote to turn off the TV. The sudden silence felt deafening, with so much tension in the air.

"I'm sorry you felt you had to get physical with Buddy at the coffee shop," she said. "Would you like to tell us what made you hit him?"

Riley reminded himself that these were good people, not only his mother's friends but fellow citizens he'd long associated with and admired. They wouldn't be acting so unreasonably if they didn't feel they had sufficient cause, if they weren't still grappling with losing a member of their family to what they perceived as another person's willful act. Riley had had a front row seat to their pain and loss, and he'd always felt terrible for them. But getting to know Phoenix again had shown him that the situation wasn't as clear-cut as they thought.

"Buddy must've provoked him." His mother inserted that protective tidbit before he could respond.

Riley had been here for five minutes, and it was already mother defending son against mother defending son. He didn't want to be the one to drive a wedge between them, but...*someone* had to stand up for Phoenix. "He was pushing around a woman. Not only that, he caused her to drop the only possession she owned of any value."

"It wasn't just a woman, it was my sister's *killer*," Buddy said. "So don't expect us to feel sorry for her. And I was just trying to talk to her. What happened to the laptop wasn't *my* fault."

Immediately outraged by this lie, Riley was about to respond when Corinne raised a hand, suggesting he let her talk first. "Buddy shouldn't have followed her into the bathroom," she said. "We'll give you that. But you know what he's been through. You know what Phoenix has done to our family. You can't understand how his pain and anger might momentarily overcome his good sense? You couldn't let other people—people who aren't so closely connected to our family—handle the situation?"

"I could if anyone else was willing to step up," Riley responded. "But I haven't found a single person, besides maybe her mother and a couple of friends of mine, who's on her side. And Lizzie isn't the strongest of defenders. I'm sorry it has to be me, but I won't allow Buddy or anyone else to torment Phoenix. It won't bring

Lori back. And Phoenix has served seventeen years of her life for that incident. She claims she's innocent. What if she's telling the truth?"

"Surely you're not serious!" Corinne said.

He didn't want to argue. There was no way to get anywhere with that, no way to establish, without doubt, what had happened. "Even if she *was* guilty, that's beside the point. Two wrongs don't make a right. I don't mean to sound callous but what Buddy's been doing to Phoenix is illegal. First of all, Jake was in that car. But even if he hadn't been, you can't run someone off the road, and you can't physically threaten someone—no matter who they are."

Buddy bolted to his feet. "I would never seriously hurt her. She's the one who jumped into that ditch when I was driving the Excursion. When she looked back and saw me, she…freaked out."

"Because you were acting like you were going to cause an accident! And don't tell me otherwise. Like I said, my son was there. He told me what happened."

"I was just messing around!" Buddy's grimace, as well as his voice, implied that Riley was overreacting. "And the laptop—she dropped that herself. I didn't touch it."

"You knocked it out of her hands, and it was all she had to be able to run her business."

"Business?" he echoed. "Like she's got anything going on!"

Riley guessed she'd soon be making more than Buddy, but he bit his tongue.

"Anyway, who gives a shit about her stupid computer or her business!" he shouted. "She's a murderer. Why are we suddenly so concerned with what she does or doesn't have?"

Riley's jaw was clenched so hard he had a difficult time speaking. "You'd better leave her alone—and my son, too. Or we're going to continue to have problems."

"Buddy would *never* hurt Jacob!" Corinne exclaimed as if she was offended by the mere suggestion.

"He almost did." This came from Riley's father. Riley was surprised when he spoke up but probably shouldn't have been. His parents were as protective of Jacob as he was.

Buddy rolled his eyes. "That's bullshit."

"What's your stake in this, Riley?" Allison, Buddy's sister, piped up. "Why are you taking it on yourself to protect her? She let you down, as much as anyone, when she killed Lori and saddled you with a child to raise alone. I'll bet anything she got pregnant on purpose, to trap you."

"That isn't true!" he said.

"How do you know?" she asked.

"Because I was there, too, remember? She wasn't the one trying to get in *my* pants. She was a virgin before I came along."

That set them back—and probably embarrassed his mother. She covered her face and shook her head but the truth was the truth. It was time to show everyone the *other* side, the things Phoenix did that made her seem perfectly normal and not a young woman unhinged by jealousy.

"You give her too much credit," Corinne snapped.

"And you don't give her enough," Riley retorted. "She was barely eighteen years old, pregnant and recently dumped by her baby's father. Most girls wouldn't be completely rational in that situation. She was frightened, panicked, hurt. But that doesn't make her guilty of anything. So, as tragic as Lori's death was, I say we live and let live rather than risk tormenting an innocent person, especially someone who's been through so much."

"You don't believe the testimony you heard in court?" Allison's husband, Jon, asked. "You think it was someone *else's* car that ran Lori down?"

"No, but someone else was in the vehicle with her," he replied. "That creates room for doubt."

"That person was Penny Sawyer, and she's confirmed that Phoenix drove into Lori," Jon said.

"Penny could've yanked the wheel herself," Riley pointed out.

"She had no reason to, so it's unlikely that she did."

Riley scooted forward. "It's still a possibility we have to consider. You don't know Phoenix."

"How come you're suddenly so sure of her character?" Allison demanded. "She's been gone for seventeen years!"

His mother placed a hand on his back. "Riley, you've always had a soft heart. I'm afraid your empathy is getting the better of you."

"It's not that. The girl I dated in high school—and the woman I'm dealing with now—would never harm anyone." He focused on one face and then the next "Look, you guys have a great family. I happen to have a great family, too. We're the lucky ones. Phoenix has never had much of anything. We're all aware of what Lizzie's like. And that Phoenix's father has never been part of her life. That her brothers took off as soon as they were old enough to get by on their own. Whatever her sins are, she's been deprived of enough. Why can't we move on? We don't have any other choice, anyway— not really. The state has done all it's going to do to punish Phoenix. We need to let that be enough."

"Easy for you to say," Corinne muttered.

"She's not welcome in Whiskey Creek," Buddy insisted. "Why should I have to run into my sister's killer wherever I go?"

"Because the law gives you no choice," Riley said. "If it helps, Phoenix told me she would go elsewhere if she could. But she can't talk her mother into leaving. Lizzie's phobias prevent her from being able to walk out of that filthy trailer. That's how hostile the world feels to her. She's too big to fit in a car, anyway."

"And whose fault is that?" Buddy yelled.

Riley wanted to punch him again. Corinne must've accurately read that desire because she got up.

"Buddy, take it easy. As unfair as it seems for Phoenix to be walking around as free as a bird when Lori will never see another sunrise, Riley's right about our legal limitations." She looked at Riley. "But what I want to know is this. Why didn't you come out as an advocate for Phoenix before now?"

"You mean when I was eighteen and being told by everyone that she wasn't worthy to be my girlfriend? That she was a terrible person—a murderer? I was pretty freaked out by Lori's death, not to mention the fact that I was going to be a father to a child whose mother was the one person in town *everyone* hated."

"But now you're convinced she's a good person?" Allison asked. "What changed?"

"I regret that I never stood up for her before. Maybe I could've stopped an innocent person from going to prison if I'd been older, stronger, more determined and less trusting of everyone else's opinion."

Allison's upper lip curled. "Oh, my God! You're going too far. You act like you're in love with her again."

His mother gasped. "No, he doesn't! He's absolutely not!"

But Riley couldn't deny it. He hoped that wasn't the case, yet he knew he felt *something*, and it was stronger than it should be.

"That's my business. Either way, I want to make it perfectly clear that I won't allow Phoenix to be bullied or tormented any longer." He turned to his mother. "Mom, I'm sorry this didn't work out the way you wanted," he said, and strode out before they could even sit down to dinner.

The next afternoon, Phoenix came out of her trailer before he could park and go to the door. Obviously, she'd been watching for him. He was grateful she was ready, since he didn't want to be late for the game. They had a forty-minute drive. But he had bigger concerns. He kept thinking about the argument he'd gotten into at the Mansfields' and worrying that her troubles weren't over.

Then there was the sight of her in those cutoffs he and Kyle had bought... That was going to make it harder to remember his determination to be her friend and only her friend.

"Why'd you have to turn out to be so damn pretty?" he muttered. For a second, he feared her beauty was blinding him. That maybe the Mansfields and his parents were right.

But he rejected that thought almost immediately. It wasn't her looks that attracted him. Not entirely. He'd dated a number of pretty women over the years. What Phoenix had was grace, and that was far more enduring and difficult to find, especially since she maintained that grace in the ugliest of circumstances.

As he leaned over to open the door for her, she gave him a tentative smile.

"Thank you." After she climbed in, she put a sack

between them. "I appreciate you coming all the way out here to pick me up."

Her sweetness was so refreshing. He tried to forget what had been said at the Mansfields'. He didn't want to let that continue to ruin his day, not when just being around her made him feel good. "Not a problem. Jake's really excited for you to see him play."

"I can't wait."

Riley indicated the sack. "What's this? Dinner?"

"Those are homemade cookies for the team," she said proudly. "Now that I have a bit of money, chocolate chips don't seem to cost their weight in gold anymore. So…I thought I'd try my hand at baking."

He found it endearing that she was so pleased to offer Jake this simple gift. She took nothing for granted, not even chocolate chips. She was so different from what the Mansfields believed… "You've taken up baking?"

"I've made the attempt. I hope they turned out okay. I mean…they aren't the best. I would've started over, but I didn't have time."

She seemed genuinely worried. "You don't think they taste good?" he asked.

"Maybe they do," she said with a laugh. "I couldn't make up my mind."

"You can't go wrong with that much butter and sugar. I'm sure the boys will love them."

She took the container out of the sack. "Would you like to try one?"

He could tell as soon as he did that they were almost burned. But that wasn't the worst of it. She'd used too much baking soda or salt. If she hadn't been sitting there, he would've spit out the bite he'd just taken.

"What do you think?" she asked, eyes wide.

He managed to choke it down. "They're…delicious."

"*Really?* Because I don't want Jake to be embarrassed if they're not."

He was also nervous about how the boys might react—but not so much for Jacob's sake. Although he didn't want his son to be embarrassed any more than she did, he knew she'd be the one to feel wounded if they complained, refused to eat them, threw them at one another or started teasing Jake.

"There's no danger of that." He manufactured enough conviction to be credible, but turned into Just Like Mom's as soon as they reached town.

"Why are you stopping?" she asked when he parked.

He chose a spot where she wouldn't be able to see the entrance to the restaurant. "I have to use the restroom."

"Why didn't you say so? You could've gone at the trailer."

"Just sit tight. I'll be right back." He hurried inside and bought two dozen chocolate chip cookies, which he hid in the bushes. Then he went back in and ordered a coffee, as though he'd just decided to get one, and returned to the truck.

He knocked on Phoenix's window.

She looked completely baffled as she rolled it down. "What's wrong?"

"Nothing. I ordered a coffee," he told her. "Would you mind going inside to wait for it while I pull across the street to get gas?"

"You want coffee in the height of the afternoon?" she asked. "Aren't you hot enough?"

"It's been a long day at work. I need the caffeine."

She unlatched her seat belt. "O-ka-ay…" She stretched out the word as if she thought he was crazy to stop for something so inconsequential when they were anxious to get to Jacob's game.

Riley waited for her to go into the restaurant before dumping the bad cookies in the nearby Dumpster and filling her plastic container with the ones he'd bought.

Fortunately, he had a full tank, because she was coming out with his coffee when he pulled closer to the door. "All set?"

"If you are." She handed him his coffee before taking the passenger seat.

He hoped she wouldn't decide to have one of her own cookies and notice the difference. He wasn't sure what he'd say then.

"We're getting a late start," she complained.

"We're on our way now."

"What is it?"

He was having a hard time stifling a chuckle, but after going to all that last-minute effort, he wasn't about to give himself away. Sobering, he shook his head. "Nothing. Just relax and enjoy the ride."

Once they arrived at the ballpark, Phoenix grabbed her cookies and hopped out of the truck. Her experience at the last game she'd attended hadn't been a good one, but Ponderosa was far enough away that she couldn't imagine there'd be many people from Whiskey Creek— just the parents of the players. And she hoped they'd be blissfully unaware of her identity and background, or at least mind their own business.

Someone she didn't recognize stopped Riley as they approached the stands. From what she could gather, it was another player's dad, eager to analyze what the Miners had to do to beat the opposing team.

When Riley paused to chat, Phoenix kept moving. This was her chance to put some distance between them and, if she was lucky, avoid becoming a point of interest. If it didn't look like she was with Riley, she probably wouldn't even be noticed in such a neutral place. So she acted as if it was mere coincidence that they'd been walking beside each other.

Because the home side was packed, she changed her mind about sitting there and climbed into the mostly empty bleachers on the visitors' side. She wasn't planning to approach Jake with the cookies right away. That would have to happen after the game, while the team was—hopefully—celebrating a win.

Selecting what appeared to be an unobtrusive spot, she sat down. Then she slowly released her breath. No one was staring at her. For the moment, she felt safely anonymous and thought she might be able to watch Jake without incident.

But the next thing she knew, Riley was making his way up the stands, coming toward her.

She gave him a subtle shake of her head to let him know she didn't expect him to keep her company. She actually preferred he sit somewhere far away. But if he recognized her attempt to dissuade him, he ignored it, even waved to various people who greeted him as he climbed up, which only attracted more attention.

Obviously, he was as popular as ever. It didn't help that Jacob was the team's starting pitcher. That came with its own cachet.

Eventually, after making sure he'd greeted everyone, he sat down beside her.

"What are you doing?" she whispered, since the people who'd said hello to him were now craning their necks to get a good look at her.

"What do you mean 'what am I doing'?" he asked.

"I understand that you're trying to be kind by befriending the outcast and all that. It's a noble thing to do, and if it involved anyone but me, I'd admire it. But I'd rather you didn't draw any more attention to me. So…could you please move somewhere else?"

"No," he said. "People have to get used to your presence. Might as well make it obvious, while we've got a small group to start with, that you're back and attending the games."

But he wasn't the one who should be making that decision. "I'd rather not be so…conspicuous, thanks."

"Just smile. You've served time. There's no way to avoid being conspicuous."

"I was managing it quite well a minute ago."

"Only because people didn't realize who you were. But they would if we were playing at home, and you want to be able to come and go as you please there, too, don't you?"

She clasped her hands tightly in her lap. "I'm hoping that will come with time."

"This is like a Band-Aid, Phoenix. Might as well rip it off and get it over with."

"You can rip off your own Band-Aids," she grumbled. "Leave me to mine."

He nudged her. "I won't let anyone mistreat you."

She looked at him, then glanced away. "There's no reason for you to be involved. Who said *you* should have to protect me?"

"I wish I'd done a better job of it seventeen years ago, I can tell you that."

She studied the ball field so people wouldn't know they were talking about anything more important than the game that was about to start. "You couldn't have stopped what happened to me."

"I didn't have to add to your problems."

"You fell in love with someone else, a better candidate. Lori was prettier, more popular, more successful in school. She had the right family, too—one that was close to your own. Those were the best credentials for a boy like you."

"Credentials?"

"What else would you call them? Attributes?" She pictured Lori walking along the side of the road in the minutes leading up to that terrible, fateful event and cringed, as she always did. It had taken her a decade not to feel nauseous. Just being in the car was bad enough, but to be blamed...

"I wish she wasn't gone, you know. I wish I'd never said a bad thing about her. Never pointed her out. Then maybe Penny wouldn't have made that joke, and I wouldn't have laughed, and she wouldn't have grabbed the wheel, and—and maybe you'd be married to Lori Mansfield today."

"I wish Lori was here, too." From the sound of his voice, she could tell that he was also facing forward. "For her sake, her family's sake, for your sake. But I wouldn't have married her. I didn't love her."

Suddenly, Phoenix wasn't so concerned about the attention she was attracting. Her heart pounded with the need to proclaim her innocence. Although she'd fought for years to overcome that compulsion, had learned that the longer and louder she protested, the guiltier she looked, the temptation welled up from time to time. It seemed so unfair that no matter what she said, no matter what she did, everyone remained convinced that she'd intentionally harmed another human being.

"I also wish you could believe me," she said softly. "That you could somehow know I didn't hit her on purpose."

She expected the old "I'll reserve judgment but I'm

not quite sure you deserve it" type of response she'd gotten before—not only from him but from others. That hurt almost as badly as open disbelief or even scorn. But she was surprised by his sincerity when he said, "I do."

She brought a hand to her chest. "Believe me, you mean? You know I didn't turn the wheel?"

He looked at her. "That's exactly what I mean."

"Hey, is that Jacob's mom?" someone called.

Phoenix had the presence of mind to slide over so they wouldn't appear too cozy. And while he confirmed her identity and various people came up to meet her, she smiled and nodded and pretended she was just like every other mom. She quickly understood that Riley had sat with her on purpose. He was establishing the tone for how the other parents should treat her, making sure they understood they'd be crossing *him* if they didn't accept her. That would have seemed monumental on its own, and yet it was dwarfed by her intense relief.

Someone finally believed her. *Really* believed her. And it wasn't just anyone.

It was Riley.

When the game ended, Riley insisted on bringing the cookies to Jake, and Phoenix didn't argue. He could tell she wasn't particularly interested in entering the fray. She was happy to stand by the fence and wave at Jake, who acknowledged her with a big smile.

Once Jake took over the cookies, they were quickly consumed, and several of the boys called out to tell her how delicious they were.

Disaster averted...

"They loved them," she said as he led the way out of the park.

Riley smiled at the wonder in her voice. "The cookies?"

She held up the empty container. "Yeah. They're all gone."

"I see. Not a crumb left."

"I'll have to bake more for the next game."

At that, Riley almost missed a step. "Sure. Of course. That would be wonderful. But...maybe next time you can bake them at my place."

"Why?" she asked, sounding confused.

"So you can show me how it's done." And he could make sure they turned out. At this point, he actually had more experience baking cookies than she did.

She seemed flattered. "You liked them that much?"

He liked *her* that much, or he wouldn't have gone to the effort of replacing the salty, rocklike results of her own baking. "Yeah."

"I'll help you," she said. "But don't think I have any special magic. I just followed the recipe on the back of the chocolate chip package."

"You've got a lot of magic," he joked.

"I do?" She gave him a quick glance. "What kind?"

The kind that had him thinking about her all the time. "You really won't come to the cabin for my birthday a week from Friday?" he asked instead of answering.

"Will Jake be there?"

She was obviously wondering if it would be a family affair. "No, he'll be at Tristan's. This is a...a friend thing." Technically it was a "friends with dates or marriage partners" thing, but he didn't want to scare her away.

"With your regular group?"

"Yeah."

"Where's the cabin?"

"Near Lake Melones. It's actually Simon O'Neal's cabin. You know him, right? The movie star?"

"No way!"

"'Fraid so. You didn't hear?"

"I've been out of the loop," she said drily. "Actually, I was never in the same loop you were."

He ignored that. "Gail DeMarco, one of the people I hung out with in high school…"

"I remember her. We had health class together."

"Well, after college, she went to LA and opened a PR firm. She did really well—had several big-name actors on her roster, including Simon. And they eventually got together."

She rolled her eyes. "You'd think my mother could've shared that with me. That's kind of big news for our little town."

"Your mother wrote you while you were in prison?"

She kicked a rock as they walked. "I told you she's not as bad as she seems."

"How often did she get in touch?"

"Once a week. She's about the only person I ever heard from, so…I guess it shouldn't be any big shock that I'd feel some loyalty to her."

He winced. "You should hate me."

"I wish I could," she said, but she grinned at him as they arrived at his truck.

"So what do you say?" he asked after he unlocked the doors and they climbed in.

"About the cabin? Will Simon and Gail be there?"

"It was their idea," he replied as he started the engine.

"Lake Melones is quite a drive."

He backed out of the parking space. "I'd take you, of course."

"But that means I'd be there for the whole weekend."

They were coming closer to acknowledging that it would be a date. Riley knew that wasn't in keeping with his decision to settle for friendship. But she was the one he wanted to take, so it was hard not to ask her. "It's a big cabin."

She seemed tempted but ultimately shook her head. "No, I'm getting a lot of bracelet orders. I'd better stay home and work. What would your parents think if they heard I showed up at your birthday party, anyway?"

He shrugged. "There'll be loads of people there."

"I don't even have a swimsuit."

"I'd be happy to get you one."

She shot him a warning look. "And you know I wouldn't be happy if you did. I'll buy my own, when I can afford to spend money on extras like that."

"*Extras?* With summer coming on, most people our age would consider it a necessity."

"I'd rather help out with Jake. I can finally do that, and it feels great."

"You're too stubborn for your own good," he muttered.

After that, they talked about the game, how well Jake had played and how excited he'd been about winning. They'd also talked about whether she'd attend the next one, even though it was at home. She said she'd probably wait, that they should take her inclusion in Whiskey Creek society in stages, and he left it at that. He didn't like the idea that she might be insulted, and coming to a home game definitely opened her up to certain things he wouldn't be able to control.

"So when are you going to make Jake and me that

spaghetti dinner?" he asked as he pulled up to her trailer.

She opened the door but didn't get out. "How about on Sunday?"

"I'm free. Jake's usually available on Sundays, too, but I'll check with him." He wanted to have dinner with her regardless, but he hoped she made better spaghetti than she did cookies.

"Let me know."

"I will." He put the transmission in Park. "Would you mind if I quickly checked out your trailer?"

She hesitated. "For…"

He thought of the hostility in his earlier exchange with the Mansfields. "I don't trust Buddy."

"Everything's been pretty quiet lately."

"It'll just take a second," he said, and felt much better once he'd walked through her place and saw that it appeared to be undisturbed.

He'd said good-night and was about to return to his truck when she surprised him by slipping her arms around his waist and giving him a quick squeeze.

"Thanks for everything but…I especially want to thank you for saying you believe me about…what happened seventeen years ago," she said. Then she smiled as he stepped outside and she closed the door.

18

"You're shopping for a *bikini*?" Jake asked.

Riley had known Jake was in the kitchen, making himself a snack before bed. But he'd been too immersed in what he was doing to realize his son had come up behind him.

He minimized the website where he'd been browsing for swimsuits, but that left Phoenix's Etsy site on the screen, which was worse. He was so tired of seeing Jake and Kyle wearing one of Phoenix's bracelets when *he* didn't have one that he'd been tempted to place an order. He'd actually considered placing *several* orders so she'd have the money to buy a suit and take the weekend off for his birthday. He just hadn't figured out where he could have those bracelets shipped without revealing himself.

"And aren't those Mom's bracelets?" Jake sounded even more perplexed.

"I wanted to see what she's working on." He got up to grab a beer. He was hoping to distract Jake from the computer. Closing out of Etsy, too, as if he'd been caught doing something he shouldn't, would only make his interest that much more obvious.

"So that's what you've been doing all night?"

"No. Of course not. I've been working, for the most part." He *had* done some work, but he'd also spent more time than he wanted to admit on sites that related, in one way or another, to Phoenix. First, he'd done some cursory searching for Penny Sawyer. He wanted to talk to her, see what she had to say about Lori's death now that seventeen years had passed. He couldn't help wondering if she'd change her story.

But he hadn't found anyone by the name of Penny Sawyer, so he assumed she was married and going by a different last name. Or she wasn't on Facebook, which was where he'd thought he might be able to track her down.

When he hadn't succeeded, he'd migrated to Phoenix's Etsy shop, considered ordering some bracelets, then set that aside to shop for swimsuits. He'd come across several options he thought would look great on Phoenix's small, compact body, but he wasn't sure what to do, since she'd made it clear that he'd better not buy her one.

"Mom's doing pretty well, isn't she?" Jake asked. "I mean, she left me a message on Facebook that she's got forty dollars she wants to give me. Do you think I can take it?"

"I don't see why not. It's fine to accept a little something every once in a while, if she offers. Just don't do it often and be careful not to let her give you too much. I'm sure you've noticed that she'd be willing to sacrifice everything. But she needs her money—she's got some serious rebuilding to do."

"That's what I was thinking. I told her I don't need anything, that it wasn't necessary. But she wouldn't listen."

Forty dollars would have been half the price of a

swimsuit, and Jake had everything he needed. But Riley understood. Jake was Phoenix's priority right now.

Jake maximized the swimsuit website on Riley's computer while Riley leaned up against the counter. "So which one are you going to get?" A mischievous grin curved his lips when he glanced up. "I think you'd look good in the white one, but please don't wear it in front of *my* friends."

Riley scowled at him. "Stop it."

Jake continued to chuckle, just to needle him, but when he'd had enough of that, he grew serious. "You like her, don't you?"

"Phoenix?"

"No, my English teacher," he said with a roll of his eyes.

As usual, Jake wouldn't let him get away with anything. Kids were so damn smart these days, so quick to catch on to the smallest nuance. "Okay, yes. I like her."

His cheek dimpled with another grin. "I could tell when we were in the pool."

Riley was already up against his parents' disapproval—and he could imagine what everyone else he knew would think. But he wasn't sure what Jake might say. "Does it bother you?"

"It worries me," he admitted. "I definitely didn't see it coming, 'cause the last time you guys got together things didn't work out so good."

"It wasn't all bad. We created you. And you know what you mean to both of us."

Jake pulled out a chair and sank into it. "Do you think she'd ever take you back?"

"No."

"I'm not convinced of that. I can tell she doesn't *want* to care about you, but…"

Riley took a sip of his beer. "But…"

"She does."

"How do you know?"

"You'd have to be blind *not* to see it. In her opinion, you can walk on water."

Riley could see that she held him in high esteem. She treated him as if he was someone special and always had. But she'd lost all confidence in her ability to be loved, and in his ability to love her. Without that confidence she'd never respond to him. "Even if that's true, she'd be better off if I left her alone."

"How do you figure?"

"I hurt her before. Badly. I don't want to do that again."

"Then don't," he said.

To Jake, life was just that simple. Riley shook his head. "When you get with another person…you don't always know how it'll end. We've got a lot of ground to cover before we make any serious decisions."

"You have to start somewhere."

"This is different because of what she's been through and my role in it. And if we become a couple, it would affect you—whether it works or not."

He lifted both hands. "Don't use me as your excuse."

"My *excuse*?"

"To play it safe. You've never been together, not in my lifetime, so I can't be too disappointed if it *doesn't* work out. I think you should take the chance."

Letting his breath go in a long sigh, he studied the liquid in his bottle. "We'll see."

Jacob dropped by Phoenix's place after practice on Wednesday, after his home game on Thursday and after school, since practice was canceled, on Friday. Phoenix had wanted to have his room perfect before he saw it, but he became a part of that process instead. They painted together and fixed things together. She was so impressed with what Riley had taught him. Jacob could do almost anything when it came to home repairs or construction. At only sixteen, he was teaching her what they could do to improve her home.

Sometimes she'd make him dinner if Riley wasn't back from work yet. She didn't have a TV or gaming system, so the home improvements gave them something to do while they talked.

On Friday, he called Tristan and had him come out, since Tristan wanted a bracelet. Then Jake used his smartphone to go on Facebook and show her the girl he was taking to prom.

Phoenix loved every minute she got to spend with her son. It all seemed rather idyllic—until he was leaving Friday night. She'd just walked him to his Jeep when Lizzie called out from her landing.

"Aren't you ever going to come see your grandma?"

Obviously, she wasn't talking to Phoenix. And, as usual, her voice sounded harsh. Guessing that Jake wouldn't know how to respond, Phoenix whispered, "Maybe you could say a quick hi. You don't have to do any more than that."

He was just getting used to having his mother in his life. She didn't want to make him uncomfortable by trying to force a relationship with his grandmother, too. But at the same time, she knew how much it would mean to her mother to see him.

With an uncertain glance, he moved into the clearing. "Hi."

Lizzie gave him the once-over from her safe place behind the door. "You're getting big."

He shoved his hands in his pockets. "I'll be a senior next year."

"You've been coming by a lot."

There was a brief silence, but before Phoenix could jump in, he said, "My mom lives here now."

"*I've* lived here forever," Lizzie said, the statement an accusation of neglect.

"Mom!" Phoenix began, but Jake cut her off.

"Right. We've never really had the chance to get to know each other."

She said nothing, and he pulled his keys out again. But she stopped him. "I have five dogs if you'd like to see them."

"He'll have to see them another time, Mom. He's got to head home," Phoenix said, but Jake surprised her by starting toward Lizzie's trailer.

"I can take a few minutes," he told her in an aside.

Phoenix couldn't help feeling panicked at the thought of him going inside that house. She was afraid he'd be so put off by what he saw that he'd be hesitant to come by again for fear that Lizzie would demand he visit with her, too.

"Jake, she has a problem," she murmured, and insisted he wait while she got the dogs herself.

Jake was sitting on the trailer steps when she returned with her mother's pets. He seemed to like them; he played with them while Lizzie stood in the doorway, peering out. She'd ask him a question every few seconds, and he'd answer. Overall, it went much better than Phoenix had feared. But when her mother suggested he come in to see her hamsters, she intervened with more authority.

"No, that's it for tonight," she said. "I don't want to make his father wonder why he's not home."

"Can't he call? Doesn't he have a cell phone like all the other kids these days?" Lizzie demanded. "If not, I've got a landline."

Apparently, she was enjoying Jake's company, even though Phoenix knew she'd deny it later.

"He has called," Phoenix said. "He was supposed to go home thirty minutes ago. Let's not get him in trouble." Jake had checked in with his dad, so it wasn't imperative that he leave right away. But she'd encouraged him to get moving because she hadn't wanted to make Riley feel their son was spending too much time with her.

"Fine!" With that, Lizzie called in the dogs and slammed the door.

"I'm sorry. She should've at least said goodbye," Phoenix whispered, but Jacob grinned as if he didn't mind and took her hand as they walked to his truck.

"I'm so lucky to have a son like you," she blurted when he let go. "I love you."

She'd meant to hold back that last part. She was afraid it was too soon, that he'd squirm in discomfort. But he turned to give her a hug.

"I'm glad you're home," he said.

"I hope my being here isn't upsetting your father. You'd tell me if anything I'm doing is causing you problems with him, right?"

"You're not causing problems. Dad really likes you. He's looking forward to dinner on Sunday."

"I bet!" she said with a laugh.

Jake opened his door. "I'm serious. He's mentioned it to me several times."

"I didn't mean to be sarcastic," she said. "I like him, too. You've got a good father."

He studied his keys before looking up at her again. "Do you think if he ever asked you out you'd go?"

She'd been so careful to hide her feelings. Had Jake noticed something in the way she watched Riley or spoke about him?

"Oh, no," she said, shaking her head. "I'm not the right kind of woman for him."

"So...who would be the right kind of woman?" he asked.

"Someone without a rap sheet," she joked, hoping to keep this conversation from becoming too intense.

"You said you didn't kill Lori."

"I didn't. But your grandparents are close friends with the Mansfields, which puts your father in a tough spot. He wants to be fair to me, but doing that risks other important relationships."

"Sometimes, when you really want to be with someone, it's hard to worry about all that other stuff."

"I would never allow him to jeopardize those relationships even if he was willing to, which I'm sure he's not. He'll find someone eventually, but that won't be me." She wished Riley would hurry up and get himself a girlfriend. Maybe then it would be easier to convince her heart to follow her head.

Jake didn't seem to know where to go with that. "Well, I hope you won't be mad if he buys you a swimsuit."

"Why would he buy me a swimsuit?" she asked.

"Never mind," he said.

Phoenix could hardly keep her eyes open. After Jacob left, she'd ridden her bike over to Kyle's office to use one of his computers and had been there for most of the night. The sun would be rising in a couple of hours, and she had a long Saturday ahead of her making bracelets, but she didn't want to quit when she was so close to being done. Riley had emailed her a hundred or more photos of Jacob growing up, which she'd been using to make a digital album for Riley's birthday next weekend. Cara, the prison guard who'd helped her run her business when she was in the Central California Women's Facility, had brought one in to show off her grandchildren before Phoenix was released, and Phoenix had fallen in love with the concept.

She was afraid Riley might already have one, but she couldn't think of anything she could afford to give him that he might like as much. And there was a certain amount of artistry involved, so he couldn't have one *exactly* like hers.

The only problem was the difficulty of figuring out the program. Although the work was easy—once she'd learned how to import the photos, crop and turn them and use all the special graphics—this was the first album she'd ever attempted. It'd had taken hours to get each page the way she wanted it.

With a tired sigh, she checked the utilitarian clock that hung on the wall. It was nearly four. Kyle had stopped by to say hello and good-night when he went to bed around eleven. She wanted to be gone when he woke up. But he returned before she could leave, wearing nothing but some jeans he'd obviously pulled on so he could walk outside.

"You're still here?"

She minimized the photo album, which she'd been looking through one final time. Kyle would probably see it at Riley's birthday party. She planned to give it to Riley before he went to Lake Melones, if it came in time. But she didn't want Kyle to realize how long and hard she'd labored over it. The number of hours she'd invested would seem disproportionate to her relationship—or lack of a relationship—with Riley.

"I'm sorry," she said. "I'm almost finished."

"You don't have to apologize. It's not as if you're bothering me."

"Then why are you out of bed in the middle of the night?"

"I got up to go to the bathroom, saw the light and thought maybe you'd fallen asleep out here."

"No. But I'm getting anxious to find my bed."

He came up behind her. "What's so important that you'd be up all night?"

"Just bracelet orders, communicating with my buyers, that sort of thing. And Riley sent me some pictures of Jacob through the years. Most of them I'd never seen, so…I've been going through them."

"That's great. It seems like you and Riley are getting along."

"He's been much nicer than I anticipated. I know having me come home has been a little scary for him."

He folded his arms. "Since you're such an ogre."

She grinned at the playfulness in his voice. "According to some."

"Have you had any more trouble with Buddy?"

"Not since that incident at Black Gold."

"Hopefully, he got the message."

"I'm just going to stay away from him. Maybe he'll see that tormenting me is more trouble than it's worth."

"Why don't I give you a ride home while I'm up?"

"No, it's too late for that. Go back to bed. I've got my bike."

"We can throw it in the bed of my truck. We've done it before."

"It's only a mile and a half. It won't take me more than ten minutes."

"You'll lock up the office, then?"

"I will. I promise."

"Okay. See you tomorrow."

He turned to go, but she stopped him. "Kyle?"

He glanced back at her.

"You're a good man," she said. "Thank you for being so kind."

"I can tell you don't realize it yet, but you're someone special."

She had no idea what he meant. "In what way?"

"Most people in your situation would've let resentment and bitterness eat them alive. But you've managed to avoid that. As far as I'm concerned, someone like you will win out in the end," he replied.

"Win what?" she muttered as he walked out. Her problems certainly hadn't disappeared. But she couldn't complain. She finally had her freedom. She was establishing a relationship with Jacob. She was making a living in spite of her past. And it felt good to have earned Kyle's respect.

19

For probably the hundredth time, Phoenix stood back to study her dinner table. She'd managed to scrounge up enough dishes. They didn't all match, but she'd improvised as best she could and, to her eye, there was a certain panache in the way her settings had come together. She doubted Riley or Jacob would notice, but she was proud of what she'd accomplished by going out into the yard and searching, making a saucer into a butter dish, a double-handled pan into a bowl for the pasta, a wooden board covered by a cute dish towel into a platter for her garlic bread. She'd cut down an old gingham tablecloth and used the extra material for napkins. They were drinking out of mason jars. But if she didn't look closely enough to see all the imperfections, she thought her efforts had been well rewarded. The food smelled delicious with all the basil, thyme and oregano she'd put in her spaghetti sauce. She'd fed Jacob before, but it had never been an arranged, sit-down dinner—just some scrambled eggs, a bean and cheese burrito or a grilled cheese sandwich.

And she'd never fed Riley.

Satisfied, she hurried into the bathroom. She didn't want them to arrive before she could shower and change.

Forty-five minutes later, she was wearing her turquoise shirt with a pretty print skirt she'd found on sale in one of the tourist shops and was beginning to watch the clock. They were supposed to show up at seven, in fifteen minutes. She eyed her table again, straightened the fork next to Jacob's plate and rearranged the wildflowers she'd picked down by the creek and put in three mason jars she'd dipped in red paint and tied together with a bow for her centerpiece. Then she went into the kitchen to sprinkle grated Parmesan on the green salad and open the oven so her garlic bread wouldn't get too crusty before going into the living room to peer out the window.

At 6:55, Riley's truck turned into the drive and she felt a fresh riot of butterflies in her stomach. She had no idea why she was so nervous. They were just having a meal together. But she couldn't seem to make her heart beat at a reasonable pace.

Maybe she was afraid her mother would try to ruin the evening. Phoenix had debated whether to invite Lizzie, or try to have dinner there, but she couldn't see the four of them together. It was too soon for something like that. So she'd carried Lizzie's dinner over earlier and told her to warm it up in the microwave when she was hungry.

At their knock, she wanted to hurry but resisted. Counting to five, so she wouldn't seem too eager, she took a deep breath and opened the door. "Hi. Come on in."

Riley held a bottle of wine and some flowers, which he handed to her. "You look beautiful," he said.

He looked pretty good himself, freshly showered and dressed in khaki shorts with a brown V-neck cotton shirt that hugged his chest and brought out the gold flecks in his eyes.

"Thanks." She smiled but told herself not to take that kind of talk too seriously. He was being polite. People said things like that when they went to someone's house for dinner.

Forcing her gaze away from him, she addressed their son. "I hope everything turned out okay. As you know, I'm new at cooking so...tell me you didn't set your expectations too high."

Jacob gave her a hug despite the objects in her hands. "If your spaghetti sauce is even half as good as your cookies, we're going to love it."

Riley coughed. "Allergies," he said when she looked at him. "It smells great."

She went to find a container to put the flowers in. Unlike her flowers, these were "legitimate"—the kind you had to pay for.

"I have another game on Monday," Jake announced as she went through her cupboards.

"Is it an away game?"

"Yeah."

"I'll be there."

"You don't even know where it is."

"Doesn't matter," she said, and heard him chuckle.

While Jake went down the hall to the bathroom, Riley came to stand in the area where her kitchen opened out to the table. "Anything I can do to help?"

He could quit looking and smelling so good. That would make it easier to keep her mind where it needed to be.

When she couldn't find any kind of container to use as a vase, he brushed past her, washed out a large tomato sauce can she'd thrown in the garbage and stuck the flowers in that.

"Good eye," she said.

He winked at her. "Stick with me."

She ignored the implications of that statement despite the grin that gave it meaning.

"Can I do anything else?" he asked.

"I've got it under control. Have a seat. You hungry?"

"Starved."

"Well, this won't resemble any meal you've ever had at your mother's place, but…hopefully it'll be okay."

"I'm just happy to be here," he said, and he sounded so sincere she turned to glance at him.

"You look beautiful," he said again—only this time Jacob wasn't around to see his expression. He acted as if he could barely keep from touching her.

Deciding that, too, should be left without comment, she grabbed the old towel she'd been using in place of oven mitts so she could take out the bread. "Are you excited about your birthday next weekend?"

"I'd be more excited if you were coming to the cabin."

"It'll be better if I stay behind. Then I can help out with Jake. There's no reason he has to go to Tristan's, you know. He could come here, if he wants."

"Tristan's parents are taking the boys to San Francisco."

"So *he'll* be gone for the weekend, too?"

He studied her. "See? Jake won't need you. You might as well come with me."

"That would only confuse everyone," she said. Especially her.

"No, it wouldn't. There'll be a lot of people at the party. You'd just be one of the crowd."

She'd never been anywhere like that before, and she hadn't joined a group of people celebrating and having fun since high school. That tempted her. Besides, she had a fabulous gift for him. If only it would arrive in the mail…

But she shook her head. She couldn't see herself socializing with his crowd, couldn't imagine he'd enjoy the way everyone would stare at her. "Wish I could," she mumbled.

He rested his hands on her shoulders. "You can come, Phoenix. All you have to do is say yes."

He was close enough that she could feel the heat of his body, and that brought back the memory of how he'd touched her in the pool. "Sometimes I don't know if you're…teasing me…"

"Of course not!"

She was a little shocked at his outrage. "Or…or testing me…"

"For *what*?" he demanded.

"To make sure you're in the clear, I guess. That you don't have to worry about me getting…too attached."

His hands tightened. "I'm not afraid of that, Phoenix."

Then what was he doing? She knew what her mother would say—that he'd use her and toss her aside again. Phoenix hated to believe it, but he'd been acting as if he was still attracted to her, even though she had nothing that would appeal to a man like him. Was her mother right? Did he hope to receive physical benefits in exchange for being so kind about Jacob?

"Don't get spooked," he added. "For now, I'm inviting you to my party. That's all."

"But having me there would be asking for trouble."

"How?"

Had he forgotten what they'd done in the pool? How easily it could've gone further? "People would talk, for one thing."

"And say what?"

"That…that I haven't learned my lesson."

"Phoenix…"

Hearing the toilet flush and Jacob's step in the hall, she brought a finger to her lips and scooted around him for fear their son would see them standing so close.

Riley pressed his thumb and finger to the bridge of his nose as he heard Phoenix tell Jacob she'd made a chocolate cake. He'd rattled her; he could tell, especially as the night progressed. She focused solely on Jacob and made small talk about prom, which was coming up, his baseball practices, his games, his friends, the various colleges he was considering.

Riley ate in silence, and marveled that the food was so good. After those cookies she'd brought to Jake's game, he'd thought they'd have to choke down whatever she'd cooked. But he'd never had tastier spaghetti, and Jake liked her dinner as much as he did. Even the cake had turned out.

Phoenix gave them each second helpings of everything, including dessert, but ate very little herself. Riley decided that he shouldn't have urged her to go to the cabin. He'd upset her—and he could see why. She'd spent seventeen years berating herself for falling in love with him, and now he'd asked her to stick her hand back into the fire.

It was too soon for something like that. If he wanted to date her again, he needed to take it slow—slower than he'd ever taken it with any other woman. But that wasn't as easy as it sounded. He couldn't get her out of his head, and his constant impulse to touch her was driving him mad, especially since he was pretty sure she wanted the same thing. She'd acted like it in the pool. Just thinking about what she'd let him do that night made him hard.

After they'd finished eating, Jake went into the living room to do his chemistry homework and Riley insisted on giving Phoenix a hand cleaning up.

"Guests aren't supposed to do the dishes," she said. "Why don't you relax? See if Jake needs any help?"

"He's fine. I don't mind carrying in a few things."

He stacked the plates on the counter but couldn't decide what to do with the leftovers. She didn't seem to have any storage containers. He figured he could put some tinfoil over each serving bowl. She had tinfoil. But when he opened the fridge, he found it crammed with old mayonnaise and peanut butter jars full of—he took one out—more spaghetti sauce?

"Wow! Why'd you make so much?" He turned as she came in with their glasses.

She shrugged as if it wasn't any big deal, but she seemed a little embarrassed. "It took a few tries to get it right."

"You made spaghetti sauce over and over?"

"This is my first dinner party. I couldn't serve something that didn't taste good," she said as though anyone else would do the same thing.

But it was only for him and Jake! He pointed to the sea of jars in the fridge. "What's wrong with these?"

She frowned. "They didn't turn out. I'm not sure what I did wrong."

"Why are you saving them?"

"No sense wasting food. I'll eat them. I just need to buy some freezer bags."

So they were good enough for *her*. Riley didn't think he'd ever met a woman as sweet as Phoenix. Who would've thought he'd admire the town pariah more than any other citizen? It was almost laughable how much he'd dreaded her return, particularly when he compared his original reaction to the way he felt now. "Well, you figured out the secret," he said. "The sauce was delicious."

"Thanks." She seemed gratified by the compliment, as if she'd hit the mark she'd set for herself. But she wouldn't engage him after that. If he stepped toward the fridge, she'd step away from it. If he went to the table, she'd go to the sink.

He found her determination not to even brush up against him quite ironic. She'd wanted him so badly seventeen years ago. And now that he wanted her, regardless of what *anyone* said, she wouldn't come near him.

They finished washing the dishes and played a game of hearts while waiting for Jacob to wrap up his homework. Riley examined her more than he did his cards, but she'd look away if their eyes ever met. After that, they all went for a walk along the creek. When Jacob took Phoenix's hand to make sure she didn't fall on the slippery rocks, Riley wished he could be on her other side.

He followed them instead.

"We could help you clean up this place," Jacob told her with a glance over his shoulder to indicate that he was talking about the yard.

Phoenix looked happier than Riley had ever seen her. There was no question she *loved* having Jacob's hand in hers. Just seeing them together made him feel guilty all over again for standing between them before. It was a miracle she didn't resent him.

Or maybe that was part of the problem. Maybe she did. He didn't feel that coming from her, but he didn't see how she could avoid hating him for denying her the one thing she wanted most.

"I'll keep that in mind," she said. "I'd like to do it sooner rather than later, but…I have to be careful with my mother. Moving things around—and especially getting rid of anything—upsets her. This is her place, after all. I'm merely a guest."

"A guest who takes care of her," Riley pointed out.

"As much as she'll let me."

"There's no rush," Jacob said. "We're here whenever you need us."

"That's very nice." She beamed up at him. Then they paused for a few seconds in the cool water to admire the sunset.

When Riley came up beside them, Jacob said, "Here, take Mom for a sec. I'm going to see if I can find some rocks to skip."

"I don't need any help," Phoenix protested, but Jacob brought their hands together and began his search.

Riley tugged on her just enough to knock her off balance. Instinctively, she cried out and grabbed hold of him, and he saved her from landing in the water.

"Are you sure?"

"You did that on purpose!" she said.

He raised their hands to show how her fingers were laced through his. "Worked, didn't it?"

"So…how'd it go?"

Riley glanced over at his son as he drove them home from Phoenix's trailer. "What do you mean? You were there. It was fine, don't you think?"

"You warned me dinner might not be very good. I

would've eaten it, anyway, like you said. But I thought the food was perfect."

"It was." He didn't mention the cookies he'd had to swap out, or that Phoenix had made who knew how many batches of spaghetti sauce. "She's learning."

"And…"

"And what?"

"How'd she treat *you*?"

Was Jake beginning to hope they'd get together? "Like I said…you were there."

"I had to do my homework while you two were in the kitchen."

Riley pursed his lips as he remembered. "She was… polite."

"That's it?"

"I got her to hold my hand."

"At the house?"

"No," he admitted, keeping his eyes on the road.

"You can't be talking about the creek." Jacob winced. "I'm not sure it counts if you have to almost pull a girl into the water."

Riley had never dreamed his son would be in a position to critique his ability to attract a woman. But their relationship was unique. The age difference wasn't as wide as that between most fathers and sons; it'd been just the two of them for sixteen years, and they often worked together. All of that tended to make Jake feel more like a buddy, at times. "She's skittish."

Jake propped his arm against the door. "Whenever I talk about you, she only has the best things to say."

"That doesn't mean she'd be willing to explore more than friendship."

"You need time to win her over."

"Getting her out of Whiskey Creek—where she

doesn't feel so hemmed in by the past—would help," he mused. "I wish I could convince her to go to the cabin with me next weekend."

"She won't go?"

He shook his head and Jacob said, "I'll see if I can convince her."

Riley told him not to. It didn't seem fair for him to involve Jacob, knowing Phoenix would do anything for their son. That gave him an unfair advantage. But his hesitancy didn't dissuade Jake. Over the next few days, he left a message on Facebook, drove out to visit her and spoke to her at his game. He told Riley that he'd said she should go to Lake Melones for the weekend. That it would be fun. That she could use the opportunity to make friends. That there was more to life than taking care of her mother and building her business. Riley had even overheard part of one conversation, since he'd given Phoenix a ride to the game. But according to what he'd heard that day, and what Jacob had told him after, Phoenix always responded with the same answer: *She says she doesn't fit in with your crowd.*

By Friday morning, he wished he could stay home himself. Kyle claimed he had a woman lined up to be Riley's date, but Riley didn't even care to meet her. The only thing that stopped him from declining was that he refused to flake out on his friends. It was *his* party, after all—and he was looking forward to seeing Gail and Simon, who hadn't been to town in a while.

The woman Kyle had invited for him was there when he arrived. Her name was Candy Rasmussen, and she was as pretty as Kyle had promised. Seemed nice, too. She smiled brightly when they were introduced, and pulled him over to sit by her almost immediately.

But once she met Simon, and she and Kyle's date,

a woman by the name of Samantha, started fawning over him like groupies, Riley knew he was in for a long weekend.

20

Riley's present was delivered on Friday afternoon. Phoenix opened it to make sure it looked as good in real life as it had on the computer, and was thrilled to see that it was even better. The minute she felt she could spare the money, she planned to order the same scrapbook for herself.

He's going to love this. Hoping to give it to him before he could leave for the cabin, she hurried over to her mother's to call Jacob's cell.

Because Lizzie was sitting at the table scowling at her—"He doesn't deserve that, doesn't deserve anything," she'd said—Phoenix turned away when her son answered and lowered her voice.

"Jake?"

"Hey, Mom. What's up?"

"I was wondering if your father's still around."

"He left for the cabin at noon. Why? Have you changed your mind about going? If so, I can give you the address. We have this app on our phones called 'Find Your Friends.' I can see where he is at any time. Plus, he gave the address to Tristan's parents."

She'd thought about going all week and had nearly relented. It almost felt…safe, once Jacob started trying to talk her into it. But there was always her mother to remind her what a fool she'd be if she ever trusted Riley again. She couldn't imagine him being interested in her—not seriously. Her mother had to be right.

"I haven't changed my mind," she told Jake. "I just… I got him a small gift for his birthday and was hoping to bring it over this afternoon, that's all."

"You should take it up to the cabin. He'd love it if you came."

Again, she nearly succumbed to the temptation. She probably would have if her mother hadn't been eavesdropping on her conversation. "I can't barge in on him and his friends. I'll wait until he gets home," she said.

But after they hung up, Jacob called back and insisted she write down the address. For some reason, he really wanted her to go—and after another three hours of deliberation, she walked back to her mother's and called to see if she could hire a car to take her.

Maybe she was crazy, as foolhardy as Lizzie said. But when she glanced around her mother's trailer and saw what playing it safe all the time looked like, she realized that fear could imprison a person just as much as the iron bars at the Central California Women's Facility.

So she decided to free herself—and attend the party.

The cabin was a mansion, a gorgeous sprawling structure made of wood, stone and glass—the wood being the only cabin-like element about it. A place like this couldn't be called "rustic."

"Nice," the driver said with a whistle.

They couldn't even see it all, not the part that lay beyond the lights in front. It had taken so long to arrange transportation it was dark, nearly ten o'clock.

Phoenix didn't say anything. His comment didn't

require a response, and she was too caught up in her own anxiety. Had she made a mistake paying this man to bring her here? What on earth had possessed her? She wasn't that good in social situations to begin with, and now she was going to barge into Riley's lake party weekend without so much as a swimsuit?

The driver came around the car. "Ma'am?"

She kneaded her forehead. It wasn't too late to drive off. She could have him take her home…

"Somethin' wrong?" he asked uncertainly.

"Yes, um, I'm sorry to change plans on you at the last minute, but I've decided to go back."

"To Whiskey Creek?"

She nodded. "Is that okay?"

"I'm sorry, but I have another fare in San Francisco at midnight," he said. "I'll barely get there in time as it is."

"Oh!" She hadn't considered that he might not be able to take her, even if she paid another hundred dollars for the return trip.

He held out his hand. "I'm sure you'll have fun here."

She climbed out. *Damn it.* She didn't belong. She should never have come…

He handed her the small, beat-up suitcase she'd borrowed from her mother and thanked her when she gave him a ten-dollar tip. Then he left her standing on the steps of movie star Simon O'Neal's cabin—*the* Simon O'Neal, one of the biggest box office stars in the country.

As if Riley's being here wasn't unnerving enough.

"I've done it this time." She looked around, wondering if there was some other way to leave, but the narrow, winding road by which she'd come was sparsely traveled. That didn't leave her with many options. It wasn't as though she could catch a bus.

In other words, she was stuck.

Letting her breath go on a long sigh, she shook her head. "What a fool." Obviously, she cared a lot more about Riley than she wanted to admit, or she wouldn't have put herself in such a terrifying position, gift or no gift.

She was here now, though. There was nothing to do but make the most of it.

She carried her suitcase up the three steps to the door—and continued carrying it across a large entry area, since it didn't have wheels like most bags made in the past twenty years.

After setting it down, she stood there for a minute, then rang the bell.

Simon himself answered. Phoenix was so tongue-tied she almost couldn't speak.

"Hello." He looked perplexed but smiled pleasantly.

"Hi, I'm, um, I'm here for Riley's party. He...he invited me."

Simon's eyebrows rose as if that was a surprise—and she could understand why. She was so different from the other people who would be here. And Riley probably hadn't mentioned her. He would have no reason to.

To Simon's credit, he barely hesitated before pushing the door wider. "Great. The more, the merrier," he said. "Come on in. We're all out back."

It felt so presumptuous to carry her suitcase inside his house, but she couldn't leave it on the stoop. Fortunately, Simon grabbed it before she could. "Let me get that for you."

She wasn't sure whether to comment on his celebrity. Should she compliment him on his last movie?

She figured that would be polite. He had to know she recognized him. There couldn't be more than a handful of people in America who wouldn't. But she'd never seen him act, never seen any of his movies. She'd only seen him in the tabloids that were sometimes available in the prison library—if one of the correctional officers, or someone else, donated them. And she didn't think it was a good idea to mention *that*. "You have a lovely place," she said instead.

"Thank you." He tilted his head as if something about her didn't quite add up, but she'd expected that type of reaction, so she wasn't offended by it.

"I'm sorry to disturb everyone this late," she said. "I couldn't get away any sooner."

"It's no problem." He set her bag in the entry. "We'll just…leave that here for now. My wife will show you to your room in a few minutes. Until then you can get yourself a giant marshmallow and make some s'mores along with everyone else."

She was grateful he was being so courteous. "Sounds delicious," she said, but was afraid she'd choke if she tried to eat anything before she could get her nerves under control.

"Right this way."

He led her through several expansive rooms that had been, no doubt, professionally decorated. She tried not to stare, but she'd never seen such an opulent home. Or maybe *opulent* wasn't the word. It wasn't pretentious; it was *quality*.

The living room area contained a huge stone fireplace and a glass wall that looked out onto a deck. Phoenix could see a large group of people gathered around a fire pit, but she didn't get a chance to determine who they all were. She didn't dare make eye contact with anyone for fear she'd find that person staring back at her in horror and disdain. Because even if that was the case, she had no choice except to walk out when Simon opened the door and ushered her through it.

"Riley, you have another well-wisher." Simon had to raise his voice against the din but, one by one, Riley's guests turned to face her and fell silent.

Phoenix's face burned so badly she felt as though she were standing *in* the fire instead of beside it. And that was *before* the person in front of Riley stepped aside, and she saw him sitting with a beautiful woman draped across his lap. That made her slightly nauseous, as if it had been an intentionally cruel joke to invite her up here.

But then she realized that *everyone* had a date...

What had she stumbled into? When he'd asked her to come, he'd made it sound like a mixed group, a big party. She'd assumed there'd be *some* couples. A lot of his friends were married. But she'd had no idea that he and Kyle would have dates. No wonder Simon hadn't known what to say about sleeping arrangements. He had to be wondering what the heck he and his wife were going to do with her—and if Riley really expected to have two women stay over.

"Phoenix!" Riley stood up so fast he almost dumped the blonde onto the floor. "I—I didn't think you were coming."

"I'm sorry. I wasn't going to, and then...and then..." She couldn't finish that sentence. She didn't have a good excuse for changing her mind, since her only reason was her desire to be with him. But she had to say *something*. Everyone was gaping at her. So she took his present out from under her arm and shoved it toward him. "I just wanted to give you this."

He was obviously taken aback. She should never

have surprised him. His date and everyone else exchanged questioning looks of *What's this?*

Fortunately, Eve Harmon, whose parents had owned the B and B in town when they were in high school—maybe they still did—jumped up right away.

"Phoenix! It's been so long! I've hardly seen you since you, er, moved back. Sit over here."

Callie and her husband pushed the chair they'd been sharing closer to Eve, so that she could sit next to her. All the other chairs were taken.

Phoenix blinked helplessly at them. She didn't want to take their seat, didn't want to disrupt their fun. At this point, she wished she could just melt into the deck. But there was no escape. Not yet. "Thank you."

She promised herself she'd sit there for thirty minutes or so and go through the motions of making s'mores, since Kyle was already pressing a fancy-looking roaster into her hands. She'd only ever used an old hanger, which told her as much as anything that she was *way* out of her element.

Thirty minutes, she reminded herself. She couldn't rush off immediately, not without creating even more embarrassment. First, she had to smooth over her mistake by acting as if it was no big thing. Then she'd figure out *some* way to escape the party and go home—even if she had to walk.

Riley felt the weight of Phoenix's present in his hands and wished he could pull her off to one side so he could reassure her and thank her for coming. But with his date standing beside him, looking as astonished as everyone else at the sudden intrusion, that wouldn't be polite. The only way he could ease Phoenix's mortification was to draw everyone's attention to him by opening the gift. "This feels heavy," he said. "I have no idea what it could be."

He'd been hoping to receive a bracelet, had nearly ordered one half a dozen times. But this was too heavy, too bulky.

Everyone moved closer as he tore off the paper, as curious as he was to see what she'd brought. They'd heard so much about her, some of it from him. He'd bought into her guilt so completely—not that he'd ever wished her ill or intended her harm, but he'd justified distancing himself and Jacob.

He wished he'd remained in touch, or at least reached out to her at some point. He realized now that cutting her off had been his loss as much as hers. If anything had become apparent to him since her return, it was that.

As the wrapping paper fell away, Riley found a photograph book that featured a picture of him and Jake on the front cover—from when Jake was two and Riley was carrying him on his shoulders. As he turned the pages, he saw that Phoenix had included most of the pictures he'd sent her. There were some of Jake alone, like the one when he was three and had a bowl on his head with spaghetti dripping down his face. There were pictures of them together. And there were group photos from Jacob's various sports teams or birthday parties. One of those showed Riley dressed up as a clown, since the clown he'd hired had backed out at the last minute.

Only true love could have made him put on that costume, he mused, remembering.

"Wow! That is *really* nice," Gail said.

Several others murmured similar praise. Riley had seen books like this before but had never gone to the trouble of creating one. He wouldn't even know where to start. It was obvious that Phoenix had put thought and effort into the project, which made it that much more meaningful to him.

He coaxed his date into taking the chair they'd just vacated, so he could finish looking through the book. When she wasn't ogling Simon, she was being too friendly with him, which he'd tolerated for the sake of "giving her a chance." As Kyle said, they had to cut these women some slack. Most women would be starstruck by Simon. He'd ignored her behavior because he didn't really care about her. But that overfamiliarity bothered him now that Phoenix was here. He didn't want her to see Candy standing so close to him. It made everything look different from the way it really was.

He loved watching Jake grow up again before his eyes, loved the graphics and quotes about fathers and sons Phoenix had added.

The last two pages weren't filled with pictures he'd provided. They were taken by Phoenix when he had her over for that barbecue and they'd wound up wrestling in the pool. This was the first time he'd seen them. They reminded him of how much fun that night had been, so he felt his smile brighten—and then fade when his eyes moved to the last one. He'd thought everything was leading up to the selfie he'd taken of the three of them together. That picture was there, as expected. But Phoenix had cropped herself out, as if she believed he'd like it better without her.

That upset him. She refused to acknowledge that his feelings were changing, as though she couldn't take him seriously. As though he'd only change his mind again. But this book was special and served as evidence that she wasn't as over him as she wanted him to think. So he propped up his wilting smile. "Thank you. This is… the best present anyone could have given me."

Although she nodded, that movement seemed slight and defensive. Her eyes kept darting to the door; he could tell that she regretted coming and couldn't wait to run out.

"Seriously," he said, hoping to convince her. "I love it."

"I'm glad," she told him. "Jake's a good boy, and you've been a good father to him."

"How'd you do this?" Gail asked. Gail had loads of money and could hire someone to make as many photo books as she wanted, but she questioned Phoenix about the program she'd used as if she might try it herself. Callie, Olivia, Levi, Noah, Addy and the others admired Phoenix's creation, too, and for that, Riley was grateful. His friends were doing what they could to make her feel welcome. But once their questions died down and the conversation turned to Baxter, a friend who'd gone through a recent breakup with his boyfriend and couldn't attend, Phoenix stood, and Riley knew what was coming next.

"I'd better get going," she said in an aside to him, suggesting she'd slip out without anyone's noticing.

But Eve heard and said, "You're not leaving *yet*, are you? You just got here!" Then everyone grew quiet again, and Phoenix found herself the center of attention, a position Riley knew she hated.

She cleared her throat. "I'm afraid so. I was never planning to stay."

That had to be a lie. Riley would've bet any amount of money that she hadn't come up here so late just to deliver his present. But he understood why she was leaving. She was trying to get them both out of an awkward situation. What astonished him was that she ventured to address Candy before she left.

"I'm sorry to have interrupted your night," she said. "I really am. That book came in the mail today, so I...I wanted him to have it in time for his birthday. But he and I aren't...seeing each other. I mean...we have a son together, but we haven't been a couple in seventeen years. We're just friends—and even that only happened recently."

Candy spread her arms, obviously surprised that Phoenix had made the effort to explain. But for all Phoenix knew, he and Candy had been dating for months. It didn't matter that, at the barbecue, Jake had implied that Riley wasn't involved with anyone. Jake wouldn't necessarily know what Riley did when he went out.

"Thanks for letting us all know," Candy said as if she was about to laugh, and that made Riley grit his teeth. His date didn't understand their history, didn't understand that Phoenix was making sure she wasn't getting in his way again, wasn't doing anything to interfere with whatever love interest he might have.

Once again, Eve made an effort to ease the awkwardness. "I'm so glad you came. I wish you could stay longer." Riley couldn't tell if she'd manufactured the disappointment in her voice, but he was relieved that she sounded sincere—and that she was attempting to support Phoenix.

Not that it would convince Phoenix to stay. She was in flight mode, and he doubted anything would change that.

Phoenix dipped her head politely. "Maybe next time."

Several of Riley's friends shot him a look as if they were asking, *Do you want us to waylay her?*

He wished he could give them some indication that

he did. He wasn't ready for her to leave, wanted to make her feel better before she took off. He hated the thought of her going home kicking herself for having trusted him again. This was his fault, not hers. But detaining her wouldn't be fair to Candy—or to Phoenix, either, since he couldn't really be with her as he wanted. So he gave no sign one way or the other and focused on more practical concerns. "You have a ride, then?"

She smoothed the sundress he and Kyle had bought her. She wore that whenever she wanted to look her best—more proof that her coming to the cabin hadn't been the whim she pretended it was. "Yeah, I have a driver waiting for me."

He could see her being cautious enough to ask whoever had brought her to wait until she checked out the situation, so he nodded. "Okay. I'll call you when I get home."

She ducked her head and disappeared through the crowd, and Riley tried to let her go without chasing her down. If she had a car waiting, she'd get home safely. He could always reimburse her for the expense, which he planned to do. Driving to the lake would've cost quite a bit.

But at the last second, he sent Candy an apologetic look and went after Phoenix. It wasn't the most courteous thing to do, but Candy hadn't been all that courteous about her obvious interest in Simon. And he couldn't let Phoenix leave without apologizing for Candy's presence, without telling her that he was glad she'd relented and come to join him. He also wanted to be sure she had enough money to pay the driver who was taking her home. "Phoenix!"

She hadn't yet cleared the living room when she turned. "Don't interrupt your evening," she said, gesturing that he should return to the fire pit. "I'm sorry I surprised you. I didn't realize this was...that kind of party."

Because he'd thought he'd have a better chance of getting her up here if he described it a different way... "Of course you didn't. I was afraid if I told you that, you wouldn't come. Then you turned me down, so Kyle had his date invite a friend. I've never even seen Candy before. She was only in my lap because we were out of chairs, and she's the one who insisted on that arrangement when I got up to offer her my seat."

"You don't have to explain," she said, as if she had no stake in his love life. "I shouldn't have changed my mind at the last minute."

"But I'm happy you did. If I'd known, I wouldn't have...made other plans."

"It's okay. Go back."

He didn't want to go back; the wrong woman was leaving... "Let me walk you out at least."

She blocked his path. "There's no need. Your friends are waiting. I'll be fine."

He'd already left the others. Another few minutes wouldn't make any difference. "I'd rather see you off. It'll give me some peace of mind."

He wondered if she'd let him take her someplace next Saturday to make up for this and planned to ask as he helped her into the car. But when he opened the front door, he found that there was no car.

She sighed as she stepped out behind him. "I guess my driver had to leave."

He frowned at her. "You knew there was no one waiting for you out here, didn't you?"

She didn't answer.

"So what were you going to do?" he asked. "Try and

walk? *In the dark?* Getting home would take all night—
and that's if you made it safely!"

Again, she said nothing.

"Do you have any idea how dangerous that would
be?"

"I can look after myself."

"Not if this is any indication!" How could she even
consider taking such a risk? Why wouldn't she just tell
him she had no way home and allow him to handle the
rest? Her safety took precedence over the politeness
he owed Candy; it took precedence over everything.

Since she'd come back to Whiskey Creek, Phoenix
was so sure he'd let her down, she refused to rely on
him for *anything.* He understood why, but he hated it.
Hated that she wouldn't trust anything he said or did.
She'd judged him emotionally unreliable and he couldn't
cry foul, even though he'd been only eighteen when he
broke up with her.

Kyle walked through the door with her suitcase.
"Hey, you forgot this!"

She hadn't forgotten it; she'd known there was nowhere to put it. And Riley hadn't even considered the
possibility of luggage. He'd been too preoccupied with
the shock of having Phoenix show up tonight and trying to figure out how to salvage what little progress
he'd made with her.

Couldn't *anything* go right? If Candy wasn't here he
could've spent some time with Phoenix in a situation
that established romantic interest, a situation in which
she couldn't tell him, or herself, that she was only with
him because he was connected to Jacob. That was exactly what he'd wanted when he invited her—to build
her trust.

Instead, he'd mishandled the whole thing, and she'd be very unlikely to take another chance on him.

"Where's your ride?" Kyle asked, looking around.

Riley didn't answer him. "You and your damn pride," he muttered to Phoenix.

"I was going to call someone," she said. "No big deal. I'm sure I can get a car."

"Not at this time of night, you can't—and I think you know that." He pointed at the thin ribbon of road winding around the mountain. "If I hadn't come out, you would've started down in the dark, on foot and…"

"And I would've been fine. People get around without cars all the time."

"Tell me, in this situation, how are you planning to do that?"

"I'll walk to the main highway and hitchhike from there."

The dread that some psychopath or rapist might get hold of her made him angry. "Like hell you will!" he said. "Do you really believe I'd let you do that?"

Her mouth dropped open. "You have no say in what I do!"

Someone had to look after her. She thought that because she'd endured prison she could endure anything, but he remembered how easy it was to toss her around in the pool. She wouldn't stand a chance if some asshole set out to hurt her. "Try walking away from me and see," he said. "I'll *carry* you back if I have to."

Casting him a look that suggested he not strong-arm her, Kyle stepped between them. "He doesn't mean it. What he means is that you should stay for a game of pool. He understands you can take care of yourself, and that what you do is entirely your business, but I need a partner, and—" he lightened his voice to persuade her, which made Riley feel like a boor because of his own behavior "—that's a real problem."

Phoenix tilted her head to look around him. "At least *someone*'s making sense."

Riley had to lean over to see her, too. "It wouldn't be safe to leave! That makes me a bad guy? Because I want to keep you from being hurt?"

"I haven't even *tried* to call for a car," she argued. "How do you know I wouldn't get one?"

"It's nearly eleven and we're in the middle of nowhere! It'll be a waste of energy." Chances were, she'd had a hard time getting a driver to bring her here in the first place. She was just trying to save face. Besides, she hadn't been heading for the phone; she'd been heading for the door. So when, exactly, and how did she plan to call limousine companies? "It'll be easier in the morning."

"In the morning?" She threw up her hands. "You have a date! Both of you have dates."

"Not really," Kyle said. "I mean, Riley's is only sort of a date, since I'm the one who asked her, right?"

She rolled her eyes. "There can't be enough room for me to stay here, anyway."

Kyle gestured at the house. "This place is huge."

"And you guys have a lot of friends, all of whom need a bed."

Riley wasn't concerned about that. He'd figure out some place for her to sleep, even if he had to take a couch. But he let Kyle respond, since Kyle seemed to have a better chance of convincing her with his kinder, gentler approach.

"Not so many that we can't squeeze in one more," he said. "Riley and I have been assigned a couple of bunk beds. We're too tall for them, anyway. You can have our room and we'll find somewhere else to sleep."

She shook her head. "I appreciate it, but..."

"But nothing." So much for letting Kyle handle this. Riley pushed him out of the way. "You might as well stay. Because if you insist on leaving, I'm going to drive you home myself, party be damned."

"No," she said. "You can't leave. It would be weird for the guest of honor to take off. And it'd be really late before you could get back. I don't want to ruin your party. You're overreacting."

"*You're* overreacting! What can it hurt to spend a few more hours here? I'll give you a ride—or arrange one—tomorrow."

"*I* invited Candy. Riley didn't," Kyle added.

She scowled at him. "Please, stop saying that. There's nothing going on between Riley and me, so none of that makes any difference."

"You didn't come here because you want to be with me?" Riley demanded.

She was obviously shocked that he'd call her on that statement. "N-not like that."

He rested his hands on his hips. "Then why'd you come?"

"What do you mean?" Her throat worked visibly as she swallowed. "It's your birthday. I—I wanted to give you your present."

That wasn't all of it. An ex didn't make the effort she'd made for no good reason. She could easily have waited until he was home to give him that photo book. "Then why won't you stay?" he asked. "If you're not interested in me, it shouldn't matter that I have a date, even if I decide to make out with Candy later."

When their eyes met, he could see the defiance his

words had sparked. But he'd meant to challenge her. Maybe she'd stay just to prove she didn't care…

"You can do whatever you like with Candy," she said.

"He's not going to make out with Candy," Kyle said. "He doesn't even like her."

Riley slapped Kyle on the back. "No need to explain. You heard her. She doesn't care what I do because she doesn't care about me."

"In that way," she clarified.

"Maybe it's time to face the truth," he said. "You care even though you don't want to. I can feel it."

Her eyes widened. "What are you talking about?"

To be honest, he wasn't sure. This certainly wasn't going to get him what he wanted. The need he felt to force her to commit herself, to respond to him, was making him push too hard. He had to ease off on the emotion and play it cool.

He didn't know how he'd gotten so far off track, anyway. "Nothing. Never mind. It's all decided. You can have my bed."

"Fine. I'll take it, even if it means you have to squeeze in with Candy!" she snapped.

He cocked his head to one side. "Maybe I'll do that."

"Don't let him fool you," Kyle said. "He doesn't want Candy."

"Kyle, I don't need your help." Riley was frustrated enough, and having Kyle step in, trying to patch things up, only made it worse.

But Kyle went on, undeterred. "The truth is, Candy and my date are both more interested in spending time with Simon. I'm guessing they'll be making s'mores as long as he's out there."

"That's too bad," Phoenix said. "I'd hate for Riley to

be deprived of her company. He's pretty used to getting whatever he wants."

"I'll be able to live with the disappointment," Riley said. Or was she trying to tell him he wouldn't get what he wanted from *her*?

"Great." Kyle clapped his hands with feigned enthusiasm. "So why don't we go downstairs and play some pool before you guys *really* get into an argument? I'll tell Candy and Samantha that they can wander in whenever they're ready."

Phoenix rubbed her arms as if she hadn't yet decided and didn't like her options.

"Should I get my keys?" Riley asked. "Are we leaving?"

She dropped her hands. "No."

"You're staying, then."

"Only until morning," she said grudgingly, and turned to Kyle. "Who will we be playing?"

"Riley and Lincoln."

Riley nearly laughed when she grimaced at his name. He'd made her mad, but he was through with pretending. They had a history, and that history might be difficult to overcome. But he couldn't believe the next guy would treat her any better than he would. He'd never intended for everything to go so wrong, had never actively tried to hurt her. He was beginning to think they'd just met too soon…

"Who's Lincoln?" she asked.

Kyle answered again. "Eve's fiancé."

"He any good at pool?"

"Yeah." Kyle jerked his head toward Riley. "He and Riley have been unbeatable so far. They're the reigning champs. But we can give it a try. It's all for fun, anyway."

"Don't count us out too soon," she said drily. "You've never seen me play."

Kyle pursed his lips as he sized her up. "You haven't seen them play, either."

"I don't care. A hundred bucks says we win."

Riley picked up her suitcase. "I wouldn't place that bet if I were you."

"I'm not worried."

As she glared up at him, he wished things weren't so complicated between them. There was such a strong attraction. He felt it even now. Knew she felt it, too.

"Suit yourself," he said.

As they went back inside, he deposited Phoenix's suitcase by the door, thinking he'd deal with it later. "Grab Lincoln," he told Kyle. "Phoenix and I will rack the balls."

21

After three beers, Phoenix wasn't feeling the same urgency to get home. Kyle's and Riley's dates hadn't come to find them, although it had been an hour or more since they'd started playing pool, so that helped ease her anxiety, too.

She and Kyle had won the first game. She still relished the surprise on Riley's face when he realized she could play as well as he could. But after that stellar start, they'd lost the second game. They would've won both, putting her a hundred bucks ahead, except Kyle had missed a couple of key shots.

Now they were competing for best out of three.

She could feel Riley watching her as she prepared to take her next turn and wondered what he was thinking. Was he wishing he'd let her leave?

Probably. He scowled every time she looked at him. And yet, whenever they passed each other, he touched her if he could do it casually, nonchalantly—and she felt his hand linger a second more than necessary.

She was afraid he was trying to make a point, and that he'd succeed. She was beginning to brush past him on purpose, just to feel that touch.

"Where'd you learn to play?" Lincoln asked. He

wasn't quite as open and friendly as Riley and Kyle, but, like her, Riley and Kyle had had a few beers and Lincoln wasn't drinking. So there was that.

"Prison." She banked the ball she'd targeted twice before sinking it in the right corner pocket.

She paused long enough to bestow a victorious smile on Riley, who lifted an eyebrow at her in return. That slight reaction was an acknowledgment of her skill. But he was also challenging her in a way she'd never expected. He was making his interest in her so plain that even his friends could tell what he wanted.

"That's interesting," Lincoln said.

She pocketed another ball. "To someone like you, my background must be more shocking than interesting, wouldn't you say?"

"To someone like me?" Lincoln repeated.

Normally she wouldn't have been so forthcoming about her past for fear of embarrassing Riley. But she was throwing out her own challenge. If he hoped to get back with her, he needed to understand everything that was part of the package these days. "Someone who's part of the 'in' crowd," she explained and, sadly, missed her next shot.

Studying what she'd left him, Lincoln circled to the other side of the table. "Given that I've served time myself, I wouldn't say I'm too shocked."

When he saw her surprise, he chuckled. Then he sank two stripes in rapid succession and walked to the far end for a third.

"Is that where *you* learned to play pool?" she asked. "Inside?"

"We didn't have a table. But I can take just about anybody in basketball, thanks to many hours in the yard."

She'd been wearing her past like armor, using it to

deflect any offer of friendship, so this made her feel a bit foolish. "How long have you been out?"

"Awhile."

That was vague, but she figured he didn't enjoy thinking or talking about his past any more than she did hers.

"A lot longer than you," he added. "Which is why I brought it up—to tell you that getting out is an adjustment. It takes time."

She conjured up a grateful smile. "Okay."

"Wow, be careful how you wield that thing," he said.

"Wield *what* thing?" she asked in confusion. "My pool cue?"

"No, that smile of yours. I'm in love, so I'm immune." He patted Riley on the back. "But I'm afraid this poor bastard has no defense."

"Mind your own business," Riley grumbled.

Lincoln didn't seem offended. He just laughed.

"What about *this* poor bastard?" When Kyle pointed to his own chest, Phoenix could tell he was doing it to goad Riley.

"In case you haven't noticed, you're not even in the running," Lincoln replied, and laughed again when Kyle flipped him off.

They teased like that as they finished the game. Without Kyle as a partner, Phoenix believed she would've won, but he couldn't hit a clutch shot at the end, and that left room for Riley to finish the game before she could get another turn.

Kyle and Lincoln were talking about a book their friend Ted had written as they climbed the stairs to get something to eat. But Riley didn't seem to be in any hurry to leave the room. He came up behind her as she was putting her stick in the rack. "I guess you owe me a hundred bucks."

She didn't bother to look back at him. "I keep trying to give you money, and you won't take it."

His hand settled on the curve of her waist, and his lips brushed her neck. "There are other things I want more."

She caught her breath. Would this be the spark that set fire to all her good intentions—and once again burned down her life? "Like…"

He didn't have the opportunity to answer. His date came into the room, and he dropped his hand and moved away.

"There you are!" she said. "I wondered where you'd gone."

Phoenix bit her tongue. Candy couldn't have wondered too much, since Kyle had told her.

Phoenix sat outside, staring into the fire while, across from her, Brandon, Kyle and Gail talked about Simon's latest movie. They'd tried to include her in the conversation by encouraging her to move closer to them, and by asking her a few questions. But when she didn't contribute more than was absolutely necessary, they let her sink into her own thoughts. She was happy just to enjoy the murmur of their voices, the cool breeze coming off the lake and the expanse of stars glittering overhead.

At least Riley had gone inside and was no longer sitting around the fire, too. It hadn't been easy to ignore his date. She'd been all over him, had even perched on his lap again, despite the fact that half the party had wandered off to different regions of the house to play pool, watch a movie or grab a snack, leaving plenty of chairs available.

Riley did nothing to stop her. He just gazed over at Phoenix as if to say, *Are you sure you don't care?*

The door opened and Eve came out. Phoenix assumed she'd join her friends, who were talking nearby, but she came around to where Phoenix was sitting and pulled up a chair. "I hear you're quite the pool player."

"I've had years of practice. Your fiancé's good, too."

She seemed pleased by the compliment. "He's good at a lot of things."

"How'd you two meet?"

Phoenix had been careful to keep to herself whenever possible tonight. She didn't want to impose on anyone who might not care to have her around. So she'd spent most of her time intermittently sipping a glass of wine while tidying up the kitchen. Despite Gail's protests that she'd worry about it in the morning, cleaning made Phoenix feel useful, gave her something to do.

Although everyone was polite, most people socialized with those more familiar to them. Eve was the exception. She kept seeking Phoenix out. Maybe, because she was engaged to a man who'd served time, she was more understanding of the things that could go wrong in a person's life, and that not everyone locked in a cell deserved it.

"Lincoln was visiting Gold Country for a little… break from work, and I ran into him at Sexy Sadie's," she said.

"He just…caught your eye?" Phoenix asked.

"That's how it started. I saw this gorgeous man across the bar and was instantly attracted." She smiled, as if there was some element of humor to the story, but she didn't expand on it. She simply added, "It was meant to be, I think."

Phoenix gave her an approving nod. "You seem happy together."

"He's been through a great deal to get to this point. He had a messed-up childhood, which set him on the wrong path. But he's put all of that behind him."

Did that mean he'd deserved to be sent to prison? Phoenix liked him so much it wouldn't change her opinion of him, but she was curious about what he might've done. It couldn't have been as bad as what *she'd* been accused of doing. "He didn't have to tell me he's had... similar experiences. I know he did it to help me feel comfortable, and I appreciate that."

"A few hard knocks makes you more sensitive to the needs of others."

Phoenix didn't want to talk about hard knocks. She'd had a few too many to be anything like the people she was currently with. Other than Lincoln... She gestured at the cabin. "This is a gorgeous place."

"It's generous of Gail and Simon to share it with us."

"Definitely."

"Has anyone shown you where you'll be sleeping tonight?"

"Gail did, about an hour ago." Instead of having her take Riley and Kyle's room, Gail had picked up Phoenix's suitcase and shown her to a small nanny's quarters.

"Are you downstairs, then?"

"Above the garage."

"Will you be comfortable there?"

Phoenix chuckled. "Of course." Surely Eve had to know that sleeping on the *floor* in a house like this would be fancier than any place Phoenix had ever stayed.

"I'm glad." She squeezed Phoenix's hand. "I'm sorry it's so hard to walk into something like this when you don't know very many of the people."

"It hasn't been too bad," she said. "Everyone's been very kind. Riley's lucky to have such close friends."

Eve studied her. "He seems to think a great deal of *you*."

Phoenix wasn't sure how to respond. "We're doing what we can to support Jacob. It's easier on everyone if we can be friendly."

Eve tilted her head. "Is that what's going on between you? You're just being 'friendly' for Jacob's sake?"

Suddenly too hot, even though she'd been chilly a few seconds earlier, Phoenix slid her chair farther from the fire. "Yeah, that's about it. I didn't mean to crash the party. I wasn't aware it was for couples when I came."

"Riley knew it was for couples when he invited you."

Phoenix hadn't let herself think about that. It didn't make sense that he'd want her with him in public. But she was new in his life, and somewhat interesting because of that. And Riley felt safe to do as he pleased. Whiskey Creek had never been the harsh and unforgiving place for him that it had been for her. "He was trying to be nice since…since I don't get out much."

"You're saying he invited you out of *pity*?"

"That's my guess."

With a chuckle, Eve stood. "I know Riley well enough to say that isn't the reason he's spent most of the night watching you while trying to get Candy to stop feeling him up."

Phoenix refused to acknowledge her jealousy of his date. "Candy's had a little too much to drink. But she's pretty, and she seems interested in him. They make a great couple."

Eve grimaced. "Are you serious?"

"Excuse me?"

"Have you talked to her?"

"Not really, but…it doesn't matter what *I* think. It's all up to him."

"I can understand why you'd say that. But I think it's pretty clear who he wants."

"Not me," she insisted.

"You won't accept what he's offering you?"

"There's no offer."

"We can all see it but you, I guess. Anyway, I'm glad he's not interested in *her*."

Despite Eve's hint, Phoenix couldn't imagine that Riley's friends would be any happier if he ended up with someone who'd served seventeen years for murder and still couldn't prove her innocence. So what if Eve was with a guy who'd done time? He didn't have any history, or enemies, in Whiskey Creek. That meant he could borrow from Eve's reputation, start with an almost clean slate.

Phoenix might've said as much, but Eve was already walking off. She seemed to be heading into the house—until Gail stopped her to ask when Callie was due.

The pregnancy was news to Phoenix, but their words became background noise in spite of her interest. Riley had come to the glass doors and was staring out at her. His date must've gone to bed because she didn't seem to be with him.

When he walked out, Phoenix got the impression that he was planning to come over to her. But she felt too beleaguered to maintain her defenses. So when one of his friends waylaid him, she hurried around the fire pit on the opposite side and slipped into the house.

She was running away from him, and she knew he'd pick up on that. But she didn't want to make matters worse by letting their feelings take control. She was afraid that if they were together for any length of time, they'd wind up in bed.

It was time to call it a night—and save her energy for the new battle tomorrow would bring.

In the light of day, maybe he wouldn't be so hard to resist.

22

"What'd she say?"

Eve, who'd gone into the kitchen, turned from pouring herself a glass of water. *"She?"*

Riley frowned at her. "Don't play games. You know who I'm talking about."

"Phoenix? She said you and Candy make a great couple."

He finished the beer he'd carried in with him and tossed the bottle into the receptacle. "I can't believe they're both here. It's been *really* awkward."

"Riley, even if you win Phoenix over, getting together with her won't be easy. She's...defensive, cautious, afraid."

"She might be all those things, but I don't believe she killed Lori. I feel like shit that I ever did."

She pulled herself up onto the counter. "The way I've always heard it, there's not much question."

"There's plenty of question. She didn't do it." He was adamant about that, felt the misgivings he'd wrestled with before had been pointing him toward the truth all along and wished he'd listened to his intuition seventeen years ago.

"She seems nice," Eve said. "Really nice." There was some reservation in her response.

"But…you don't think I should date her?"

"I don't know her well enough to make that call. Either way, I like her a heck of a lot more than Candy." She twisted around to peer out into the darkened living room. "Speaking of which…where *is* your date?"

He lowered his voice. "She finally passed out."

"She's okay, though?"

"Yeah. She's fine. Just drunk. And I'm grateful for the break."

"She was…quite forward."

"*Too* forward. She tried to pull me into a bedroom several times."

"How'd you say no?"

"I just kept guiding her back to the party."

"Yikes."

"I hope she recovers by morning. Maybe it isn't polite, but I'm going to ask her to leave."

Eve leaned back on her hands. "Didn't she come with Samantha?"

"Kyle can give Samantha a ride later if he wants her to stay."

"Actually, I doubt he'll mind if Samantha goes home," Eve mused. "From what I've seen, he avoids her whenever he can."

Riley went to the fridge to rummage for the fruit he'd seen Phoenix put in there earlier. "I told him he didn't know this woman well enough to spend an entire weekend with her."

Eve swung her legs against the cupboards, giving them a gentle tap. "It's too bad they're not a better fit. Losing Olivia was hard on him. And with her and Brandon both here…"

"Samantha's not the one who's going to help Kyle get over Olivia," he said, popping some grapes into his mouth.

She sighed. "I agree. So where's Samantha now?"

"She went to bed. I saw her for a few seconds not too long ago, and she apologized for her friend's behavior."

"That's nice at least."

"I've never had anyone feel me up the way Candy has."

"Once Simon went to bed, she really turned it on."

"I guess if she can't have him, she'll settle for someone who's in his circle."

"She's *that* shallow?"

"You haven't noticed?"

Eve shrugged. "I can't say I've been impressed with her."

He thought of how quickly Phoenix had disappeared once Candy had gone to bed. "So you don't think I have a chance with Phoenix?"

"Everything she's suffered has to have changed her. I worry about that."

"I do, too. But—" he frowned at the grapes in his hand "—what she's suffered has only changed her for the better. In any case, nothing seems to stop me from wanting her."

"Then maybe you should quit fighting it, give it a shot," she said, obviously trying to be open-minded.

"*I'm* willing, but...you can understand why she might be reluctant."

"Of course. I also understand that people like Lincoln, who have trust issues, can sometimes recover—if they get enough love and reassurance."

"But I'm the *last* man she could ever trust."

"I wouldn't say *that*. You're the father of her son.

You're whole and healthy, emotionally and physically. And she cares about you. Who'd be more capable of giving her what she needs?"

He smiled.

"You like the sound of that."

"Yeah," he admitted, and gave her a quick hug.

Since Kyle was watching a movie with some of the others who were still up, Riley had their downstairs room to himself. But he didn't stay put for long. He couldn't get comfortable in that small bed. It didn't help that he had so much on his mind. He kept thinking about the photo book Phoenix had made for him, how thoughtful it had been. He felt bad that she'd summoned the nerve to come all the way up here—even paid a goodly sum to hire a driver—and had such a terrible surprise waiting for her when she arrived.

He wanted a few minutes alone with her so he could thank her for the birthday present. He also wanted to make it clear that he wasn't sleeping with Candy. When they'd been sitting around the fire, he'd only left because Candy had been crawling all over him. He wouldn't have abandoned Phoenix otherwise, not when she felt so out of place.

"Where are you going?" Kyle glanced up from the TV when Riley walked by.

"Getting a drink," he replied.

Kyle must've realized that wasn't the truth, because he came around the couch and handed him something. Riley couldn't see what it was in the dark, but the smooth texture of an individual condom package was distinctive enough that he knew.

"In case you didn't come prepared," he whispered.

"I *didn't* come prepared," Riley said. "I wasn't expecting Phoenix to be here. But I won't need this. I'm just going to talk to her. There's no way she'd let me touch her."

"It won't hurt to have one on you," Kyle muttered, and returned to the movie.

The water was freezing. Phoenix knew she shouldn't be swimming in the lake—not alone and not in the middle of the night. She wasn't even dressed appropriately; she'd had to wear her bra and underwear, since she didn't have a suit. But she'd found a small balcony and stairs off her suite above the garage, with a little path leading to the water, and she'd needed to do *something* to curb the thoughts and desires that were bombarding her from all sides.

After seventeen years, she'd accepted that Riley would never love her. She'd come home with a plan to build a life that didn't include him, except in the role he'd always play as Jacob's father. And now he wanted her back?

That couldn't be. Even if it was true, they didn't stand a chance. Not in the world they knew, the one beyond this gorgeous cabin.

Problem was, her body didn't seem to be getting the message. She thought of him constantly, burned for his touch. This whole night felt like some kind of mating dance.

The shock of the cold water helped. At least it gave her something else to concentrate on. Her mother had been right; she shouldn't have come here. It tempted her to forget who she was and why she had to be more careful than most women—women like Candy, who seemed far more capable of taking a sexual encounter in stride.

Telling herself she'd eventually find someone else, someone who could *really* love her, she kept swimming, farther and farther from shore. When she turned back, she could see that the lights of the cabin were growing dim, but she didn't care. She would've swum all the way home, if possible. Out here there was silence and peace, and she no longer had to watch Candy with Riley, no longer had to see the intense expression on his face that let her know she was the one he wanted.

Maybe she should ask Jake to create a profile on Match.com. If she started dating, that could distract her, maybe keep her from making another mistake...

She thought she heard her name. But it was late. She couldn't imagine that anyone had noticed she'd left her room.

She kept swimming.

Then the sound came again.

It was Riley. He was standing on shore. She couldn't make out his face—the cabin's floodlights created a halo around him—but she identified him out of instinct. Who else would come looking for her? He'd been tracking her all night—while trying to pry Candy away.

The shivering she'd experienced for the past few minutes grew worse. She couldn't face him alone and in the dark. She wouldn't be able to separate what was real and what was part of this fairy tale.

She thought if she ignored him, he might go back inside and leave her alone. But he didn't. The next thing she knew, he stripped down to his boxers and waded in.

"You're too far," he yelled.

"Don't worry," she called back. "I'm fine. I'm just... out for a relaxing swim."

He didn't return to shore. He swam toward her. When he was within five feet, he stopped and treaded water. "Let's head to land," he said. "We'll talk there. This isn't safe. You've been drinking."

"I'm not drunk. I don't even have a buzz." She'd been a little tipsy earlier, but she'd been careful to drink only in measured amounts since then.

"No one swims into the middle of a lake in the dark, especially when it's so cold," he said. "What's going on?"

"Nothing. I needed to clear my head. That's all."

"I don't think freezing to death will help. This water is the spring runoff from the Sierra Nevada Mountains, for God's sake. It doesn't get warm until midsummer. And with the wind tonight…"

"You go. I'll come in a few minutes."

"Is it Candy?" he asked. "Because I don't have any feelings for her. If I had my choice, she wouldn't even be here."

She wiped the water from her eyes. "Why am *I* here? That's what I can't figure out. Why did you invite me when you knew all your friends would be around?"

"Why do you think?" he asked.

"I get that you want to sleep with me. But you could've approached me at home. Asking me to join you at something like this, where everyone has a date— that makes a public statement."

"Exactly. That statement was meant for you, not them. This isn't about sex, Phoenix. I'm not asking you to be my dirty little secret."

"Then what? I'm struggling with all the contradictions. I finally got it through my head that you don't want me…and now you do?"

He flipped his hair out of his face. "It's not fair, I know. I don't understand why everything went the way it did. But since you came home it feels…it feels as if you're what I've been waiting for."

"You must be even more confused than I am." She started putting some distance between them.

"Don't go any farther!" he yelled. "You're making me nervous out here!"

She ignored that. "I wasn't good enough for you in high school and, after seventeen years in prison, I haven't exactly come up in the world. I'm fighting day to day for the most basic things. How could I possibly attract someone like you?" And even more importantly, what did she have to hold him? She couldn't go through what she'd been through before, especially with the same man.

He powered through the water to close the gap between them. "I've *never* believed you weren't good enough for me—not in my heart. And that's what I should've trusted. I would have if…if everyone else had stayed out of it."

"But those people are your parents, your friends. They haven't gone away," she argued. "They'll come at you again, saying all the same things!"

"They won't sway me, Phoenix. Not this time. I'm sorry I let them before."

When he was close enough, he grabbed hold of her, and she didn't fight him. He was too strong. She didn't want to fight him, anyway. She wanted to *believe* him, she just wasn't sure she could. Not after nearly two decades of getting only one or two letters a year from him. "You don't have to apologize again. That's not what I'm looking for…"

"But I need you to understand." He hugged her close, obviously trying to share his body's warmth, since she was shivering. "I thought I was too young and inexperienced to be the only one to see how amazing you are. I doubted myself, caved in to the pressure and blindness of the people I trusted to guide me. I didn't realize they were looking at all the wrong things. They saw the junk around your mother's trailer. Your mother's weight and her phobias. Your black secondhand clothes. Your…nonconformity. And they missed what's really important."

Now she was more confused than ever. "And that is? I'll always be Lizzie's daughter, Riley. When I get on my feet, I plan to try and find her some help, but I doubt she'll even let me. You can't *make* someone go to therapy. I suspect my mother will always be just as she is now."

"It's not your mother I want to be with. It's you."

"But she's part of my life! And so is the stigma of what I supposedly did!"

"What matters is that you have the biggest heart imaginable." Resting his forehead against hers, he cupped her face with one hand. "And you are the most forgiving, unassuming, generous person I've ever met. What man wouldn't be happy with someone like you?"

She tried to pull away. "You can't mean that."

He grabbed her arm before she could escape. "I mean every word. I know it's hard for you to believe in me. But I have a lot more confidence in myself now that I'm older, a lot more confidence in *you* and what we can be together. Because of that, I hope…"

Her breath froze in her lungs as she looked up at him. "What?"

"I hope you'll give me another chance," he murmured.

How could she? They both lived in Whiskey Creek, and that meant the past would always stand between them.

"Phoenix?" he prompted.

She'd closed her eyes, but when he said her name she breathed deeply and opened them. "It's more than seventeen years since I've been with a man. You know that. You *were* that man. I won't be any good. I can barely remember what a penis looks like, let alone what I'm supposed to do with it."

His voice sounded stricken. "You just discounted everything I said. You think I'm just hoping to get laid."

"No, I think you mean well."

"But…"

"You meant well seventeen years ago, too. Sex tonight, while we're away from our normal lives, that's all I can offer you. Tomorrow we'll…go on as if it never happened."

"Don't say that! I can fight everyone else, tell them to go to hell, that we'll be together if we want. I'm happy to do all the fighting, for both of us. But I have to have *you* on my side. I have to know I'm fighting for something I can actually win."

She shook her head. "Being with me wouldn't be good for you. I can't let you do it."

"Shit." He started swimming off, but when she didn't follow, he turned back. "I can't leave you out here. At least let me take you in and get you warm."

She couldn't stay in the water, anyway. She could no longer feel her arms and legs. "I'm coming."

23

Sex tonight, while we're away from our normal lives, that's all I can offer you.

Riley had rejected that offer on principle. But that'd been easier to do when they were both freezing in the lake. As soon as they hurried into Phoenix's room and she unfastened her wet bra, it became next to impossible to remember *why* he'd said no.

She was the one who'd suggested they spend the night together. He would never have pressed her for anything physical, not until he'd done more to prove himself and knew she felt confident in him. He had to be careful with her. For so many reasons, she wasn't an average woman. But...

This sudden boldness of hers took him off guard. She seemed to be acting with reckless abandon, a sense of fatalism, throwing all caution aside—as if she'd take what she wanted and then accept whatever "punishment" or disappointment followed.

That wasn't the right frame of mind.

And yet...there she was, dropping what little she was wearing, along with her defenses—which challenged him in a whole new way.

"You're getting naked right in front of me," he said, his eyes riveted on her breasts.

She hesitated. "Isn't that why you're here?"

"I'm pretty sure I said no while we were in the lake."

"But you didn't *have* to come to my room. I'm capable of drawing my own bath."

That was true. In his defense, he'd wanted to take care of her, see that she was warm, safe and dry before he went to bed. But now that he was confronted with the choice again, he also wanted to feel her legs hug his hips as she drew him inside her. And the fact that she'd removed her wet bra held him like a high-powered magnet.

His muscles bunched as he fought the testosterone coursing through him. "Then tell me this. What do I stand to lose?"

She was still shivering. *"Lose?"*

"I want to make sure that it's not going to convince you of something terrible if I *don't* walk out that door."

Suddenly uncertain, she crossed her arms, leaving her panties on. Riley recognized them as one of the lacy pairs he and Kyle had purchased for her and wondered if they were the same pair she'd had on in the pool. But that was a memory he shouldn't have summoned, not if he still planned to sleep in his own bed. Remembering the way she'd gripped his wrist as he'd explored her warmth made him far too eager to do it again.

"Phoenix? Tell me it'll be okay."

Her voice sounded husky when she said, "It'll be okay. I don't expect you to leave. I don't even *want* you to."

The look on her face seemed to confirm her words.

Except for his boxers, which were wet, he already had his clothes off. After getting out of the lake, they'd both been in too much of a rush to stop and dress. They'd paused only long enough to grab their clothes from the shore. "You're not afraid to let me make love to you after so many years?"

Her gaze slid over his chest to the erection that was obvious under his boxers. "I think it's inevitable."

She also thought it was inevitable that he'd be finished with her afterward. But maybe the easiest way to convince her otherwise was simply to prove her wrong.

He went into the bathroom and turned on the water. "Come here."

Obviously nervous now that she'd made the commitment, she bit her lip as she met him in the bathroom.

"You're beautiful," he told her, and purposely touched her face instead of her breasts. "You know that, right?"

When she grimaced and started to shake her head as if she didn't expect such effusive compliments, he pressed both hands to her cheeks and made her look at him. "It's true."

"I have too many scars…"

"They don't detract from your beauty." He touched the one on her abdomen. "What happened here?"

A muscle moved in her cheek. "I was shanked."

There was that "take me or leave me, this is what you get" attitude she'd had while they were playing pool. It was almost as if she pointed out everything she figured he wouldn't like, to prove that he couldn't really be interested in her.

But she was wrong. The less appealing aspects of her life and her past didn't scare him, not like they used to. The thought of her lying on some dirty cement floor, bleeding, made him furious at himself. Why hadn't he done more to help her during the past seventeen years?

To make her time at the correctional facility less difficult?

He'd been stuck in denial, determined to relegate Jacob's mother to the past.

"Why and how were you attacked?" he asked softly.

"Let's not talk about my scars. They're...unsightly."

He'd thought it might help to address such things; he wanted her to know that she had nothing to be insecure or self-conscious about. He understood who and what she was—and wanted her, anyway. "They're not unsightly to me. They're just...part of who you are. I wish you'd never had to go through what you did..."

"Don't," she said. "Let's not bring the past in here with us—at least not the parts we can avoid."

"Okay, but other than the regret I feel about your pain, I don't mind this scar or any of the others." He ran his thumb over the elastic of her panties. "How about I take these off?"

When she nodded, he slid them down and gazed up at her.

"Well?" she said, obviously feeling self-conscious under his silent regard.

"This is going to be good." He stripped off his boxers. Then he scooped her into his arms and carried her into the hot water.

Riley was on his knees in front of her. Phoenix knew that a more confident woman—a woman like Candy—might've clenched her hands in his hair and pulled him up to bring their mouths together. She wanted to do that, wanted to kiss him as he pushed inside her.

But experience had taught her not to express what she felt, especially when it came to him.

She lay without moving as he lifted her halfway out

of the water and licked the drops from the insides of her thighs. When he moved higher, the pleasure grew so intense she started to tremble, but she couldn't encourage him by arching toward him or vocalizing it, or doing anything else. The memory of the pain, rejection and degradation that'd come after the pleasure seventeen years ago was simply too powerful, no matter how hard she tried to block it out.

"Don't you like this?" he murmured, his eyelids heavy as he looked up at her.

She'd closed her eyes, but when he spoke she opened them. He was asking why she wasn't responding. He probably felt as if he was in this alone. But she couldn't even bring herself to assure him that she *did* like it. A lot. Probably because she liked it too much. This wasn't the frenzied coupling she'd imagined. A hit-and-run would be one thing. But…this was slow and seductive. She was breaking every rule she'd set for herself before leaving prison, and those rules had been her way of making sure she stayed out of trouble.

"Phoenix? Don't I have the right spot?"

He knew what he was doing, but every woman was different. Given her lack of response, she could see why he might wonder. But this was *her* problem, not his. Even though her heart was racing, she felt…frozen.

He's going to leave now. You aren't capable of going through with this. Not with him.

"I told you I'd be terrible," she said. "You—you don't have to stay."

He narrowed his eyes. "What are you talking about? I *want* to stay. I'm *dying* to stay."

"I'm too damaged." She started to get out of the tub, but he held her in place.

"I don't believe that," he said, then put his mouth on

her again. The water flowed around her breasts as his hands gripped her buttocks and his tongue moved over her. She could barely breathe, and yet she still tried to contain herself. Somehow, acting on her desire didn't seem as dangerous as letting him know how much she enjoyed this. That had to be where she'd gone wrong before. She'd been too needy, too eager, too transparent; she could never let herself be that vulnerable again. They were just bodies, two bodies acting on instinct...

"Quit holding back," he murmured.

"I—I can't help it."

"All you have to do is relax."

"I keep hearing my mother telling me I'm a fool."

"We've both let you down. And yet you're trying to trust her again, trying to make a life with her in it. That's all I'm asking for you to do for me."

"But I think she might be right about this. There are *always* consequences, and what comes next?"

"You're going to climax. That's what comes next," he said and, holding her legs apart, he lifted her out of the water again.

She was doing everything she could to sabotage her own pleasure. Riley had never been with anyone who tried to remain so aloof. She was resisting the very thing she wanted, which confused him at first. Still, it didn't take long to figure out what was going on. Phoenix was trying to participate physically but not mentally. She seemed to believe that would somehow protect her, keep her from becoming vulnerable.

Tomorrow we'll just...go on as if it never happened. She was determined not to let this change anything.

But he was just as determined to make her feel the intensity of their connection, and see her react to it.

He'd never worked so hard to bring a woman pleasure or felt as gratified as he did the moment Phoenix cried out.

He looked up at her then, in triumph, and saw the realization hit her—that fighting him had been a waste of time and this night would change everything.

That was when he helped her out of the tub and guided her to the bed. They didn't even take the time to dry off. He'd broken through all her defenses. She was finally ready to make love with him the way *he* wanted—with passion and tenderness, but most of all with meaning.

When Riley touched her in bed, it was with a reverence that hadn't been there before. Positioning himself beside her, he rose up on one elbow as he trailed a finger between her breasts. He gave Phoenix the impression that he wanted to take their lovemaking slow, to savor every moment.

His gaze swept over her, seeing everything, since they hadn't turned off the light. "I like the way you look." He lowered his mouth to hers and kissed her gently, sweetly. "And the way you taste." He breathed in as he ran his nose down her neck and over one breast. "And the way you smell."

Phoenix didn't dare speak. She was feeling far too much to express any of it in words, was frightened by what might come out if she tried. The last thing she needed was to tell him that no man could ever mean as much to her as he did. That whether they were together or not, she'd love him until the day she died. Anyone who could hang on for seventeen years, through the rejection she'd faced and everything else she'd been through, had to be built for one man and one man only. And, for whatever reason, *he* was that man.

His hand cupped her breast as he suckled her, and the other hand found its way to her hair. Then he raised his head and stared down at her as his fingers sought even more intimate places.

"I've imagined the two of us together so many times," he said. "At Sexy Sadie's, in the pool, at night in my bed. But the reality is so much better than all of that."

She began to explore his body. She figured this might be her only chance to act on the desire he aroused in her. Why not take what she wanted, too? Forget about caution and control and what might happen later. Add another night to her small but treasured cache of memories, this one of Riley as an adult?

He seemed slightly surprised that she'd become more aggressive. So far, all she'd done was try to remind herself that this probably wouldn't lead to anything permanent. That would be too much to ask, and she'd learned long ago not to wish for a lot. But if she *had* to love Riley, she might as well enjoy the next few hours.

"Phoenix?" he whispered. "What are you thinking?"

"I'm not. Let's not waste our time talking, either," she said, and felt his body go taut when she wrapped her hand around him. "I—I need…"

"What?" He closed his eyes. "What do you need?"

"I need to feel you inside me," she replied. "And I'm not willing to wait."

He didn't require any more encouragement. After that, everything grew intense. His kisses changed to hungry and purposeful and she thought he'd enter her right away. But he didn't. He got out a condom and put it on. Then he held her arms above her head and paused to look down at her. "Being with you, it's…amazing," he said. "Thank you for taking the chance, even though I don't deserve it. I'll prove myself. You'll see."

She groaned as she felt him fill her. "Yes," she whispered, trying to ignore his words—in case she made the mistake of counting on them. "God, that feels good."

It'd been so long—and never, in all that time, had she wanted anyone else.

Phoenix woke a few hours later. It was still dark, so she wasn't sure what had awakened her, until she felt movement. After sleeping alone for seventeen years, she had someone else in her bed—and not just anyone. This was the one man she'd sworn to avoid.

Swallowing a sigh at her weakness—she'd made love to him not just once but *twice*—she leaned on one elbow to gaze at him in the moonlight shining through a skylight overhead. He was even more beautiful asleep…

"What are you thinking about?" he murmured.

She hadn't realized he was awake, and she wasn't about to tell him the truth. She grinned instead. "That you're good in bed."

"You're not bad yourself. You really underestimated your own ability, you know that? That second time… you just about killed me."

She knew he was referring to how wantonly she'd straddled him before they fell asleep, and felt the heat of a blush. "What are you talking about? You were fine."

"I was hanging on for dear life. I've never been ridden quite like that."

"Stop teasing me," she said, and gave him a playful punch.

He grasped her hands. "Why? I liked it—so much that I nearly humiliated myself. It was all I could do to last. Just thinking about the look on your face when you came makes me hard."

"We don't have any more condoms, and we already had to use the withdrawal method once. We shouldn't risk it. With my luck, history will repeat itself."

"Wouldn't that be ironic—if I got you pregnant again?" he said, but he sounded more wistful than horrified by the idea.

"At least we're older. Now it doesn't matter what anyone says about our choices."

"Being an adult has its advantages."

"But if I *am* pregnant, I get to raise this one."

She sounded adamant, as if she wouldn't allow herself to be robbed again. He stroked her hair. "You're assuming you'd have to do it on your own."

"I don't expect anything from you, Riley. I'm stronger than I thought I was. You can go your way, and I'll be fine."

He ran a finger down the side of her face. "I'm not going anywhere," he said, pulling her back down beside him.

It was almost eleven o'clock when Riley woke up. He wasn't sure how he'd slept so late, since he was used to getting up early. But when he saw that Phoenix wasn't in the room, he worried that she might've tried to leave the cabin on her own. He wanted to be the one to drive her home, so he threw on his clothes without bothering to shower, raked his fingers through his hair to get it to lie down and hurried over to the main house.

Fortunately, Phoenix was there, in the kitchen, helping with breakfast—and Candy was nowhere in sight. Was it too much to hope that *she* was the one who'd left?

He didn't see Samantha, either, also a hopeful sign.

"Morning." Gail smiled brightly as she carried out a platter of scrambled eggs. Eve followed with sausages.

Riley's gaze sought out Phoenix, who was frying potatoes. At the sound of his voice, she glanced behind her and curved her lips in a brief smile before returning to her work. But the uncertain nature of that smile made him walk over, wrap an arm around her shoulders and kiss her on the top of her head. "Hi, gorgeous."

She looked over at the kitchen table, where all his friends were watching them. "You'd better grab a plate while the eggs are hot," she said, going red. "I'll bring over the potatoes in a second."

Simon stood next to her, making waffles. His grin slanted to one side, and he nudged Riley, who was walking by. "You sleep okay in that small bed?"

"Best night I've had in a while," Riley said.

Simon chuckled. "Glad to hear it."

Everyone smirked at him. But Riley didn't care if they were catching on that he'd been with Phoenix. It didn't embarrass him in the least. He'd gotten what he wanted; now he just had to figure out how to hang on to her. Jacob had said he didn't mind their being together. But there were also his parents, the Mansfields and all the other people in Whiskey Creek who thought she was guilty of killing Lori. And Lizzie wasn't likely to forgive him for the pain he'd caused Phoenix.

But first things first. He had to start his second chance with Phoenix by asking Candy to leave. "Where are Candy and Samantha?" he asked.

Callie jerked her head at Kyle, who was sitting at the table. "Someone did you a solid and told them that having them here wasn't really working out."

Riley felt his mouth drop open. "You?"

Kyle took a sip of his orange juice. "Don't say I never did anything for you."

"Thanks. But you *are* the one who got her up here." He lifted his hands. "Just sayin'."

He scowled in mock anger. "Because you couldn't get your own date."

Relieved to think he'd been spared *that* obstacle, he poured himself a cup of coffee and joined the others at the table. "So…how'd it go? What'd she say?"

"She'd already figured out you weren't all that interested in her. She was packing when I knocked on the door."

"There's nothing like sobriety to put things in perspective."

Everyone laughed.

"What about Samantha?" Riley asked. "She could've stayed."

Kyle clicked his tongue. "That wasn't really working, either."

Riley put his coffee down and squeezed Kyle's shoulder. "Sorry, bro."

He shrugged, and focused on Olivia, who was just coming into the room with her husband, Brandon. "Attraction's a funny thing."

He'd been in love with Olivia for a number of years but had lost her to his stepbrother. Riley could only imagine how hard it was to see them together all the time.

"Definitely." Riley certainly hadn't been able to pick the woman *he* was attracted to. Phoenix had tried, more than once, to warn him that being with her wouldn't be easy, but she was the one he wanted, and he couldn't seem to escape that.

"Who's ready for a waffle?" Simon asked, but then the phone rang, and he raised a finger for quiet.

"Riley, it's Jacob," he said a moment later.

Riley felt Phoenix's interest as he walked over. But when everyone went back to talking, he had to take the phone into the other room in order to hear. "What's up, buddy?"

"Why aren't you answering your cell?" Jake asked.

It was on the nightstand by the bed he was *supposed* to sleep in, but he wasn't about to reveal that. "I forgot my charger," he lied. "But I'll borrow one, so you can reach me later if you need to."

"I'm glad you gave Tristan's parents the number to the cabin."

"Why? Is something wrong?"

He didn't answer that question. "Did Mom ever show up?"

Riley peered around the corner to see Phoenix scooping potatoes into a bowl. "Yeah."

"And? Did that work out?"

He had to smile. Last night had been a little rocky at first. She'd been determined to shut him out and protect herself, but after they'd reached the bed she'd started feeling comfortable with him... "It sure did. I'm happy she's here."

"Is *she* happy?" Jacob asked.

Riley remembered almost pulling her into the creek the last time Jacob had tried to help him and felt his smile grow bigger. "I think so."

"That's a relief, anyway."

Jacob didn't sound as pleased as Riley would've expected; he sounded more upset or preoccupied than anything else. "So what's wrong?"

"We stopped at the Gas 'n' Go to fill up and get some snacks before heading to SF this morning, and…"

Riley felt a tremor of unease, not from anything Jacob had said, but from the way he was acting. "*And? What is it?*"

"Buddy Mansfield was there."

Tightening his grip on the phone, Riley propped one foot against the wall. "He'd better not have said anything to you!"

"He didn't threaten me or anything. But…I don't like him anymore. Not even a little. He's a jerk."

Riley had never liked him a whole lot to begin with, but he had liked Corinne and the rest of the family. "Just ignore him."

"I wanted to, but he said Aunt Corinne's found Penny Sawyer, and that Penny would finally set us both straight on exactly who and what my mother is."

Oh, God… Riley leaned around the corner again to see Phoenix sitting at the table beside Noah. When she glanced up at him, he slipped back behind the wall. "Your mother didn't kill Lori on purpose, Jake. Penny grabbed the wheel."

"*I* know that, and *you* know that. But…I didn't get the feeling Penny's going to admit it. And it sounded to me like she's coming to town. If that happens, it'll stir everything up all over again. Everyone will hate Mom, no matter what we say. I'm afraid they'll make her life so miserable she won't be able to keep living here."

Riley had tried to find Penny himself on Facebook, had hoped to get her to tell the truth. Last night, as he was drifting off, he'd even considered hiring a private investigator to clear Phoenix's name. But if the Mansfields had found her and were bringing her to town, he doubted she'd be saying the things he wanted to hear. *"When?"*

"He didn't say—not that I heard, anyway. Tristan dragged me out of there pretty fast, so Buddy and I wouldn't wind up in an argument."

"It was getting heated?"

"Mostly on my part. I told him to leave my mom alone. But he won't. And neither will Aunt Corinne. It's *so* unfair."

Riley rubbed a hand over his face. What was he going to do now? "Dad?"

"Don't worry about anything," Riley said. "Go to San Francisco and have a great time. I have your mother here with me. Nothing's going to happen to her."

"She'll be there the whole weekend?"

"Yes."

"Okay. I was afraid to leave in case that Penny person showed up, and we wouldn't be here when she did."

"I'll take care of it, like I said. Everything'll be fine," he insisted, but he was uneasy when he hung up.

24

As soon as she saw Riley return the phone, Phoenix walked over to the breakfast bar to get the juice she'd forgotten. She'd wanted to speak to Jacob, had been hoping he'd ask for her. Apparently, he hadn't. "Is everything okay?" she asked as Riley began to load up his plate.

He nodded but didn't seem quite as carefree as he'd been when he first came down to breakfast. "Yeah. Jake's on his way to the city."

"Is he excited?"

"I think so. He couldn't talk long. They were all in the car."

That made sense, but there still seemed to be... something that had brought a dark cloud. "He was just checking in, then?"

"He wanted to make sure you arrived safely."

She grinned, remembering how often Jake had pushed her to come to the party. "He's the one who got me up here."

"He's a hell of a wingman. I don't know anyone else who could've managed that."

"So...what time are we heading back?"

"We're not." He elbowed her, but his playfulness

didn't seem as natural as it had earlier. "Not today. You're locked in for the entire weekend, so I hope you're ready to have some fun in the sun."

She lowered her voice. "I don't even have a swimsuit. I came on the spur of the moment. I wasn't really prepared."

"I should've bought you one. I'll do that when we get home."

"I'll buy my own…" she started, but he cut her off.

"For now, we'll see if Gail has an extra."

She was smaller than Gail, than all his friends, but she figured she could always go wading in her clothes. With her scars, she actually preferred that.

As she walked back to her seat so she could finish her breakfast, he clasped her upper arm.

"You're okay with staying, aren't you?"

Her heart nearly tripped over itself as she looked up, into his face. She wasn't going to complain about spending another night with him. "I'm fine with it."

"Thanks." He held her chin while giving her a quick peck. "This is the perfect birthday."

But if he truly felt that way, why did he seem sort of…troubled?

Phoenix sat on the deck of Gail and Simon's houseboat with Riley and several of his friends. Music played in the background while Noah—who'd fixed her bike— blended and served margaritas. Several people braved the cold water.

Gail had lent Phoenix a pretty bikini that didn't fit too badly. She wore a T-shirt of Riley's over it, which he kept encouraging her to take off, so she wouldn't get a farmer's tan. She wasn't ready for his friends to see her scars, though. She already stood out enough. Last night she'd shown up at the party as a fifth wheel. Now his official date had left and most people guessed that he hadn't slept in his own bed. Every once in a while, she'd catch one of his friends eyeing her curiously. They'd always smile when she looked up, but she could tell they were a little unsure about his latest decision.

She couldn't blame them for being concerned. From their perspective—from almost anyone's perspective—he could do a lot better.

"You're awfully quiet."

Riley had gone to get some chips and bean dip. This remark came from Levi, Callie's husband, who was lying on her opposite side.

"I'm just…enjoying the sun," she said, but she was enjoying more than that. Rubbing sunblock on Riley's back or seeing him flash her that smile of his made her stomach do flip-flops. She was living a dream, being with him like this, especially with the houseboat and cabin and all the beautiful people he hung out with. They were the crowd she'd admired back in her high school days, although she'd tried to pretend she *didn't* envy them.

"So you're having a good time?"

She'd been having a *great* time. Just when she'd resigned herself to going without sex for another two or three years, she'd had the night of her life, and it'd been with Jake's father. But she had to wonder where it would all end. So much of her relationship with her son still depended on Riley. If he decided she wasn't innocent, after all, or that there was something else wrong with her, Jake's opinion could change, too.

But they weren't back in Whiskey Creek yet. Why ruin these few days by worrying about the future?

"It's been nice to get away," she replied.

Levi sat up in his lounger and took off his sunglasses. "I hope so. Because…people are always going to talk. Or stare at someone who's new or different. That's life, and you can't let it bother you. I can tell you that everyone here…they mean well."

She glanced around to make sure no one could overhear what she said in response. Fortunately, Callie, Levi's wife, was in the galley, trying to help Noah get the blender going again, since it had jammed. "I appreciate that. I really do. But I understand they're Riley's friends—that *you're* Riley's friend, too. You're all afraid he's making a mistake getting involved with me, and I can't fault you for that."

"If he cares about you and believes in you, there must be a reason."

"He's better off without me," she said solemnly. "So are the rest of you."

"Because…"

"Befriending me would be pitting yourselves against everyone else in Whiskey Creek."

"If that's what it takes, that's what it takes. But why don't you let us worry about what we should or shouldn't do?" He stood and peered over the side.

"Hey, jump in," Brandon called the second he saw Levi. "Feels great!"

Levi turned to her and gestured at the water. "Shall we?"

Phoenix sensed that he was issuing a challenge—*Be who you are*—and realized how futile it was to hide anything. She'd been through a hard time, but she hadn't deserved it. So she'd hold her head high and let people make up their own minds about her past.

With a nod, she stood up and peeled off Riley's shirt. She felt Levi's eyes lower to the scar on her abdomen.

Then he grinned at her as if no one would ever care about that—and they both dived over the side.

The entire weekend was idyllic. Phoenix had never had more fun in her life. After Levi coaxed her into swimming with Brandon, she became less guarded around Riley's friends. She began to see that she wasn't as different as she'd always thought. Sure, she had a scandalous past, and everyone knew the terrible details. But Lincoln had served time. Levi hinted that he hadn't been perfect. And as the group talked about Cheyenne and Dylan, who weren't there because they hadn't wanted to leave their baby, she began to remember Dylan's reputation in high school. He'd been trouble with a capital *T*, and so had his younger brothers. Simon had made frequent appearances in the tabloids. Riley and his friends even teased Simon about his past. Then there was Callie, who had to be cautious about what she ate and what she came in contact with because of health issues, and Addy and Sophia, who hinted that life had, at times, been difficult for them, too. Eve had tried hard from the beginning to be welcoming, and the rest grew friendlier the more she interacted with them.

Riley's friends added to the overall fun. But the best part was, of course, Riley and the nights they spent together. Sex had never been that good in high school. Phoenix hadn't realized it *could* be so good.

When Sunday evening came around, she was even more reluctant to leave the cabin than she'd expected. Somehow she'd lost the fatalism that had insulated her from the worst blows of life, and she'd begun to hope. That hope was fresh and exhilarating. But it was also frightening because it meant she could get hurt again.

The fact that she could so quickly forget the lessons

and scars of the past was a testament to the resilience of the human spirit. It'd taken only three days with the man she'd dreamed about for most of her life, a few new friends and plenty of good times and laughter to feel almost as if those years in prison had never occurred.

"Too bad we have to go back so soon," she lamented as she zipped her suitcase.

Riley was a few feet away, packing his bag since he'd moved into her room after their first night together. He glanced up when she spoke, then walked over to take her by the shoulders. "This weekend was just the beginning. At least when it comes to us."

She nodded. "Right."

He frowned. "You believe that, don't you?"

"I'm open-minded about it," she joked.

He looked worried as he dropped his hands. "There *is* something I need to tell you, though," he said. "Something I've been putting off."

Now? Just when she'd let down her guard? Phoenix felt herself tense. "What is it?"

"Nothing to do with us, but…it will upset you. I waited because I didn't want it to ruin the weekend, but I want you to be prepared."

Her nails curled into her palms. "For…"

"When Jacob called?"

Her stomach plummeted. "You said he was okay!"

"He was, and he is. But…he was calling to tell me something that has him worried."

"And that is…"

"The Mansfields have managed to track down Penny Sawyer."

The memories of everything that had destroyed her life came rushing back. Lori's death, the guilt she felt about being unable to control the car after Penny yanked on the wheel, the horror of what had happened afterward, that sick feeling of despair when no one would believe her… For a few days here at the cabin, she'd felt like a different person, a regular person. She'd begun to believe she might have the chance to outdistance all of that. So she'd relaxed—and here was the next punch.

"Let me guess. She isn't coming clean." It wasn't hard to predict where this was going.

"She *must* be standing by her story," Riley agreed, "or they wouldn't be bringing her to town."

She was coming to Whiskey Creek?

Phoenix moved away from him to sit on the bed. "Why are they doing this? I served my time. They can't try me again. So what do they hope to accomplish?" she asked. But the answer was obvious. They were angry that Riley and Jacob had defected and befriended Lori's "murderer." The Mansfields wanted to convince them, and anyone else who might consider accepting her, that she was really the evil person they believed her to be. They wanted to push her out of their world completely.

"They're looking for some way to feel better about what happened to Lori. That's all. And punishing you makes them feel they're doing what they can to avenge her."

"It's not enough that an innocent person sat in prison for half her life?"

"An eternity wouldn't be long enough, since they think you're guilty."

She shoved a hand through her hair. "I'm afraid they'll turn Jacob against me. I wish…I wish they'd leave me alone."

"That would be nice, but at least you're not on your own with this anymore," he said.

She stared at him.

"I won't let them hurt you."

"You can't get involved!" she cried. "If you and Jacob stand up for me, they'll just become more determined to prove you're wrong."

He sat down next to her and took her hand. "I don't have any choice."

"Of course you do. You need to distance yourself, keep a low profile."

"That isn't possible."

"Why not?"

He brought her knuckles to his lips and kissed them, then waited for her to look up at him. "Because I'm in love with you."

She wanted to believe that. She'd longed to hear him say those words again. Maybe she could've believed him if they'd been able to stay in the idyllic world of the cabin. But they had to deal with the real world. They'd be back in Whiskey Creek within hours.

"Then you'd be smart to fall out of love," she said. *Like last time.* She didn't add that, but it was implied.

When he winced, she regretted throwing the past in his face. He'd obviously been hoping she'd slip into his arms and say the same thing to him. So far, she'd been careful not to declare herself. She'd given him everything else, but she'd held back those words, because she was afraid they'd break the spell he seemed to be under, and she'd lose him again.

Besides, by pushing him away, she was doing him a favor. There were plenty of women in the world. Why would he want to be with someone he had to constantly defend when he could just as easily fall for someone else?

"My feelings aren't as changeable as you think," he said, and pulled her to her feet.

* * *

It was dark when she got home, but her mother must've been watching for her. As soon as Riley turned into the drive and Phoenix hopped out, the dogs came running from Lizzie's trailer while Lizzie hid behind the door as she so often did.

"Home at last?" she called through that two-inch gap.

Phoenix managed a smile and waved. "Yeah."

"You had fun?"

Riley climbed out, too, and glanced over but said nothing.

"It was...nice," Phoenix told her.

"I suppose you got what *you* wanted, Mr. Stinson," Lizzie said to Riley.

A muscle moved in his cheek. He knew she wasn't being friendly to him, but he made a stab at responding politely. "I'm glad she came."

"I bet," her mother said with a cackle. "So does that mean you're satisfied? You've accomplished your goal, and we won't be hearing from you anymore?"

Phoenix came around the front of the truck and grabbed Riley's arm as he started to head toward Lizzie's trailer. "Ignore her," she muttered, but he wouldn't. He shook off Phoenix's hand and stalked over.

Lizzie slammed and locked her door before he could even reach the steps.

"I'm not going to hurt you," he yelled. "I just have a few things to say, and I want you to listen." He knocked, but she wouldn't open up.

Phoenix knew she was more afraid he'd see how big she'd become than anything else. Her mother relished a good confrontation; it gave her an outlet for all the anger and resentment that made her so bitter.

"Riley, don't bother," Phoenix mumbled.

"I'd like to talk to her."

"There's nothing to say."

"There sure as hell is!" He banged again but had to resign himself to speaking through the panel. "Hey, I get what you were implying, but you're wrong, okay? I care about your daughter."

Lizzie's voice rang out loud and clear. "Oh, yeah? We'll see how much!"

"You're just afraid of losing her," Riley retorted. "She's the only one who's shown you any kindness, and you don't want to be left alone again."

"Now you're a fucking shrink?" Lizzie fired back.

"I don't have to be a shrink to see you're scared shitless of just about everything," he said. "But don't let those fears ruin your daughter's life, too. That's all I ask. She deserves more than that."

"Does that mean she deserves *you*?"

"Whatever I can give her."

"Oh, and any woman would be so lucky to have that."

He didn't make a rejoinder. Although clearly unhappy with their exchange, he walked back to Phoenix and insisted on checking out her trailer, as he had once before, to make sure Buddy hadn't done anything in her absence.

"Tell Jacob I said hello," she said when he was finished and stood at her door. She knew her son had gotten home because he'd called them while they were driving back.

Riley stared down at her. "I know you love me, so quit pretending you don't," he said, then swept her into his arms and kissed her. "Tonight's going to suck without you," he said, giving in to the more exuberant and boyish side of his personality.

"I'd come over if I could, but I'm afraid it would totally freak Jake out if I stayed the night," she told him. She suspected it would freak out everyone else, too— except his close friends, who already knew they were together.

"He's probably guessed that we've been to bed. It didn't take your mother long to figure it out. And I told him things went well between us at the cabin."

"*Things went well?* That means we've been to bed? Is that some kind of guy code?" she said with a laugh.

"He doesn't want the details. Like you said, that would only creep him out."

"I'm afraid it'll be too weird for him to see us as... more than friends."

"He acts as if he likes the idea, but...some of that might be because he wants me to protect you."

She shook her head. "That's exactly what I *don't* want—for you, or him, to make enemies when you've always been so well loved."

"*I* won't be picking the fights."

The memory of him and Buddy hitting each other in that bathroom turned her stomach. "It doesn't matter. Don't fight."

"Stop worrying. You try to carry the whole world on your shoulders. I'll see you tomorrow when I pick you up for Jake's game."

She braced one hand on the lintel and held the door with the other. "I can't go to the game!"

"Why not?"

"It's at *home*?"

"You love seeing him play and you have every right to be there."

"That could cause Whiskey Creek's first riot, especially if any of the Mansfields come. And they could do that in some misguided attempt to defend their turf.

Now that they're all fired up about finding Penny and they're so certain she'll confirm my guilt, who knows how far they might take it?"

He shrugged. "Kyle will be there to help me. Maybe I'll get Noah and Ted to come, too."

"Riley?"

He'd turned to go, but paused to look at her. "What is it?"

"I do love you."

A tender smile curved his lips. "See? That wasn't so hard, was it?" And he walked back to kiss her again.

25

His mother frowned when she opened the door to see him standing on her stoop. He would've walked in, but the door was locked—and at ten on a Sunday, he could see why they'd think they were in for the night.

"What's wrong?" she asked. "You don't look happy."

He opened the screen. "I'm not."

She stepped aside as he entered the house. His childhood home was well built and well maintained. He'd done most of the repairs on it himself, at least over the past fifteen years, and that included reroofing. He'd also remodeled the kitchen and both bathrooms, helped his father chop down some diseased trees in the backyard and put up shelving in the garage. So his parents' three-bedroom rambler was updated but not particularly large or ostentatious.

He could hear the TV in the living room, where he'd find his dad in his favorite recliner.

"Do I want to ask what's wrong?" His mother went to get the cookie jar. Since he was a kid, he'd gone to that ceramic monkey almost first thing whenever he came into the house, so she was familiar with the routine.

"Maybe not," he said. "Because I'm going to need you to fix it."

She removed the monkey's head and tilted the jar in his direction. She kept his favorite oatmeal scotchies on hand for him and Jake, but for the first time since he could remember, he refused them.

"Now I have no doubt that this is a serious problem." Although she was mostly joking, there was a vein of seriousness in her voice. She put the cookie jar on the kitchen table. "So what is it I'm supposed to fix? Will I have any choice in the matter?"

"Not if you love me," he told her.

The TV went on pause. "Hey, who was at the door?" his father called.

"It's me, Dad." Riley led his mother into the living room.

"What timing. You've got to see this," his father said, and rewound part of the program he'd been watching.

Riley marveled at ESPN's Top Ten Plays—especially a half-court buzzer beater in professional basketball. But then he asked his father to turn it off.

"Why?" he asked in surprise. "What's going on?"

"I want to talk to you and Mom."

The TV went off as requested, and Riley took the love seat while his mother perched on the edge of the sofa. "Tell me this has nothing to do with Phoenix," she said. "Because I'd do anything I can for you. But there's nothing I can do to make *that* right."

"There's a lot you can do," he responded.

"So it *is* Phoenix that's brought you here so late? Riley, there've been some developments over the past few days that you need to be aware of—"

"Let me guess," he cut in, "you and Corinne have found Penny Sawyer."

Her eyes widened. "*I* had nothing to do with it, but Corinne has found her, yes. How'd you hear?"

"Buddy told Jacob Saturday morning, and Jacob called me while I was at the cabin."

"So that's what has you so upset?" she asked. "Corinne just wants to have a meeting where we can all hear what Penny has to say."

"And the point of that is…?"

"She's worried about us, trying to do us a favor. No one has more to lose than we do if Phoenix isn't what she's pretending to be."

"Pretending?" He shook his head. "Never mind. We know what Penny's going to say, so what's the point?"

"The fact that she's standing by her story after seventeen years lends even more legitimacy to her statement," his mother said.

"So Corinne told you she *is* standing by her story."

"Yes."

"Well, that might add legitimacy for you," he argued. "To me, it simply indicates what I already knew—she doesn't want to be blamed."

"We should at least listen to her. If she's lying, maybe we'll be able to tell from her facial expression or her manner."

Helen looked to Tom for support.

"We should at least listen to her," he confirmed.

"She was the only other person in the car, Riley," his mother went on. "The only other person who can tell us what happened. I realize Phoenix seems nice these days, but—" she made a gesture to keep him quiet "—just go with me on this for a minute. What if she's a fraud? What if she *did* mean to kill Lori?"

"I don't believe that for a minute."

"But what if…?"

"Lori's gone, Mom. We can't bring her back."

"I couldn't agree with you more!"

"So what good will it do to continue persecuting Phoenix?"

"No one's persecuting anyone. But do you really want Jacob to embrace an individual like that *as a mother*?"

Riley had been embracing Phoenix in more literal ways, which his parents would soon learn. Admitting his romantic interest right now would only work against him, however. They'd be convinced his judgment was too clouded for him to see her clearly. "Penny *can't* tell the truth, Mom. Not unless she wants the Mansfields and everyone else to hate her the way they've hated Phoenix."

"Penny doesn't even live here anymore. Why would she care about that?"

"Because that anger could lead to prosecution if they go to the police, and they probably would."

"Good Lord, do you hear yourself? You're accusing Penny of something almost as terrible as hitting Lori in the first place. What kind of person blames someone else for such a horrendous incident?"

"It happens, Mom. All the time. It's good ol' self-preservation at work."

She scooted forward. "I still think we should listen to what Penny has to say. If you're afraid to do that much, it tells me you just don't want to see the truth."

He swallowed a sigh. He was frustrated, but he could see why his mother believed what she did. He could see why the Mansfields and everyone else did, too. That had been the problem all along. It didn't make a whole lot of sense for Penny to do what she'd done. "What type of person is Penny now?" he asked.

"I have no idea. Like I told you, I had nothing to do with looking her up. The day you got into that fight with Buddy, Corinne hired a private investigator to find Penny. That's about all I know."

If Penny was going to add to Phoenix's grief, he was glad he hadn't bothered paying to track her down.

"So...will you hear Penny out or not?" she asked.

Riley couldn't very well refuse. His mother was right—it would only make him look like he was resisting the truth, and that wouldn't help him convince anyone of anything. "Fine. I'll listen to what she says. But I want two things in return."

"And they are...?"

"I want the PI's contact information. If Corinne can do a little research before that meeting, I should have the same right. And I want Phoenix to be invited. She should have the chance to defend herself."

"I can get you the PI's information easily enough. Corinne forwarded me one of his emails. But there's no way she'll ever allow Phoenix inside her home."

"Then we do it elsewhere. I'd offer my place, but I'd rather not worry about Jake walking into the middle of it."

"Why can't we do it here?" his father asked.

His mother pursed her lips. "I guess we could."

"Then it's solved," Riley said. "When will Penny be here?"

"Corinne's still making the arrangements. I'll let you know at Jacob's game tomorrow."

That meant he needed to get to work. "Then forward me that private investigator's email tonight."

"I'll go do it right now."

"And just so you know, Phoenix will also be at Jacob's game."

"She's been there before," his father pointed out. "We'll just ignore her," he added for Helen's sake.

"But this time she'll be with me," Riley said.

Helen got to her feet. "Riley, please hold off being with her in public. Just...give it a week. Wait until we've talked to Penny."

"I've already told Phoenix I'll pick her up."

His mother exchanged a concerned look with his father. "Son..." she started.

"Don't interfere," Riley broke in. "Jake wants her there."

"Fine," she said. "But I hope you know what you're doing."

"So?"

Phoenix glanced up from where she was stirring oatmeal on the stove. "So what?" she repeated, but there was no mystery as to where her mother hoped to take this conversation. Although Lizzie would never admit it, she was dying to learn the details of Phoenix's cabin trip, especially after what Riley had said to her last night.

"Was it worth it?" Lizzie asked.

"Worth what?"

Lizzie rolled her eyes. "What do you think?"

"I had a great time," she said.

"With Riley."

Phoenix lowered the heat. "Yes, with Riley."

Her mother hesitated for a moment. Then she said, "How long do you expect it to last?"

"I couldn't tell you," she replied. "I can't predict the future, and neither can you. So don't throw any more dire warnings at me. I'm just taking it one day at a time."

"You think he's going to carry you away from all of

this?" She gestured at their surroundings, but Phoenix knew she meant the entire property. "Is that the dream?"

"No! I'm not trying to get him to do anything for me. I love him, okay? Maybe it'll work out for me, and maybe it won't, but I seem to have the most stubborn heart in history, because I can't stop loving him."

"He and his folks don't like me," she mused. "They'll make you ashamed of your own family."

"I can't speak for them, but…he's not that way."

"Bullshit!" Lizzie barked out a laugh. "You'll see. If you start going with him, it won't be long before you won't even give me the time of day."

Her mother was acting belligerent again, but there was an underlying note of petulance that allowed Phoenix to recognize the fear that inspired it. Lizzie believed that Riley would try to shut her out of Phoenix's life, so she was trying to get rid of him first.

Once Phoenix realized that, the impulse to snap back at her mother disappeared. Turning off the stove so the oatmeal would cool a bit, she walked over to sit down across from Lizzie.

"What are you doing?" Her mother nodded at the pan that held her breakfast as if she couldn't understand why Phoenix wasn't dishing it up. "What's wrong? Why are you looking at me like that?"

"Because I want to make sure I have your attention."

"You had my attention before. Wasn't I talking to you?"

"You were, but you weren't making much sense. I won't abandon you, regardless of what happens. Do you understand? I'm. Not. Going. Anywhere. Not even if I get back with Riley." She wasn't convinced that would happen, anyway, wasn't sure where the experience they'd shared at Lake Melones would lead. "Not even if I move away from Whiskey Creek at some point. I will always be your daughter and I will always do whatever I can to love and help you. It may not be everything you'd like me to do," she clarified, "but I won't turn my back on you the way my brothers have."

Lines appeared in Lizzie's forehead as she feigned a "what are you talking about?" expression. "I'm not afraid of that. I don't care if you *do* abandon me," she snapped. But those words were such a transparent lie Phoenix couldn't take her seriously.

She bit the inside of her cheek so she wouldn't smile. "Well, you're never getting rid of me, whether you want to or not," she said, and noticed how much nicer her mother became after that.

Phoenix was nervous, but she didn't want Riley to know exactly *how* nervous. Once he picked her up, she acted as if going to a home game wasn't any different from attending an away game.

"I hope Jake does well," she said.

Riley slung one arm over the steering wheel. "He will. He's on a roll."

She wiped her palms on her shorts. Then she rummaged in her purse for some lip gloss. She'd wanted to bake more cookies for the team but, after being gone all weekend, there'd been no time. She'd been too busy trying to catch up on her bracelet orders.

"You okay?" Riley asked, glancing over at her.

"Of course," she said with a smile.

"My parents will be there, but don't worry about that."

Don't worry about it? Her stomach burned from the acid caused by her anxiety. "Okay. But…do they know *I'll* be there?"

"Yes. I told them, so…they won't do anything to make you uncomfortable."

Just being around them made her uncomfortable, but even if Helen and Tom glared daggers at her, she'd smile in return or simply avert her eyes. She didn't want Riley to get into another argument with his folks, didn't want to come between him and his family. Costing him some of the most important relationships in his life wouldn't be an act of love. That would be pure selfishness, and she knew it. "I'll be fine."

He turned down the radio. "It's going to be okay. Trust me."

She let him take her hand. "When's Penny coming to town? Have you heard?"

"According to what my mom told me on the phone this morning, she'll be here Saturday."

"That soon?"

"Yeah. They're pressing her to come as quickly as possible."

"Before I can get my hooks into you," she murmured.

"Except it's too late for that," he teased. When she didn't react, he sobered. "My mother has asked that I hear Penny out, and I said I would."

Phoenix's breath caught in her throat. "You did? *Why?*"

"Because it could be important, give us a chance to present our own case."

"Our case?"

"I was going to tell you that next. You'll be there. My mother has agreed to include you."

Phoenix had reconciled herself to the fact that she'd likely never see Penny again, so she wasn't sure how she felt about coming face-to-face with her. The mere thought of Penny evoked anger, the old anger—and the futility of that anger, which was worse. It had always been difficult to get beyond the injustice she'd been dealt, and now that she was home, she had to confront Penny's lies all over again? "What have they promised her?" she asked.

"What do you mean?"

"She can't *want* to come back here. If I'd lied like she did, I'd never want to see this place again."

He scowled. "What are you saying? You think the Mansfields are paying her?"

"Unless she's started believing her own lies. Or she's looking forward to being in the spotlight again. She has to have *some* reason. I've fulfilled my sentence, so it can't be for a conviction."

"That's why we both need to be there. To figure it out. So...what do you say?" He lowered his head to see into her face. "It won't be easy to confront her, but *I* think we should take her on."

"Why?" Phoenix asked. "They'll believe her, like they already do. What they're really hoping for is to convince *you*."

He squeezed her hand. "She won't be able to, Phoenix. That's not why I'm going. It's been so long. Things change. I'm hoping we can get the truth out of her."

Phoenix didn't even dare to hope, not after all the letters she'd sent Penny that'd gone unanswered. And not after all the days she'd prayed for a miracle, to no avail. "*How?* How could we possibly make her admit anything?"

"I've been working on that."

They passed the hardware store, the soda fountain, the dress boutique. "Excuse me?"

"I don't want to tell you about it yet, don't want to get your hopes up in case it falls through. But I also don't want you to worry too much. They're not going to have quite the advantage they think."

"What are you talking about?" she asked.

"You'll see."

She felt her eyebrows draw together as she looked over at him. "Tell me," she insisted, but they were already turning into the high school.

"Just trust me," he said as he parked.

He got out, but she couldn't bring herself to follow him. Not immediately. So he came around and opened her door.

"I'll be right by your side," he said. But in some ways that was worse. They were making a statement and almost everyone would have *some* reaction to it.

Closing her eyes, she took a deep breath, then let it go in a rush. "I hope Jake does well," she said again, and climbed out.

26

Phoenix was quiet at the game. Riley was sure she didn't say more than two words through nine innings. She sat surrounded by his male friends, kept her gaze trained on the baseball diamond and shook her head every time anyone offered her anything—a hot dog or gum or sunflower seeds.

Plenty of people stared at them. Riley could hear whispering, too. *Isn't that the woman who killed Lori Mansfield?...You don't think Riley's taking her back, do you?...She's pretty, you gotta give her that, but shit, how do you take a murderer back into your life, let alone your bed? If he's not careful, she'll stab him in his sleep.*

He knew that Phoenix could hear them, too, even though she pretended she couldn't. He wished he could go around and make them all shut up, but those wagging tongues were just something they'd have to endure. Interest would fade with time, as everyone got used to having Phoenix back and seeing them together.

His parents didn't end up coming. Riley guessed his mother would give him some lame excuse later. She'd say they got too busy or were too tired, but he figured they'd purposely avoided the high school once they learned Phoenix would be there. They didn't want to be seen with her, didn't want to be perceived as giving their blessing to his acceptance of her. They were waiting for the big confrontation this weekend, hoping *that* would set him straight and put them all back on the same footing.

But, God willing, by then he'd have some interesting show-and-tell of his own.

Jake came over after practice the next few days, and Riley stopped by after work. Phoenix's trailer was small and hot and far humbler than their house, but they spent a lot of time in it. She assumed they liked that she made them dinner—she had to cook for her mother, anyway—and maybe they enjoyed getting out of their usual surroundings. Because they didn't even mention the heat or the things she lacked. Neither did they try to convince her to come to their house instead. They seemed content just to be wherever she was.

On Friday, Riley brought over a small TV and a stack of DVDs, and they had a marathon movie night. When Jake fell asleep on the couch around midnight, Phoenix could tell that Riley was tempted to take her into the bedroom. They hadn't slept together since the cabin. They'd both been working too hard. Or, if they weren't working, Jake was with them. But as much as Phoenix craved Riley's touch, she was afraid their son might wake up.

"God, I miss feeling you beneath me," Riley whispered as he stood behind her in the kitchen, where she'd carried the bowls they'd used for popcorn.

"Maybe we'll have some time alone this weekend," she whispered back. But they both knew what was happening tomorrow. He was picking her up at ten and taking her over to his parents', where the Mansfields and

Penny Sawyer would meet them. She wouldn't be able to sleep a wink, not with that on the horizon.

"You're not scared to see Penny, are you?" he asked, turning her to face him when she kept on washing dishes.

"I'm terrified," she said. "I'm afraid you'll believe her. I wish you didn't even want to hear what she has to say."

"I'm not as excited about it as I was."

She dried her hands. "What does that mean?"

"I had something hopeful going, like I mentioned when we were driving to the game. But—" he grimaced "—it sort of fell apart."

"What was it?"

"I hired Corinne's private investigator to do a little work for me, too. Had him do a background search. He even managed to track down Penny's ex-husband."

"What did you want with her ex?"

"People share secrets with their spouses all the time. I was hoping he'd tell me that she admitted she was the one who caused the accident."

"But she didn't?"

"I personally think she did, but he still feels too loyal to divulge anything that could get her in trouble."

"So we have nothing. Just more of her lies."

He rested his forehead against hers. "I'm sorry. I really hoped for better."

"Does that mean we can cancel tomorrow? Just go on the way we've been?"

"Canceling will make me look scared, as if I'm afraid to hear the truth, or I won't face it. *I* should go. But I can stand up for you. You don't need to be there."

"Heck, no!" she said. "If you're going, so am I. At

least if Penny sees me, it won't be as easy for her to lie—although she certainly managed it in court."

"Nothing she could say will ever persuade me that you're anything less than the wonderful person I know you to be," he said. Then he kissed her, several times, until their kisses grew heated and she pulled away.

"Not with Jake here."

He didn't complain. He just woke Jake and followed him home.

Phoenix thought she'd be alone for the rest of the night, with the next eight hours to dread their meeting. But Riley returned less than an hour later, alone, and stayed until dawn before going back home to slip into his own bed before Jacob could wake up.

"This feels like *Groundhog Day*," Phoenix said as Riley parked at the curb outside his parents' house.

"Groundhog Day?"

"Haven't you seen that movie? My mother has a copy. We watched it the night I got home. Bill Murray's in it. I wasn't interested enough to pay a whole lot of attention. I was mostly indulging her. But he lives the same day over and over again."

Riley seemed confused by the comparison. "This day isn't like any other. You haven't seen Penny for seventeen years."

"But I'm heading into treacherous territory—like at the baseball game yesterday, the cabin before that, the restaurant when I first got out of prison. Only—" she bit her lip "—this is the most terrifying."

"I won't let Penny treat you badly," he said.

"It's your mother I'm worried about. This'll be the closest I've come to her since we broke up."

He chuckled. "She's not as scary as you think. And we're not broken up anymore. That changes things."

"We're not broken up right now. But what happens after we walk into that house and Penny starts spewing her poison?"

"I told you. It won't change anything between us. I thought last night would've convinced you of *that*."

"Last night was...memorable." She smiled playfully. "Let's go back, take off our clothes and forget all about this."

He walked around to open her door. "Appealing as that sounds, we have to get through this first. We can't flinch from it or they'll think they've won."

She leaned around him to see the front door. "They always win."

He studied her for several seconds, then frowned as if he was growing uncertain. "Maybe you *should* stay out here. I have no idea what they might say to you. I can't stop them from talking, and I don't want to see you hurt. I'll call you in if...if it could help."

"No. I've come this far. Let's see if Penny can lie like she did before, now that I'm no longer a pregnant, panic-stricken, eighteen-year-old facing extensive prison time."

She climbed out, and he took her hand as they approached the house.

"You don't have to hang on to me," she said.

"I know," he responded, but didn't let go.

They weren't late and yet everyone else was already inside. It felt as though her enemies had gathered in advance, so they'd be able to launch a unified attack.

For all her tough words, she found herself gripping Riley's hand a little tighter.

All eyes immediately turned her way. Phoenix ignored the malevolence on Buddy's face as well as the somber expressions of the others. She even ignored Riley's mom. She was most interested in Penny, who glanced up but would not hold Phoenix's gaze.

"Thanks for coming." Riley's mother nodded at Phoenix in a stiff yet polite greeting.

Phoenix nodded back but didn't speak.

"You two remember Penny." Helen motioned toward the tall, bone-thin woman several seats away. "I suggest we go ahead and start, get this over with as quickly as possible."

Corinne took the lead. "Penny, I know it's difficult to recount what you went through. We cried about it together on the phone. But Helen's right. It's better to just...lay it out there."

They were treating Penny so gently. Lori's murderer! Phoenix couldn't believe the irony...

Penny cleared her throat and shifted, but still didn't speak. So Corinne prompted her again. "Can you tell us what happened the day my daughter was killed?"

It was almost imperceptible, and yet Phoenix thought she saw Penny cringe before squaring her shoulders.

"It's like I said before. In court. Nothing's changed."

Phoenix had expected to be self-conscious, to feel as she usually did whenever she left the safety of her trailer. But all of that fell away as she studied Penny. *This* was the person who'd caused her to spend seventeen years in prison for a crime she didn't commit, who'd cost her all that time with her son. Penny was the one who'd gotten away without consequence, and yet... there was an air of desperation about her, as if she'd fared even worse than Phoenix since they'd last met.

Why? What was it? Penny was still somewhat attractive, with her long blond hair and high cheekbones. She was dressed nicely, too—in a long skirt with sandals and a pretty blouse, sheer in the sleeves. Her clothes looked brand-new, which gave Phoenix the impression that she'd dressed up for this occasion.

Or that she'd been dressed up...

Phoenix's mind reverted to what she'd believed about the Mansfields paying Penny to come. There had to be *something* in it for her. This couldn't be about justice; it was Penny who'd escaped justice.

"Can you give us more details?" Corinne asked. "Go over it step by step?" She continued to speak softly, as though she was addressing a frightened child. That galled Phoenix, but it was effective.

Once Penny started talking, she told basically the same story she'd given the jury. Only she wouldn't look at Phoenix when she spoke. She kept stopping and Corinne would have to persuade her to start again. Soon, Penny grew so agitated that she began biting her cuticles—and interrupted herself to ask how long it would be until they drove her back to the airport.

That was when Phoenix noticed the sores on her hands.

"Why do you think Phoenix aimed for Lori?" Corinne asked, once again trying to keep Penny focused.

"Phoenix hated Lori." Penny sounded like a robot. Phoenix suspected she'd rehearsed this part. "She was... jealous of her. She wanted Riley."

That was the same motive people here had ascribed to her since it happened. There was nothing new or unexpected about that, since they'd also said it in court. Penny didn't embellish the original story, didn't re-create any dialogue from when they were in the car, as the Mansfields were obviously hoping she would. But it was the best they could get out of her.

Bringing Penny here didn't seem to be adding *any-thing* new. Maybe that was why Helen seemed frustrated when she took over. "To be fair, we also need to hear from Phoenix." She gave a grudging nod to Riley. "Phoenix, do you have anything to say?"

"It's a lie," Phoenix said. "*I* didn't turn the wheel. Penny did, and she knows it."

Penny didn't jump up in indignation as she'd done in court. She shrank in on herself.

"Why?" Helen asked. "*Why* would Penny turn the wheel?"

"Let's ask *her*," Phoenix said. "Penny? *Why did you do it?* And why did you let me go to prison for it?"

Jiggling her leg, Penny seemed to zone out, as if she were just putting in time, and again gave no discernible response.

"Penny?" Helen prompted.

Scowling, Penny grew slightly belligerent. "I didn't. I don't care what anyone says. Why would *I* want to hurt anybody? *I* had nothing against Lori."

"I don't believe you meant to hurt anyone," Phoenix said. "It was an accident, right? Something stupid you did just to be funny. And it wound up having tragic consequences."

Penny shook her head. "No, of course not! You're wrong. She—she's lying," she said, pointing at Phoenix. "I told you she'd just accuse me."

Riley spoke up. "All we want is the truth."

Penny got to her feet, then swayed and nearly fell over before regaining her balance. "I told you the truth. I can't believe you'd question my integrity. I shouldn't have to sit through this. I'm done. I came and I told my story, like you asked. Now, who's going to take me back to the airport?"

"Hold on," Riley said, raising his hand. "*My* story? That's revealing, isn't it?"

"I meant *the* story," Penny corrected, looking a bit rattled.

Riley's eyes narrowed. "Sure you did. Then maybe you won't mind answering a few questions."

Her gaze darted to Corinne before moving back to him. "What questions? I told you everything. You can't keep me here against my will!"

"We paid for your trip," Corinne said. "And we're paying for your time, since you said you'd miss work."

So there *was* money involved. That answered at least one of Phoenix's questions—why Penny would be willing to do this. Phoenix was almost certain she had a drug habit. Maybe she didn't make enough at work. Maybe this was the only way she could get another fix. Drug addicts had been known to rob minimarts for fifty bucks or less.

"She doesn't even have a job," Riley said, but Corinne was too focused to react to that.

"I think you owe us a few more minutes at least," she told Penny.

Riley waited until he had Penny's undivided attention. Then he said, "Do you know a man by the name of Roger Hume?"

"That—that's my ex," she said.

"We agree on one thing, then. Roger is your ex. You were married to him for nearly ten years. Is that correct?"

Phoenix had no idea where he was going with this. Riley had told her when they were cleaning up last night that Roger hadn't given him what he wanted.

"What does *that* matter?" Penny said. "We haven't been together in a long time. He's ancient history."

The Mansfields—and Riley's parents—were so caught up they watched with open mouths.

"You were officially divorced four years ago," Riley went on. "But the marriage fell apart much sooner. From what he told me, you two fought constantly because of your drug habit."

She seemed stunned and confused that he knew so much. "No..."

"I had a background check done."

She blinked at him. "Which means...what?"

"I have the police records to prove it. You've been arrested for trying to run Roger down with your car, striking him with your fists and trying to set fire to your own apartment. Once you were arrested for being naked in the street, so high that you didn't know who you were or where you were, and—"

"I want to go," she broke in.

Phoenix could hardly hear above her own heartbeat. What was Riley doing?

"What kind of drugs do you use?" he asked. "Because you clearly haven't stopped."

"That's none of your business. This has nothing to do with my habit or my marriage or anything else."

"It has *everything* to do with your habit," he said. "You came here for the money, am I right?"

"No." She shook her head but it was a pretty obvious lie. "I suffer from depression, so...so I'm on medication for that. But a lot of people suffer from depression."

Riley clicked his tongue. "This is a little different. Roger said things would get so bad you'd disappear for a week at a time. He told me you were haunted by a terrible tragedy that occurred during your senior year, said you just couldn't put it behind you."

She waved a hand to indicate the room at large. "Haven't we *all* been haunted by Lori's death? I was in a vehicle that struck and killed another human being!"

Riley lowered his voice but spoke as if there was no question about the veracity of what he said. "Because you grabbed the wheel."

She blinked repeatedly. "No. And if Roger said that, he's lying! He doesn't know what happened because he wasn't there."

"But you told him, didn't you? When you were high or sad or unable to forget, you shared your dark secret."

"You tricked me into coming here!" She turned on Corinne. "You said all I had to do was show up and tell my story, and you'd give me two hundred dollars for my time and pay for my flight. I want my money, and I want out of here."

"Two hundred dollars?" Phoenix said. "That's all it took to get you to try and hurt me again?"

"How can anything I say hurt you now? You're out, aren't you? There's nothing more they can do to you. I might as well get the money."

Corinne pressed a hand to her throat as if she needed to pry someone's boot off it. "Is it true?" she gasped. "What Riley's saying?"

Wearing an expression of concern, Corinne's husband stood and rested a hand on her shoulder.

"Don't listen to her, Mom," Buddy said. "This is all Phoenix, trying to confuse us. She did this…"

"That's ludicrous!" Riley shouted. "You guys are the ones who brought Penny here! But now that we've got the chance to talk to her, I want the truth. If you don't— or can't—accept being wrong, feel free to walk out."

Tears were beginning to run down Penny's face. "I didn't do it."

"Then why would your ex-husband say you did?" Helen asked.

Penny's eyes took on a look of fear that reminded Phoenix of a cornered animal. "He's bitter, angry. He's an *ex*, for Christ's sake. Some exes will do *anything* to get back at their former partners."

"He didn't sound bitter to me," Riley said. "He told me part of him will always love you, but that you need help. That you've fallen so far, he doesn't know if you'll ever get back up."

Closing her eyes, she covered her face, but the tears continued. Phoenix could see them dripping off her chin.

"Tell the truth," Riley said, unyielding, insistent. "For once in your life, tell the fucking truth!"

She began to tremble. "I didn't mean to hurt her," she whispered through her fingers. "God knows I didn't mean to hurt anyone. It was—it was an *accident*. No one should be punished for an accident."

Phoenix was so surprised that Penny had finally admitted her culpability that it took a second to sink in. She looked at Riley to see if he'd heard it, too. Then she looked around the room and saw that everyone else was equally stunned.

"And yet you made what you did even worse by letting an innocent person take the consequences," Riley said. "For an accident like that, with no ill intent, you probably would've been sentenced to five years, if that. Instead, you let everyone believe Phoenix *tried* to run Lori down, and you let her sit in prison for *seventeen years*. She missed out on raising her son, and she had to come home to face the anger of the people who believed she'd murdered a member of their family."

"I know! But I can't fix that now! It's in the past." Penny crumpled to the carpet, sobbing so loudly that they could no longer understand her. Something about, "I never meant to hurt anyone. It was a joke."

When she curled into a fetal position, Phoenix stood up to go to her. She wasn't sure what she felt. It wasn't forgiveness exactly. That would take a lot more time. But it was a profound sadness that even though Phoenix was the one who'd been punished, Penny *hadn't* avoided the consequences. The lie she'd told had destroyed everything admirable about her.

"Come on." Phoenix took her arm to help her up. "I'm guessing you won't be getting the two hundred dollars you were hoping for. But Riley and I will drive you to the airport."

It wasn't until later, when they were on their way home, that Phoenix was able to ask Riley about Roger. "You told me he *didn't* tell you that Penny yanked on the wheel," she said.

He glanced over as he drove. "He didn't—but *she* didn't know that."

"You *tricked* her into admitting the truth?" Phoenix cried.

Riley tucked a length of hair behind her ear as he gave her the same smile she'd dreamed about for seventeen years. "It was a bluff. But it was all I had. Thank God it worked. But I wish we could've gotten her to sign a statement accepting responsibility." They'd tried, but by the time Riley had come up with the idea on their drive to the airport and they'd stopped to buy some paper, Penny had pulled herself together and refused.

They'd sat in silence all the way to Sacramento. Then she'd gotten out, slammed the door and stalked off.

"It probably wouldn't have held up in court, anyway," Phoenix said. "Not without being notarized."

"We should hire a lawyer," he said. "I wish I'd thought of bringing one with us today, but I was too worried about how you'd be treated and the fact that I couldn't come up with anything solid. It never even crossed my mind." He shook his head. "Even if I'd thought of recording the conversation on my cell once we got there, we would've had *some* proof of what she admitted."

"We have witnesses. Your parents won't lie, will they?"

"No, but I'm sure the Mansfields would rather keep the truth quiet. They were so sure you were at fault, it'll be more than a little embarrassing when everyone learns just how wrong they were. Fortunately, as much as my mother loves her best friend, she loves me more. We can depend on her to tell the truth."

"Then that's enough for me," Phoenix said. "Let's not waste our time fighting for more. I've heard about ex-cons suing for compensation. But it's not easy to get, especially if there isn't some sort of forensic proof that'd make the question of guilt *un*questionable. With someone like me? Even if we got Penny to repeat what she said to us today, they could say that memories are faulty. That she was coerced or whatever. There'd be so much red tape we'd never collect. As a matter of fact, we'd spend more money going after it than we'd ever receive."

"But the system failed you. It took seventeen years of your life! And what about clearing your name? Isn't that important to you?"

"I might pursue that at some point. Who can say if it'll become more important to me later on? I just don't want to deal with it right now, not when the people who matter to me the most know the truth. I just want to put it behind me, start over. Besides, it wasn't the system that failed me. It was the integrity of one person. No system can compensate for a lack of integrity."

"You're serious."

"Absolutely. At least it's over. At least *you* know the truth and your family knows. That's more than I've dared to hope for in a long, long time. And I have so much to look forward to."

"Being with me and Jacob—that's enough?"

"What more could I ask for?" Phoenix felt lighter than air. She'd be able to walk through Whiskey Creek with her head held high. She wouldn't have to fear the Mansfields or endure the hatred that had barraged her before. She could go to Jake's games without any hesitation and feel he had no reason to be ashamed of her. "I'll never forget the way the Mansfields hung their heads after Penny broke down, and how apologetic your parents were."

"They were wrong, and now they know it." He threaded his fingers through hers. "So what do you think?"

She studied his profile as he drove. His tone indicated that he was taking the conversation in a different direction, but she had no idea *which* direction. "About what?"

He grinned. "Isn't it time for you to make *me* a bracelet?"

Riley couldn't wait to tell Jake what had happened with Penny, and he knew Phoenix was even more excited. She kept wringing her hands and shifting her weight while they stood outside the entrance of Just Like Mom's and watched Jake park in the restaurant lot. Jake knew they were happy about something, because they'd invited him to join them for a celebration sundae. But he didn't know what they were going to tell him.

"Hey!" The cleats on Jake's shoes clicked on the walkway as he approached. He'd come straight from baseball practice, so he was sweaty and his uniform was covered in dirt. He'd asked if he should stop and shower first, but they'd been too eager to see him.

"Hi!" Phoenix rushed toward him and hugged him, which probably wasn't a good idea, because she broke down in tears almost immediately.

Jake glanced at Riley as he returned the embrace, looking a little uncertain, and Riley winked to say he shouldn't be concerned.

"We met with Penny today," Phoenix announced with a sniff as she let him go.

Jake removed his baseball cap and put it on backward. "And?" He sounded even more uncertain than he looked.

"She finally told the truth." Riley spoke up since Phoenix's tears had welled up again, and she had to keep wiping her face. "She admitted that she was the one who caused Lori's death."

"Are you kidding?" Jake nearly yelled, he was so excited, which drew the attention of a party walking past. But Riley felt like shouting it to the whole world, anyway, and he was confident Phoenix felt the same.

Smiling through her tears, she shook her head and Jake swept her into his arms again. "Mom! Do you realize what this means?"

She laughed as he swung her around. "It means you

no longer have to wonder about me or feel as if other people believe the worst," she said.

"We believed you even before. Didn't we, Dad?" he said. "Someone like you could never do anything like that."

The sight of Jake clasping his mother with such happy relief made Riley emotional, too. He was afraid his voice could crack, so he cleared his throat in an attempt to conceal his emotions and nodded instead of speaking.

"Did Grandma and Grandpa hear it?" Jake asked, setting her down.

"They did," Phoenix replied. "The Mansfields heard it, too. And we owe it all to your father. He's the one who got her to admit that she pulled on the wheel."

"How'd he do that?" Jake asked.

Riley had recovered enough to speak without losing control, so he interrupted before Phoenix could retell the story. "Let's go in, and we'll give you all the details."

"This is awesome!" Jake told Phoenix.

Her smile stretched wider than Riley had ever seen. "It's so good to be free—really free—at last," she said, and slipped under Riley's arm as they walked into the restaurant.

Epilogue

June 2

Dear Coop,

So much has happened since I got out that I don't even know where to start. I'm happy. I guess that's a good place to begin. I'm happier than I've ever been in my life—so happy that I'd go through ten more years of prison if I had to, in order to get where I am now. I still live on my mother's property in a run-down trailer, but it's not so bad, since I've made it my own. It lets me stay close to her and take care of her. She needs that. I haven't even pressured her to get rid of the junk yet. I figure there's time. We can take it in small increments, work with her limitations so that she's not too miserable about the whole thing.

My bracelet business is growing like crazy. I'm surprised by how fast. I can barely keep up with the orders. Who knew they'd catch on? I just bought myself a new laptop (it's a used one but that's all I need for now) and ordered internet service. Hallelujah for the small things! I'm saving up for a car next. But that will take a while. I put some money on your books, by the way.

I've included a picture of Jake. Isn't he handsome? He's the best son a mother could have. He comes to see me often, and I go to all his baseball games. You should see him pitch! I'm sure he'll get a college scholarship (and I'll be weeping in the audience when they award it to him).

Now you're probably chuckling about the other picture. You always teased me that I'd get with a man right away after going so long without... you know. But that's me and Riley. Yep, *the* Riley. LOL! I never could get over him. I think you knew that. Only now being in love isn't such a bad thing, since he claims he wants to marry me. It might take a few months to actually convince me that he means it. But he's trying, and I'm fine to let him keep trying—for a while.

At least he knows I didn't kill Lori on purpose. That's the important part. How he figured it out is a long story—too long to write now—but Penny (the other girl in the car when the accident happened) finally admitted the truth. You're probably wondering if that means Lori's family is going to try and have her prosecuted. I doubt it. I think they understand there's not much to be gained by punishing someone who never meant to do anything wrong in the first place. And even if they want their vengeance, prison would be an improvement over the life Penny's leading now. Turns out she's a junkie, living here and there and all over, with few friends and very little contact with her family. Things never got *that* bad for me. I've had my fair share of enemies—this heart of mine has been shattered in a million pieces—but even during the worst of times, I had you. One of God's tender mercies.

Love,
Phoenix

* * * * *

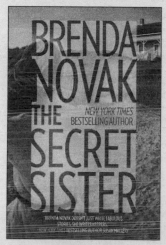

REQUEST YOUR FREE BOOKS!

2 FREE NOVELS
FROM THE ROMANCE COLLECTION
PLUS 2 FREE GIFTS!

YES! Please send me 2 FREE novels from the Romance Collection and my 2 FREE gifts (gifts are worth about $10). After receiving them, if I don't wish to receive any more books, I can return the shipping statement marked "cancel." If I don't cancel, I will receive 4 brand-new novels every month and be billed just $6.24 per book in the U.S. or $6.74 per book in Canada. That's a savings of at least 22% off the cover price. It's quite a bargain! Shipping and handling is just 50¢ per book in the U.S. and 75¢ per book in Canada.* I understand that accepting the 2 free books and gifts places me under no obligation to buy anything. I can always return a shipment and cancel at any time. Even if I never buy another book, the two free books and gifts are mine to keep forever.

194/394 MDN F4XY

Name _____ (PLEASE PRINT)

Address _____ Apt. #

City _____ State/Prov. _____ Zip/Postal Code

Signature (if under 18, a parent or guardian must sign)

Mail to the Harlequin® Reader Service:
IN U.S.A.: P.O. Box 1867, Buffalo, NY 14240-1867
IN CANADA: P.O. Box 609, Fort Erie, Ontario L2A 5X3

Want to try two free books from another line?
Call 1-800-873-8635 or visit www.ReaderService.com.

* Terms and prices subject to change without notice. Prices do not include applicable taxes. Sales tax applicable in N.Y. Canadian residents will be charged applicable taxes. Offer not valid in Quebec. This offer is limited to one order per household. Not valid for current subscribers to the Romance Collection or the Romance/Suspense Collection. All orders subject to credit approval. Credit or debit balances in a customer's account(s) may be offset by any other outstanding balance owed by or to the customer. Please allow 4 to 6 weeks for delivery. Offer available while quantities last.

Your Privacy—The Harlequin® Reader Service is committed to protecting your privacy. Our Privacy Policy is available online at www.ReaderService.com or upon request from the Harlequin Reader Service.

We make a portion of our mailing list available to reputable third parties that offer products we believe may interest you. If you prefer that we not exchange your name with third parties, or if you wish to clarify or modify your communication preferences, please visit us at www.ReaderService.com/consumerchoice or write to us at Harlequin Reader Service Preference Service, P.O. Box 9062, Buffalo, NY 14269. Include your complete name and address.

ROM13R

BRENDA NOVAK

32993	INSIDE	___ $7.99 U.S.	___ $9.99 CAN.
32904	WATCH ME	___ $7.99 U.S.	___ $9.99 CAN.
32886	DEAD GIVEAWAY	___ $7.99 U.S.	___ $9.99 CAN.
32831	KILLER HEAT	___ $7.99 U.S.	___ $9.99 CAN.
32803	BODY HEAT	___ $7.99 U.S.	___ $9.99 CAN.
32725	THE PERFECT MURDER	___ $7.99 U.S.	___ $8.99 CAN.
31639	THE HEART OF CHRISTMAS	___ $7.99 U.S.	___ $8.99 CAN.
31591	COME HOME TO ME	___ $7.99 U.S.	___ $8.99 CAN.
31546	TAKE ME HOME FOR CHRISTMAS	___ $7.99 U.S.	___ $8.99 CAN.
31423	WHEN SUMMER COMES	___ $7.99 U.S.	___ $9.99 CAN.
31371	WHEN SNOW FALLS	___ $7.99 U.S.	___ $9.99 CAN.
31351	WHEN LIGHTNING STRIKES	___ $7.99 U.S.	___ $9.99 CAN.
28858	DEAD SILENCE	___ $7.99 U.S.	___ $9.99 CAN.

(limited quantities available)

TOTAL AMOUNT	$ _____
POSTAGE & HANDLING	$ _____
($1.00 for 1 book, 50¢ for each additional)	
APPLICABLE TAXES*	$ _____
TOTAL PAYABLE	$ _____

(check or money order—please do not send cash)

To order, complete this form and send it, along with a check or money order for the total above, payable to MIRA Books, to: **In the U.S.:** 3010 Walden Avenue, P.O. Box 9077, Buffalo, NY 14269-9077; **In Canada:** P.O. Box 636, Fort Erie, Ontario, L2A 5X3.

Name: _____

Address: _____ City: _____

State/Prov.: _____ Zip/Postal Code: _____

Account Number (if applicable): _____

075 CSAS

*New York residents remit applicable sales taxes.
*Canadian residents remit applicable GST and provincial taxes.

MIRA®

www.MIRABooks.com

MBN0415BL